Quigley's Quest

When rancher Dan Quigley's teenage sister is brutally raped and murdered by the Snell gang of outlaws, Dan immediately embarks on a quest to bring them to justice.

By chance he meets with Marian Foley, who is also seeking vengeance against the Snells for the murder of her father. Joining forces, their quest takes them to Kansas and deep into Indian Territory, a popular refuge for outlaws on the run. Here, the Snell gang has friends.

Can Dan and Marian possibly stay alive long enough to overcome the formidable forces ranged against them? Will justice be served?

By the same author

Billy Dare
Bodie
The Long Trail
The Trouble Hunter
Danger Valley
Showdown at Deadman's Gulch
Branagan's Law
Law of the Noose
Marshal of Borado
Valley of Fear
Buzzards in the Sky
The Man from Dodge
Brady's Revenge
Trail Dust
The Range Robber
Trail of the Killer
Raiders of the Panhandle
Law of the Frontier
Ringo's Revenge
Panhandle Drifter
The Vengeance Riders
The Brannigan Boys
The Vengeance of Vickery

Quigley's Quest

ALAN IRWIN

ROBERT HALE · LONDON

First published in Great Britain 2005

ISBN 0 7090 7661 4

Robert Hale Limited
Clerkenwell House
Clerkenwell Green
London EC1R 0HT

Typeset by
Derek Doyle & Associates, Liverpool.
Printed and bound in Great Britain by
Antony Rowe Limited, Wiltshire

ONE

It was a hot afternoon on the Circle Q. Rancher Dan Quigley was engaged on some repair work on the corral fence at the small ranch which lay not far south of Pueblo in Colorado. He paused for a moment to mop his brow.

Dan was in his late twenties. He was a shade under six feet, with broad shoulders. He had a strong face, square-jawed, topped by a mop of unruly fair hair.

Before resuming work on the fence he glanced along the trail towards Blantry, a small town six miles to the south. During the past hour he had glanced frequently in that direction, expecting to see his sister Rachel riding back from a visit to town.

The two were very close, especially so since their parents, who had established the ranch, had died tragically of cholera just over a year ago. Rachel, ten years younger than Dan, was an attractive, lively girl, with her mother's fair hair and good looks.

At the time his parents died, Dan was serving as town marshal at Blantry, but he had decided to quit the job to join Rachel on the ranch, and take over the running of the Circle Q.

Once again, Dan looked along the trail to the south. He had originally intended to accompany Rachel to town and back, but he was especially busy on the ranch owing to one of the two ranch hands being laid up temporarily with a damaged leg.

He worked on for another hour to complete the repairs. There was still no sign of Rachel, and he was beginning to feel concerned. It was three o'clock in the afternoon, and he knew that his sister had intended to arrive back at the ranch around one o'clock.

He decided to ride towards town to meet her, and five minutes later he was heading south along the trail. There was still no sign of his sister ahead. Two miles further on, he caught sight of a riderless horse standing close to a small grove of trees about a hundred yards to the west of the trail.

The horse looked like Rachel's mount, and Dan's concern deepened as he rode fast towards it. As he drew closer, he was able to confirm that the horse was the one which Rachel was riding when leaving the ranch for town. But there was no sign of his sister.

He rode completely around the grove, but there was still no sign of Rachel. He rode up to her horse, dismounted, and examined it. It was not injured, and showed no signs of a fall.

He tethered the horses at the edge of the grove and walked among the trees, searching for Rachel, calling out her name at intervals. But there was no response.

He had reached a point about half-way towards the centre of the grove when he came upon her. She was lying on the ground, face up and motionless. Her clothing was disarranged, and her neck was severely bruised. He knew at once that she was dead. He knelt down beside her and took one of her hands in his. Overcome by the enormity of his loss, he stayed motionless for a while. Then he stood up and examined the ground around his sister's body. He could see the footprints of at least two men. He picked up the slender body and walked back to his horse.

Gently, he laid his dead sister across his horse's shoulders, mounted, and took her in his arms. He headed for Blantry. As he rode along he felt an overwhelming surge of anger against the persons responsible for the death of his sister.

As he entered Blantry, a small but growing group of townspeople followed him in silence as he rode up to the livery stable and stopped outside.

The liveryman, Hank Taylor, a distant relative

and close friend of the Quigleys, was working inside. He saw them through the door and ran outside. Shocked, he stared at Rachel, lying motionless in Dan's arms.

'What's happened, Dan?' he asked.

'Rachel was late getting back to the ranch,' Dan replied. 'I rode out to look for her. Found her like this, not far off the trail. She's dead.'

He spoke to the onlookers.

'Would somebody please ask Doc Sawyer and the marshal to come here,' he said.

As a man hurried off towards the doctor's house, another one told Dan that Marshal Benteen was out of town for a few days. Dan handed Rachel down to Taylor, then followed him into the house beside the stable. Taylor carried the body into a bedroom and laid it on a bed.

Moments later, the doctor knocked on the door. Taylor let him in and led him to the bedroom. Shocked, Sawyer bent over Rachel. It was clear to him that she had been dead for a while. He straightened up.

'I can't say how sorry I am about this,' he said. 'I know how you both felt about Rachel. What happened, Dan?'

'I found Rachel lying in a grove of trees between here and the ranch,' Dan replied. 'Close to the body I found the footprints of two, maybe three, men. What I'd like you to do, Doc, is examine Rachel and tell me exactly what happened to her.'

'All right, Dan,' said Sawyer. 'You two can wait outside. I'll be as quick as I can.'

He came out of the bedroom fifteen minutes later.

'Rachel was raped,' he said, 'then she was strangled. There are clear signs of a man's hands around her throat. She has a few bruises on her arms and there are some broken fingernails on both her hands.

'There were signs of blood on her fingers, and I reckon there could be some scratch-marks on the faces of the villains who attacked her. And clenched in one of her hands I found a few strands of sandy coloured hair.'

As he handed the strands over, he looked closely at Dan, sensing his deep anguish at his loss and his feeling of intense anger against the men who had violated and murdered his sister.

Dan asked the liveryman to see the undertaker and make arrangements for Rachel's burial the following morning.

'I'm going back to the place where I found Rachel,' he said. 'While it's still light, I want to take a good look at the sign the killers left behind them.'

He went outside and scanned the faces of the group of people still standing there. He was looking for a friend of his, Jim Shafto, an ex-Army scout, now retired and living in Blantry. Jim was a half-breed Indian, noted for his skill as a tracker, and the law occasionally enlisted his help in tracking criminals. Of late, he had increasingly been plagued with rheumatism.

Dan spotted Shafto standing at the rear of the group of onlookers. He walked round to him and drew him aside.

'Jim,' he said, 'I need your help. Rachel was killed by two or three men. Will you go with me to where I found her and tell me as much as you can about what happened there?'

'I will go,' said Shafto. 'Wait here while I get my horse.'

Ten minutes later he reappeared, and Dan rode off with him to the place where he had found Rachel's body. When they reached the grove, Shafto told Dan to wait for him outside it.

Then he slowly circled the grove once, on foot, before entering it and walking up to the place where the body had been found. It was some time before he reappeared and walked up to Dan.

'There were three men,' he told Dan. 'They all walked into the grove, taking Rachel with them. She was struggling as they dragged her along. One of them was a big, heavy man. The other two were smaller, and one of them was lame. He dragged his right foot as he walked. They all wore boots.

'When they met up with Rachel, they were riding in a direction a little south of east, and after they killed her they carried on in the same direction. Maybe they were heading for Indian

Territory. Are you going to follow these men?'

'I am,' Dan replied. 'I'll follow them either until I'm dead, or until I've made them pay for what they've done.'

'A few years ago I would have come with you,' said Shafto, 'but now I am too old. I cannot walk or ride far without pain. But there is something I *can* do. I will follow their trail for a few miles before it is dark, and I will let you know if they are still riding in the same direction as they were when they left here.'

Dan thanked his friend, then headed for the Circle Q, where he found his two ranch hands, Ben Drury and Hal Jenkins, in the bunkhouse. Jenkins had just ridden in from the range.

Dan broke the news to them about the murder of his sister. Both men, who had come to be friends as well as hired hands, were badly shocked by the news. Dan repeated what Shafto had told him about the three men involved in the murder.

'I'm going after those three,' he told them, 'before the trail gets cold. If you're willing, Ben, I'd like you to take charge here and keep the place running till I get back. I can't say when that'll be. If you need any help, hire another hand. Is that all right with you both?'

Both men nodded.

'We'll be glad to look after the ranch for you,' said Drury, 'but that's a dangerous job you're taking on. Don't you need some help?'

'When I find them,' said Dan, 'I'll bring the law in if I can. I'll be leaving right after the burial tomorrow.'

The following morning there was a large attendance at the burial in the small cemetery on the edge of town. When the ceremony was over, Dan received the condolences of friends, and took his leave of them. Then he stood alone for a while, grieving by the graveside, before turning away.

As he left the cemetery, Jim Shafto came up to him.

'I followed the tracks for five miles,' he told Dan, 'as far as Eagle Rock, and they were still heading in the same direction they were going when they left Rachel. Maybe you can pick up their tracks at Eagle Rock, maybe not. They are not very clear. And I think that if you do see them, you will soon lose them further on.'

'I guess you're right, Jim,' said Dan, 'but at least I know in which direction they're heading. I'm obliged to you.'

He went for his horse, then headed for Eagle Rock, a well-known landmark in those parts. He was wearing a gunbelt which carried a Colt .45 Peacemaker. In the saddle holster on his mount was a Winchester .44 rifle.

TWO

When Dan reached Eagle Rock he found what he thought were the tracks of the three killers he was seeking. But after following the tracks with difficulty for about a mile, he lost them. He decided to continue riding on in the same direction, with as little rest as possible.

Two days later, and still twenty miles from the Kansas border, he passed through a narrow gap between two ridges. Dismounting to look at some horse tracks, he was sure that they had been made by the mounts of the riders he was following.

In the late afternoon, after crossing the border into Kansas, he saw the buildings of a homestead off to his left. He left the main trail and headed for the house. He could see no movement around the buildings, or in the fields. He dismounted outside the house, and as he approached the door, he caught a brief glimpse of somebody looking out through a window.

Dan knocked on the door, which was opened

after a brief interval by the homesteader, Starkey, a short, slim man in his fifties. He was holding a rifle and was wearing a bandage around the top of his head. He looked suspiciously at Dan.

'Howdy,' said Dan, wondering how the homesteader had come by his injury. 'I dropped in to see if you could help me. I'm trailing three killers who might have passed by here. I thought that maybe you'd seen them before dark yesterday.'

Starkey swayed a little and grabbed hold of the doorpost to steady himself. Then he stepped backwards.

'Come on in,' he said.

Dan walked inside and the homesteader closed the door behind him. On the far side of the room, Starkey's wife was seated on an armchair. She also had a bandage running round her forehead and the back of her head. One side of her face was badly bruised.

Starkey gestured towards a chair and Dan sat down. The homesteader followed suit.

'If it's killers you're after,' said Starkey, 'then I reckon they were here yesterday. Maybe we're lucky to be still alive.'

He went on to tell Dan how three men had ridden on to the homestead before dark the previous day with a lame horse. Looking through the window of the house he had seen one of them start to remove the saddle from the animal.

When Starkey left the house to see what was

happening, he was told that the men were taking Starkey's saddle horse, which was in the corral, and were leaving the lame one behind.

When Starkey protested, he was pistol-whipped from behind by one of the men. When his wife came out to help him she was punched so savagely on the side of her face that she fell down. As her head hit the ground she suffered a bad cut on the temple.

The men had plundered provisions in the house to make themselves a meal, and had stayed on the homestead all night. They took a further meal at daybreak, then rode off to the east, after telling Starkey that they were staying in the area, and if he or his wife left the homestead during the next two days they would be shot.

Dan could see that the Starkeys were still suffering from the effects of their injuries.

'Can I ride for a doctor to come out and see you?' he asked.

'There ain't no need,' said Starkey. 'We'll be all right in a couple of days.'

'Those three men,' asked Dan,'was one of them bigger than the other two, and did he have sandy hair?'

'Yes,' replied Starkey. 'The leader was bigger than the others. I reckon he was about six feet tall. And he had long sandy hair down to his shoulders. The other two were around five-six, and just as mean-looking as their leader. One of them walked with a limp.'

'I'm certain now,' said Dan, 'that they were the three men I'm trailing.'

He went on to tell Starkey and his wife of Rachel's death at the hands of the three men, and of his own resolve to bring them to justice. He said he would be grateful for anything else they could tell him about their unwelcome visitors.

'I heard some names,' said Starkey. 'First names, I reckon. The big man was called Vince. The one who walked with a limp was called Tom.'

'Don't forget the marks on the big man's face,' said Mrs Starkey.

'That's right,' said her husband. 'They looked like scratch-marks to me.'

He went on to tell Dan that the horse that had been stolen from him was a chestnut with a white stripe down its face, and a scar left by a flesh wound just above its right front knee. When the men left, it was being ridden by the man with the limp.

He also said that he had overheard the big man, when talking to his partners, mention a small town called Jessop to the east, a place which had been visited only very occasionally by the Starkeys.

Dan thanked the couple, and when they once again declined any offer of help, he headed for Jessop, in the hope that the three men he had been trailing had called there.

It was early evening when he arrived. When Starkey had mentioned Jessop earlier, Dan was sure that he had heard the town mentioned to him at some time in the past, but he couldn't remember in what connection.

As he rode along the one and only street, he glanced at the buildings on either side. A sign on one of them caught his attention. It read LIVERY STABLE H. TAYLOR PROP.

Suddenly, Dan remembered that Hank Taylor, the liveryman in Blantry, had once casually mentioned that a cousin of his, Henry Taylor was running the livery stable in Jessop, Kansas.

He rode up to the stable door and dismounted. As he did so, the liveryman came out of the stable.

'Howdy,' said Taylor, a short, pleasant-looking man in his fifties.

'Howdy,' Dan replied. 'I wonder if I'm talking to a cousin of Hank Taylor, who runs a livery stable in Blantry, Colorado?'

Taylor's face broke into a smile.

'You sure are,' he said. 'You know Hank?'

'I'm a friend of his, Dan Quigley,' said Dan.

'Hank mentioned you and your folks in one of his letters,' said Taylor. 'Said you were a lawman.'

'Until a year ago,'said Dan, 'when my parents died. Then I started running the Circle Q Ranch with my sister Rachel.'

He went on to tell of Rachel's murder and his pursuit of the three men responsible for her death.

When Dan had finished, the shocked Taylor was

quiet for a few moments. Then he expressed his sympathy for Dan.

'Hanging's too good for the likes of them,' he said. 'You reckon you can catch up with them?'

'I aim to,' Dan replied, and described the three men to Taylor. 'They might have passed through Jessop,' he said. 'Did you see anything of them?'

'I sure as hell did,' Taylor replied. 'They rode in this morning, and went into the store. I happened to be in there at the time, and got a good look at them. After a couple of hours the big man and the lame one rode out of town to the east. As for the third one, he's still here.

'His horse is in the stable. He told me he's staying overnight at the hotel. Said he'd be leaving town in the morning. I don't know why he stayed on after the other two left.'

'Was one of the three riding a chestnut with a white stripe down its face?' asked Dan.

'Yes,' replied Taylor. 'I'm pretty sure the lame man was riding a horse like that.'

For a few moments Dan considered the situation. Then he spoke again to the liveryman.

'What I'd like to do,' he said, 'with your help, and if you ain't got no objection, is capture the third man when he comes for his horse, and hand him over to the law. It's a stroke of luck for me to find him here alone.'

'You can count on me helping you any way I can,' said Taylor.

'I'm obliged to you,' said Dan. 'I wonder if the hotel-owner has any idea where the big man and his partner were heading when they left town earlier today.'

'I'll go to the hotel right now,' said Taylor, 'and have a word with Rennie, who owns the place. He's a good friend of mine.'

He was back in fifteen minutes.

'We're in luck,' he said. 'Rennie's daughter was serving breakfast in the dining-room, and when she was clearing the table next to the one where the three strangers were sitting, she happened to hear the big man say to the one who stayed behind something about meeting up with him near Topika, in a week's time.

'I happen to know that Topika's a town in Indian Territory, not far south of the Kansas border. It's roughly south-east of here, maybe ninety miles away.'

'How can I get hold of the county sheriff?' asked Dan.

'That's Sheriff Cassidy,' said Taylor. 'As a matter of fact, we're expecting him the day after tomorrow.'

'Good,' said Dan, 'that gives me a bit of time to squeeze some useful information out of the man who stayed behind.'

For a while Dan and the liveryman discussed Dan's plan for dealing with the man they were expecting to turn up for his horse the following morning. It was decided that Dan would stay in the stable overnight, using a bunk placed in an empty stall.

The next morning Taylor, standing just inside the stable door, watched out for the man they were expecting. It was just after eight o'clock when he called out to Dan.

'He's coming,' he said.

Dan crouched down in the empty stall, out of sight. As the man entered the stable Taylor walked up to him.

'Come for your horse?' he asked. 'It's ready, but I just noticed one of the shoes is going to need attention before you go much further. Let me show you.'

The man cursed, and followed Taylor into a stall near the front of the stable. The liveryman lifted one of the hind legs of the horse and both men bent over to look at the shoe.

Dan slipped silently into the stall behind them and lifted the man's six-gun from its holster. He forced the muzzle of his Peacemaker into the back of the man's neck.

Involuntarily, his victim made a grab towards a holster which he found empty. Then he froze.

'Let's straighten up, slow and easy-like, and move out of the stall,' ordered Dan.

When all three had left the stall, Taylor tacked a notice on the outside of the stable door. It read CLOSED. BACK IN THIRTY MINUTES. He closed and locked the door and returned to Dan, who was holding his gun on the prisoner.

The man in front of Dan was slim and not more than five and a half feet tall. He had a long, narrow face, with lips set in a perpetual sneer. He stood motionless, his eyes fixed on Dan's face. Taylor moved up and searched the man's pockets. He found a large sum of money in banknotes, but nothing to establish the man's identity. Then Dan spoke to the prisoner.

'A few days ago,' he said, 'three men attacked a young woman a few miles north of Blantry in Colorado, and left her dead. I'm the woman's brother, and you are one of the three men who killed her.'

Momentarily, a hint of fear showed in the prisoner's eyes.

'For a while,' Dan went on, 'I was aiming to shoot you on sight, but now I'm figuring on handing you over to the law. But before I do that, I aim to find out from you who you and your two partners are, and just what happened when you killed my sister.

'I know that you're due to meet up with your two partners near Topika a week from now. You and your partners were heard talking about it and I figure to be waiting for them when they turn up there. You'd be wise to start telling me everything right now.'

'You go to hell!' said the prisoner. 'I ain't talking.'

'Right,' said Dan, and he and Taylor proceeded to gag the prisoner and truss him so thoroughly that he was unable to move. They dragged him into the stall where Dan had spent the night, and laid him on the floor, well out of sight of anyone who might enter the stable. Then they walked out on to the street.

'I don't reckon it's going to be that easy to get this man talking,' said Dan. 'I think I'd better work on him outside of town.'

'You can take him on the buckboard,' said Taylor. 'We can cover him with sacking, and you'd better keep off the street.'

During the next half-hour, Taylor hitched a horse on to the small buckboard which he kept behind the stable. They bundled the prisoner on to it, and covered him with sacking.

Dan drove the buckboard along the backs of the buildings lining the street, then joined the trail which he had followed into Jessop the previous day. He had covered just over three miles when he spotted a small clump of trees, well off the trail, which he had noticed previously. He left the trail and headed towards it.

When the buckboard reached the grove Dan dragged the prisoner out of it, then took a look at the trees. He selected one which had a high, almost horizontal, branch, and dragged the bound man up to it.

He tied the end of a length of rope around the

prisoner's ankles, then threw the other end over the branch. Exerting all his strength, he gradually hoisted his captive upwards until he was suspended, head down, about three feet clear of the ground. Then he tied off the free end of the rope on a shorter, lower branch which was within easy reach.

As he took the gag out of the prisoner's mouth, Dan could see the beads of perspiration and the worried look on his face. The look of concern deepened as Dan walked around, picking up material from under the trees which would produce the fire he wanted. Leaving a space through which he could insert some paper which he had brought with him, he piled the material under the prisoner's head.

He spoke to his captive.

'This is your last chance to talk before I light this fire, and start lowering you down on it,' he said. 'I've told you what I want to know.'

Either the man was not without courage, or he did not believe that Dan would carry out his threat. He remained silent.

Dan poked a lighted piece of paper into the centre of the pile, then another piece. Quickly the flames took hold, and soon the timber was burning. Dan untied the free end of the rope, lowered the prisoner a few inches, then retied it.

His victim tried to swing himself out of the area of rising heat, but he was too tightly bound. Dan could see that his hair was singeing.

He untied the rope and lowered the man another two inches. Before he could retie it, the man, staring into Dan's implacable face, yelled out in pain and desperation. 'I'll talk!' he shouted, 'as soon as you pull me out of this.'

Dan pulled on the rope until, although the man's head was out of the area of intense heat, he was still experiencing some discomfort. He tied the rope off.

'I want the truth,' he said. 'I'll know for sure if you're lying, and if I think you are, I'm going to lower you down again, put some more wood on the fire, and leave you here to burn to death.'

As he questioned his badly shaken victim, the facts gradually emerged that his name was Ike Benson, and his partners were Vince Snell and Tom Pearce. Benson had joined the gang a year ago, to replace a gang member killed in a bank raid. The gang, led by Snell, specialized in bank and stagecoach robberies, and operated mainly in Kansas, Nebraska and Indian Territory.

They were on their way from Nebraska to Kansas, by way of Colorado, when they happened upon Rachel. It was Snell who had decided to intercept her, and under his orders Benson and Pearce had helped him to surround her, pull her from her horse, and drag her into the trees, where Snell had sexually assaulted and strangled her.

Snell and Pearce, who were related, had parted

from Benson in Jessop because they wanted to visit relatives who were farming in Kansas, before heading for Indian Territory. The exact whereabouts of these relatives was not known to Benson. All he could say was that some time ago Snell had received a telegraph message from one of them, and he had noticed that it had been sent from Dodge City, in Kansas.

The plan was that when Benson was reunited with the other two in a small ravine half a mile north of the trail, and five miles east of Topika, in six days' time, they would all move on to meet up with an old partner of Snell in Indian Territory. Who this partner was, and where they were due to meet, Benson didn't know.

Convinced that he had heard the truth, Dan finished the interrogation, pulled Benson away from the fire, and lowered him to the ground. He took one of the water bottles he had brought with him and slowly poured the contents over Benson's head. The prisoner's hair was singed and the skin on the upper part of his head was reddened.

While waiting till after dark, Dan untied Benson's hands and he and his prisoner took some food and drink. Then, after he had tied Benson's hands again, he hoisted him on to the buckboard and drove it back to town. As he stopped behind the stable Taylor walked out and helped him take the prisoner inside, and into the empty stall.

'He talked?' asked the liveryman, looking at the

state of Benson's head.

'He talked,' replied Dan, grimly, 'and I'm sure I got the truth out of him.'

He told Taylor all that he had learnt from Benson.

'What d'you aim to do now?' asked the livery-man, when Dan had finished.

'We'd better stay quiet about holding him here as prisoner,' said Dan, 'just in case any of his friends turn up. When the sheriff gets here tomorrow, I'll hand Benson over to him. He was a wanted man before Rachel was killed – maybe for murder as well as robbery. We'll see what the sheriff has to say.'

'Right,' said Taylor. 'Until the sheriff turns up, we'll keep him tied up here, and supply him with food and water.'

THREE

Around mid-afternoon on the following day Sheriff Cassidy rode into Jessop. He was a tall middle-aged man, riding straight in the saddle, with a neatly trimmed beard and moustache. He wore a smart white Texas hat. Taylor saw him coming, and intercepted him on the street outside the stable. He took him inside to meet Dan.

After the sheriff had heard Dan's story, and what he had learnt from the prisoner, they took him to the stall to see Benson. He eyed the prisoner with grim satisfaction.

'That's Benson, all right,' he said. 'He's on our wanted list, with Snell and Pearce. They've all committed robbery and murder in Kansas. And I know they're wanted in Nebraska and Indian Territory as well.'

He looked at the prisoner more closely.

'What's happened to his head?' he asked.

'A bad case of sunburn,' said Dan. 'Only a fool would go around without a hat in weather like this.'

Cassidy's lips twitched.

'You're right,' he said. 'Only a fool would do that.'

'I aim to ride to Topika tomorrow to see if I can locate Benson's partners,' said Dan. 'What d'you aim to do with the prisoner?'

'Take him back with me to the cells in my office,' Cassidy replied. 'I'll leave in the morning. But I have to call in at Pardoe on the way to meet Nelson, one of my deputies. That's about forty miles east of here. Likely I'll stay there overnight.

'I'm going to the telegraph office right now, to send a message to the federal marshal at Fort Smith, Arkansas, telling him about you expecting to meet up with Snell and Pearce near Topika in Indian Territory. Maybe he can fix it for a deputy US marshal to get there and lend you a hand.

'I'll ask him to send a reply to you here about whether he can help. So you'd better wait till you get an answer. Shouldn't be more than a day or two.'

The following morning two strangers rode into Jessop and went into the hotel dining-room for breakfast. They were travel-stained and roughly dressed, and the hotel-keeper wouldn't have been surprised to learn that they were members of the criminal fraternity.

The men's table was against a window looking out on to the street. Having finished the meal, they were just about to leave the table when one of them glanced out of the window.

Riding along the street outside was Sheriff Cassidy. He was riding slightly behind a horse which was carrying Benson, his hands tied in front of him.

The man looking out of the window spoke urgently to his companion. The other joined him in looking intently at the two riders outside, who passed out of view as they watched. After a few minutes of earnest discussion, the men paid their bill and went out on to the street.

Looking along it, they could see the sheriff and his prisoner riding out of town to the east. They made a few purchases at the store, then walked over to their horses, mounted them, and rode out of town in the same direction.

The reply to the sheriff's telegraph message came the day after Cassidy and his prisoner left town. The telegraph operator brought it to Dan at the livery stable, an hour before noon. The message advised Dan that the US marshal would try and get two deputies to Topika by the time Snell and Pearce were expected there. They would contact Dan at the Palmer Hotel.

Dan showed the message to Taylor.

'I reckon I might as well set off for Topika right now,' he said, 'and keep a look-out for Snell and Pearce when I get there.'

'Your best way to Topika,' said Taylor, 'is to follow Sheriff Cassidy on the trail he took from here to Pardoe. Then, ten miles this side of Pardoe, you can fork right, on to a trail that takes you across the border into Indian Territory. After that, you head east, keeping pretty close to the border.'

Twenty minutes later, Dan took his leave of Taylor, promising to let the liveryman know the outcome of his quest for the two killers.

Almost thirty miles out of Jessop, just after following the trail through a narrow, steep-sided gully, he caught sight of something white poking out of a clump of long grass, just off the trail.

Curious, Dan rode over to investigate. He dismounted, and out of the grass he pulled a white Texas hat. It looked identical with the one worn by Cassidy when Dan had last seen him. At the back of the hat, just above the brim, was a hole which could have been made by a bullet.

Examining the ground closely, Dan walked along the trail in the direction that Cassidy would have been riding. He came to a spot where there were signs of horses and men moving around. There were also signs of something being dragged off the trail to a patch of brush twenty yards away. Parting the brush, Dan found himself looking down at the dead body of Sheriff Cassidy. He was lying face down, and there was a bullet-hole in the back of his head.

Dan had to climb both sides of the gully before he found the place where two men had waited in ambush until one of them fired the shot which killed the sheriff. A spent cartridge case lay on the ground. It was possible, thought Dan, that the object of the ambush had been to free Benson.

Picking up the spent case, Dan returned to the body and covered it well with loose brush. Then, ignoring the trail which, half a mile ahead, forked right for Indian Territory, he headed for Pardoe.

Night was falling as he rode into town and headed for the livery stable. He asked Butler, the liveryman, whether Nelson, the deputy sheriff, was in town.

'He is,' said Butler. 'That's his horse in the stall behind you. There's a good chance you'll find him in the hotel dining-room just now.'

Dan thanked the liveryman, handed his horse over, and walked across the street to the hotel. Going into the dining-room, he stopped, and looked around. Sitting alone, facing him, was a fresh-faced young man in his early twenties, wearing a deputy sheriff badge. Dan walked up to him.

'My name's Quigley,' he said. 'I've got to talk with you. I've got some bad news about Sheriff Cassidy.'

The deputy motioned to Dan to take a seat.

'I was expecting him here yesterday,' he said.

'He's dead,' Dan told him. 'He was ambushed and killed on his way here yesterday.'

Obviously badly shaken by the news, Nelson listened as Dan told him of his own pursuit and capture of Benson, and Cassidy's decision to escort the prisoner to Pardoe.

Nelson stood up, leaving an unfinished meal on the table. 'I'm going for him now,' he said. 'I'll get a buckboard at the livery stable. I'd be obliged if you'd come along and show me just where the body is.'

'Sure,' said Dan.

At the livery stable Nelson asked Butler to tell the town undertaker to be ready to take the sheriff's body over on their return.

'I'll take him back to headquarters,' he said. 'I figure he'd like to be buried at the cemetery there. He ain't got no kin alive, so far as I know.'

On their way to collect the body, Nelson asked Dan to repeat all that he had told him in the hotel dining-room. Then he asked him what he was planning to do next.

'I'm wondering,' said Dan, 'if it could have been Snell and Pearce who killed the sheriff in order to rescue Benson. Or maybe the killers didn't even know Benson, but had a grudge against the sheriff. If it was Snell and Pearce, they sure ain't going to turn up near Topika now.

'All the same, I'm going to ride there to meet up with the two deputy US marshals. Maybe they can give me some more information about Snell and the others.

'I'll tell them about Benson being freed, and if there's no sign of him and his partners in the area, I'll ride to Dodge and have a word with the sheriff there. There's a chance that Snell has relatives around there, and maybe I can pick up his trail again.'

'I'm going to get a posse together as quick as I can,' said Nelson, 'to go after the men who killed the sheriff. But I don't reckon there's much chance of us catching them. The trail's too cold.'

When they arrived at the scene of the ambush, Dan helped the deputy to carry the sheriff's body to the buckboard. Then he returned to Pardoe with him. The following morning he left town, heading for Topika.

Arriving there in the afternoon, two days before Benson had originally planned to meet up with Snell and Pearce in a ravine close by, he took a room at the Palmer Hotel. Enquiries revealed that no one resembling Snell, or either of his partners, had been seen recently around town.

Dan took a meal at the hotel, then rode out of town towards the ravine where Benson had been due to meet up with his partners. He approached it cautiously, and established that there was no one there. Nor was there any sign of recent occupation.

Riding to a suitable vantage point nearby, he kept watch on the ravine through his field glasses for the rest of that day, the following day, and up to noon on the day after.

It was then that two riders came into view, heading not towards the ravine, but in the direction of Topika. Dan could see that neither of them was big enough to be Snell. It was possible, he thought, that they were the two deputy marshals he was to meet.

He left his vantage point and rode off in a direction which would intercept them. As he drew closer, they saw him coming and slowed down, then stopped. As he came up to them Dan could see the deputy US marshal badges on their vests.

'I'm Dan Quigley,' he said. 'I've been expecting you.'

The older of the two deputies spoke.

'I'm Deputy Ridley,' he said, 'and this is my partner Deputy Sloane. Have you seen any sign of Snell and Pearce yet. We're sure itching to get our hands on them.'

'I've got bad news for you,' said Dan. He told them about Sheriff Cassidy's murder and Benson's escape.

'I don't think it's likely Snell and the others'll turn up here now,' said Dan,'because I think they probably know that Benson was arrested and escaped. They've probably gone into hiding somewhere. But just in case, I'll stay on here till the day after tomorrow, watching that ravine where they were due to meet. I'm sorry if you've had a wasted journey.'

'That weren't your fault,' said Ridley. 'We'll stay here with you. We've covered a lot of miles lately. We could do with a day's rest. What're you aiming to do if they don't show?'

'Pick up the trail of those three again,' Dan replied. 'Has either of you any ideas that might help?'

Sloane shook his head. His partner thought for a short while before replying.

'I reckon they're more likely to be in Kansas than in the Territory,' he said. 'I remember hearing a rumour a few years back that Snell had some kin not far from Dodge City in Kansas, and whenever they've done a job down here, they've generally headed north and slipped over the border into Kansas before we could catch up with them.

'It might be a good idea for you to have a talk with a man called Mark Dunster. He was a county sheriff in Kansas for a long time until he retired about a year ago. I heard he lives in Dodge City.'

'I've heard of him,' said Dan. 'I reckon I'll pay him a visit.'

When the rifle bullet drilled into the back of Sheriff Cassidy's head, killing him instantly, Benson heard the sound of the shot a brief moment later. It came from the top of one of the sides of the gully.

The sheriff slumped forward, then fell sideways out of the saddle. His mount ran on for a short distance, then stopped. Benson calmed his horse, and brought it to a standstill, facing the direction from which the shot had come. He stayed in the saddle, his bound hands raised in the air.

Two men appeared in sight, both carrying rifles. They climbed down the side of the gully, and approached him. As they drew nearer, he recognized one of them. He was a man called Granger, a relative of Snell's, who had helped in a stage-coach hold-up carried out by the Snell gang six months earlier. He had left the gang after the robbery, and Benson had not seen him since.

Granger walked up to Benson and cut the rope around his wrists. Benson dismounted.

'Lucky for you,' said Granger, 'that we spotted Cassidy riding out of Jessop with you.'

He pointed to his companion.

'This is my partner Pete Warner,' he said. 'Seeing that Cassidy was holding you prisoner, and that he shot Pete's brother dead just over a year ago, we figured he had this coming to him.'

'I'm obliged to you,' said Benson, and explained how he came to be in Cassidy's hands.

'I've got to find Snell and Pearce before they get to Topika,' he said. 'The law might be waiting there to pick them up. D'you know where I'm likely to find them?'

'There are two homesteads, side by side, between Dodge City and the border with Indian Territory,' said Granger. 'They were settled by relatives of Snell. They'll be there, for certain. It's a safe hiding-place for them.

'I reckon they'll decide to stay on there till the hunt for the sheriff's killers dies down. And if I were you, I'd make sure before I rode on to the homesteads that they aren't being watched by the law.'

He gave Benson directions for finding the homesteads.

'Take the sheriff's weapons,' he said. 'When we've collected our horses we're heading south for Indian Territory.'

FOUR

After Dan had spent two days with the deputies near Topika, there was still no sign of Snell and Pearce. He took his leave of Ridley and Sloane, and headed for Dodge City.

Arriving there early the following day, Dan soon located ex-Sheriff Dunster in his small, new, freshly painted house on the edge of town. Dunster, a slim man, still keen-eyed and sprightly despite his years, listened as Dan introduced himself. He invited his visitor inside and they sat down in the living-room.

Dunster listened with keen interest as Dan told him of Rachel's murder and his own pursuit of the Snell gang.

'I heard about Benson escaping, and Sheriff Cassidy being found dead,' he said. 'I met Cassidy a couple of times. D'you reckon Snell had something to do with it?'

'I'm not sure,' said Dan, 'but I think it was either him or friends of his. Now, from something Benson told me, I think there's a chance that Snell and Pearce, and maybe Benson, are staying with kinfolk of Snell not far from Dodge right now.'

'As far as I can recollect,' said Dunster, 'Snell arrived in Kansas from Illinois five years ago, with his parents Rufus and Matilda. With them were a cousin of Rufus, called Nat Sherwin and his wife Emily.

'Each of the two families claimed a quarter section of land about twenty miles south of here, and started growing a few crops. Snell dabbled in horse-trading as well. The two homesteads were adjoining, and the two houses were close together. The Snell house was a lot bigger than the other.

'Vince Snell didn't stay at the homestead for long. He recruited some criminal types to form a gang, and they started out on a series of bank and stagecoach robberies.

'I know the homesteads well, because after two robberies in the county which I was pretty sure were the work of the Snell gang, I had a strong suspicion that they were hiding at the homesteads. So I took a posse there, and we made a thorough search. But there was no sign of the gang. It looked like they'd vanished into thin air.'

'If you'd tell me just where the homesteads are,' said Dan, 'I think I'll ride down there and nose around a while. It's the only lead I have.'

'Seems like a good idea,' said Dunster. 'Before I retired I made some enquiries in the area, and it seemed like Rufus and Matilda were living a lot better than your average homesteaders, and weren't working anything like as hard. I figured that they were getting some of the money from the robberies.'

Dunster proceeded to give Dan directions for reaching the homesteads.

'Thanks,' said Dan, when he had finished. 'Before I go I'll have a word with the sheriff.'

'His name's Carter,' said Dunster. 'He's the man who took over from me. He's sure going to be interested in what you've just told me. But I happen to know he's out of town right now. He's due back on the noon stage day after tomorrow. I'll pass on the information you gave me when he gets back. He's a good law officer, and a friend of mine. If you locate Vince Snell and his men in the county, get a message to him, and I'm sure he'll lead a posse out to help you.'

'I'll do that,' said Dan.

He left Dunster and went to a nearby store for some provisions. Then he set out for the two homesteads whose location Dunster had described.

He planned to arrive in the area before dark, then to find a suitable vantage point from which he could keep the homesteads under observation during daylight. During the night he would move up to observe the buildings more closely.

Dan got his first sight of the buildings through his field glasses when he was still some distance away. He swept the surrounding terrain with the glasses. The homesteads were on flat ground, but to the south, well off the trail, a long, low ridge, running roughly east to west, was visible. He estimated that from the top of this ridge, using field glasses, effective surveillance of the two homesteads would be possible.

He left the trail and headed for the ridge, aiming for a narrow gap that he could see through the glasses, and keeping sufficiently far away from the homesteads to make it unlikely that he would be spotted from there.

He rode through the gap, then turned eastward along the foot of the south side of the ridge. He stopped when he judged that he had reached a point where the ridge was closest to the homesteads.

Leaving his horse in a large recess in the side of the ridge, Dan climbed up to the top, to find that he was opposite the homesteads. The ground was littered with boulders, large and small, and Dan selected a suitable place from which he could watch the homesteads.

He could see nobody working in the fields, but two men were moving around the buildings. He started to sweep the surrounding area with his glasses, and as he looked along the top of the ridge, to the east, he caught sight of a distant moving figure which sank down on top of the ridge as he watched.

Keeping his glasses trained on the position where the figure had sunk down, Dan saw an occasional movement. He got the impression that somebody, like himself, was keeping a watch on the homesteads. But who could it be? He decided to find out.

He went back to his horse, mounted it, and rode further along the foot of the ridge to a point which he judged to be directly below the location of the person he had just seen.

There he found a tethered horse. He dismounted, and slowly climbed up the ridge, keeping a close watch on the top of the slope. When he reached it, he flattened himself on the ground and looked across the top of the ridge.

He could see a figure lying on the ground beside a boulder, looking towards the north. Intrigued by the possibility that someone else shared his interest in the two homesteads, he decided to find out the identity of the watcher. He drew his Peacemaker, in the use of which he had acquired considerable expertise. He advanced cautiously on the figure on the ground. As he drew closer he could see that it was slim, and of medium height. He could see a six-gun in a right-hand holster and a Winchester rifle lying on the ground.

Dan had almost reached his objective when there was a slight sound as something moved under his foot. The figure rolled over, pulling the revolver from its holster, but Dan kicked the weapon out of its owner's hand before it was cocked and lined up on him. His victim froze at the sight of the Peacemaker in Dan's hand.

Startled, Dan found himself looking into the face of a slim young woman with auburn hair cut short, brown eyes, and of such beauty despite her look of alarm, as to make Dan catch his breath. He had the feeling that she suspected he was there to do her harm.

He holstered his gun, and as she sat up, rubbing her hand, he squatted down beside her.

'I ain't here to do you harm,' he said, 'but I'm sure curious to know what you're doing, all by yourself, on top of this ridge, carrying a six-shooter and a rifle, and keeping watch on those homesteads down there.'

She looked relieved.

'I might ask you the same thing,' she said.

'D'you live around here?' asked Dan.

'No,' she replied, 'I've come a long way to get here.'

'Same here,' said Dan. 'I'm here to keep watch on those homesteads down below. One of them belongs to the parents of the outlaw Vince Snell.'

'Yes, I know,' she said. 'It looks like maybe we came here for the same purpose. I'd sure like to know why you're here.'

'I'll tell you my reason, then you tell me yours,' offered Dan.

'Agreed,' she said. 'I'm Marian Foley.'

'Dan Quigley,' said Dan, and went on to tell her the full story of Rachel's death and his pursuit of the killers.

She listened in silence.

'I'm sorry about your sister,' she said, when Dan had finished. 'The same three men were responsible for the murder of my father.'

Haltingly, she told Dan how she and her father, John Foley, after the death of her mother two years ago, and with a strong bond of affection between them, had continued to run a small ranch in Nebraska.

Then, one fateful day a few months ago, Snell, Benson and Pearce had called at the ranch to water their horses at the water trough near the foot of the tall windmill standing near the house.

Marian and her father had been working near the windmill when the men arrived and asked leave to water their mounts. As she stood watching the men, Marian began to feel uncomfortable at the way Snell was eyeing her.

When the horses had been watered, Snell said something to the other two, and they suddenly took hold of John Foley's arms, while Snell grabbed Marian and started dragging her, kicking and screaming, towards the house.

The rancher, with a superhuman effort, had broken away from the two men holding him, and he rushed towards Snell. Hearing Pearce's cry of warning, Snell had turned and shot Foley through the heart, while still retaining his hold on Marian.

Pausing for only a moment, while Pearce ran up to the rancher, who was lying motionless on the ground, Snell had continued to drag Marian towards the house. Shocked by the sight of her father going down, she was still struggling violently.

Then Benson had called out urgently, pointing towards the north. Snell came to a halt, still holding Marian tightly, and he and Pearce looked in the direction of Benson's pointing finger. In the far distance, barely visible, a group of nine riders was heading fast in their direction.

Benson had yelled that it looked like a posse, and they'd better move out pronto. Snell had hesitated, before quickly tying Marian's hands and feet. Then he and his two companions rode off fast to the south.

'I managed to roll over to my father,' said Marian, 'but he was dead. I could see the bullet hole over his heart. The posse turned up soon after, and they told me who the three men were, and that they had robbed a stagecoach further north. Then they rode off after them, leaving one man to help me. But they never caught up with Snell and the other two.

'I sold the ranch, then I went to Laramie, Wyoming, to stay with an uncle of mine who'd been a lawman there until his wife eventually persuaded him to retire. I knew he was pretty handy with firearms, and I asked him to recommend a rifle and a six-shooter for me, and to show me how to use them. I told him I was going after the men who'd killed my father.

'He and my aunt did their best to change my mind, but when they could see it was no use, he helped me as much as he could. Like you see, he got me a Sheriff Model Peacemaker .45 and a Winchester .44 carbine, and spent some time showing me how to use them.

'When I was in Laramie, we heard the news from the sheriff there that Benson had been captured in Kansas, and had later been freed when the lawman escorting him to jail had been ambushed and killed. The sheriff said he'd also heard that Snell had kinfolk homesteading not far from Dodge City, Kansas.

'So I got the idea that if I watched the homesteads for a spell, maybe Snell would turn up there. So I took a stage to Dodge, and hired a horse there. As it happened, the liveryman who let me have the horse knew where the Snell homestead was located. So here I am. I only arrived about four hours ago, and so far nothing interesting has happened down there.'

'I had pretty much the same idea as you,' said Dan. 'I'm sorry about your father. Maybe we can work together on this.'

'I was hoping you'd say that,' said Marian, 'I ain't exactly had a lot of experience in chasing criminals around.'

'I have a strong feeling that Snell and the others are down there right now,' said Dan. 'The homesteads have been searched for them in the past, but they've never been found there. Maybe that's because they were too well-hidden. I aim to go down there after dark and look for any evidence that they're there.'

'I'll go with you,' she said.

Dan admired the courage of this young woman who had set out alone on such a perilous mission.

'All right,' he said. 'We'll watch the homesteads from here until dark, then we'll ride down there after midnight and take a good look around. It's the bigger of the two houses that belongs to Snell's parents.'

In the period before darkness fell, Dan, watching through his field-glasses, saw two men occupied around the buildings for a while. Then they disappeared, one into each of the two houses. Dan was fairly sure that they were not members of the Snell gang. He guessed that they were Rufus Snell and his relative Sherwin, the owner of the adjacent homestead.

After dark, Dan and Marian took some food and drink, then lay down and rested. When midnight came, they went for their horses, led them over the ridge, then rode to the homesteads. They tied their mounts to the pasture fence on the Snell homestead, some distance from the buildings. No lights were showing. It was a clear night and a half-moon was shining.

Looking into the small pasture, Dan could see the dim shapes of about twelve horses.

'I've just had an idea,' he said to Marian. 'Wait here.'

He climbed over the fence and moved slowly around, quietly approaching, calming and examining the horses.

He had almost finished the task when his efforts were rewarded. As he gently ran his hand over the right foreleg of the chestnut horse with a white stripe down its face which he was examining, he could feel the scar just above the knee. He was sure that this was the horse taken from the homesteader Starkey to replace Pearce's lame mount when the Snell gang had called at the homestead. He returned to Marian.

'There's a horse in there,' he said, 'that I know for certain was being ridden by Pearce soon after they killed Rachel. This means either that Pearce could be here now, with the rest of the gang, or that they've been here and gone, leaving the stolen horse behind. I think they're still here, hiding somewhere till the search for them eases off a little. They know that folks get pretty riled when a law officer's been killed.'

'So the first thing we have to do,' said Marian, 'is find out for certain whether or not they're here.'

'That's right,' said Dan. 'If they *are* here, it's

likely they'll come out into the open during daylight now and again, when they think it's safe.

'We've got to find a place to watch from that's a lot closer to the buildings than the ridge is. If they happen to be there we want to be able to identify Snell and his men.'

'How about that patch of brush that lies about half-way between the ridge and the buildings?' suggested Marian. 'It's well outside the boundaries of the homesteads.'

'A good choice,' said Dan. 'Let's go and take a look at it. But first, I'll see if they've posted any guards outside the buildings. I won't be long.'

He melted into the darkness, and was back in twenty minutes.

'No guards,' he said,'and close up, I could see that the Snell house is a fair bit bigger than the other one. Plenty of room inside for guests. Let's go.'

When they reached the brush patch that Marian had referred to, they decided that it would be suitable for close-range observation of the homesteads in the daytime. They returned to the top of the ridge, where they rested until an hour before dawn.

Then, leaving their mounts on the south side of the ridge, and carrying food and drink with them, they walked back to the brush patch and settled down inside it. They chose a position from which they would, come daylight, have a clear view of the homestead buildings.

It was around eight o'clock in the morning before the watchers saw any sign of activity. A man came out of the Snell house, collected some logs, and went back inside. Shortly after this a man came out of the other house, filled a pail with water from the water trough, and disappeared inside. Neither of the men was recognized by Dan or Marian.

'They must be Vince Snell's father and the other homesteader, Sherwin,' said Dan, watching through the field glasses.

An hour later, Rufus Snell reappeared, and went into the barn. Forty minutes later, Sherwin left his house, collected some tools, and walked to one of the fields. As he started work there, his neighbour Snell left the barn and returned to the house.

Twenty minutes later, he came out again. He was carrying a pair of field glasses. Circling the group of buildings, he surveyed the terrain in every direction. As he looked towards them, Dan and Marian shrank further down into the brush. A little later, they saw him go back into the house.

Five minutes after this, two men emerged from the Snell house. Dan stiffened as he recognized, firstly, Vince Snell, then Pearce. He handed Marian the glasses, and heard her quick intake of breath as she recognized the two outlaws.

'Maybe Benson hasn't turned up yet,' said Dan, 'or maybe he's still inside, and we'll see him later today. Whether there's three, or only two of them, we've got to let the law know that they're here, waiting to be picked up.

'Tomorrow morning, Marian, will you ride into Dodge, and let Sheriff Carter know that the outlaws are here. I happen to know that he's due back in Dodge on the noonday stage. I'll carry on watching them from here in case they leave. If they do, I'll follow them.

'We'll have to wait here till after dark. Then we'll go back to the ridge and get some sleep. You can leave for Dodge before daybreak. When you leave, I'll come back here.'

'All right,' said Marian, 'but if they've left, and crossed over the border before the posse catches up with them, I want you to telegraph me at the sheriff's office in Dodge City the first chance you get, telling me where I can join up with you. After all, we're partners in this, aren't we?'

'All right,' said Dan, 'the first chance I get.'

As the day passed, the watching couple saw Vince Snell and Pearce go back into the house, then reappear for a short while in the afternoon. The two women showed up outside at various times, and Rufus Snell and Sherwin occupied themselves on various tasks around the home-steads.

When darkness fell, Dan and Marian walked back to the ridge, and took some food and drink. When they had finished, Marian spoke to Dan.

'I ain't too happy about leaving you here on your own,' she said.

'I can't see any other way,' said Dan. 'Now that we know for certain that Vince Snell and Pearce are here, the right thing to do is to let Sheriff Carter know. And I sure don't want to leave you here on your own.

'We'd better get some sleep now. Judging by this morning, there's no need for me to leave earlier than half an hour before daybreak. You might as well leave at the same time.'

FIVE

When Benson parted from Granger and Warner after the murder of Sheriff Cassidy, he knew that as soon as the body was found, there would be intense activity for a while in the search for the people responsible. He decided not to ride directly to the Snell homestead, but to head southeast, and find a safe hiding-place for a while, before heading for the homestead to find out if Vince Snell and Pearce were, or had been, there.

He had ridden fifteen miles when he came in view of a distant homestead straight ahead. A buckboard, with two people on the driving-seat, was just pulling away from it, heading south.

Benson waited till the buckboard was out of sight, then rode up to the homestead, confirmed that there was nobody there, and helped himself to sufficient provisions from the house to last him until he reached the Snell homestead. Then, striking east, he came, after an hour's ride, upon a secluded gully, well off the trail, where he considered it would be safe for him to hide.

He stayed there until he judged that the hue and cry in Kansas had died down. He left after dark, and headed for the Snell homestead, whose exact location he had been given by Granger.

Just after daybreak, and only a few miles from his destination, he was riding along a narrow trail between a small thicket and a large rock-outcrop, when he saw a distant rider approaching him. Quickly, he turned, rode round to the rear of the thicket, and dismounted. Leaving his horse there, he moved through the thicket until, although still concealed inside it, he was close to the side of the trail.

He watched the approaching rider as the horse cantered towards him, then slowed down to a walk as it approached the narrow gap between thicket and outcrop. Benson could see that the rider was a woman. As the horse drew closer, he realized with a shock that he had met the woman several weeks earlier on a small ranch in Nebraska, where her father had been shot dead by Vince Snell.

How she came to be there, he could not surmise, but he figured that her presence so close to the Snell homestead was extremely suspicious, and could indicate the presence of a serious threat to his two partners if they were hiding there.

As Marian walked her horse past him, Benson decided on his course of action. He waited a moment, then drew his six-gun and left the thicket. He ran up quietly behind Marian, and before she realized what was happening, he had grabbed her horse's bridle.

At the sudden appearance of Benson by its head, the horse reared, and Marian was thrown from the saddle. She fell awkwardly, and lost consciousness as her head hit the ground hard.

When she came to a few minutes later, her hands were tied in front of her, and her six-gun had been removed from its holster. She shook her head and sat up, staring at Benson. She immediately recognized him as one of the two men who had been with Vince Snell when her father was killed.

'Well, well,' said Benson, 'you sure are a long way from home. Maybe you'd like to tell me just what you're doing here.'

Forcing herself to stay calm, Marian stared straight back at the outlaw, but made no reply.

'All right,' said Benson, 'maybe we'll get some answers when we meet up shortly with my partners. Mount up, or I'll put a rope on you and drag you behind me.'

Slowly, her head throbbing, Marian rose to her feet, then climbed on to her horse. Benson led it to the place where he had left his own horse, which he mounted, then led Marian's mount towards the Snell homestead.

Rufus Snell, splitting some logs outside th[e] house, saw them approaching, and ran insid[e] house. He came out and walked up to them as the two riders neared the house.

'Howdy,' said the outlaw. 'My name's Benson. I'm a friend of Vince. I thought maybe he's staying with you. He's going to be mighty interested in what this woman with me was doing when I came across her a few miles from here.'

Rufus Snell started to speak, then stopped as the door of the house opened and his son stepped out, followed by Pearce, who was carrying a pair of field glasses.

'Make sure,' said Vince Snell to Pearce, 'that there's nobody coming this way.'

Then he called out to Benson.

'We was wondering where you were,' he said. 'See you've got company.'

He walked up to Benson, curious about the woman with him. He glanced at his partner, then noticed that the woman's hands were tied. He looked up into her face, shaded by her wide-brimmed hat. He recognized her immediately. Startled, he turned to Benson, who had dismounted.

'Spotted her on the trail, a few miles north of here,' said Benson. 'She was heading north. When I saw who she was, I figured I'd better bring her along with me.'

'She was alone?' asked Snell.

'Yes,' Benson replied. 'I didn't see no sign of ody else around. I asked her what she was doing there, but she weren't inclined to talk.'

'Maybe we can remedy that,' said Vince Snell. 'She's a long way from that ranch in Nebraska, where her father was foolish enough to get himself shot. Maybe she's got some crazy idea of revenge. We'll take her inside, and see if we can get her talking.'

Just then, Pearce returned to report that he could see no sign of anybody in the surrounding area. All the men went inside, taking the prisoner with them. They went into the living-room, where Marian saw Matilda Snell, seated on a chair.

Matilda was a small, careworn woman, with a deep sense of shame, not shared by her husband, about her son's criminal activities. Rufus Snell, unlike his wife, was happy to accept, from time to time, a small share of the proceeds of the Snell gang's robberies.

Marian was ordered to sit down in the living-room, and the four men followed suit.

'Who's the woman?' asked Rufus Snell.

'She's a rancher's daughter from Nebraska,' his son replied. 'I had to shoot her father in self-defence.'

'That's a lie!' shouted Marian. 'You murdered him.'

Ignoring Marian, Vince Snell spoke to his two partners.

'We've got to find out what she's doing around here,' he said. 'It shouldn't take long to make her talk.'

For Matilda Snell, this was the last straw. She stood up, and faced her son.

'It's bad enough,' she said,'that we have to hide you and your friends from the law, but while I'm still alive, nobody's going to be tortured or molested or murdered on this homestead.'

Her son glared at her, then looked at his father. Rufus Snell shrugged his shoulders. He knew that his wife was no coward, and once she had made up her mind about something, there was no changing it.

'We'll take her with us, then,' said Vince Snell.

'And when'll that be?' asked his mother.

'Day after tomorrow,' he replied sullenly, still smarting from his mother's remarks. 'It looks like whatever she was doing, she was doing alone, but just in case, we'd better keep a watch on the door of the house during the night.'

They took Marian to the smaller of the two bedrooms upstairs, after Vince Snell had screwed the window tight shut. The other bedroom was the one used by the homesteader and his wife. They left the prisoner with her hands tied and the bedroom door locked from the outside.

Marian sat on the bed. Worried about what the gang might do to her when they took her away with them, she wondered what Dan was doing. She was sure that he would have seen her arriving at the homestead with Benson.

*

From inside the thicket, Dan had watched with grave concern as he saw Benson and Marian ride up to the Snell homestead, and shortly after go inside with Pearce and the two Snells.

Worried about the danger Marian must be facing at the hands of Vince Snell, he decided to make a rescue attempt as soon as there was any chance at all of success. The best time, he thought, would be during the night, after the occupants of the house had turned in.

He continued to watch the homesteads throughout the day. Both Rufus Snell and Sherwin did some work in the fields, and the wives appeared outside from time to time. But there was no sign of Marian or the outlaws.

When darkness fell Dan walked back to the ridge, took some food and drink, then rode back to the thicket. Desperately anxious about Marian's welfare, he watched until no lights were visible in the Snell house, except one which seemed to be coming from an upstairs room. It was possible, he thought, that this was the room in which Marian was being held. It was now eleven o'clock in the evening.

He waited for a further hour, then rode to the pasture fence, to which he tied his horse. He circled the Snell house on foot, and could see no guards outside. A light was still showing through an upstairs window. He decided to see if he could enter by the front door.

Inside the house, Pearce, sitting in the darkness on a chair close to the wall at one side of the door to the outside, stiffened as he heard a faint creaking sound as the door handle slowly turned. Quietly, he rose from the chair, drawing his six-gun, and stayed behind the door as it slowly opened.

Dan, standing against the wall outside the door, pushed it half-open with one hand. After listening for a short while, he stepped into the doorway, opened the door further, and moved forward into the room. Pearce, peering from behind the door, could just make out the dim shape of the man who had entered the house.

He moved quietly sideways and pistol-whipped the intruder on the side of his head. Dan fell down on to his hands and knees, then began to rise to his feet again, and started to reach for his Peacemaker. Before he could draw it, Pearce fired a shot into his body, and Dan fell to the floor and lay motionless, temporarily stunned by the combined effect of the blow on the head and the gunshot wound. Pearce felt for the intruder's six-gun, and lifted it from its holster.

The sound of the shot brought the two Snells and Benson into the room, where Pearce was lighting a lamp. They were followed by Matilda Snell. The four men looked down into Dan's face.

'Well, I'm darned,' said Benson. 'This is Quigley, the man who captured me. Like I told you, he's the brother of that girl we met a few miles north of Blantry, in Colorado. He's the one who hung me upside down, over a fire. I'm sure looking forward to getting my own back for that.'

Dan stirred, then slowly raised himself to a sitting position.

'You can get your own back later, Ike,' said Vince Snell, glancing at his mother. 'We'll take him with us when we leave.'

Looking up at the four men standing above him, and feeling the pain in his head and side, Dan realized that his desperate attempt to rescue Marian had failed. Pearce bent over and looked at the damaged clothing and the bloodstain on the prisoner's side.

'Looks like my bullet hit him in the side,' he said.

'You were a fool to come after us, Quigley,' said the outlaw leader, 'and so was the woman. We'll put you in a room upstairs with her till we figure out what to do with you both.'

He searched Dan's pockets and took out a roll of banknotes. He took Dan's Peacemaker from Pearce, and put it, with the notes, in a drawer in a chest at the side of the room. Then he spoke to Pearce.

'Bring that rope we've got back there, Tom,' he said, 'and later on, find Quigley's horse, and put it in the pasture.'

Dan watched as Pearce walked towards what

appeared to be the blank rear wall of the house. Near the far right-hand corner, he pressed on the wall, and a section of it, pivoted half-way along the top and bottom edges, swivelled open. Pearce passed through the aperture, and returned shortly after with a length of rope.

Dan could see now why past searches on the homestead for the Snell gang had proved fruitless. A false end wall had been constructed, behind which they could hide when the law was searching for them in the area.

Marian's heart sank when the door of her room opened and Dan stumbled in, with Vince Snell and Pearce close behind. Dan sat down on the double bed. Matilda Snell came in, carrying a bowl of water, a cloth, and some bandaging. She placed them on a table, and then spoke to Marian as she untied the rope around her wrists.

'See to his wounds,' she said, then left the room.

The two outlaws watched while Marian bathed the wounds on Dan's head and side. The flesh on his side was torn, but there was no bullet inside, and the wound did not appear to be serious.

After Marian had applied two bandages, she and Dan were ordered to lie on the bed, and were trussed by the outlaws in such a fashion that they could barely move. Snell and Pearce left the bedroom, locking the door behind them. Down in the living-room, Vince Snell told Benson to stand guard over the outside door for the rest of the night. Then he and Pearce went to their beds behind the false wall.

In the upstairs bedroom, Marian told Dan how she had been waylaid by Benson, and Dan told her about his reception as he entered the house.

'What's going to happen to us?' asked Marian.

'I don't know,' Dan replied. 'They're making up their minds. But knowing Vince Snell as we both do, I'd say our prospects ain't too good. All the same, we ain't finished yet. Any chance of us getting away that might crop up, we've got to be ready to grab it with both hands.'

'I'll do my best,' said Marian. 'How're you feeling?'

'Not so bad now,' Dan replied. 'You done a real good job tending to the wounds, and stopping the bleeding.'

'D'you think we can get these ropes off?' she asked.

'Not a chance,' Dan replied. 'We'd better try and get some rest, and see what tomorrow brings.'

They chatted for a while, then both lay silent. Half an hour passed before they heard the faint sound of the bedroom door being unlocked. The door opened and somebody came into the room and placed some things on the table. A moment later, a match flared, and a lamp standing on the table was lit. A rolling-pin was lying beside it. Standing by the table was Matilda Snell. She spoke in a whisper to the two prisoners.

'I'm going to set you both free,' she said, 'on two conditions. First, while you're getting away from here, I don't want nobody killed. Hurt maybe, but not killed. And second, I don't want you to tell anybody about you being held here, or about the hiding-place behind the wall. I figure that if you both give your word, you'll keep it.'

'You have my word,' said Dan. 'And thank you.'

'And mine,' said Marian. 'And thank you too.'

Mrs Snell nodded, then untied Marian, who did the same for Dan. The homesteader's wife picked up the rolling-pin and handed it to Dan.

'You'll need this,' she whispered. 'There's a guard down below. Put it back in the kitchen when you're done with it. And give me a few minutes to slip back into bed before you leave this room.'

She extinguished the lamp and left the room, taking the lamp with her. As she got back into bed with her husband, he was still sleeping as soundly as when she had left him.

'That guard down below,' said Dan. 'If we can put him out of action quietly, we stand a good chance of getting away.'

After a short wait, they left the room. Marian was carrying some rope. They went to the head of the stairs, which ended half-way along a short passage on the ground floor below. One end of this passage led into the room where Dan expected to find a guard.

With Dan in the lead, they crept down the stairs

and into the passage. They could see a faint light coming from the living-room. They moved towards it, then stopped near the end of the passage. Dan peered into the room.

Benson was sitting on a low-backed chair, facing the door to the outside. Beside him was a small table on which a lighted lamp, with its wick turned well down, was standing. The outlaw's head was slumped forward, and a faint snore was audible.

Motioning to Marian to stay where she was, Dan crept up behind the outlaw, and raised the rolling-pin. It was not a weapon with which he was familiar, but he reckoned it was just right for the job of putting Pearce out of action for a short while.

He struck the outlaw on the back of the head, and as Pearce fell forward off the chair, Dan caught him and eased him to the floor. Marian brought the rope, and they trussed the outlaw thoroughly, and gagged him. Then they took his gun, and tied him to a leg of a heavy settee, so that he could not move along the floor. As they finished this, he was showing signs of recovery, and Dan put a blindfold on him.

Then Dan returned the rolling-pin to the kitchen, and recovered from the chest drawer the banknotes, and the six-guns belonging to himself and Marian. He found their rifles standing against the side of a cupboard. They left the house, and paused for a moment outside.

'There's a good chance,' said Dan, 'that both our

horses are in the pasture. Let's go and see.'

Searching in the dark, they found their horses in the pasture, and their saddles and bridles on the ground outside, near the gate. They put the saddles and bridles on their horses, and mounted. A sudden wave of nausea washed over Dan, and he gripped the horn of his saddle. When he recovered he noticed that the wound in his side was bleeding again.

'I reckon I need to see a doctor, Marian,' he said. 'We'd best go to Dodge City.'

Back at the Snell homestead, it was dawn before Benson was released and it was realized that the prisoners had escaped. Vince Snell and his partners made a hurried departure from the homestead, and headed for Indian Territory.

SIX

It was well after daybreak when Dan and Marian rode into Dodge City. Marian watched Dan anxiously as he swayed in the saddle. She led him to the house of a doctor whose shingle she had noticed on her previous visit. She dismounted and knocked on the door.

It was opened by Doc Fleming, who took one look at Dan and ran to help him down from his horse and into the house. Marian followed them inside. Quickly, the doctor examined the wound in Dan's side, then the damage to his head.

'I reckon you'll live,' he said, 'and it ain't likely there'll be any permanent damage. But if you take my advice, you won't climb into a saddle for at least two weeks. Rest is what you need. The less you move around for a while, the better.'

He proceeded to clean and bandage the wounds, then asked Dan where he would be staying.

'In the hotel across the street, I reckon,' said Dan.

'I'll drop in there tomorrow to see how things are going,' said the doctor. 'You mind telling me how you come by these wounds?'

Dan had his answer ready. He had discussed the matter with Marian as they rode towards Dodge City. They had decided on the story Dan would tell in order to honour their agreement with Matilda Snell, the woman who had almost certainly saved their lives.

'My own fault,' he said. 'Like a darned fool, I was playing around with a loaded six-gun, trying to quicken up on my draw, and managed to shoot myself in the side. The shock bowled me over, and I hit my head hard on the ground. I can tell you for sure, it's something that ain't never going to happen to me again.

'I'm a mite embarrassed by the fool thing I did, and I'll be obliged if you don't mention it to anybody.'

'Sure,' said Fleming. 'You have my word on that.'

Dan and Marian took adjoining rooms at the hotel, and the doctor looked in periodically over the next two weeks, at the end of which he pronounced Dan fit to ride.

'I reckon,' said Dan, after the doctor had left, 'that when Vince Snell and his partners found we'd escaped, they wouldn't lose no time in leaving the homestead themselves. And I figure they'd be likely to head for Indian Territory.

'So we've got to try and pick up their trail again. And that ain't going to be easy. But I've got an idea that might help. Let's go and see Mark Dunster. He used to be the sheriff here.'

They found Dunster in his house. Dan introduced Marian to him, and she told the ex-sheriff how Vince Snell had murdered her father, and how she had decided to do all she could to bring him and his men to justice.

'I met up with Miss Foley not far from the Snell homestead,' Dan explained, 'and we joined forces to watch it. We had a good look around the buildings during the night, and watched them during the day. We're sure that the outlaws ain't there now. But we thought that maybe you know something that might help us to find them.

'When I captured Benson in Jessop, and got some information from him about the gang, he told me that Vince Snell was aiming to meet up with an old partner of his in Indian Territory. He couldn't give me a name, or tell me where the meeting was to take place. D'you recollect anything about an old partner of Snell's, who left the gang for some reason?'

Leaning back in his chair, and closing his eyes, Dunster searched his memory. Then his eyes snapped open.

'Of course!' he said. 'It must be Halliday. He was one of the first men Snell recruited for his gang. He was captured during their first bank raid. The rest of them got away with a small haul. If my memory's correct, Halliday was sentenced to four years in the state prison.'

'Does that mean,' asked Dan, 'that he might've been released already, or that maybe he's due for release any time now?'

'Could be,' Dunster replied. 'It's just about four years since I caught him.'

He rose to his feet.

'Let's go and see Sheriff Carter,' he said. 'Maybe he can help.'

They went to Carter's office, and found him seated behind his desk. Dunster introduced him to Dan and Marian, and explained the situation to him.

'What I'll do,' said the sheriff, 'is telegraph the prison governor and find out whether Halliday's been released, and if he has, whether anybody knows where he was going. Should get a reply in a day or two. I'll get in touch with you when it comes.'

Dan thanked the sheriff and Dunster, and he and Marian went for a meal at the restaurant near to the hotel.

On the following day, early in the afternoon, Carter located them in the restaurant and sat down at their table.

'I've just heard from the prison governor,' he said. 'Halliday was released a week ago. The governor found out that he enquired at the nearest stage office about the best way to get to a small town called Larita in Indian Territory. It's pretty well at the centre of the Territory.

'According to the message I got, Halliday took the next stage south after making his enquiries. There ain't no stage running through Larita, but maybe he was going by stage as far as he could, before carrying on on horseback. Are you two aimimg to ride down to Larita?'

Both Dan and Marian nodded.

'It's the only lead we've got,' said Dan. 'We're obliged to you. Before we go, we'll call on Mr Dunster and get a description of Halliday.'

A little later, when they saw Dunster, he described Halliday as now around twenty-five years old, slim, of medium height and fair-haired. He had a scar across the back of one of his hands. As they left the old lawman, he wished them well in their quest.

During the long, uneventful ride to Larita, Marian, under Dan's guidance, had several sessions of target practice with her six-gun and rifle. They reached Larita early in the day. Looking for the store, Marian spotted it a little way ahead, on the right, and they rode towards it.

On the boardwalk outside it, Rob Sinclair, twenty-year-old son of widower Herb Sinclair, who owned the store, was standing with a small tin of paint in one hand and a paint-brush in the other. He was applying a lick of paint to the outside of the store.

A short, slim youth, Rob, due to a childhood illness, had failed to develop mentally beyond the age of fourteen, but he was good-tempered and willing, and a great help to his father.

Just before they reached the store, Dan and Marian stopped at a convenient hitching rail and dismounted. Two men walked past them on the boardwalk. Both men were outlaws, seeking temporary sanctuary in Indian Territory.

The younger of the two, a man called Renton, was wearing a six-gun and carried a whip in his hand. He had a mean, scowling face. His partner, Weller, only slightly less villainous in appearance than Renton, was also wearing a six-gun. Dan looked searchingly at the two men as they passed.

As the two outlaws came towards him, Rob Sinclair stepped back to admire his handiwork. Instead of swerving slightly to avoid him, Renton pushed Rob roughly aside, causing green paint to splash out of the tin on to Renton's pants and boots.

The outlaw's temper flared. He flung Rob to the ground, and started lashing him with his whip. Yelling with pain, his victim curled up and covered his face with his hands.

Dan jumped on to the boardwalk, ran up behind Renton, and just as the outlaw was about to lash the boy for the third time, he wrenched the whip from Renton's hand, and pistol-whipped him. Then he pushed him so that he fell off the edge of the boardwalk on to the street. The outlaw lay there, momentarily stunned.

As Dan was pushing Renton on to the street, his partner Weller made a move for his six-gun, but stopped abruptly as the muzzle of a revolver was jabbed into the small of his back.

'I wouldn't do that,' said Marian. 'Just leave that gun be, and stay where you are.'

She lifted Weller's gun from the holster and threw it on the boardwalk behind her.

Dan, seeing that Weller was no threat to him, holstered his gun and stood facing Renton, who was rising to his feet.

'What a bad-tempered bully you are,' said Dan. 'That paint you got on you was your own fault. There ain't room for both of us in this town. You and your partner'll have to leave.'

Renton, recovered from the blow to the head, was quivering with rage.

'Nobody orders me out of any town,' he said. 'You're as good as dead.'

He reached for his six-gun, confident that his own gun-handling ability would quickly dispose of this meddling stranger.

But his confidence was misplaced. Dan's Peacemaker was lifted out of the holster, lined up and cocked fractionally before the gun in Renton's hand. Dan's shot penetrated the outlaw's heart, while Renton's shot went wild as he staggered back and fell to the ground, his gun falling from his hand.

Dan stepped down on to the street and picked up the gun, before bending down over Renton. He could see that the outlaw was dead.

He stepped back on to the boardwalk, and went over to Rob Sinclair, still lying curled up against the wall of the store. As Dan bent down over him, the storekeeper came out to investigate the shooting, and ran over to his son.

'What's happened here?' he asked.

'The man lying on the street gave the young fellow here a couple of lashes with a whip, before he was stopped,' said Dan. 'Does the youngster live in the store?'

'Yes,' Sinclair replied. 'He's my son.'

'Better take him inside, and tend to his wounds,' said Dan. 'I'll come in and see you later.'

Dan saw that Marian was still holding her gun on Weller. He spoke to the small group of people which had collected at the scene.

'Did any of you see all that happened here?' he asked.

'I did,' said a burly man standing at the front. 'I own the livery stable across the street. I saw it all. This man had no call to whip Rob. And he went for his gun first. You didn't have no option but to shoot him.'

'Is there an undertaker in town?' asked Dan.

'That's me,' said another man in the group, 'and I agree with what was said about you having to shoot. I'll take care of the body, and see it gets buried right.'

Dan turned to Weller.

'If you've got a notion to take revenge for what just happened to your friend,' he said, 'maybe you'd like to pick up your gun and we'll settle it right now.'

Having seen Dan in action, Weller knew he was no match for him in a gun battle. He shook his head.

'You'd best go with the undertaker then,' said Dan. 'We'll keep the six-guns in the store here till you leave town.'

Dan picked up the two weapons and Marian holstered her six-gun. Weller walked over to the undertaker and Dan joined Marian.

'Thanks for the help,' he said. 'If you hadn't taken a hand, I reckon there was a good chance of me getting shot.'

'That's what I figured,' said Marian, as Dan led the way into the store.

The storekeeper, in the living-quarters with his son, heard them come in and came into the store to meet them.

'I'm Herb Sinclair,' he said. 'My son's called Rob.'

He led them to the room where his son was lying on a bed with his shirt removed. There was a nasty weal on his back and cuts on his arm and the side of his face.

'I'll just carry on bathing these,' said Sinclair, 'then I'll bandage them. It's lucky the whipping was stopped. Maybe you'll tell me exactly what happened out there.'

When Dan had done this, he asked the storekeeper if he knew the two men.

'Never seen them before,' said Sinclair. 'We get a lot of strangers passing through. And it's a pretty safe bet most of them are criminals. Indian Territory's a favourite spot for outlaws on the run.'

As Sinclair continued to bandage his son's wounds, with Marian lending a hand, Dan explained to the storekeeper the reasons for the presence of himself and Marian in Larita. He described Vince Snell, Pearce, Benson and Halliday.

'We think these four may be around here,' he said. 'Have you seen them?'

Sinclair hesitated.

'Because of some bad things that's happened in the past,' he said, 'us townsfolk don't pass out any information about strangers that we see in town. It's safer that way. But seeing as how you helped Rob here, I feel obliged to tell you that I've seen all four of the men you just described. Snell and his two partners arrived about two weeks ago. They all came into the store to buy a few things, then booked in at the hotel.

'About five days later, the other one, Halliday I think you said, rode in about noon. I saw him go into the hotel. Not long after, all four of them came in here and bought a couple of sacks of provisions – the sort of things they would need if they were fixing to camp out and cook their own food for a spell.

'Then they all left. They were pretty close-mouthed. I ain't got no idea where they were heading.'

'We're obliged for the information,' said Dan. 'D'you happen to know which direction they took when they left town?'

'No,' replied the storekeeper, 'but I've got a friend who spends most of his time sitting on his porch just along the street. Maybe he knows.'

He tied off the last bandage.

'I'll go and ask him,' he said, 'and I'll see if the hotel keeper heard anything that might help you.'

He turned to his son.

'I'll be back soon, Rob,' he said. 'These folks'll stay here till I get back.'

Dan and Marian chatted with Rob until Sinclair returned fifteen minutes later.

'As soon as they cleared town they headed south,' he told them, 'and they kept going south as long as my friend could see them. They weren't following a trail, just heading across country. And the hotel keeper didn't hear anything that might help you.'

'Thanks,' said Dan. 'I reckon we'll have a meal, then head off in the same direction as Snell and the others.'

'The next town south of here is White Rock,'

said Sinclair, 'It's about seventy miles away. I've been there a couple of times. It's a bigger town than Larita. There's a telegraph office there, and there's a regular visit by a deputy US marshal.'

A little later, Dan and Marian discussed the situation over a meal in the hotel dining-room.

'I've got a feeling, Marian,' said Dan, 'that those four want to lie low for a while, and that they're hiding out somewhere south of here, and not that far away. Are you happy about us going to search for them?'

'Of course,' she replied, 'it's the only thing to do.'

'All right,' said Dan, 'but maybe you'd like to stay here and sleep in a proper bed for one night, before we carry on?'

'No,' said Marian, 'let's carry on as soon as we can.'

'Right,' said Dan. 'We'll buy some provisions, then we'll be on our way.'

SEVEN

Dan and Marian left Larita in the middle of the afternoon, and rode to the point where Vince Snell and his companions had disappeared from the view of Sinclair's friend. Looking out for possible hiding-places, they continued south until dark, without seeing or encountering anybody on the way.

They camped out for the night, and continued south the next morning. After riding for two hours, they were rounding the base of a knoll which lay in their path, when Dan suddenly called on Marian to stop and retrace their path around the knoll.

They dismounted, and walked back a little way round the knoll until they could look to the south again. Dan looked through his field glasses, then handed them to Marian.

'Look,' he said, pointing. 'It ain't easy to spot, but can you see that smoke? It could be from a camp-fire or a chimney.'

'I see it,' said Marian, 'but I don't see anybody near it.'

'It's a good way off,' said Dan. 'I reckon that maybe the smoke's rising out of a gully or a basin.'

Marian stiffened. 'There's a man just come into sight this side of the smoke,' she said. 'He's standing against a boulder.'

She handed the glasses to Dan, who watched the distant figure until, a few minutes later, it disappeared from view.

'It's too far away to be sure,' he said, 'but from what Dunster told us about Halliday, it could be him. He's the same sort of build. Maybe Snell and the others are hiding out over there, and Halliday's on guard.

'One thing's sure. We can't get anywhere near there in daylight without being seen. We'll stay here till after dark.'

They waited for an hour after the sun went down, then rode towards the position from which they had seen smoke rising earlier. Stopping well short of it, they tethered their mounts and advanced cautiously on foot. Dan was carrying a coil of rope.

Eventually, they found themselves standing at what appeared to be the top of the wall of a shallow ravine. Looking down to the left, they could just distinguish the outline of a small shack, with chinks of light showing at the windows.

'I'm going down there, Marian,' said Dan.

'We've got to find out if Snell and the others are in that shack. You stay here, in case I get into trouble.'

'All right,' she said, 'but take care.'

Dan sat down, and inched his way down the sloping side of the ravine until he reached the bottom. Then he slowly approached the shack. He could see no sign of anyone outside it, but from the inside came the faint sound of voices.

As he crept closer to the shack, he stopped suddenly, as his foot touched something protruding from the ground. Bending down, he could feel that it was a short wooden stake which had been driven firmly into the ground. The top of the stake was about six inches above ground level.

Dan could feel a taut wire passing through a hole near the top of the stake. Feeling the wire gently with his hand, he traced it from stake to stake as it circled the shack, then approached the rear wall and disappeared inside. Dan was sure that disturbance of the wire by anyone approaching the shack would trigger some device inside which would alert the occupants to danger.

Thankful for a lucky break, he stepped over the wire and cautiously moved up to a shuttered window in the rear wall of the shack. He could now see that the shack was old, and in a somewhat dilapidated condition. There was a gap in the shutters to which Dan applied one eye.

He drew a deep breath as he recognized the

four men seated around a table, finishing a meal. They were the four men whom he and Marian were seeking. They were talking to one another, but the sound of their conversation was so faint that Dan could not make out what was being said.

Looking towards the front wall of the shack, he could see that the door was held closed by a stout timber bar dropped in place across it. In the corner, close to the door, four rifles were resting against the wall.

Dan left the window, stepped carefully over the alarm wire, and went to look for the horses. He found them, picketed together, a little way up the ravine. Then he returned to Marian.

She heard him climbing the slope, and was waiting for him when he reached the top. He told her that their search was ended, and they sat down together, looking down at the shack below. They discussed their next move, then rested till just after midnight, half an hour after the light in the shack had been extinguished.

Taking the rope with them, Dan and Marian descended to the floor of the ravine and walked to the place where the four horses were picketed.

Dan untied one of them and, with Marian by his side, led it towards the front of the shack. As they reached the alarm wire, Dan kicked it purposely with his boot, and they heard a faint jangling sound coming from inside the shack. Dan led the horse up to the door, then he and Marian ran up the ravine and hid behind a boulder close to the picketed horses.

Inside the shack, the sound of the alarm brought Snell, lying on the only bunk, and the other three, lying on the floor, to their feet. Each of them was holding a gun in his hand. They listened for a short while, then Snell lifted the bar off the door, opened the door a few inches, and peered out. Standing just outside was an unsaddled horse which, even in the darkness, he was able to recognize as his own.

'Dammit!' he said. 'My horse is just outside the door. Must've broken loose. Take it back to the others, Tom, and make sure they're all picketed right this time. And when you come back, set the alarm again.'

Benson lit a lamp inside the shack and Pearce went out and led the horse back to the others. Inside the shack Snell lay down on the bunk again, and the other two lay down on the floor.

When Pearce reached the picket line, he tied Snell's mount to it, then bent over to check the rope holding the next horse in line. Silently, Dan came up behind the outlaw, and pistol-whipped him hard on the back of his head. Pearce collapsed on the ground.

Quickly, Dan and Marian took his gun, gagged him, and bound him securely, hand and foot. Leaving him lying there, and taking the remainder of the rope with them, they walked back towards the shack. They stepped over the alarm wire and moved silently up to the window in the rear wall. Dan looked through the gap in the shutters, then whispered to Marian.

'They're all lying down,' he said. 'Two on the floor, and one on a bunk.'

They walked round to the door. Dan pushed it open and stepped inside, with Marian close behind. She moved up to stand beside Dan as they looked at the three men, all apparently asleep. Dan fired a shot into the wall of the shack, and as the three men came fully awake, and started to sit up, he called out to them.

'Anybody reaching for a gun is a dead man,' he shouted. 'Just stay still while my partner collects them.'

Halliday, whose hand was on the floor, only inches from his six-gun, unobtrusively picked it up, then raised his arm quickly to shoot at Dan. Dan's eye caught the movement, and he shot Halliday through the head before his opponent had triggered his gun.

At the same time, Marian fired a warning shot close to Snell, followed by one which narrowly missed Benson's ear. Dan held a gun on Snell and Benson, while Marian collected the weapons. Then, after confirming that Halliday was dead, he and Marian securely bound the outlaw leader and his companion, and laid them down on the floor close to Halliday. During this procedure neither of them spoke, but Dan noticed them glancing towards the door.

'Don't expect Pearce to take a hand,' he said. 'We took care of him before we came in here.'

'Watch them, Marian,' he went on, 'while I bring Pearce here. Shoot them if they don't lie still. Like you, I don't much care whether we take them in dead or alive.'

Dan found Pearce conscious. He untied his feet, pulled him upright, and forced him, with a gun at his back, to walk to the shack. Inside, he ordered Pearce to lie down beside his partners, and secured his feet again. He told the prisoners that if they talked to him or Marian, or among themselves, he would gag them all. Then he took Marian outside.

'You sure done good, Marian,' he said. 'I'll drag Halliday outside, and bury him in the morning. For the rest of the night, we'll stay inside the shack and watch those three. Don't forget for one minute that they're very dangerous men. We'll spell each other off for the rest of the night, so's we each get a little sleep.

'I reckon our best plan is to get the prisoners to White Rock, the place Sinclair told us about. Once we get there, we can arrange for the law to pick them up. What d'you think?'

'I think you're right,' Marian replied, 'and I know how dangerous they are. We'll have to watch them every step of the way.'

When daylight came, Dan went outside and buried Halliday, leaving Marian to guard the prisoners. When he had finished the job, he walked a little way down the ravine to inspect what looked like the remains of a prairie schooner, one of the covered wagons which had accompanied many thousands of pioneers heading westward from Missouri into what they fervently believed was to be a brighter future for themselves and their children.

The canvas or cotton cover, and the bows which had supported it, had long since disappeared, and much of the timber which had formed the sides of the wagon bed was missing. But the floor of the wagon bed, the timber parts underneath it, and the tongue, were in reasonable condition.

He looked at the wheels. The iron tyres were rusted a little on the outer surface, but were still intact, and the wheels looked to be sound. Partially embedded in the ground underneath the wagon he saw the harness. When he'd pulled it free, he could see that it was still serviceable.

He returned to the shack and called Marian outside.

'I wasn't too happy,' he said, 'about the idea of us taking those three to White Rock with them on horseback. It could be hard work for us. They'll all be looking out for the slightest chance to escape.

'But I reckon I have the answer. There's an old prairie schooner down the ravine that might just make it to White Rock. We'll hitch a couple of horses to it, and carry those three on the wagon bed, tied so's they can't move, except when we give them a break, one by one, and feed them. If we take it easy, and there's still some grease left on the axles, maybe we'll make it. Could be there by late tomorrow.'

Using the provisions in the shack, they made a meal for themselves, then gave food and drink to the prisoners, who, mindful of Dan's threat to gag them, made no attempt to talk to their captors.

Dan went to collect his horse, and that of Marian. On his return, he led two of the outlaws' horses to the wagon, and hitched them to it. Then, sitting on the front of the wagon bed, he managed to persuade the horses to pull it up to the shack. He was relieved to note that the wheels were rotating fairly smoothly.

With Marian's help, he dragged the cursing figures of the bound outlaws outside, and hoisted them on to the wagon bed. They used rope to secure the prisoners to the wagon bed in a horizontal position. They placed some provisions on the wagon, then, with Marian on horseback, and three horses tied behind the wagon, they were on their way.

The journey went well that day, and they camped out overnight. The following morning, they started early, and stopped at noon for a short break. They arrived at White Rock an hour before nightfall.

Their arrival caused a stir as they headed for the centre of town. A growing group of people accompanied them, pushing up to the wagon to get a good look at the three prisoners. Dan stopped the wagon and spoke to the onlookers.

'Who's the head man in this town?' he asked.

'That would be Mr Halley,' said a man at the front of the crowd. 'He owns the hotel and the store.'

'You know where I might find him?' asked Dan.

'In the hotel, I reckon,' said the man. 'I'll run along and tell him you're looking for him.'

Following the man, Dan drove the wagon along the street and pulled up outside the hotel. Hailey was standing on the boardwalk outside. He was a tall man, middle-aged, well-dressed, and wearing a neatly trimmed beard and moustache.

Dan jumped down off the wagon and introduced Marian and himself to Hailey. He explained their presence and that of the three prisoners. Hailey stepped down into the street and had a good look at the outlaws. He stared hard into the face, flushed with rage, of Vince Snell, crammed uncomfortably between his two partners on the floor of the wagon.

'That's Snell, for sure,' he said. 'I saw a Wanted poster for him a while back, when I was in Dodge City. It's a face you ain't likely to forget.'

'Can you hold them in town till the law picks them up?' asked Dan.

'Sure,' said Hailey. 'We're expecting a couple of deputy US marshals to call here in two or three days' time. They call in regular, but not always the same ones each time. You'd probably be surprised if you knew how many deputies are patrolling Indian Territory.

'We've built a jail behind the hotel, where we can hold criminals until the deputies turn up. There's room for those three in there.'

'I'll help out with guarding them till the law turns up,' offered Dan. 'Are there any other men in town you can call on? These prisoners have got to be watched pretty close. They're all killers.'

'Sure,' answered Hailey. 'I can get as many as we'll need. We'll put two armed guards over the prisoners day and night, with the guards being relieved every four hours. Drive the wagon around the back, and we'll slap them in jail right now.'

Round at the jail they took the ropes off the prisoners and fastened them in a single barred cell, furnished with three bunks. The cell, and the passage leading to its door, were separated from the other room in the building by a partition, with a communicating door. This other room, furnished with a small table and two comfortable chairs, was intended to accommodate the guards.

Two men, who had been sent for by Hailey, arrived to take up guard duty. The hotel-keeper spoke to Dan and Marian.

'I reckon you two are glad to see Snell and the

others behind bars,' he said. 'Come over to the hotel with me. I've a couple of rooms there you can use. And maybe you'd like to take a meal with me. I'd like to hear a lot more about how you came to be trailing those three outlaws.'

Dan and Marian accepted the offer, and accompanied Hailey to the hotel. After the meal, Hailey left them, telling Dan that he would let him know later when he was required for guard duty. He said that it would probably not be until the following day.

At the time the three prisoners were being taken off the wagon and put into the jail, a man who had earlier walked up to the wagon as Hailey was inspecting the prisoners, pushed to the front of the group of onlookers to watch the proceedings.

As the prisoners disappeared from view, he left the group, and walked to his horse, which was tied to a hitching rail in the street. He picked up a sack of provisions which he had purchased earlier, and rode fast out of town in a westerly direction.

After travelling five miles, he left the trail, rode north-west for a further two miles, and entered a deep gully. He rode along it to join a group of four men, seated on the ground, who had been awaiting his arrival.

The rider was Lou Perrin, and the men waiting for him were Grant Henderson, and the other members of the Henderson gang of outlaws, whose criminal activities ranged from Kansas to East Texas. Henderson, the leader, was a stocky man, hard-faced and beetle-browed, with a considerable reputation as a gunfighter. The three men seated by him were Clancey, Wiley and Porter.

Perrin dismounted and walked up to Henderson.

'I've got bad news for you,' he said. 'Three of the four men we were supposed to meet up with in that ravine north of here are in jail in White Rock. They were brought into town on a wagon, all tied up, by a man and a woman. The man was called Quigley.'

'Damnation!' said Henderson. 'Who were the three?'

'I got a good look at them,' said Perrin. 'They were Snell, Benson and Pearce. The one missing was Halliday.'

'We really need those three for that job we've got planned,' said Henderson. 'What's the jail like?'

'It's a small building behind the hotel,' Perrin replied, 'and they were fixing to post a couple of guards inside it, day and night, until two deputy US marshals turn up in two or three days' time. The guards were going to be relieved every four hours.'

'This man Quigley and the woman with him,' said Henderson, 'did you get to know anything about them?'

'No,' replied Perrin, 'I figured I'd better come and tell you about Snell and the others as quick as I could.'

'You done right,' said Henderson. 'We're going to bust those three out of jail before the deputies turn up. We'll do it tonight. Soon after midnight would be a good time.'

He walked to his horse, and from one of the saddlebags he took a couple of deputy US marshal badges taken from two lawmen who had been chasing them in Indian Territory several months earlier. They had ambushed the two deputies, and had killed them, then buried them on the spot.

He walked back to the others, fastening one of the badges to his vest. The other one he handed to Clancey, his second in command.

'I figured these might come in useful one day,' he said. 'Let's talk about how we're going to free Snell and the others.'

EIGHT

Henderson and his men left the gully late in the evening. Clancey and the outlaw leader were wearing the deputy US marshal badges on their vests. They rode towards White Rock, and stopped on the edge of town. Perrin went on ahead to look at the jail from a distance. He was back in twenty minutes. The time was just on midnight.

'There's nobody outside the jail,' he reported, 'and while I was watching, two men turned up to relieve the two guards inside.'

'Good,' said Henderson. 'That means that we've got four hours before the next change-over.'

Half an hour later, leaving Porter with the horses, Henderson and Clancey started walking towards the jail, and Wiley and Perrin headed for the livery stable. All four men, who were carrying rope with them, kept off the main street, and moved silently in the shadows.

When Wiley and Perrin arrived at the stable, they went to the door of the liveryman's house, which was located behind the stable. The house was in darkness. Perrin knocked hard on the door a couple of times, and a light showed from inside.

The door was opened by Stone, the liveryman. A short man in his early sixties, he was holding a lamp in his hand. He saw the guns in the hands of the two men outside, and hurriedly attempted to close the door, but they forced it open. Wiley grabbed Stone and held a gun against his head, while Perrin closed the door behind them.

They went into the bedroom, where Stone's wife was sitting up in bed, and securely gagged and bound the couple, leaving them lying on the bed.

'That should hold them long enough,' said Perrin.

The two men left the house and walked over to the stable. Inside, they lit a lamp, and looked at the five horses inside. They selected three, put saddles and bridles on them, and led them out of the stable, leaving it in darkness. Leading the horses, they made their way to the place where Porter was waiting.

Meanwhile, Henderson and Clancey walked up to the door of the jail and stood outside.

'Remember,' whispered Henderson. 'No shooting.'

Clancey nodded his head, then rapped on the door. After a brief interval they heard a voice inside asking who was there.

'Deputy US marshals Green and Bradford,'

shouted Henderson. 'We'd like to take a look at the prisoners.'

There was a pause, then the door was unfastened and opened half-way. The two guards, Hartford and Meaker, peered out. Hartford was holding a lamp, and Meeker was pointing a two-barrelled shotgun at the two men outside. The guards could see the deputy marshal badges on Henderson and Clancey.

'We've just seen Mr Hailey at the hotel,' said Henderson. 'That's great news about you holding the Snell gang here. We sure would like to see them.'

'We didn't expect you for a couple of days,' said Meeker.

'That's right,' said Henderson. 'We've altered our schedule. Better for you, though. We'll take charge of the prisoners in the morning, after we've had some sleep.'

'I'd like to check with Mr Hailey before you come in,' said Meeker.

'All right,' said Henderson, 'we'll go and bring him here. Mind you, it may take a little while. He was on his way to bed when we left him.'

He and Clancey turned, and started walking towards the hotel.

'Stop!' said Meeker. 'There's no need. Come on in.'

He opened the door wide and the two outlaws entered. As Meeker turned to stand his shotgun in the corner against the wall, Henderson struck him savagely over the head with the barrel of his six-gun. Simultaneously, Clancey handed out the same treatment to the unsuspecting Hartford as he placed the lamp on the table.

Both men collapsed on the floor, and Henderson took their six-guns while Clancey went for the rope they had left lying on the ground outside. The outlaws gagged the two guards and bound them securely. Then, taking a key from a hook on the wall, they walked through the door to the pasaage outside the cell. In the passage was a lighted lamp.

Snell left his bunk as the two men came in to the passage and walked up to the bars of the cell. He did not recognize them for a moment. When he did, his relief was patent.

'Mighty glad to see you, Grant,' he said. 'We was wondering whether you'd heard about us being picked up.'

'Perrin just happened to be in town to pick up some provisions when you were brought in,' said Henderson, as he unlocked the cell door. 'We've got horses waiting for you just outside town, and I reckon it'll be three hours or more before the alarm's raised.'

They dragged the two guards into the cell, and locked them in. Hartford was conscious, but Meeker was still not moving. Henderson handed the guards' six-guns to Snell and Pearce, then the five men went to join the other three waiting just outside town.

On the way, Snell explained how he and his men had been captured, with the loss of Halliday, by a man and woman seeking vengeance.

'This man and woman who brought you in,' asked Henderson, 'd'you reckon they'll still try to find you even though they know there are at least seven of us?'

'I have a strong feeling,' said Snell, 'that that's exactly what they'll do.'

'In that case, we'd better watch out for them,' said Henderson, as they joined the three men waiting for them.

The combined force of outlaws rode off to the north. Their destination was South Kansas. Henderson had, a while back, received information from a hitherto reliable source, that a freight wagon carrying a large shipment of gold, and travelling west to east, was due to arrive in Dodge City in about a week's time. The wagon was to be escorted by three armed Wells Fargo guards. The intention of Henderson and Snell was, with their combined gangs, to steal this shipment.

At fifteen minutes past four o'clock in the morning, Dan and Marian were woken by Hailey. He told them that Snell and his men had escaped, with the help of four strangers, probably friends of theirs, about three and a half hours earlier.

'Was anybody hurt?' asked Dan.

'The two guards, Hartford and Meeker, were both pistol-whipped by two men wearing deputy US marshal badges,' said Hailey. 'Hartford came round all right, but we're worried about Meeker. Looks like he was hit real hard, and he ain't come round yet. The doc's tending him right now.'

He went on to give Dan and Marian more details of the night's happenings.

'Come daylight,' said Dan, 'we'll see if we can find out which way those men were headed when they left here. Then we'll take off after them.'

'You sure?' asked Hailey, looking at Marian. 'You'll be up against seven men, maybe more, if you do.'

'I'm sure,' said Dan, looking at Marian. He was confident about what her answer would be.

'Me too,' she said.

When daylight came, Dan examined the ground just outside town, and found the place where the men who stole the horses had assembled with Snell and his men, and their rescuers, before riding off. The men had all left together, heading in a northerly direction. He walked back to the hotel to join Marian and Hailey. He told them what he had found.

'We'll follow them after breakfast,' he said.

'Right,' said Hailey. 'When the real deputies turn up, I'll let them know exactly what happened here.'

Dan and Marian left an hour later, and followed the tracks for five miles, then lost them, when they were still heading north, on a stretch of terrain unsuitable for tracking by anybody other than an expert. After a fruitless attempt to pick them up again, they continued in a northerly direction.

Dan spoke to Marian.

'I've been thinking about the men we're following, Marian,' he said. 'Maybe Snell was due to meet up at the ravine with the men who rescued him. Maybe they found out, somehow, that Snell and his men had been captured.

'It could be that they planned to join forces for a big job like the robbery of a large gold shipment being carried by train, or maybe freight wagon. If that's true, it's more than likely that the robbery would take place in South Kansas, which is exactly where we're headed. So let's carry on till something turns up.'

'All right,' said Marian, 'it's all we can do. But I must say I was some disappointed when we heard about Snell and the others being rescued. I'd figured that our job was finished.'

'Me too,' said Dan.

They continued north to Larita, camping out overnight on the way, and rode up to the general store around mid-morning. Sinclair was at the counter inside. They described the events which had taken place since they last saw him, and asked if a bunch of riders, at least seven, had been seen in town the previous day.

Sinclair shook his head.

'No,' he replied, 'I'd sure have noticed them if they'd been here.

'Just a minute, though,' he went on, after a brief pause. 'I had a freight wagon call here yesterday evening, delivering some supplies. The driver mentioned that earlier in the day, when he was ten miles west of here, he spotted a bunch of riders crossing the trail ahead of him. They were heading north.'

'Is the driver still in town?' asked Dan.

Sinclair looked out of the window.

'There's his wagon,' he said, pointing, 'just along the street. I reckon he'll be moving off soon.'

Dan and Marian left the store and walked along to the wagon. The driver was just about to climb on to the driving seat when Dan spoke to him.

'The storekeeper figured that maybe you could help us,' he said. 'He told me you saw a bunch of riders yesterday when you were heading this way.'

'That's right,' said the driver, 'about ten miles west of here.'

'How many riders, would you say?' asked Dan.

'They were quite a ways off,' replied the driver, 'so I can't be sure. But I'd say there were seven or eight, and one of the riders looked to be on the big side. They were heading north.'

Dan thanked the driver, and turned to Marian.

'Looks like those riders the driver saw could be the ones we're after,' he said. 'Let's angle off a little to the west, and maybe we'll get more news of them.'

But they were disappointed. Two days later they reached the Kansas border without hearing of any further sightings of the outlaws. Then their luck changed.

In the small town of Padlow, just over the border, they spoke with a man working on the roof of a building on the edge of town. On the previous day, he had noticed a group of eight riders, who stopped well outside town. One of the group had ridden to the store, and later, carrying a large sack, he had rejoined the others. The group had then ridden off to the north.

Dan and Marian went to see the storekeeper. He told them that the sack contained provisions, and gave a close description of the man who bought them. The description tallied with Benson.

'Dodge City's roughly north of here,' said Dan to Marian as they left the store. 'It's a little over fifty miles away. Let's ride in that direction, asking on the way if anybody's seen the eight riders. If we get no news of them, we'll carry on to Dodge City and have a talk with Sheriff Carter.'

'All right,' said Marian. 'I can't think of a better idea.'

They reached Dodge City the following day, without hearing any further news of the eight outlaws. They headed straight for the sheriff's office, to find there was a note tacked to the door saying that he would be out of town till eight o'clock on the evening of the following day.

They took rooms at the hotel nearby, and went to the sheriff's office the next day, in the evening.

Sheriff Carter was inside, and he listened with mounting interest as they told him of all the events which had occurred since their last meeting.

'You could be right,' said the sheriff, 'in thinking that the two gangs have joined up for a big operation. And it looks like it could be in my territory. They could be after a big gold shipment going east by rail, or maybe by express wagon. The last would be easier to rob.'

He called a deputy over, and asked him to go to the Wells Fargo office and see if the agent, Josh Pallister, could come over to see him.

Pallister, a neatly dressed middle-aged man, returned with the deputy. Carter introduced him to Dan and Marian.

'Mr Quigley and Miss Foley have been chasing the Snell gang,' he told Pallister. 'They captured them in Indian Territory, but through no fault of theirs, the gang escaped. They know that Snell and his partners joined up with a group of five men, and all eight of them crossed the border into Kansas, south of here, two days ago.

'They don't know who the other five are, but it looks like they could be planning a big operation some time soon. I was wondering if you knew of any valuable shipments in the offing in this area?'

Pallister, glancing at Dan and Marian, hesitated before he replied.

'Whatever I tell you, Matt,' he said, 'has to be in confidence.'

'Agreed,' said the sheriff, 'and I think I can say the same for Mr Quigley and Miss Foley.'

Dan and Marian both nodded.

'Right,' said Pallister, 'in that case, I have two pieces of information that might interest you.

'Firstly, I received a coded message by telegraph only half an hour ago, that an express wagon's coming into Dodge from the west, the day after tomorrow. It'll be carrying a quarter million dollars' worth of gold, to be transferred to an east-bound train.

'Though I've only just heard about it, the shipment could have been planned a while back. As well as the gold and the driver, the wagon's carrying four Wells Fargo armed guards.'

'That shipment could be the target that Snell and the others are aiming for,' said Carter, 'and I reckon they're aiming to make the steal before the wagon reaches Dodge.'

'You could be right,' said Pallister. 'The other piece of information I have is that I happen to know that about three years ago in Texas, the Snell gang joined up with the Henderson gang to carry out a big bullion robbery. Maybe the same thing's happened again.'

'We've got to warn the men on that wagon,' said Carter. 'D'you know what trail they'll be on?'

'Yes,' replied the agent. 'They'll be on the trail from Twin Springs to Dodge. The trail heads south-west from Dodge, then runs fairly close to the border with Indian Territory.'

'I can get a posse organized by daylight,' said the sheriff. 'We'll ride out then, to meet the wagon.'

He looked at Dan and Marian. 'You want to come along?' he asked.

They both nodded.

'Figured you might,' said Carter. 'Glad to have you along. We'll leave just before daybreak.'

NINE

When the posse left Dodge City, in the direction of Twin Springs, the sheriff set a brisk pace, with an occasional rest for the horses. He was hoping that by sundown they would meet up with the express wagon carrying the gold shipment.

They had reached a point twenty-eight miles out of Dodge City, with no sighting of the wagon, when Dan, riding with Marian on one flank of the posse, noticed some marks on the ground between the edge of the trail and a patch of tall thick brush which stood nearby.

He called out to the sheriff, and the posse came to a halt as Dan dismounted to look at the marks. Carter joined him a moment later. It looked as though several heavy objects had been dragged off the trail, and over to the brush. Then they saw several patches of what looked like dried blood on the ground.

Dan and Carter walked over to the brush patch, parted it, and pushed their way inside. They came to a sudden halt. In front of them, piled up on the ground, lay the bodies of seven men.

Deeply shocked, the sheriff cursed. Then, with Dan's help he had a close look at each of the bodies. When he had done this, they both turned and walked out of the brush. The sheriff spoke to the posse.

'This is bad,' he said. 'There are seven bodies here, all with gunshot wounds, and all dead. There are four Wells Fargo guards, one man who looks like the wagon driver, and two others, likely from the gang that attacked the wagon.'

'One of those two,' said Dan, 'is Pearce, a member of the Snell gang.'

They carried the bodies out of the brush, then looked at the tracks left by the wagon wheels. They could see where the wagon had stopped, and had later been driven off the trail, towards the south.

'They're heading for Indian Territory, for sure,' said Carter.

Leaving two members of the posse behind to arrange for the bodies to be transported to Dodge City, the rest of the posse followed the wagon tracks for a little over a mile, where they led into a gully. Here they found the empty wagon. Horse tracks indicated that the outlaws had continued in a southerly direction, and the posse followed suit.

A few miles further on, they came across the owner of a small ranch which lay in their path, and they enquired whether he had seen any sign of the outlaws.

'Maybe,' he replied. 'I saw a bunch of riders over to the east yesterday, but I didn't get a close look at them. There were six, I think, and they were leading two horses. And another thing, I found four stray horses on my range this morning, and they weren't saddle-horses.'

'Probably the ones that were hauling the express wagon,' said the sheriff.

They thanked the rancher, picked up the trail of the outlaws, and followed it up to the border with Indian Territory. Here the posse halted.

'My jurisdiction ends here,' said the sheriff to Dan. 'I want these outlaws just as much as you do, but I can't take my posse over the border. I'll get a message to the US marshal at Fort Smith as soon as I can. I'll tell him about the hold-up, and about the robbers crossing into his territory.'

'We'll be leaving you, then,' said Dan.

'I figured you would,' said Carter, and watched Dan and Marian for a while as they crossed the border and rode on to the south. While wishing them well, he was in no doubt about the hugeness of the risk they were taking.

The outlaws appeared to be sticking to a well-defined trail to the south, and Dan and Marian followed this until darkness fell. They made camp for the night, and on the following morning they continued along the trail.

They had covered about four miles when they came in view of a solitary building a little way ahead. As they drew closer, they could see the words SULLY'S STORE painted in large white letters on the front of the building.

They dismounted outside the store and went inside. Sully, the storekeeper, standing near some shelves at the back of the store, turned and walked slowly up to them, taking a good look at Dan, then Marian. He was a short man of middle age, balding, with a plump face.

'Howdy,' he said. 'You folks need some supplies?'

'A few,' Dan replied, 'and maybe some information if you have it.'

'Sure,' said Sully. 'Just now, I'm dealing with a customer out at the back, but it won't take long. Have a look round inside here while you're waiting.'

He left through the back door of the store, closing it behind him, and went over to a half-breed Indian, employed by him, who was opening some packing cases.

'Chato,' he said. 'Ride fast to the outlaws' hideout. Tell them that the man and woman they told us about are here, and will soon be riding on through the pass.'

Chato ran to a pony standing behind the store, untied it, and leapt on to its back. A moment later, he was racing towards the south.

Sully went back into the store, and spoke to Dan and Marian.

'Now folks,' he said, 'what can I do for you?'

'We'd like some supplies,' said Dan, 'but first, did you see a bunch of six riders pass here yesterday, leading two horses?'

'I did,' Sully replied. 'One of them came into the store for some supplies. The others waited for him well away from the store. I figured that maybe they were criminals on the run, and didn't want me to get a good look at them.'

'They were heading south?' asked Dan.

'That's right,' Sully replied. 'Let me show you.'

He led them outside, and pointed towards a low ridge in the distance.

'You see that gap in the ridge,' he said. 'I happened to be outside the store not long after the riders had moved on, and I saw them riding into that gap. As to who they were, I ain't got no idea. I learnt a long time ago that it pays not to be curious about any strangers passing this way.'

Dan and Marian bought a few items, then rode on towards the ridge pointed out by Sully. As they drew closer they could see that the floor of the narrow gap was scattered with large boulders, up to ten feet high. Only a narrow zigzag passage was available for riders passing through.

When they reached the gap Dan took the lead, and they threaded their way through the boulders. They had reached a point about half-way through the gap when four men holding six-guns suddenly came out from behind a large boulder just in front of them. The men blocked their path and one of them ordered the two riders to raise their hands.

Dan recognized Benson, and he realized that any resistance would be suicidal. The other three men were strangers to him. He raised his hands. Marian did the same. Quickly, they were relieved of their weapons, and their hands were tied. Then Benson spoke to them.

'Snell ain't around just now,' he said, 'but he'll be back with Henderson day after tomorrow. He's sure going to be pleased to see you two, thanks to Sully, after all the trouble you've caused us. One thing's sure. You ain't going to die easy.'

Leading the prisoners' horses, the four outlaws walked back along the gap to the place where they had hidden their own mounts. Then they all rode on through the gap, turned to the left, and rode along the foot of the south side of the ridge. Half a mile further on, they turned into a small ravine which cut into the side of the ridge, and stopped, close to an opening in the side of the ravine. The prisoners were ordered to dismount, and were then led through the opening and along a short passage into a large cave. It was roughly circular in shape, with a high ceiling, and was about thirty feet in diameter. From the objects lying in the cave, it was apparent that it was being used by the outlaws.

The prisoners' feet were tied and they were ordered to sit on the floor of the cave, with their backs to the wall. Their rifles and six-guns were placed on the floor at the far side of the cave. Wiley, a member of the Henderson gang, kept watch over the cave entrance, while Clancey and Perrin, also Henderson's men, sat inside, chatting with Benson.

Clancey noticed that Perrin, a stocky, swarthy individual, with a pock-marked face, appeared to be showing an excessive interest in the young woman seated on the far side of the cave. His eyes seldom left her, and when they did, they quickly returned.

'Forget it, Lou,' said Clancey, aware of Perrin's lecherous nature. 'I know what you're thinking. But nobody harms the man or the woman till Grant and Vince get back.'

Benson's eyes strayed to Dan from time to time as he recollected their encounter in Jessop.

'When Quigley over there captured me in Jessop,' he told the others, 'he took me out of town, built a fire under a tree, and hung me over it, head down. I damn near lost all my hair, and it didn't do the skin on my head any good either.'

'He was trying to make you talk?' asked Clancey.

'That's right,' Benson replied. 'It was only by telling him a pack of lies that I managed to stop him from lowering me right down on to that fire. After what he did to me, it galls me to see them sitting there so comfortable.'

He stood up, walked over to the two prisoners, and inspected the wall of the cave above their heads. He could see, at a height of about eight feet above the floor of the cave, a narrow horizontal fissure in the wall, about five feet in length.

He walked to the far side of the cave, and picked up a rifle and a stout wooden box, one of several which were being used as seats. He returned to Dan and Marian, and standing on the box, he poked the barrel of his rifle into the fissure, to confirm that it was deep enough for his purpose. He walked back to Clancey and Perrin.

'What I aim to do,' he said,'is ride to the store and get a couple of lengths of iron bar and a heavy hammer from that old blacksmith shop behind the store.

'I reckon I can fix it so's we can hang these two up with their feet clear of the floor. That way, they ain't going to be exactly comfortable, and they won't be able to get up to any mischief while we're asleep. We'll slap gags on them so's they can't make a lot of noise if they can't stand the pain.'

'All right,' said Clancey, 'and bring back some tobacco and coffee. We're running short of both.'

When Benson reached the store he told Sully about the capture of Dan and Marian.

'Henderson and Snell are away on business just now,' he said, 'but I reckon that when they get back there'll be a reward for you for helping us to capture Quigley and the woman.'

He went into the disused blacksmith shop and rummaged around until he found two pieces of iron bar of the right dimensions, and a heavy hammer.

Back at the cave, he stood on the box and hammered the two metal bars well into the fissure, about three feet apart. Each bar projected horizontally from the wall for about two feet. He tested each bar by grasping it, and hanging from it for a while with his feet clear of the floor. Each of the bars remained firmly in place.

Later in the evening, when the outlaws decided it was time for sleep, Perrin went outside, to start his period of guard duty, and Wiley came in.

Benson checked the ropes around the wrists and lower legs of the two prisoners, and gagged them both. Then, with the help of Clancey and Wiley, they lifted Dan, with his back to the wall, and positioned him so that one of the bars ran between his upstretched arms, immediately below the rope which was firmly binding his wrists together. Using the second bar, they repeated the process for Marian.

Hanging from the bars, the two prisoners could feel them digging painfully into the flesh of their arms, close to the ropes.

The three outlaws lay down at the side of the cave opposite to that where the prisoners were hanging. A lighted lamp stood on the floor near them. Within twenty minutes, all three appeared to be fast asleep. Benson, who had been observing Dan with grim satisfaction, was the last to go.

Dan turned his head to look at Marian. She stared back at him. Her face showed the increasing pain caused by the combined effects of the strain on her arms as they supported the full weight of her body; and the metal bar digging into the flesh on her arms.

He looked up at the bar from which he was suspended. Perhaps, he thought, he could move his arms along it to the end of the bar, and so drop to the floor. Keeping watch on the three sleeping men, he used his feet to push himself away from the wall, and at the same time he tried to move his arms along the bar.

But after fifteen minutes of concentrated effort, he was in exactly the same position as when he started, and the pain in his arms was intense. Then it occurred to him that the bar was possibly made of malleable material, capable of bending.

Gritting his teeth, he raised his body by bending his elbows, then let it drop back freely to its previous position. This produced momentary additional downward pressure on the bar.

Despite the severe pain, and keeping a close watch on the three sleeping men, he slowly repeated the procedure a dozen times, then looked up at the bar. He was certain that it was now slightly bent towards the floor. As he took a short rest, he turned his head to look at Marian. She was looking up at the bar above his head, and he guessed she had realized what he was trying to do.

He continued his efforts, pausing from time to time, encouraged by the fact that the bend in the bar was becoming more pronounced. But it took another thirty agonizing drops before the bar bent to such a degree that he slid off it and collapsed silently on the floor of the cave.

He lay there for a moment, watching the three outlaws. They were still sleeping soundly. He sat up, bent forward and, with his wrists still tied, managed with some difficulty to untie the rope around his legs. He stood up close to Marian, and passed his hands under her feet. Then he encircled her legs with his arms, lifted her off the bar, and lowered her to the floor.

They both froze as a snorting sound came from one of the sleeping men. As they watched the outlaws, praying that their escape attempt was not to be nipped in the bud, Clancey turned over, snorted once again, and shortly after, started snoring gently.

Dan untied the rope around Marian's legs, then they both stood up and she untied the rope around his wrists. He performed the same service for her and they removed the gags from their mouths.

'We've got to move quick,' said Dan, 'before they wake up or the guard comes in. I think I'd better put the guard out of action first. Let's get our six-guns. They're on the floor over there.'

They moved silently across the cave, and picked

up and checked their six-guns, which were lying not far from the sleeping men. Each of the outlaws had placed a six-gun on the floor, close to his side.

'Remember, Marian,' whispered Dan, 'these men are all killers of the worst kind. If we're forced to shoot, we must do our best to shoot to kill. All right?'

Pale-faced, but resolute, Marian nodded her head.

'I'll go and attend to the guard,' said Dan. 'I'll pistol-whip him, and tie him up with that rope they used on us, and gag him. You stand just inside that passage leading out of the cave, and watch those three. If they wake before I'm back, come out to me.'

Marian nodded, and while Dan was creeping across the cave to pick up the rope and a gag, she turned to move towards the passage. As she did so, her foot caught the butt of her rifle, which was standing against the wall. As it fell, it dislodged Dan's rifle which was standing against it, and with a loud clatter both weapons fell on the floor.

Clancey was instantly awake, his hand reaching for his gun. The reactions of his two partners were a little slower. Clancey's gun swung towards Dan, but Dan's bullet hit him in the head before the outlaw fired.

Marian saw that Benson was sitting up and reaching for his gun. As he picked up the revolver, then turned it towards her, she shot him in the chest.

Wiley and Dan fired simultaneously at one another. Dan directed a lethal shot into Wiley's chest, whereas the bullet from the outlaw's six-shooter grazed Dan's left temple, and sent him, temporarily dazed, to his knees.

A moment later, Perrin, alerted by the shooting, ran into the cave. Immediately, his attention was riveted on the scene in front of him – the three outlaws lying on the floor of the cave, and Dan on his knees, still dazed, and shaking his head.

For the moment, the outlaw failed to notice Marian, standing to one side of him, against the wall of the cave, with a six-gun in her hand. As he moved towards Dan, intent on administering a fatal shot, Marian steadied herself, took careful aim, and shot him in the back. Perrin collapsed on the floor of the cave without firing.

Moments later, Dan staightened up, and was able to check each of the four outlaws lying on the floor. When he had done this, he walked over to Marian, who was standing, white-faced and shaken, watching him.

'They're all dead, Marian,' he said. 'Never forget, it was either them or us.'

She nodded, then looked at the wound on Dan's temple.

'Your head!' she said.

'Just a graze,' said Dan, feeling the wound. 'It's hardly bleeding. Could have been a lot worse if you hadn't shot Perrin down.'

He walked over to a small pile of something against the wall of the cave, which was covered by a canvas sheet. Removal of the sheet revealed a heap of small stout bags, each tied firmly at the top. He picked one up, opened it and looked inside.

'I thought so,' he said, as he retied the bag and dropped it back on the pile. 'This must be the gold dust they stole from the express wagon. Let's go outside, and decide what we do next.'

They walked through the passage and sat on the ground outside. The night was warm, and Marian was beginning to regain her composure.

'Come daylight,' said Dan, 'we'll have all day to get ready for Snell and Henderson when they get back tomorrow. Let's work out a plan to catch them both.'

After half an hour's discussion, Dan suggested that they rested there, and they lay on the ground until dawn, when they had a meal. The pain in Dan's arms and shoulders was easing.

Leaving Marian outside the cave entrance, Dan walked over to a large dense patch of brush growing at the foot of the opposite side of the ravine. He examined this closely, then climbed out of the ravine and walked up to look at a nearby level patch of ground which was cluttered with innumerable small fragments of rock.

He returned to the brush patch, and forced his way to the centre, leaving a narrow passage behind him. It was a difficult task which took some time. When he had finished, he came out of the brush and rejoined Marian.

'I've found a hiding-place for the gold,' he said, 'and a spot where I can bury the four outlaws.'

With Marian's help, he removed all the bags of gold from the cave to the ground at the centre of the brush patch, where they would be completely hidden. When all the bags had been transferred, Dan carefully rearranged the thick brush to close the passage he had made. He also removed all trace of their footprints near the brush.

'The next thing,' he said, when the job was finished, 'is to get those four bodies to that burial place I found. But I can do that myself.'

'We're partners, ain't we?' said Marian. 'I'm going to help you. How do we get the bodies over there?'

'We'll use their horses to carry them,' Dan replied. 'We'll lead them out of the ravine, and circle round to the place I found.'

They dragged the bodies out of the cave, and slung them on the backs of the outlaws' horses. Then, riding their own mounts, they led the horses to the flat stretch of rock-strewn ground which Dan had visited earlier.

They selected a place where the rock fragments were thickly piled, and removed sufficient rocks over a small area to produce a shallow trench in which the bodies were laid, side by side. Then they replaced sufficient pieces of rock to fill in the grave, and level it off with the surrounding undisturbed ground. When they had finished, there was no indication that anything was buried there.

'I'm glad that's over,' said Marian. 'I wasn't sure I could go through with it.'

'You did fine,' said Dan, 'and I'm sure glad of your help. Our next job is to find somewhere to hide the horses. Let's take them, and have a look around.'

About three quarters of a mile from the ravine, and not visible from it, they found a grassy hollow which seemed suitable for the purpose. They hobbled six horses, including the two belonging to the two outlaws killed when the express wagon was robbed, and left them there. Then they rode back to the cave.

Inside it, they removed all traces of blood on the floor, knocked out the two bars protruding from the wall, and carried the outlaws' belongings and provisions outside. The cave now gave the appearance that the occupants had left of their own accord – with the gold.

Dan looked along the tops of the sloping sides of the ravine. A little further up the ravine, he could see a small grove of trees. He pointed it out to Marian.

'That's where we can wait for Snell and Henderson,' he said. 'Let's carry all this stuff up there.'

When they had done this, they tethered their horses inside the grove, well back from the ravine, and settled down to await the arrival of the two outlaw leaders the following day.

TEN

Snell and Henderson had ridden to Talako, a small town further south in Indian Territory, to visit a man called Brewster, who had, a while back, served a prison sentence for bank-robbery. They had heard that Brewster had contacts which would enable him to take the gold off their hands and pay them a reasonable price for it.

They had contacted Brewster in Talako, and had made a deal with him. He would send three armed men back with them to take over the gold. One of Brewster's men would carry the cash payment to be handed over in exchange for the gold when they reached the cave. An hour after the deal was agreed, the five riders left Talako for the cave.

They arrived at the ravine the following day, and as they rode up it towards the cave entrance, Henerson and Snell came to a halt. The others did the same.

'Something's wrong,' said Henderson. 'There should be some horses up there.'

He drew his gun and advanced slowly up the ravine. The others followed suit. When they reached the cave entrance they could see no sign of a guard.

They dismounted, and Henderson and Snell walked into the cave, holding their six-guns. The others remained outside.

Inside the cave, Snell and Henderson saw that the gold was missing, and that the indications were that the four men they had left there had gone with it.

'Damnation!' said Henderson, his face red with rage. 'I never figured they'd do this. One of us should've stayed behind.'

'It's the gold,' said Snell angrily. 'It makes men do some crazy things. What do we do now?'

'We'll find them, of course,' said Henderson savagely, 'and when we do, we'll kill all four, and get the gold back.'

They went outside and spoke to Craven, the leader of the three men who had accompanied them to the cave. They explained that their men and the gold were both missing.

'You reckon they've taken off with it?' asked Craven.

'We can't think of any other explanation,' said Snell.

'We ain't much good at tracking,' said Craven, 'but if we can get on their trail, we'll help you to deal with them. But it's going to cost you.'

Snell looked at Henderson, who nodded.

'All right,' he said.

'If we can't pick up their trail,' said Craven, 'we'd best go back to Brewster. If anybody in the Territory's trying to sell stolen gold, he's bound to hear about it.'

'It'll be dark soon,' said Henderson. 'We'd better stay here overnight. I'm going to ride to the store now, to see if Sully the storekeeper knows anything about our men leaving.'

He was back an hour and a half later, with the news that Dan and Marian had been captured soon after he and Snell left to see Brewster. According to Sully, the two prisoners had been taken to the cave, and were being kept alive.

'Sully says that he knows for sure that our men and the prisoners were all in the cave two days ago,' Henderson went on, 'and nobody said anything to him about leaving.'

'This ain't good tracking ground just here,' said Craven, 'and I think we'll stand a better chance of picking up their trail if we ride out a little way, then circle this spot. If we don't strike lucky, then we'd better head for Brewster, in Talako.'

Keeping watch from the grove, Dan and Marian saw Snell and Henderson arrive with Brewster's men. The presence of the latter scuppered the plan they had hatched of capturing the two gang leaders as they came out of the cave after discovering that their men and the gold were missing.

They saw Henderson ride off, while the remaining four men took the saddles off their horses, and went into the cave.

'Looks like they're staying overnight,' said Dan, 'and I'll wager that Henderson has ridden to the store to find out if Sully knows where his men are.'

After dark, they heard the sound of a horse moving up the ravine to the cave entrance.

'That'll be Henderson,' said Dan. 'I guess he knows now that we were captured. But I reckon that all he and Snell are thinking of right now is how to get the gold back. We'll follow them tomorrow, and wait our chance to capture them.'

Dan and Marian kept watch in turn until ninety minutes before dawn, but there was no sign of the men moving out. They left the grove, and climbed on foot to the top of the ridge, where they found a place from which they could watch the ravine below, without the danger of being spotted. Dan had his field glasses with him.

The five men below breakfasted shortly after dawn, then rode down the ravine, and after pausing for a short while, they rode north for three-quarters of a mile before they stopped. Three of them then moved slowly off to the west, gradually circling south, while the remaining two moved off to the east. They, too, were riding slowly, and gradually circling south.

'They're seeing if they can cut the trail of Clancey and the others,' said Dan. 'They'll likely be joining up again south of here.'

He was proved right when, around an hour and a half later, looking southward through his glasses, he saw the five riders unite, and after a brief delay, move off towards the south.

'This is where we start following them,' said Dan, 'but first we've got to take the hobbles off those horses in the hollow.'

They hurried back for their own horses, freed the horses in the hollow, and rode towards the place at which Snell and the others had last been sighted. Continuing on to the south at a fast pace, it was not long before Dan, using the field glasses, spotted the five riders in the distance. They were giving no indication of suspecting that somebody might be following them.

Keeping well back, Dan and Marian shadowed the riders ahead until nightfall, when they stopped at a point from which the camp-fire lit by their quarry was visible ahead.

'I don't think,' said Dan, 'that we should try and take Snell and Henderson just yet. Not with those other three there. I reckon we'd better wait until we can catch them on their own.'

'I think you're right,' said Marian. 'Have you any idea who those three are?'

'I reckon,' said Dan, 'that they might have something to do with taking the gold off the hands of

Snell and Henderson. It can't be that easy to change gold into cash.'

They continued their pursuit the following morning. Around noon, they saw a small town in the distance. The five riders in front of them were making straight for it.

Dan and Marian hid their horses in a deep, curving recess in the side of the gully through which they were passing. The horses were not visible to anyone riding through the gully. Then, for a clearer view, from cover, they climbed up the side of the gully and watched the five riders as they entered the town.

As the riders disappeared from view, they were passed by another rider leaving town and heading towards the gully. Dan and Marian stayed where they were, watching the rider from cover. Soon, it was clear that it was a woman, probably around thirty, slim, with light-brown hair.

Marian touched Dan's shoulder, and pointed to a rider coming along the trail from the north, and approaching the gully. He was a thickset, bearded man, roughly dressed, and wearing two guns. It was apparent that he and the woman would pass one another close to the point where the watchers were hidden.

When the two riders met, the man barred the woman's progress. Then they exchanged a few words, and the woman tried to move forward around him. The man grabbed the bridle of her horse, jumped down from his own mount, and pulled her out of the saddle.

She screamed as he forced her to the ground and bent down over her, trying to pin her down. Struggling desperately, she raked one side of his face with her fingernails. Cursing, he recoiled for a moment, slapped her hard on the face, then resumed his attempt to pin her down.

Dan ran down to the floor of the gully. Marian followed him. The woman's attacker caught sight of Dan out of the corner of his eye and swung round, drawing his six-gun. But before he could trigger it, Dan's bullet hit him in the head, and he fell on top of the woman.

Dan ran up, saw that he was dead, and lifted him off the woman, who stopped screaming as she saw Dan and Marian. Marian bent down, and helped the woman to her feet. She was obviously badly shaken, and it was a while before she regained her composure.

She thanked them for their help.

'I'm Sarah Varley,' she said, haltingly. 'I was just out for a ride, like I do once or twice a week. My husband Greg owns the livery stable in Talako. The man who attacked me is called Slade. I think he'd been drinking. He's a hired gunman, working for a man called Brewster. He's pestered me in town a few times, but I couldn't tell Greg about it. I was scared he'd get killed if he faced up to Slade, which he was bound to do if I told him.'

'This man Brewster,' asked Dan, 'does he run some sort of business in town?'

'He owns the saloon and the boarding-house,' Sarah replied, 'and he's been trying to buy us out. We heard a rumour that he's served a prison sentence, but he seems to have plenty of money now, and he's got several tough-looking characters like Slade on his payroll.'

'When you rode out of town,' said Marian, 'we saw you pass five riders on their way in. Did you know any of them?'

'Three of them,' Sarah Varley replied, 'are Brewster's men, don't know who the other two are, but they were both in town a few days ago, seeing Brewster.'

Marian introduced herself and Dan to Sarah, and gave her a brief account of the circumstances which brought them to Talako.

'So the two men we're after,' said Dan, when Marian had finished, 'seem to be doing some sort of business with Brewster.'

He paused for a moment, then spoke to Sarah.

'I think you'd best keep quiet about what's just happened here – except to your husband, of course. You go back now, and after dark I'll drop Slade's body somewhere on the edge of town. That way, Brewster won't know how he came to die. And as for us, we'll have to wait our chance to take Snell and Henderson.'

Sarah was visibly relieved.

'I'd be very grateful if you'd do what you just suggested,' she said. 'It would make things a whole lot easier for me and Greg. But when you bring the body in after dark, why don't you both come and hide in our place? We've got a big house with plenty of rooms and a good view of the street.'

'We're obliged,' said Dan. 'That'll be a big help, because we can't risk Snell seeing us in town. We'll ride in around midnight. Just where is your house located?'

'There's only one street,' she replied. 'The stable's on the right, in the middle of town. You can't miss the sign. The house is the building just before the stable. Knock on the door at the back. We'll be expecting you.'

When Sarah had ridden off towards town, Dan hid Slade's body, and his horse, well away from the trail, to be collected later. Then he and Marian waited until it was time to leave for Talako.

They had left the body a little way off the trail just outside town, and released his horse at the same spot. Then they rode along the deserted street to the livery stable and knocked on the back door of the adjacent house.

It was opened by Sarah Varley, who showed them in and introduced them to her husband, a pleasant-looking man of about forty. They all went into the living-room.

'Sarah's told me what happened,' said Varley, 'and we're mighty beholden to you both. We're aiming to help you any way we can. You left Slade's body outside town?'

'Yes,' Dan replied,'and his horse.'

'Brewster won't know what to make of it,' said Varley. 'He'll be wondering who it was that got the better of a top gunfighter like Slade.'

While Varley took care of their horses, his wife showed Dan and Marian into two small rooms with beds, where they could spend the night.

After taking breakfast just before dawn, Dan and Marian sat in Dan's bedroom watching, through a gap in the curtains, the activities in the street outside. On the opposite side of the street were the saloon and a single-storey boarding-house, side by side.

They had barely settled down when a man came running along the street and entered the boarding-house. Shortly after this, two of the men who had accompanied Snell and Henderson back to Talako came out, followed by a big, bearded, aggressive-looking man who tallied with Varley's description of Brewster.

The three men hurried along the street. They returned soon after, with Brewster leading the way, followed by the other two men carrying the body of Slade. They all disappeared round the back of the saloon.

Fifty minutes later, Dan and Marian felt a sudden surge of anger as they saw Snell, only thirty feet away, as he left the boarding-house with

Henderson. Both men went into the saloon.

Varley came into the room, and told Dan and Marian that he was going over to the saloon to see what was happening. He was back half an hour later.

'Brewster's hopping mad,' he said. 'His best man's dead, and he ain't got no notion of who killed him. Right now, he's sitting in the saloon with those two men Snell and Henderson.'

'I've got a feeling they're hoping Brewster can help them get the gold back,' said Dan. 'Maybe Brewster was going to take the gold off their hands.'

'What d'you aim to do now?' asked Varley.

'I saw Snell and Henderson come out of the boarding-house earlier,' said Dan. 'They must have rooms there. Maybe we could capture them during the night and take them out of town. Then we could meet up with the law somewhere, and hand them over. What d'you think, Marian?'

'I can't think of a better idea,' she said.

'We need to know which rooms they're in,' said Dan, 'and what's the best way of getting into the boarding-house during the night.'

'I can help there,' said Varley. 'I've been in once or twice to see customers of mine. There's a passage runs down the middle of the accommodation part of the building, with rooms on either side. One end of the passage leads out through a door to an alley at the side of the building.

'The boarding-house keeper works for Brewster. Now and again he goes into the saloon. Next time I see him do this, I'll walk into the boarding-house and take a look at the register.'

Varley's opportunity came twenty-five minutes later. Dan and Marian, watching through the window, saw a man leave the boarding-house and enter the saloon. Moments later, Varley entered the boarding-house. Five minutes later, he came out and reported to Dan and Marian.

'Snell and Henderson are staying in the last two rooms down the passage,' he said. 'Their rooms are opposite one another, and close to the door leading to the alley. The two rooms next to theirs are empty, according to the register. Brewster's men have rooms near the other end of the passage.

'I had a quick look at the doors. The room doors and the door into the alley don't have proper locks on. They can be opened from either side, just by turning the handle. It looked like the alley door could once have been fastened from the inside by dropping a bar across it, but there ain't no sign of any bar now.'

'That sounds good,' said Dan. 'Now if we manage to capture those two, we need to hand them over to the law as soon as possible. What's the quickest way of getting a message to the US marshal at Fort Smith?'

'Twenty miles north-east of here, there's a home

station on the stagecoach route,' said Varley. 'They've got a telegraph office there. I have a friend in town who owes me a favour. He helps me out in the stable now and then. He'll ride there with the message, without asking any questions. I'll warn him it's likely he'll have to leave in the middle of the night.'

'Good,' said Dan. 'Now when we leave here with Snell and Henderson, I reckon we should head east, so's to meet up with the deputies as soon as possible.'

'That's right,' said Varley.

'Is there some sort of landmark, well away from here, where we could wait for them?' asked Dan.

Varley pondered for a moment before he replied.

'Taking those two outlaws with you will slow you down some,' he said, 'but I reckon that by sundown tomorrow you'd be able to reach Buffalo Bluff, due east of here. You can't miss it. It's a well-known landmark. It stands in the middle of a big stretch of flat country, except for a big basin close by, with some brush at the bottom.'

'That sounds like just the place,' said Dan. 'I'll write that message now. Sheriff Carter in Dodge City telegraphed the US marshal in Fort Smith a while back, to let him know that me and Marian were following six outlaws, including Snell and Henderson, into Indian Territory. So he won't be surprised to get a message from us.'

Varley produced a pen and some paper, and Dan scratched out his message and passed it to Marian, who read it and passed it on to Varley. The message read:

HOLDING SNELL AND HENDERSON PRISONER. HEADING EAST FROM TALAKO FOR BASIN CLOSE TO BUFFALO BLUFF. WILL WAIT THERE FOR DEPUTIES. GANG MEMBERS BENSON, CLANCEY, PERRIN AND WILEY ALL DEAD. GOLD RECOVERED. DAN QUIGLEY AND MARIAN FOLEY.

Varley folded the paper and put it in an envelope.

'I'll hold on to this for now,' he said, 'and as soon as you ride off with Snell and Henderson I'll get my friend to take it to that telegraph office I told you about.'

'I'd like to help you pull this off,' Varley went on. 'What else can I do?'

'You've done a lot already,' said Dan, 'but if you're set on doing more, you could get our horses, and those belonging to Snell and Henderson, ready to leave when the time comes. When we take the two outlaws, we'll blindfold and gag them, so that, if things should go wrong, they won't be able to identify you to Brewster as somebody who was helping us.'

Dan and Marian spent the rest of the day, apart from the time taken over meals with the Varleys, watching the street from Dan's bedroom. The two outlaws remained in the saloon all day, except for two visits to the boarding-house for meals. Then, late in the evening, the watchers saw them leave the saloon for the boarding-house again, presumably with sleep in mind.

Dan and Marian rested till half past one in the morning. Looking out on to the street, they could see that all the buildings were in darkness. They went to the rear of the stable, and found Varley there with four saddled horses.

'They're all ready,' he said. 'I've tied them to the rail here.'

The three of them crossed the street and entered the alley by the side of the boarding-house. Dan was carrying some rope and two sacks and Marian held an unlighted oil-lamp in her hand. Outside the door, Marian lit the lamp and turned the wick well down. Varley remained where he was, while Dan opened the door and he and Marian crept inside.

They stood listening for a few moments, but the only sound they could hear was a faint snore coming from a room along the passage. There was no sign of a light in any of the rooms.

Dan cautiously turned the door handle of the room to his left, slowly opened the door, and stepped inside. Marian, carrying the lamp, followed close behind him and placed the lamp on a table, then quietly closed the door. As Snell stirred, Dan walked over to the bed and jammed the muzzle of his revolver into the side of the outlaw's neck.

Snell's eyes opened, and he instinctively reached for the pistol on the table by his bed. But Dan had already handed this to Marian. Dan pressed his gun more forcibly into the outlaw's neck as Snell stared incredulously into the faces of the two intruders.

'Just one sound out of you, Snell, and you're a dead man,' said Dan. 'Let's gag him, Marian.'

Marian tied the the ends of the gag at the back of the outlaw's head while Dan forced it into his mouth with the barrel of his six-gun. Next, he ordered the outlaw to dress himself. When he had done this, his hands were firmly bound and he was blindfolded. His personal belongings were placed in a sack, and he was led outside, where Varley held a gun against his back.

Dan and Marian then went into Henderson's room, and meted out the same treatment which Snell had received. Before Marian put the blindfold in place, the fuming outlaw recognized her and Dan from Snell's descriptiom of them. They led Henderson outside, then the two outlaws were escorted by Varley and Dan to the horses behind the stable. Marian extinguished the lamp and closed the three doors, before joining the others. Throughout the operation, there was no sign that anyone, other than the two outlaws, had been disturbed.

'Those two sacks of belongings,' said Dan to the liveryman, 'can you hide them in a safe place?'

'Sure,' said Varley. 'Leave it to me.'

The outlaws were led to their horses, and were helped into the saddle.

Varley took Dan aside, out of earshot of the prisoners.

'That message'll be on its way to the telegraph office in twenty minutes,' he said. 'Good luck to both of you.'

He stood and watched as Dan and Marian, leading the horses carrying the two prisoners, faded into the darkness along the backs of the buildings lining the street.

ELEVEN

It was ten o'clock in the morning when Brewster came to see Varley in the stable.

'You seen those two men who rode in with Craven the other day?' he asked abruptly.

'If you mean Mr Snell and Mr Henderson,' said Varley, 'they knocked me up in the middle of the night. Said they'd decided to leave, and wanted their horses. So I opened the stable, got the horses for them, and they left. Didn't say why they were going, or where they were headed, and I didn't ask.'

Brewster frowned.

'There's some mighty odd things happening around here,' he said. 'First, we find Slade with a bullet through his head, and nobody knows who done it, then those two ride off in the middle of the night for no good reason I can think of. I'd sure like to know where they've gone. D'you know if there's anybody in town that's good at tracking?'

'Not that I know of,' Varley replied.

Brewster cursed angrily, and walked out of the stable.

Dan and Marian led their prisoners to the east during the rest of the night, and continued on during the following day, with an occasional short break. There was still an hour to go before sunset when they first caught sight of Buffalo Bluff in the distance. As they drew closer, they could see, close to the south side of the bluff, the basin which Varley had mentioned.

It was roughly circular in shape, with gently sloping sides, and the bottom was dotted with boulders and large patches of dense brush. They rode down to the bottom of the basin, and found a place where they could camp.

They ordered Snell and Henderson down from their mounts, told them to sit on the ground, then tied their feet together. They took a meal themselves, then fed the prisoners, retying their hands and gagging them when the meal was finished.

'This is where we stay until those deputies turn up,' said Dan to Marian, speaking out of earshot of the prisoners.

'I can hardly believe it's nearly over once again,' said Marian. 'It's been a long chase.'

They were both tired after a long day in the saddle, and ready for some sleep. But they were aware that it was essential at night, as well as during the day, to keep a close watch on such a dangerous pair of criminals.

They decided to keep the fire going, and to take turns in standing guard over the prisoners. As an added precaution, they trussed the two outlaws so that they were barely able to move.

Dan took the first watch. He woke Marian at two o'clock in the morning to relieve him. She rose, walked over to a small boulder, and sat down with her back against it, facing the two prisoners. Dan put some wood on the fire, lay down, and was instantly asleep.

Marian looked across at the two outlaws, who were lying motionless on the ground. She felt relief that her mission was almost completed, and realized that, like Dan, she must start thinking about her future.

Several times, she caught herself nodding, and rose to walk around for a while. She sat down again, but soon her eyelids drooped and her head nodded once again.

A slight sound from behind alerted her, but it was too late. Her six-gun was removed from its holster, a large hand was clamped over her mouth, and a strong arm held her firmly from behind.

Moments later, two more intruders came silently out of the darkness. One of them ran up to Dan, jammed the barrel of a six-gun against his head, and took his revolver. The other man ran up to Henderson and Snell, and stood looking down at the two trussed figures.

The man holding Marian dragged her towards Dan, and threw her on the ground beside him. He spoke to one of the others.

'Hold a gun on these two, Walt,' he said.

He walked over to the two bound men, lifted Snell's head so that he could get a better view of his face, then did the same with Henderson.

'Damn me!' he said. 'It's Grant Henderson! Let's get those gags and ropes off the two of them. We'll use the ropes to tie the man and woman.'

Minutes later, Dan and Marian were lying helpless on the ground, side by side, and Snell and Henderson, who had armed themselves with the prisoners' six-guns, were glaring down at them. The look on their faces boded ill for the two captives.

The three men who had burst into camp were the members of the Barry gang of outlaws, led by Morgan Barry. Henderson had, a while back, spent some time with Barry, acting as his second in command. Then, when Henderson had decided to form a gang of his own, they had parted amicably. Recently, Barry and his men, Hart and Ford, finding things too hot for them in Kansas after two robberies committed by them, had decided to move down to Texas for a while.

They had been riding through the night across Indian Territory, when one of their horses had stumbled, damaging a leg so badly that it could not carry a rider. At the time this happened, the three riders were skirting the basin where Snell and Henderson were being held. Glancing down into the basin, Barry caught a glimpse of the faint light from the camp-fire.

'Looks like there's somebody down there,' he said. 'We need a horse. Let's all sneak down there on foot, and see if we can get hold of one.'

Cautiously, they approached the fire until, looking from cover, they could see two men lying together, apparently bound, on the ground, one other man lying alone, and what looked like a woman keeping watch. They decided to overcome the woman and the man who was lying alone.

'How in hell d'you come to be in this fix, Grant?' asked Barry, 'and where are your men?'

Almost overcome with rage at the indignities suffered by himself and Snell at the hands of Dan and Marian, Henderson fought to control himself. He introduced Snell, then explained the situation to Barry.

'That's quite a story,' said Barry, when Henderson had finished. 'So you've no idea where your men have gone with the gold?'

'No,' Henderson replied. 'We were hoping Brewster might be able to help us find it. We'll ride back to Talako and see him again.'

'You got any idea where Quigley and the woman

were taking you?' Barry asked.

'Somewhere further east, where they could hand us over to the law, I reckon,' Henderson replied.

'What're you going to do with them?' asked Barry.

Snell butted in.

'One thing's sure,' he said. 'Neither of them's going to leave here alive.'

'We'll take one of their horses, then,' said Barry.

Snell walked over to the prisoners, and stood looking down at them. His face was distorted with rage.

'You two are finished,' he said, 'but you ain't going to die easy. I know where a bullet hurts most. And when you're dead, we'll leave you here to rot. But before I put those bullets into you, I have some unfinished business with the woman.'

He bent down, took hold of Marian's arms, and overcoming her attempts to resist, he started dragging her away from the fire towards the surrounding darkness. Dan struggled in vain to free himself of his bonds.

Snell halted abruptly, and dropped Marian on the ground as a single shot rang out, followed by a voice speaking out of the darkness.

'That was a warning shot,' it said. 'There's a party of deputy US marshals out here. You're all covered. If you've got any sense, you'll drop your guns on the ground, and lift your hands. And I mean right now.'

The warning was ignored. All five outlaws, desperate to avoid capture, dashed away from the fire towards the nearest cover, firing wildly as they ran, and leaving Dan and Marian lying on the ground.

But for four of them, the attempt to escape capture was doomed to failure. Instant and accurate fire from the three deputies brought them all down.

Snell, the one furthest away from the camp-fire, bent double as he ran. He was hit, but continued running until he was swallowed up by the darkness. He passed half-way between two of the deputies, one of whom was standing near the four picketed horses. He made his way out of the basin.

There was silence for a while. Two of the outlaws lay motionless on the ground. The other two were moving, but looked to be in no condition to offer any further resistance.

The three deputy US marshals, holding their rifles at the ready, emerged from the darkness and approached the four outlaws. They took their weapons, then two of them took the ropes off Dan and Marian, and helped them to their feet. Walker, the leader of the three, spoke.

'I reckon you're Quigley, and this is Miss Foley with you,' he said. 'I'm deputy US Marshal Walker, and my two partners here are deputies Horne and Quinn. It looks like we got here just in time.'

'You sure did,' said Dan.

'There ain't no doubt that this is your lucky day,' said Walker. 'The reason that help's turned up for you sooner than it might have done, is because we were already in Indian Territory, waiting to start another operation, when we got a message to drop everything and ride here to meet you.

'When we got here, we snuck down into the basin quiet-like, to check up on the situation here. When we saw you two tied up and lying on the ground, we knew something was wrong.'

Horne, who had been taking a close look at the four outlaws, spoke to Walker.

'Two of them are dead,' he said. 'The other two are still alive, and likely to stay that way. One of them has a bullet in his leg. The other's been hit in the shoulder. I'm pretty sure I've seen their faces on Wanted posters, but I can't recall the names.'

Walker took a close look at the four outlaws, while Dan checked that Marian had not been hurt during her struggle with Snell.

'We've got the whole Barry gang here,' said Walker. 'Hart and Ford are dead. Barry's the one with a bullet in his shoulder. I don't know the one with the bullet in his leg.'

'That's Henderson, the leader of the Henderson gang,' said Dan. 'That just leaves Snell. I saw him run off, but I think he was hit.'

'I think you're right,' said Walker. 'I got one shot at him before he ran out of sight. I'm sure I hit him, but it weren't bad enough to stop him running. We'll have a look for him come daylight.'

Walker put some more wood on the fire, then spoke to Dan and Marian.

'This is a great haul we have here,' he said, 'and that's on top of those four dead outlaws you mentioned in your message to Fort Smith. Were they all Henderson's men?'

'Three of them were,' Dan replied. 'The fourth was the only remaining member of the Snell gang, apart from Snell himself.'

'So mainly due to you two,' said Walker, 'three outlaw gangs have been put out of action, and Snell's on the run. There's a lot of folks going to be mighty pleased to hear that.'

Waiting for daylight, the deputies did what they could for the wounded men, and Walker said they would get them to a doctor as soon as they could.

He told Dan and Marian that his partner Quinn had a white father who had taken a Pawnee woman for his wife. After his father died, he had lived with the Pawnees for several years when his mother returned to the tribe. Then he had been recruited by the army as an army scout. When the army no longer required his services, he had become a deputy US marshal, based on Fort Smith.

'He's the best tracker I ever met up with,' said Walker. 'As soon as it's daylight, he'll find out what's happened to Snell.'

At dawn, Quinn walked to the point at which Snell had disappeared from view when under fire. Studying the ground, he gradually worked his way out of the basin, and moved out of sight of the watchers below. Thirty minutes later he reappeared, riding his own horse. He was leading the mounts belonging to his two partners, also two of the three horses which had been left at a different location by the Barry gang.

'Snell's wounded all right,' he said, as he rejoined the others. 'I saw spots of blood near his tracks. He picked up one of the Barry gang's horses near the top of the basin, and rode off to the south. And we know he was carrying a six-gun when he left the basin.'

Walker reflected for a short while before he spoke.

'What we'll do is this,' he said. 'Me and Horne'll take charge of Barry and Henderson, and get them to Fort Smith for trial. The two dead men, we'll bury here. And Quinn'll go after Snell right now, and he'll bring him to Fort Smith when he catches up with him.'

Dan had a brief word with Marian, then he spoke to Walker.

'We'd like to go with Mr Quinn,' he said. 'We've been a long time on the trail of Snell, and we'd like to be there at the end. You know that Snell murdered Miss Foley's father, and also my sister?'

'Yes, I heard that,' said Walker, 'and I reckon

you deserve what you're asking for. And maybe Quinn'll be glad of a bit of help, chasing a man like Snell.

'I could deputize you both, though I ain't heard of a lady deputy before. But you'd have to swear to uphold the law, which says that, if possible, criminals like Snell must be arrested and taken in for trial.'

'That's what we've been aiming to do all along,' said Dan.

'All right,' said Walker, and he swore them both in. 'Whatever happens with Snell,' he said, 'don't forget we'll need you at Fort Smith, to testify against Henderson and Barry.'

'We'll be there,' promised Dan, 'just as soon as Snell has been dealt with.'

Fifteen minutes later, Dan and Marian rode out of the basin with Quinn. The deputy was a slim, lithe man of average height, whose face betrayed little of his Indian blood. He appeared to accept their presence with equanimity.

Once they were out of the basin, Quinn ranged ahead, dismounting only occasionally, and generally maintaining a southerly course at a brisk pace. Dan and Marian followed behind.

'Beats me how he can pick out Snell's tracks on ground like this,' said Dan. 'Darned if I can.'

'Me neither,' said Marian. 'With Quinn on the job, and Snell wounded, I'm beginning to think that the end of the trail ain't far away.'

'You're right,' said Dan, 'but we've got to remember that a wounded Snell can be a very dangerous man to follow.'

Late in the afternoon following his flight from the basin, Snell was still riding south. His progress had been slow. He had been forced to make several stops to try and stanch the bleeding from the wound in his left arm, below the shoulder. The bullet had not lodged in the arm, but the flesh was badly torn.

An hour before nightfall, he dismounted, and climbed to the top of a knoll that he had just rounded. He lay down to rest for a while, and looked searchingly to the north. He could see no signs of pursuit, but twenty minutes later, he stiffened and cursed as he caught sight of three riders in the far distance, moving in his direction. One was riding a little in advance of the other two.

He was too far away to identify the riders, but he felt fairly sure that they were Dan and Marian, accompanied by one of the deputies who had fired on him and the others in the basin.

He descended the knoll and continued riding south in the gathering darkness. He knew that five or six hours ahead lay the small town of Brannock, which he and his men had visited briefly about a year ago. He decided to continue in that direction, riding through the night. His pursuers, he felt sure, would be camping for the night, with the intention of picking up his tracks again at daybreak.

He knew that there was no escape unless he could get rid of his pursuers. And with three of them after him, that was not going to be easy. He cursed again as he felt a surge of pain in his wounded arm.

He reached Brannock, near to exhaustion, soon after midnight. It was a small town, and the single street was deserted. He tied his horse to a hitching rail outside what appeared to be an abandoned building in an isolated position right on the edge of town. He stood for a while, looking along the street. There were no signs of life.

He was certain that his pursuers would follow him into town, probably around noon, and he wondered if he could find a suitable place from which to ambush them when they arrived.

He walked to the centre of town. He passed the general store on his left, and further on, on his right, he came to the livery stable. He walked round to the rear of the stable, then returned to the store and took a look behind it. He noticed a small wooden hut, well away from the main building.

As he walked up to the hut, he could just distinguish a notice painted on the door. It read: DYNAMITE – KEEP OUT. He guessed that the hut contained a small number of sticks of dynamite, for occasional use by customers of the store.

Snell walked away from the store, then stopped as a thought struck him. He returned to the hut and felt the padlock which was holding the door closed. He pulled hard on it, exerting all his strength, and suddenly the fixing into which the padlock was engaged, came away from the door.

He pulled the door open and stepped inside. Carefully, he struck a match, then opened the lid of a stout wooden box standing on the floor, and took out two sticks of dynamite. He closed the box and left the hut, pushing the door to behind him. He hoped that it would be some time before it was noticed that the door had been forced.

He walked back to the building where he had left his horse, and went inside, through a door which was standing slightly ajar. Lighting a match, he could see that the building had not been occupied for some considerable time. There was a window in the north side of the building, one facing on to the street, and one which gave a view along the street towards the centre of town.

Snell decided that he would stay in the building until he saw the three riders who were following him come into town. He would have to risk his presence in the building being discovered before then. He led the horse inside the building, and closed the door, then ate a small quantity of food which he had found in one of the saddlebags.

When he had finished the meal, he sat on the floor, with his back to the wall, tried to ignore the throbbing pain in his arm, and dozed fitfully until dawn.

TWELVE

Dan and his two companions made camp shortly after Snell had spotted them in the distance. At daybreak, they resumed the chase, and three hours later, Quinn told Dan and Marian that it looked as though Snell was heading for a town called Brannock, to the south.

'It's only a small place,' said Quinn, 'and judging by the time these tracks were made, he could have got there during the night. So, by the time we turn up, there's a chance he might have left.'

Round about noon, they could see in the distance the town of Brannock, and it was clear that the tracks of Snell's horse were heading straight for town, soon to be lost, among many others, on the street of Brannock.

'We'll see if anybody in town's seen him,' said Quinn, 'and a good place to start would be the livery stable.'

'While you're doing that,' said Marian, 'I'll go in to the store. I need to buy a few things. And while I'm in there, I'll ask the storekeeper if he's seen Snell.'

'All right,' said Dan, 'but keep an eye open for him, in case he's still around.'

Snell, peering through the north-facing window of the building in which he had taken refuge, saw the three riders approaching town. As they drew closer, he was able to identify Dan and Marian. He kept them under observation as they passed the building in which he was hiding and rode along the street towards the centre of town.

He cursed as he saw Marian break away from the other two and tie her horse to the hitching rail outside the store. For the operation he had in mind, he would have preferred the three to stay together. He saw Dan and Quinn dismount outside the livery stable and disappear through the wide-open doors leading into the stable.

Snell, who, during the course of his criminal activities, had gained some experience in the use of dynamite, picked up the two sticks that he had stolen. Quickly, he estimated the length of fuse-cord required for his purpose, and using his knife, he cut off the remainder.

He left the house and walked along the side of the street, deserted at the time, towards the livery stable. The two sticks of dynamite were concealed under his vest. There was a maniacal glare in his eyes.

When Marian entered the store, there was no one inside. She called out several times, then knocked on the door leading to the living-quarters. But there was no response. She opened the door at the rear of the store and walked outside, but there was still no sign of the storekeeper. She closed the door behind her, and walked along an alley leading to the street, intending to rejoin Dan and Quinn at the livery stable, before returning to the store later.

As she reached the end of the alley she stopped short. Along the street from her, standing on the same side as herself, directly opposite the livery stable, she saw Snell. She could also see Dan and Quinn, their backs to the street, standing just inside the stable entrance, talking to the liveryman.

When Marian caught sight of Snell, he had just finished lighting with a match the two fuse-cords attached to the two sticks of dynamite. Grasping the two sticks firmly in his right hand, he drew his arm back, preparatory to throwing the two sticks across the street into the open door of the stable.

Marian knew that swift action was needed to avoid disaster. She drew her Peacemaker, steadied herself, and fired. The bullet hit Snell squarely in the side, just before he was ready to release the dynamite. Still holding it, he staggered sideways, then fell forward, face down, with the dynamite underneath him. An instant later, his body took the full force of the explosion.

As soon as Marian had fired, she dodged back into the alley, and emerged, after the explosion, to stare, badly shaken, at the remains of the outlaw. At the sound of the shot, followed immediately by the explosion, Dan and Quinn came out of the stable with the liveryman. They both ran up to Snell, who was recognizable, but quite obviously dead. Then they ran on to Marian.

Dan could see that she was trembling, and he put his arm around her.

'What happened, Marian?' he asked, when she had calmed down a little.

'The storekeeper was missing,' she said, 'so I was coming to join you two at the stable. I saw Snell with two sticks of dynamite, with short burning fuse-cords. I could tell he was aiming to throw them across the street at you two. I knew I had to stop him, and there was only time for one shot. I was praying I wouldn't miss.'

'We're both beholden to you, Marian,' said Dan, and Quinn nodded assent. 'I reckon we'd both be dead for sure if that dynamite had landed anywhere near us.'

He and Quinn walked back to the group of townspeople who had collected. Only slight damage had been done to buildings close to Snell's body, and no one but the outlaw had been harmed. Quinn explained the situation, and arranged for the body to be buried. Then he spoke to Dan and Marian.

'Looks like you've finished the job you set out to do,' he said. 'But like Deputy Walker told you, you'll be needed at the trial of Barry and Henderson. Let's all have a good night's sleep here in town, and we'll set off for Fort Smith in the morning.'

During the evening, Dan had a chance to talk with Marian alone.

'How d'you feel, Marian, now it's all over bar the trial?' he asked her.

'It feels like a big weight's been lifted off my mind,' she replied.

'It's the same with me,' said Dan, 'and it means we can start thinking about what we're going to do with the rest of our lives.

'One thing that scares me,' he went on, 'is the thought that when the trial's over, maybe I'll never see you again. The thing is, I'm so darned used to having you around, saving me from criminals who're out to kill me, I ain't sure I can manage on my own.'

'What gave you the idea that we'd be parting company?' asked Marian, smiling. 'Like you, I figure that we belong together.'

'You mean to say,' asked Dan, 'that if I asked you whether we could get hitched, you'd say yes?'

'I'd jump at the chance,' Marian replied. 'I know what a good man you are.'

'And if I suggested that after the trial, we headed back to the Circle Q ranch in Colorado, with the idea of running it together, how would you feel about that?' asked Dan.

'Can't think of a better idea,' Marian replied. 'I'm looking forward to it.'

The trial of Henderson and Barry took place a week later in Fort Smith, Arkansas. The judge was

Isaac Charles Parker, dubbed by some as the 'hanging judge'. Appointed by President Grant for the task of administering the law in Indian Territory, he held the post for twenty years, showing considerable sympathy for the plight of the Indians.

At the trial, attended by Dan and Marian, the judge sentenced both Henderson and Barry to death by hanging. After the trial, he asked to see Dan and Marian in his private rooms. When they arrived there, Parker and his wife Mary greeted them, and all four sat down.

'I know,' said Parker, 'that although you have been responsible for the deaths of a number of criminals, it has never been your intention to take the law into your own hands.

'Mainly through your efforts, three gangs of vicious and rapacious criminals have been destroyed. My wife and I wish to thank you for the courage and tenacity you have both displayed in achieving this.

'I don't know what plans you have for the future, Mr Quigley, but I wonder whether you'd consider taking up a post as a federal marshal? Men of your calibre are badly needed. I have no doubt that such an appointment could be arranged.'

'Sorry, judge,' said Dan, 'but the situation is that Marian and me are getting married before we leave here, then we're heading for my ranch in Colorado, where we aim to raise both cattle and a family.'

'Congratulations!' said Parker. 'Can we take it

that we're invited to the wedding?'

'We'll be proud to have you there,' replied Marian.

They left the Parkers shortly after, and Dan went to the telegraph office, where he sent two telegraph messages. The first was to his hand Ben Drury, who was running the Circle Q ranch in his absence. It told Ben that Dan was returning with a bride, to take over the running of the ranch.

The second message was to Pallister, the Wells Fargo agent in Dodge City, to say that Dan and Marian would soon be calling on him to tell him exactly where the stolen gold shipment could be found.

When they arrived in Dodge City, they gave both Sheriff Carter and Pallister a brief account of events since they had last seen them. Then Dan gave Pallister detailed instructions as to where the gold was hidden.

'There's a big reward on offer to anybody who helps to get the gold back,' said Pallister, 'and that'll be yours if we find it where you say it is.'

'It's well hidden,' said Dan. 'I'm pretty sure it'll still be there.'

The following morning, Dan and Marian left Dodge City on the last stage of their journey to the Circle Q. Four days after their arrival there, they received a message from Pallister to say that the gold had been recovered.

MONTREAL &
QU

Edited by Paul Waters

FORMAC PUBLISHING COMPANY LIMITED

CONTENTS

CONTENTS

Canadian Cataloguing in Publication Data

Main entry under title:

Montreal & Quebec City colourguide

(Colourguide series)
ISBN 0-88780-474-8

1. Montreal (Quebec) – Guidebooks. 2. Quebec (Quebec) – Guidebooks.
I. Waters, Paul. II. Series

FC2947.18.M6535 1999 917.14'28044 C99 931382-7
F1054.5.M83M6535 1999

Formac Publishing Company acknowledges the support of the Department of Canadian Heritage and the Nova Scotia Department of Education and Culture in the development of writing and publishing in Canada.

Canadä

Formac Publishing Company Limited
5502 Atlantic Street
Halifax, Nova Scotia
B3H 1G4

Printed and bound in Canada.

Distributed in the United States by:
Seven Hills Book Distributors
1531 Tremont Street
Cincinnati, Ohio, 45214

Distributed in the United Kingdom by:
World Leisure Marketing
9 Downing Road
West Meadows Industrial Estate
Derby DE 21 6HA
England

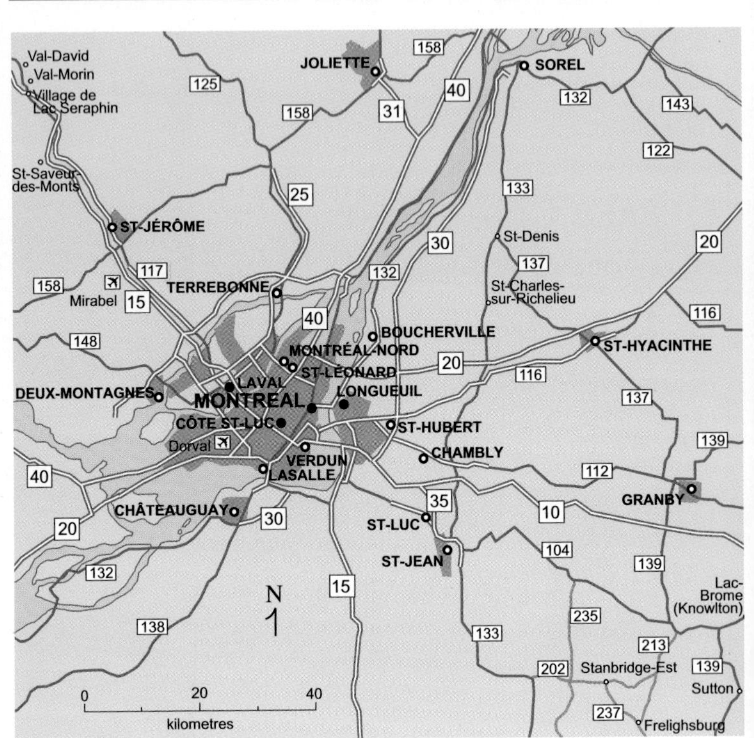
Val-David
Val-Morin
Village de Lac Seraphin
St-Saveur-des-Monts
ST-JÉRÔME
Mirabel
TERREBONNE
JOLIETTE
SOREL
St-Denis
St-Charles-sur-Richelieu
BOUCHERVILLE
MONTRÉAL-NORD
ST-LÉONARD
LAVAL
DEUX-MONTAGNES
MONTREAL
LONGUEUIL
CÔTE ST-LUC
Dorval
ST-HUBERT
ST-HYACINTHE
VERDUN
LASALLE
CHAMBLY
GRANBY
CHÂTEAUGUAY
ST-LUC
ST-JEAN
Lac-Brome (Knowlton)
Stanbridge-Est
Sutton
Frelighsburg
N
0
20
40
kilometres

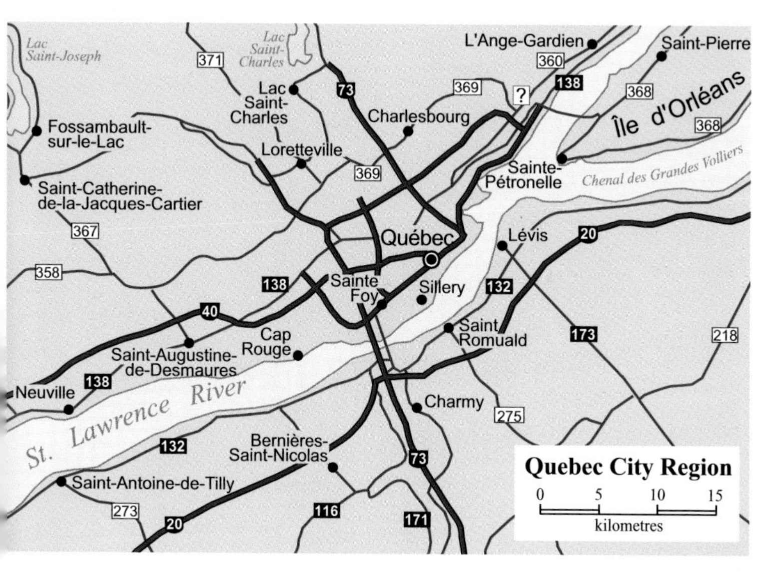
Quebec City Region
0 5 10 15
kilometres
Lac Saint-Joseph
Lac Saint-Charles
L'Ange-Gardien
Saint-Pierre
Île d'Orléans
Lac Saint-Charles
Fossambault-sur-le-Lac
Charlesbourg
Loretteville
Sainte-Pétronelle
Chenal des Grandes Volliers
Saint-Catherine-de-la-Jacques-Cartier
Québec
Lévis
Sainte Foy
Sillery
Saint Romuald
Cap Rouge
Saint-Augustine-de-Desmaures
Neuville
St. Lawrence River
Charmy
Bernières-Saint-Nicolas
Saint-Antoine-de-Tilly

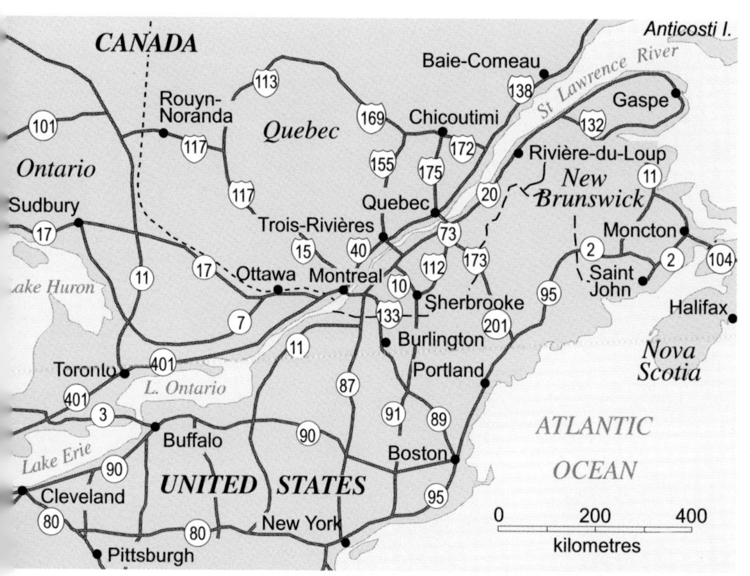
CANADA
Anticosti I.
Baie-Comeau
St Lawrence River
Gaspe
Rouyn-Noranda
Quebec
Chicoutimi
Rivière-du-Loup
Ontario
New Brunswick
Sudbury
Quebec
Trois-Rivières
Moncton
Ottawa
Montreal
Saint John
Lake Huron
Sherbrooke
Halifax
Burlington
Toronto
Portland
Nova Scotia
L. Ontario
ATLANTIC OCEAN
Buffalo
Lake Erie
Boston
Cleveland
UNITED STATES
New York
Pittsburgh
0 200 400
kilometres

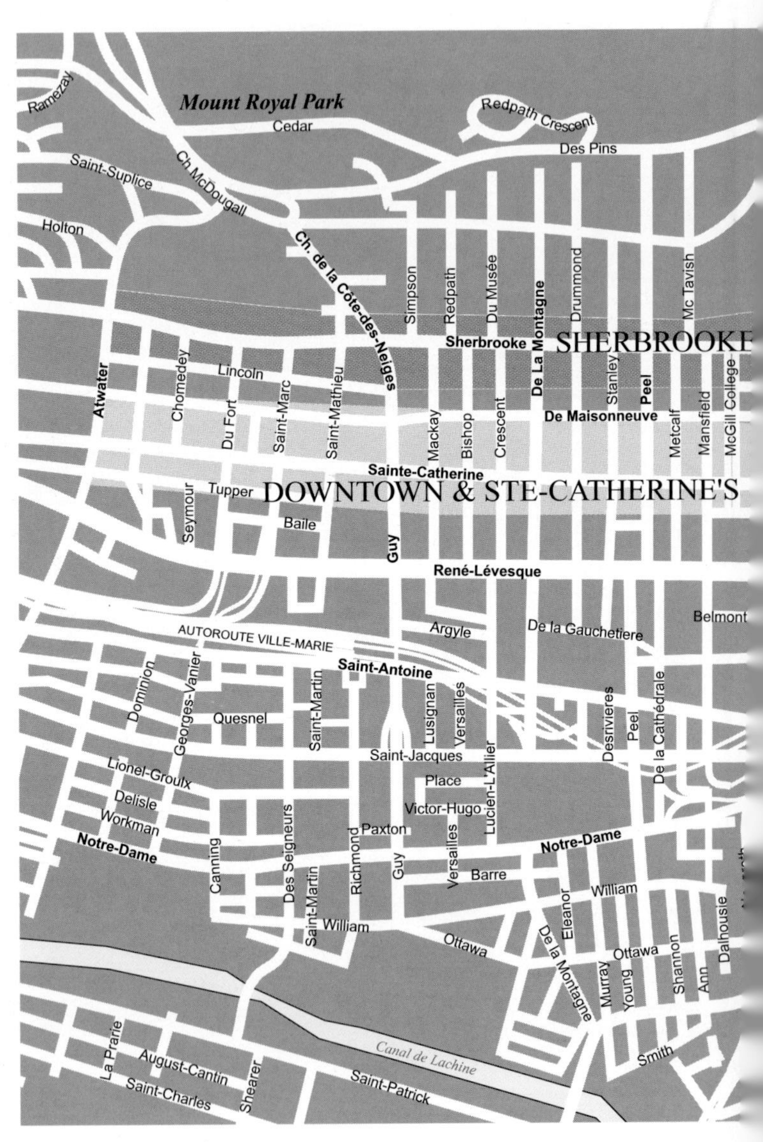
Mount Royal Park
Ramezay
Cedar
Redpath Crescent
Des Pins
Saint-Suplice
Ch McDougall
Holton
Ch. de la Côte-des-Neiges
Simpson
Redpath
Du Musée
De La Montagne
Drummond
Mc Tavish
Sherbrooke
SHERBROOKE
Atwater
Chomedey
Lincoln
Du Fort
Saint-Marc
Saint-Mathieu
Mackay
Bishop
Crescent
Stanley
Peel
De Maisonneuve
Metcalf
Mansfield
McGill College
Sainte-Catherine
Tupper
Seymour
DOWNTOWN & STE-CATHERINE'S
Baile
Guy
René-Lévesque
Argyle
De la Gauchetiere
Belmont
AUTOROUTE VILLE-MARIE
Saint-Antoine
Dominion
Georges-Vanier
Quesnel
Saint-Martin
Lusignan
Versailles
Desrivieres
Peel
De la Cathédrale
Saint-Jacques
Lucien-L'Allier
Lionel-Groulx
Place
Delisle
Victor-Hugo
Workman
Paxton
Notre-Dame
Canning
Des Seigneurs
Richmond
Guy
Versailles
Barre
Notre-Dame
William
Eleanor
Saint-Martin
William
Ottawa
De la Montagne
Ottawa
Murray
Young
Shannon
Ann
Dalhousie
Smith
La Prarie
August-Cantin
Saint-Charles
Shearer
Canal de Lachine
Saint-Patrick

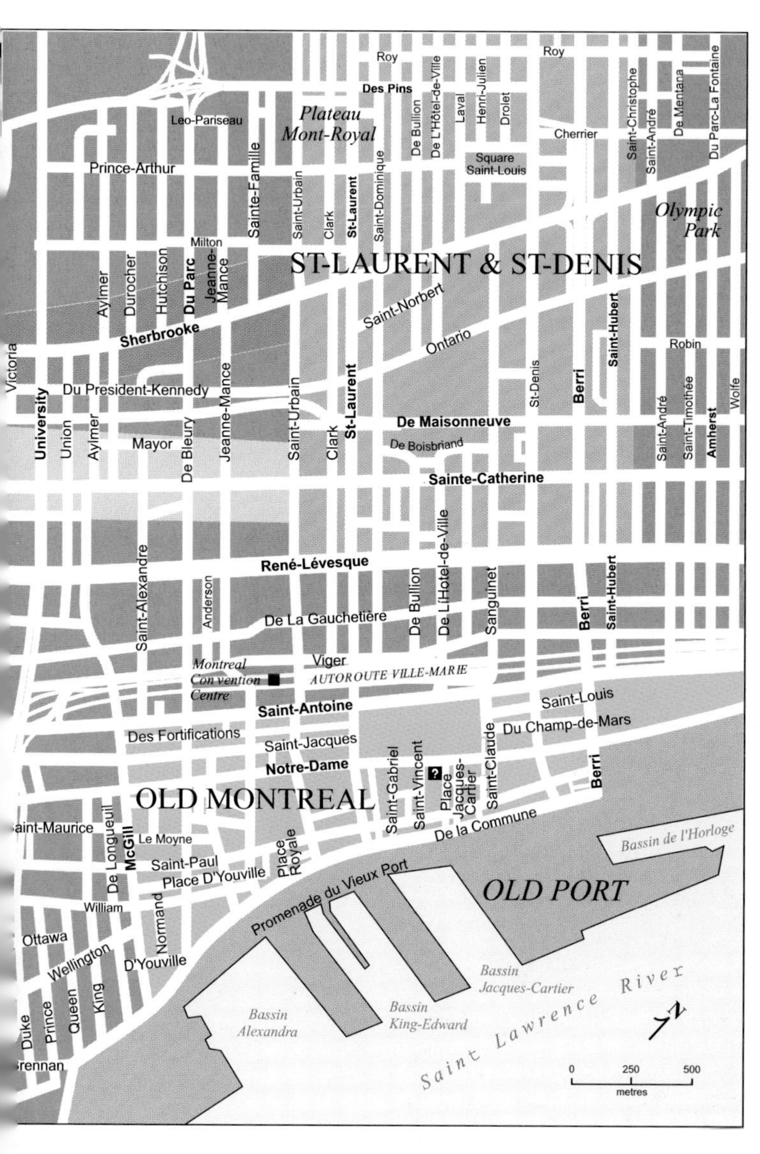

ST-LAURENT & ST-DENIS
Plateau Mont-Royal
Olympic Park
OLD MONTREAL
OLD PORT
Montreal Convention Centre
AUTOROUTE VILLE-MARIE
Roy
Des Pins
Leo-Pariseau
Prince-Arthur
Milton
Sherbrooke
Saint-Norbert
Ontario
Cherrier
Square Saint-Louis
Robin
Du President-Kennedy
De Maisonneuve
De Boisbriand
Mayor
Sainte-Catherine
René-Lévesque
De La Gauchetière
Viger
Saint-Antoine
Saint-Louis
Du Champ-de-Mars
Des Fortifications
Saint-Jacques
Notre-Dame
De la Commune
Saint-Paul
Place D'Youville
Le Moyne
William
Ottawa
Wellington
D'Youville
Promenade du Vieux Port
Bassin de l'Horloge
Bassin Jacques-Cartier
Bassin King-Edward
Bassin Alexandra
Saint Lawrence River
Victoria
University
Union
Aylmer
Durocher
Hutchison
Du Parc
Jeanne-Mance
De Bleury
Sainte-Famille
Saint-Urbain
Clark
St-Laurent
Saint-Dominique
De Bullion
De L'Hôtel-de-Ville
Laval
Henri-Julien
Drolet
Saint-Christophe
Saint-André
De Montana
Du Parc-La Fontaine
St-Denis
Berri
Saint-Hubert
Saint-Timothée
Amherst
Wolfe
Saint-Alexandre
Anderson
Sanguinet
Saint-Gabriel
Saint-Vincent
Place Jacques-Cartier
Saint-Claude
Place Royale
McGill
De Longueuil
Normand
King
Queen
Prince
Duke
Saint-Maurice
Brennan
0 250 500
metres
N

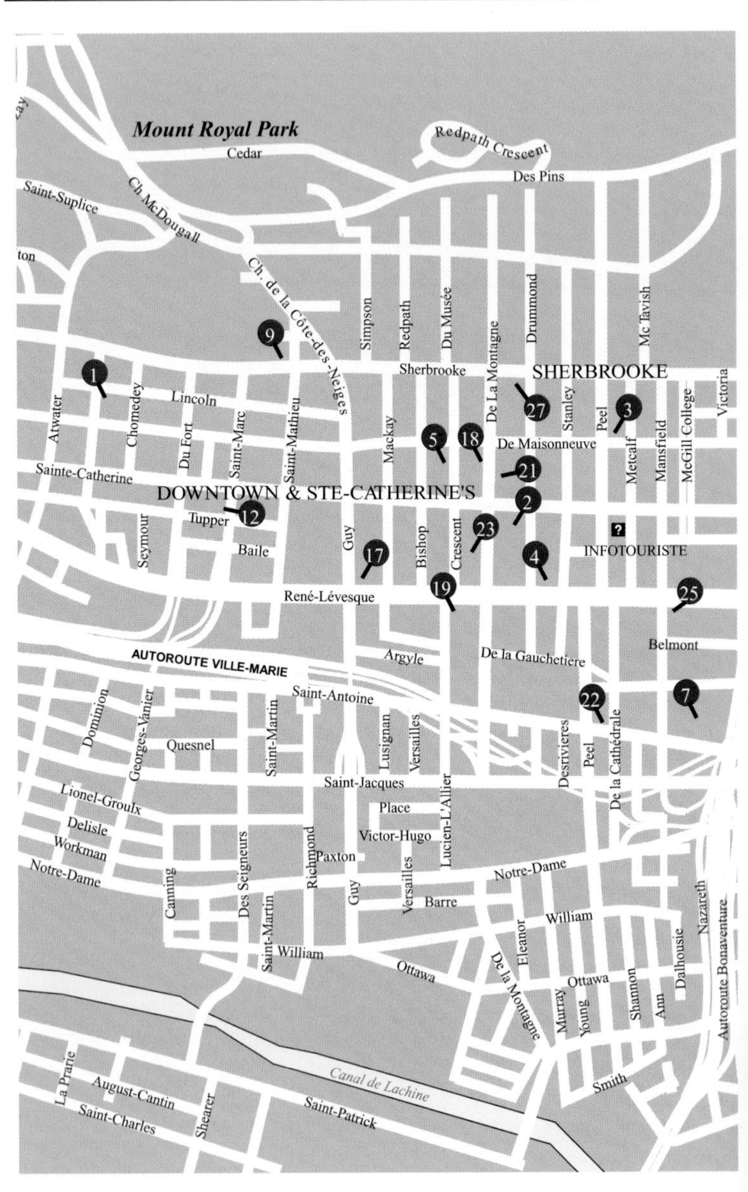

Montreal Hotels
1 Appartement-Hôtel Le Riche Bourg
2 Best Western Europa Centre-Ville
3 Best Western Ville-Marie Hôtel
4 Le Centre Sheraton
5 Château Royal Hotel Suites
6 Day's Inn Montréal Centre-Ville
7 Hilton Montréal Bonaventure
8 Holiday Inn Montréal-Midtown
9 Hôtel Château Versailles
10 Hôtel Courtyard Marriott Montré
11 Hôtel Delta Montréal
12 Hôtel du Fort
13 Hôtel du Parc

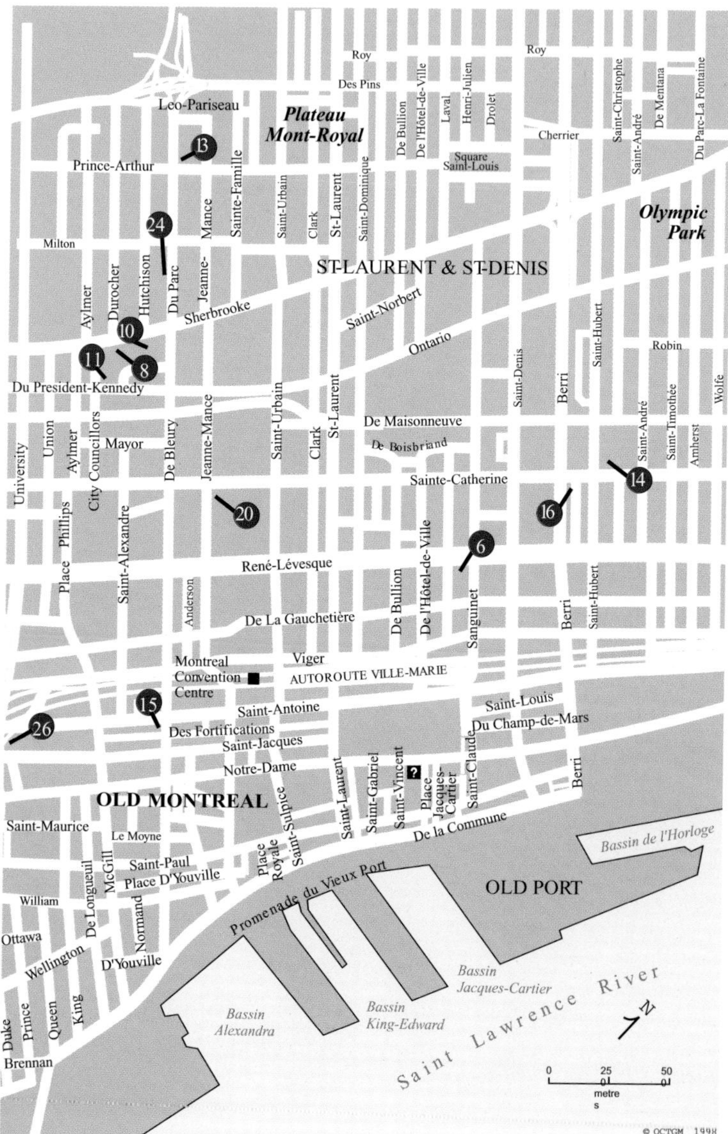

4 Hôtel Gouverneur Place Dupuis
5 Hôtel Inter-Continental Montréal
6 Hôtel Lord Berri
7 Hôtel Maritime Plaza
8 Hôtel de la Montagne
9 Hôtel Montréal Crescent
0 Hôtel Wyndham Montréal

21 Loews Hôtel Vogue
22 Marriott Château Champlain
23 Novotel Montréal Centre
24 Quality Hotel (Journey's End)
25 The Queen Elizabeth Hotel
26 Radisson Hôtel des Gouverneurs
27 Ritz-Carlton Kempinksi

Welcome to Montreal and Quebec City!

This guide has been written to help you get the most out of your stay in and around the province of Quebec's two largest cities: Montreal and the provincial capital, Quebec City.

The introductory chapter provides an overview of each city as well as an historical introduction to the province of Quebec. The maps in the preliminary section of the book provide a general view of each city and the major road arteries, while more detailed downtown and specific area maps give key locations such as hotels. In addition, a neighbourhoods map for Montreal shows the districts covered by separate chapters later in the book.

The guide is divided by city and then, within these sections, into the best each city has to offer and then its distinct areas. The chapters "Montreal's Best" or "Quebec City's Best" are thematic, covering topics such as museums, architecture and heritage, shopping, and excursions; the chapters under "Montreal by Area" or "Quebec City by Area" are divided into well-recognized streets or neighbourhoods that define how most people experience each city.

The final section of the guide contains select listings, with practical information on everything you'll want to do or find in either Montreal or Quebec City: accommodations, dining, night life, museums and galleries, attractions, festivals and events; shopping; galleries — along with special travel services and tips.

This book is an independent guide. Its editor and its contributors have made their recommendations and suggestions based solely on what they believe to be the best, most interesting and most appealing sites and

attractions. No payments or contributions of any kind are solicited or accepted by the creators or the publishers of this guide.

In a city as lively as Montreal things change quickly — even in a solid bastion of francophone culture such as Quebec City. The safest thing to do about information you're relying on in this book is to confirm it with a brief phone call. If your experience doesn't match what you read here — or if you think we've missed one of either city's best features — please let us know. Write us at the address on the contents page (page 3).

This book is the work of a team of talented writers, editors, and photographers. You can read about the people associated with this colourguide below.

LOUISA BLAIR is a freelance journalist, editor and translator who lives in Quebec City.

CATHERINE BOUCEK is a Montreal journalist. She writes a regular column, Virtually There, for the Travel section of the Montreal *Gazette*.

PHIL CARPENTER is a freelance photojournalist working out of Montreal. His photos have appeared in the National Post and the Montreal *Gazette*.

SOVITA CHANDER is a historical researcher and freelance writer. Her Quebec City home affords her much grist for both avocations.

BRAM EISENTHAL is an entertainment publicist and freelancer, and a founding member of the Travel Media Association of Canada.

SEAN FARRELL is a Montreal journalist specializing in sports and travel.

PIERRE HOME-DOUGLAS is a Montreal writer and editor who contributes travel stories and opinion pieces to newspapers and magazines.

THÉODORE LAGLOIRE is a professional photographer working out of Quebec City.

DONNA MacHUTCHIN is a Montreal writer with a passion for travel and her city. She is the librarian at the Montreal *Gazette*.

JIM McRAE is a partner in a Montreal communications firm who freelances as a journalist and book editor to local newspapers and trade magazines.

ANASTASIA MICHAILIDIS-RISACHER is a television journalist who grew up in Montreal's Greek community.

SARAH MORGAN is a Montreal-born freelance writer and translator.

LORRAINE O'DONNELL is a freelance researcher and writer based in Quebec City. Her doctoral dissertation, currently underway, looks at the history of women at the Eaton's department store.

MONIQUE POLAK teaches English literature at Marianopolis College in Montreal. In her spare time, she cultivates a widely varied career as a freelance journalist and dines out as often as possible.

MARY ANN SIMPKINS is a travel writer who contributed to the *Ottawa Colourguide*. She now lives in and explores the culture of Quebec City.

MARK STACHIEW works for the Montreal *Gazette* and is married to a woman who loves to shop.

EILEEN TRAVERS is a Montreal journalist.

When not teaching mentally handicapped children, SARAH WATERS explores the nooks and crannies of her home city.

Introducing Montreal and Quebec City

Downtown Montreal

The Château Frontenac in Quebec City

Quebec City and Montreal are easily Canada's two most historic cities. These two urban sisters — the capital and the metropolis — have been rivals since birth, but they both owe their existence to the same mighty forces: French ambition (both commercial and spiritual) and the St. Lawrence River. And in the end, it was the river that was more enduring.

It's interesting to note that in French the St. Lawrence is not a rivière but a fleuve. The difference is important not just because fleuve suggests heft and flow — it is to rivière as river is to stream — but also because fleuve suggests majesty. And the St. Lawrence is nothing if not majestic. As it journeys from the Great Lakes to the Atlantic it absorbs into itself two of the grandest rivers in eastern North America — the Ottawa and the Saguenay — and it constitutes the heart and soul of French Canada.

THE CITADELLE IN QUEBEC CITY

Together, Quebec City and Montreal formed the opposing sentinels of New France, and New France, in the words of geographer/historian Luc Bureau, was all about water: "Water is what France sought to master. Water is what characterized the initial settlement.... Quebec, incomparable strategic outpost for the defence of the river ... Montreal, at the junction of the waters of the west and northwest."

Between those early cities were two thin strips of barely cultivated, sparsely settled shoreline set in a forest that stretched to the Arctic — Canada's shaky beginnings.

Quebec is the senior of the two river cities. Its name comes from an Algonquin word that means "where the river narrows," and it is that narrowing that first attracted the attention of Samuel de Champlain when he came sailing up the river in 1608. He could guard this spot from Dutch and English rivals with a few cannon. So he landed on the shore at the foot of the great cliff that is now surmounted by the towers and turrets of the Château Frontenac Hotel, and built a shelter. The city was born.

De Champlain was never as successful as he'd hoped he'd be in attracting settlers. Things were fairly prosperous back in the mother country and French farmers were quite happy at home. But he did attract fur traders and merchants and the city became quite wealthy. Wealthy enough, anyway, to keep attracting the attention of those pesky Englishmen. And wealthy enough for the merchants to find the money to build fine stone homes and churches on the banks of the St. Lawrence.

THE PLAINS OF ABRAHAM

Eventually, the governors, the military and the clergy moved literally up market, abandoning the cramped quarters along the river for the airy heights atop Cap Diamant. Easier to defend, they argued. Not that those

PLACE D'ARMES IN QUEBEC CITY

heights did them much good when General James Wolfe turned up with his mainly Scottish soldiers in 1759.

Montreal's beginnings were more pious. When Paul de Chomedey, Sieur de Maisonneuve, landed on the island in May 1642, he and his 50 or so followers dreamed of converting the natives to Christianity and creating a new Catholic society in the wilderness. Their plans didn't really come to much, partly because they tried to establish their utopia at the juncture of the St. Lawrence and Ottawa rivers, which was a little like building a monastery on Wall Street — commercial goals soon drowned out spiritual intentions. Even the name of the settlement — Ville-Marie, in honour of Christ's mother — has virtually vanished, surviving only as the name of an expressway and a skyscraper.

So much for origins. The French regime ended in 1763 with the Seven Years' War (what Americans call the French and Indian Wars) and the Treaty of Paris gave all of New France to Britain. English and Scottish settlers, greedy for commercial conquest, poured into the new territories, and both cities, it must be said, did very well in their new empire. But Montreal was the main beneficiary. By the mid-19th century, millionaire barons with Scottish names, Protestant values and grand stone mansions on the slopes of Mount Royal controlled most of the wealth in Canada.

CALÈCHE IN MOUNT ROYAL

This long history of commerce and conquest, of linguistic and cultural tensions, of religious fervour and conflict, of prosperity and poverty, has created two complex and endlessly fascinating cities. They both have layers and layers of history, much of it, as you'll learn in this book, carefully preserved. And none of it is dull. Quebecers in both cities have far too much joie de vivre to get pedantic about the past. Ancient stone mansions, they figure, make great settings for good restaurants, and 200-year-old cobbled streets aren't of much interest unless there are a couple of sidewalk cafés along the side where you you can spend an afternoon sipping a cappuccino or a glass of wine.

Both cities are rich in culture and entertainment. Both have superb restaurants, lively nightclubs and trendy shops. They have, not surprisingly, the finest French theatres in

MONTREAL AT NIGHT

North America, and Montreal's symphony is one of the best on the continent. On a more frivolous level, French Canada, because of its long linguistic isolation, has developed its own vast pop culture — movies, rock stars, soap operas, folk singers — that is virtually unknown outside Quebec. Céline Dion didn't develop in a vacuum.

The two cities are very different. Montreal is the metropolis, a jumble of conflicting and competing cultures. Smoked meat and souvlaki are as much a part of its traditional diet as tourtière and pouding au chômeur. Quebec is more solidly French — it's hard to find even an English novel — and the centre of government. It's staid and assured without Montreal's jittery edge.

In fact the two cities don't really like each other very much. Montrealers view Quebec City as a bastion of smug bureaucrats dedicated to milking the metropolis of profits to squander on silly government dreams. Quebec City residents often seem to regard Montreal as a kind of polyglot intrusion, a foreign body that doesn't really belong in Quebec at all. The truth is, however, the two cities complement each other (even if they seldom compliment each other), and to explore one without at least visiting the other is like eating cake without frosting — pleasant, perhaps, and certainly less fattening — but missing something.

LOCAL COLOUR IN MONTREAL

The sensible thing to do to start where the history started — in Quebec City. The only problem with this approach is that those old walls are pretty seductive. You might never make it to Montreal. Of course, the same problem would arise if you started at the other end of the axis.

The chapters that follow will give you a good idea of how best to explore each city. But that leaves the question of how to travel between the two. A boat would be your best choice if you could swing it — romantic, adventurous and historically appropriate. But for most people it's fairly impractical. That leaves road and rail.

MONTREAL METRO

The main highway between Quebec City and Montreal is the Autoroute Jean-Lesage — or Highway 20. It's a very efficient piece of civil engineering — and perhaps one of the dullest stretches of road in Canada. It has no hills, passes through no towns and has no access to the river. Leave it to the trucks, and drive the along the north shore instead.

The main north shore road — Highway 40 — is an efficient piece of engineering as well (except for the little jog you have to make at Trois-Rivières), but the scenery is much more pleasing and the history far more interesting. If you get bored with the four lanes you can get off and follow the old route along the river.

Whatever you do, stop in Trois-Rivières. It might seem a grubby little industrial city when you sweep through on the highway, but it is in fact older than Montreal, and the historic section along the river has some beautiful little 17th- and 18th-century gems. Just across the Mauricie River in Cap de la Madeleine is a major marian shrine, Notre Dame du Cap. The Pope stopped here to say Mass on his visit to Canada and the setting along the river is quite lovely.

Train service between the two cities is frequent and efficient, especially now that Via Rail has restored its service to the centre of Quebec City. It once moved the train station from the magnificent structure on the waterfront to a tacky little outbuilding in suburban Ste-Foy, with a predictably disastrous drop-off in passenger use. Unfortunately, the train follows essentially the same route as that truck-bearing Highway 40, so the scenery on the trip isn't very arresting. On the other hand, if you sleep it doesn't matter, and you'll arrive well rested.

PLACE DU CANADA IN MONTREAL

MONTREAL'S
BEST

Montreal's Top Attractions

Sarah Waters

Basilique Notre-Dame

God and Mammon seem to have the corner on Montreal's attractions. If you measure these things by the number of visitors alone, two Christian shrines and the Casino de Montréal top the city's popularity charts.

The shrines are of course much older than the casino and are a reminder of the days when Quebec prided itself on being the most loyal province of the Roman Catholic Church. That fervent piety seems to have petered out, but it has left behind some glorious monuments. Two of the most famous and most visited honour Christ's earthly parents: Mary has Notre-Dame basilica in Vieux-Montréal, and her husband is the patron of St. Joseph's Oratory on the other side of Mount Royal.

Basilique Notre-Dame-de-Montréal, at 116 Rue Notre-Dame O./W., (514-849-1070), is probably the most celebrated church in Canada. Its vast blue interior spattered with thousands of 22-carat-gold stars graces postcards, posters, calendars and place mats. It's where Céline Dion married her manager and it was the venue of one of Luciano Pavarotti's most famous appearances, a Christmas concert that has been endlessly recycled by the Public Broadcasting System in the United States.

All this fame sits well on the old place. It's a truly magnificent building, which could accommodate just about every Catholic in the city when it first opened in 1829. It was, oddly enough, designed by an American Protestant named James O'Donnell, who was so pleased with his work that he converted to Catholicism and is buried in the crypt. The decor is the work of Victor Bourgeau, who filled O'Donnell's vaulted stone cave with dozens of paintings and pine and walnut carvings, ornate panelling, fanciful pillars and stained-glass windows from Limoges. The reredos features a larger-than-life-size depiction of the crucifixion surrounded by four life-sized scenes of sacrifice from the Old Testament — all carved in wood by local artisans. The pulpit with its curving staircase and the baptistery with murals by Ozias Leduc are works of art. Behind the main altar is the Chapelle du Sacre-Coeur, the most popular wedding chapel in Montreal. In 1978 an arsonist torched the place and destroyed much of its Spanish-style Gothic Revival interior. Architects rescued what they could and added a very modern roof with a huge skylight as well as a plexiglass altar with an enormous bronze sculpture rising above it. Although not to everyone's taste, somehow it all blends in.

Oratoire Saint-Joseph

The interior of the Oratoire Saint-Joseph de Mont-Royal, at 3800 Rue Queen Mary (514-733-8211), is drab by comparison. But what this huge church lacks in opulence it makes up for in size and setting. It sits on the northern side of Mount Royal surrounded by gardens and trees. Thousands of pilgrims visit it every year, seeking favours and cures from both St. Joseph and Blessed Frère André Bessette, the humble little Christian brother who was responsible for getting the oratory built. Successful supplicants have left behind hundreds of canes and crutches that are used to decorate the walls of the votive chapel. The building actually houses two churches — the

CASINO DE MONTRÉAL

nondescript little crypt church on the ground floor and the immense but sombre oratory church under the dome. The latter is the home church of the Petits Chanteurs du Mont-Royal, the finest boys' choir in the city. The complex also has a museum dedicated to Frère André, a cafeteria, a souvenir shop and a hostel for pilgrims.

It's hard to make the jump from all this piety to the glitz and glitter of the Casino de Montréal (514-932-2746). But then, the casino is on an island named after the same Notre-Dame as the basilica, so in a way it all fits. The casino is a success story. It gets more than 15,000 visitors a day and at last count had 1,835 slot machines, 88 tables for baccarat, blackjack and roulette, five restaurants, a dinner theatre and — just in case you should run short of cash — lots of automatic teller machines. It opened in the futuristic glass, aluminum building that was the French pavilion at Expo '67. When that got too full, the government agency that runs the casino took over the adjoining Quebec pavilion. (First, though, it tinted the cubic building an alluring and appropriate shade of gold.) Lest you should be misled into thinking this is Las Vegas North, there are some rules: no jeans, no running shoes and no drinking alcohol on the gaming floors (one vice at a time, please). Some of the restaurants are buffet joints that would be familiar to Nevada gamblers, but one of them, Nuances, is very posh indeed, and offers great views of the Montreal skyline.

SAILING PAST THE CASINO

So much for God and Mammon on Montreal's must-see list. It's time to make a little trek east on the Métro to the Viau station to take a peek at one of the great white elephants of all time — the Stade Olympique at Ave. 4141 Pierre-de-Coubertin, (514-252-8687). English-speaking Montrealers call the place the Big Owe, which describes

THE STADE OLYMPIQUE

both its shape and the shape of Montreal's finances after it was built. Mayor Jean Drapeau hired French architect Roger Taillibert to design the building for the 1976 Olympics. It was supposed to be the prince of stadiums and a monument to sport, and it is indeed a dramatic structure rising like a great white mirage out of the low-lying architecture of Montreal's east end. But it never really functioned very well as a sports stadium and it makes most of its money from trade shows and mega-concerts. Céline Dion and the Rolling Stones do a better job of filling its vast interior than baseball or football ever did. So why go look? Well, there are at least four reasons. First, the stadium's spectacular. It looks like a giant clamshell, and while the collapsible fabric roof never worked, and then was replaced by an equally disastrous permanent one, the interior does have a bright and airy feel. Second, the leaning tower, which was intended to hold up the collapsible roof, features a neat tram that climbs its shaft to a great viewing platform overlooking Montreal. Third, the Olympic swimming pools under the tower are open to the public. Finally, the stadium is right next door to at least two very successful attractions.

Examining at the Insectarium

The Biodôme (514-868-3000) is housed in the velodrome built for the Olympic bicycle races. In fact, it's designed to look a bit like a '70s-style cyclist's helmet. But the building has been gutted and transformed into an indoor outdoors (see Nature & Natural History). It re-creates four habitats — a rain forest, a Laurentian forest, a polar landscape and the St. Lawrence marine ecosystem — complete with all the requisite plants and animals.

For those who prefer their plants in a more natural setting, the Jardin Botanique de Montréal at 4101 Rue Sherbrooke O./W. (514-872-1400) is right across the street from the Biodôme. This is one of the biggest such gardens in the world, with 185 acres of gardens, 10 greenhouses and a bug-shaped Insectarium that's full of live and dead insects (see Nature & Natural History).

But enough about bugs and flowers. It's time for some history. Just about every visitor to Montreal makes a trip at some point to Vieux-Montréal and the adjoining Vieux-Port. This was a rundown area until the late '60s when Montreal finally woke up to the treasures it has along the waterfront. Now its narrow cobblestone streets are packed in summer and still well populated in winter, with visitors admiring the fine

Vieux-Port marina

examples of 18th- and 19th-century architecture that line its sidewalks. Vieux-Montréal is also home to some of the city's most popular museums — the Musée d'Archéologie Pointe-à-Callière and the Centre d'Histoire de Montréal (see Museums) — and an art gallery dedicated to the work of one man, Marc-Aurèle Fortin (see Galleries). All this borders the Vieux-Port, a strip of wharves, grassy expanses and once dilapidated warehouses that has evolved into one of the city's most popular parks. (See Old Montréal and Old Port.)

Musée d'Archéologie Pointe-à-Callière

The Vieux-Port also offers a pleasant way to get to another great park. In summer, shuttle boats carry passengers from the Jacques-Cartier pier to Parc des Îles in the middle of the St, Lawrence. (Less romantic and more practical visitors can take the Métro instead.) The park was the home of Expo '67, the world's fair that trumpeted Montreal's arrival as a modern metropolis and the party capital of Canada. In fact, one of the two islands the park comprises — Île Notre-Dame — didn't exist before Expo. It rests on a solid foundation of stone rubble excavated for the construction of the Métro system.

Centre d'Histoire de Montréal

Some of the Expo buildings are still in use. The flamboyant French pavilion and the neighbouring Quebec pavilion, as already noted, house the Casino de Montréal, and Buckminster Fuller's gigantic geodesic dome — originally the United States pavilion — houses the Biosphere, an interactive exhibit on the Great Lakes/St. Lawrence waterways (see Nature & Natural History). One of the most successful reminders of Expo's

Bateau mouche and Biosphère

glory days is La Ronde amusement park (514-872-4537 or 1-800-797-4537). The Expo symbol — a circle of stick men (or chicken feet, depending on how you look at it) — still decorates the park's giant Ferris wheel. But La Ronde is now a lot better than it was during Expo, when it was, frankly, a little short on thrilling rides. Now its has a couple of giant roller-coasters that rival the best in the world.

LA RONDE AMUSEMENT PARK

Within the sound of the roller-coaster screams is a completely different attraction, the Old Fort and Stewart Museum (see Museums). The fort was built to fend off an American attack that never came and is now used as a drilling ground for the Olde 78th Fraser Highlanders and the Compagnie Franche de la Marine, so sometimes the sound of muskets drowns out the shrieks from La Ronde.

Beyond this, the park has enough to keep even the most casual visitor content for a day or two. It has the city's only natural beach (a cleverly disguised filtration system keeps the water clean), a rowing basin, a vast floral display called Floralies and a couple of hundred acres of trees and walkways. Grand Prix drivers compete here very summer in North America's only Formula One auto race, and pyrotechnicians from a dozen countries spend summer weekends trying to outdo each other with fireworks displays.

OLD SOLDIERS AT THE STEWART MUSEUM

As we're on the subject of parks, let's finish this roundup of Montreal's highlights with a visit to the largest and most famous of the city's parks, Mont-Royal. It's named for the steep but modest little knoll that rises 234 metres above the city centre, a prominence Montrealers call, without any sign of embarrassment, "the mountain" or "la montagne." The city bought the land on Mount Royal's slopes in 1876. In an inspired moment, the administratrion hired Frederick Law Olmsted, the man responsible for New York's Central Park, to turn it into a park. Olmsted's dream was to keep the whole 101 hectares (250 acres) as natural as possible. He built a few lookouts and laced the meadows and hardwood forests with a series of footpaths. Others spoiled this dream by adding a man-made pond (Beaver Lake), a 30-metre-high cross made of steel girders and the Voie Camilien Houde, a thoroughfare that cuts right through the park from east to west. Still, Parc Mont-Royal is Montreal's favourite and easiest escape from the stone and concrete canyons of the city.

BOARDWALK IN MONT-ROYAL

Heritage & Architecture

Jim McRae

Rue Peel
downtown

Montreal is a city of many spoils. It brims with cultural diversity, flourishes with art and fashion and serves up fine dining and entertainment in banquet-like proportions. And all of this is celebrated in an urban setting decorated with some of the richest architecture on the continent. Since its founding in 1642, Montreal has grown from a frontier settlement of New France to a cosmopolitan city on the edge of the new millennium. Along the way, pioneer settlers, Victorian industrialists and international masters of the classical school have all added their touches to the city's architectural heritage.

Fragments of 17th- and 18th-Century New France

While it is commonly believed that Old Montreal is full of buildings that date to the French regime, in fact there are only a handful of gems from that epoch still standing (not including the church of the Visitation, which is located in the north end of the city). These are, however, historical jewels — some of them over three centuries old.

The old Saint-Sulpice seminary, dating to 1685, is one such gem. Located beside Basilique-Notre-Dame, it is the oldest building in Montreal, constructed to house Sulpician priests. The seminary features several medieval characteristics: cradle-vaults in the foundation, corner towers with staircases and building practices common to artisan tradesmen of the period. The low storeys and small windows are signatures of French regime architecture. The central door is engraved with the year 1740, the year the portico was added to the seminary.

Several blocks to the southwest, the Grey Nuns general hospital at Rue St-Pierre and Place d'Youville was built in 1693 as the second hospital in the city. It was given its name after Marguerite d'Youville founded the congregation of the Sisters of Charity, also known as the Grey Nuns, sometime around 1750. The hospital was destroyed by fire in 1765 and the walls that were left undamaged were used in the rebuilding. It was later partially demolished to be replaced by a grand greystone warehouse.

Château de Ramezay

Roughly a kilometre's walk from the old hospital, the Château de Ramezay on Rue Notre-Dame E. stands as a well-preserved monument of the French regime. The residence was constructed for the governor of Montreal, Claude de Ramezay, and work on it began in 1705. The Château is a blend of urban row house and detached rural home, a trend in Montreal-area dwellings at the time. It was converted into a museum in 1895. Although there is little doubt as to the year work began on the Château, there is some debate as to whether the Maison du Calvet on the northeast corner of rues Bonsecours and St-Paul actually dates back to 1725. Early city maps show a building in the location, but it's not certain that this was the original house. Other reports indicate that the fieldstone structure with a steeply sloping roof was built in 1770, a decade after the city was taken over by the British. Nonetheless, it is a fine example of 18th-century architecture. The house is named after Pierre du Calvet, a Frenchman and partisan of the American Revolution who became a resident of Montreal. It now houses a charming little inn and one of the city's better French restaurants.

Maison du Calvet

Victorian Influence, 1837–1914

Victorian architecture is an influence, not a single style. And in Montreal, rich Scottish and British industrialists would wield considerable influence over the city's buildings for seven decades — well past the reign of Queen Victoria. These nouveau riche of the New World borrowed from classical traditions, putting their own elaborate stamps on the business addresses where they plotted their economic conquests. Some say that Notre-Dame Basilica, although constructed prior to the reign of the famed British monarch, heralded the era of Victorian architecture in Montreal. Built in 1829, Notre-Dame is the neo-Gothic creation of Irish-American architect James O'Donnell. He used decorative components of the Gothic style to produce a monument resembling the celebrated cathedrals of Europe: majestic façade, elaborate portico and soaring bell towers. A Protestant by birth, O'Donnell converted to Catholicism before his death in 1830 and is buried beside the altar in his famous creation.

Notre-Dame Basilica

Opposite Notre-Dame on Place d'Armes is the Bank of Montreal Building, perhaps the richest example of Victorian architecture in the city. It was designed by Englishman John Wells and dates to 1847. Although a major expansion at the turn of the century left only the façade as part of the original construction, it alone is considered a magnificent architectural achievement. Its detailed and expert stonework, often compared to that of the Bank of the United States in Philadelphia, evoked the power of Montreal's commercial elite. A short distance to the southeast, William Footner's Marché Bonsecours on Rue St-Paul is an example of the level of extravagance associated with the Victorians. Costing a staggering $70,000 when completed in 1842, Bonsecours market features cast-iron Doric columns in its portico while an imposing dome rises above its roof line. Located on the harbour, the three-story-high, 152-metre-long building was a beacon for the era, sending a message of the city's commercial success to those arriving by river. Bonsecours once served as parliament and town hall. Today, cultural events and exhibitions are frequently held here.

Bank of Montreal

Marché Bonsecours

Montreal's current city hall, or Hôtel de Ville, is also a Victorian structure. Designed by architect H. Maurice

HÔTEL-DE-VILLE

Perrault, it is an example of the Second Empire style, which originated in France. Built between 1872 and 1878, it fell to fire in 1922. The remaining walls were used in its reconstruction and a tall mansard roof was introduced. Elaborately decorated and massive in size, the building sits across the street from Château de Ramezay. Juxtaposed, the two illustrate the difference between the simple lines of the French regime and the frills of the Victorian era.

THE SQUARE MILE

While the mercantile elite of the Victorian era were branding their edifices with labels of commercial success, they were also building domestic monuments to themselves in an area known as the Square Mile, later dubbed the Golden Square Mile. This neighbourhood was bordered by Rue Sherbrooke to the south, the slope of Mount Royal to the north, Chemin de la Côte-des-Neiges to the west and Rue Bleury to the east. Its residents controlled 70 percent of Canada's wealth at the turn of the century. The status symbols built to house these magnates were some of the most extravagant private homes ever constructed on the continent.

RAVENSCRAG

Unfortunately, many of these urban palaces were razed in the late '60s and early '70s during a time of careless city planning. The few examples that remain, however, offer a glimpse of the lifestyle of Canada's early business barons. Principal among these estates is Ravenscrag (now the Allan Pavilion of the Royal Victoria Hospital on Ave. des Pins) home to Sir Hugh Allan, the richest of all of Montreal's elite. The sprawling house features a mixture of architectural styles but borrows mostly from the Italian Renaissance. From its location on the flank of Mount Royal, it represented the pinnacle of personal success for the rest of the growing metropolis to see.

While not as ostentatious as Allan's mountainside monument, Trafalgar House at 3015 Ave. Trafalgar is a fine example of a wealthy Victorian domicile. Built in 1848, it was designed by John George Howard, an English draftsman and engineer who emigrated to Toronto. He incorporated Gothic and Tudor features into the design of the house. Its red-brick facade and stone-framed windows and doors display considerable craftsmanship and contribute to an overall look of solidity. The former Engineers' Club (now a popular restaurant, part of the Mother Tucker chain) is another example of an opulent Victorian residence. Located at Place du Frère André (formerly Beaver Hall Square), just north of Blvd. René-Lévesque, the mansion was completed around 1860. It is said to be designed by William T. Thomas, one of the most accomplished architects of the period and the mastermind behind St. George's Anglican Church on Dorchester Square. The residence has the flavour of an Italian Renaissance mansion.

St. George's Anglican Church

Residential Architecture

If the homes of the Victorian era's elite were an expression of the individual through elaborate decoration and outward displays of wealth, the row houses of the working class of Montreal were the opposite: nondescript structures designed to huddle the masses close to the industries that kept the Square Mile golden.

Multifamily vertical housing, one or two flats above a main-floor flat, first appeared in Montreal between 1850 and 1860 in Pointe St-Charles. These were erected to house Irish immigrants who worked either on construction of the Victoria Bridge or in the yards and shops of the Grand Trunk Railway. Streets such as Sébastopol, Charon and Le Ber are lined with these dwellings. Wooden frame in construction, they are finished with red brick and extend right to the sidewalk, with no balcony. Twin doors share a common landing, one leading to the main floor, the other to an inside staircase that accesses the second level. The roof is either flat, mansard or with a steep, sloping side with dormers looking out onto the street. Any decoration on the façade usually occurs at the roof line, incorporating the dormers and simple cornices.

Multifamily vertical housing

Although the working-class homes closer to the city core exhibit more architectural flair than those in the Pointe, they are still models of simplicity. Apart from some examples of upscale, stone-faced British-style row houses on Rue Laval and Carré St-Louis, they are typically, like those on nearby Rue Hutchison, two storeys high with greystone façades and picturesque architectural motifs; this style became common throughout the city. Stone — a grey limestone quarried on Montreal island — is also a common façade in the solidly built apartment blocks on rues St-

FLAT-ROOFED HOMES

Hubert and St-Denis between Ste-Catherine and Sherbrooke.

In the more densely populated areas of Verdun, Rosemont and Plateau Mont-Royal the row houses feature two or three levels of flats finished in brick. These flat-roofed homes have porches, balconies and outside staircases in front and back. This type of dwelling became typical housing for the city's working class, and, because it is more prevalent than any other building type in the city, represents a de facto Montreal architectural style. These buildings were erected to house the 400,000 people who moved to the city between 1891 and 1921.

When duplexes and triplexes were springing up all over the city to handle the influx of rural migrants, builders began to standardize their techniques and to use prefabricated building materials, such as the outside staircase. Montreal's distinctive outside staircases were seen as a space- and cost-saving feature: having the stairs on the outside meant more living space inside and less fuel needed to heat an area that would be used just for stairs. Curved versions are used where homes have little frontage. The drawbacks are that the stairs can be slippery in winter (many people affix outdoor carpeting to combat this problem) and tend to block sunlight from the front of the house.

DISTINCTIVE OUTSIDE STAIRCASES

CHURCH ARCHITECTURE

Mark Twain once said that you couldn't throw a brick in Montreal without breaking a church window. And although there is no hard evidence to prove that the American literary icon ever put his theory to the test during his visit in 1881, several important churches dominated the core of the city at the time, their spires and domes competing for space on the skyline.

ST. PATRICK'S BASILICA

Notre Dame, located at Place d'Armes, was principal among these historic houses of worship, its chapel having been part of the main fort in 1642; the present building dates to 1829. St. Patrick's Basilica on Blvd. René-Lévesque, completed in 1847, also punctuated the landscape, as did Christ Church Cathedral, dating to 1859, near Phillips Square. The Cathédrale Marie-Reine-du-Monde (originally named St-Jacques) or in the heart of the business district was over halfway throughout its construction by 1881 when Twain visited Montreal. While many of the churches mentioned were merely a stone's throw from the Windsor Hotel, the spot where he made his quip, further afield stood the only church that dated back to the French regime. Located at Sault-au-Récollet, west of Ave. Papineau on Blvd. Gouin, the church of the Visitation was begun in 1749 and ready for Mass by 1751. Charles Guilbault, a parishioner, supplied the rough masonry of the main building, which also features classical arched windows. In the early 1850s the prolific Montreal architect John Ostell added a new front in a severe English neo-Baroque style. The interior is equally rewarding, as master sculptors like Philippe Liébert, Louis-Amable Quévillon and David Fleury-David lent their skills to different aspects of the church over time. The tabernacle of the main altar was completed in 1792, the altars between 1802 and 1806 and the vault and much of the present interior between 1816 and 1831.

1000 DE LA GAUCHETIÈRE, MARIE-REINE-DU-MONDE, SUN LIFE

SKYSCRAPERS THEN AND NOW

Although church steeples and bell towers defined Montreal's skyline from its earliest days, the city's first office towers began to challenge them near the end of the 19th century, when the elevator and the use of iron and steel framing allowed architects to push buildings higher than their standard five or six storeys.

Oddly enough, the city's first "skyscraper," or gratte-ciel featured neither of these innovations. Still, the New York Life Insurance Co. building on Place d'Armes, completed in 1888, was the city's first eight-storey office building. Although Notre-Dame's 66-metre-high twin spires still rose above any other structure in the city, taller buildings were soon to follow.

Basilique Notre-Dame relinquished its title when the Royal Bank building, reaching 23 storeys, was completed

BNP AND LAURENTIAN BANK

in 1928. Located on Rue St-Jacques, not far from the renowned church, the bank's exquisite ground floor was a symbol of Montreal's mercantile elite. Another example of the increasing wealth of the city was the Sun Life Building on the east side of Dorchester Square. Built in three stages between 1914 and 1931, it was the largest building in the British Empire when completed. Its steel framing is wrapped in Stanstead granite and Corinthian columns line its ground floor.

The era of the modern-day Montreal skyscraper began in the early 1960s and involved the efforts of several world-renowned architects. Place Ville-Marie, an I.M. Pei creation, was conceived in the late 1950s but not fully completed until 1966; the tower dates from 1962. Its cruciform design makes it one of the most recognizable structures in Montreal.

Slightly to the east at Square Victoria, Luigi Moretti and Pier L. Nervi put their finishing touches on La Tour de la Bourse in 1964. It is the first earthquake-proof building ever constructed and, at 47 storeys, was the tallest concrete structure in the world. In the main lobby, a 13-metre-tall stalactite comprising 3,000 pieces of Murano glass welcomes visitors. Slightly to the west of the city core, the black-metal and tinted-glass office towers of Westmount Square, unveiled in 1965, are considered masterpieces of Ludwig Mies van der Rohe, the former director of the Bauhaus.

In recent years, other significant towers have staked their claim in the celebrated skyline. The quiet elegance of the 672-foot-high 1000 de La Gauchetière is one example, the 47 storeys of glass and granite at Le 1250 boulevard René-Lévesque is another. The former has a glass-domed exhibition hall that features a skating rink, the latter a 25-metre-high interior garden.

The glass and steel of the downtown skyscrapers may punctuate Montreal's modern skyline, but in no way do they supersede the structures that are cast in their shadows. The city has been under construction for over 350 years and its architecture is rich and diverse. It reflects the influences of its founding fathers and incorporates the styles, and often the personal tastes, of those who followed. Just as few cities in North America can match Montreal's history, few can match, in age and diversity, its architectural heritage.

Museums

Sarah Morgan

McCord Museum

It would be hard to find a North American metropolis with more history than Montreal. The city's roots reach back to the middle of the 17th century, and it's hard to dig a sewer or repair a street without turning up some artifact from the past in Montreal. There was a time in the 50s and 60s when history was viewed as something you knocked down or pushed aside to make way for another skyscraper or freeway. But Montrealers have learned to revere, even revel in, their rich heritage. You can see that pride in the cobbled streets of Vieux-Montréal, the Victorian row houses of the McGill ghetto and the comfortable Second Empire homes built by the francophone elite in the Quartier-Latin.

A gift from Sir William Cornelius Van Horne to his grandson

You can also see it in the city's museums, where every effort is made to bring the past to life and render it vivid and relevant for modern visitors. Some museums are tiny. The Bank of Montreal, for example, has squeezed a modest but interesting little display on early banking practices into one room on the ground floor of its head office on Place d'Armes. Some focus on the contributions of one person; others, like the McCord and the Musée d'Archéologie Pointe-à-Callière, take a much broader view.

19th century Mohawk beadwork

The Broad View

The broad view is probably a good way to start any exploration of the city's history, and it would be hard to find any museum broader than the McCord Museum of Canadian History at 690 Rue Sherbrooke Street O./W. (514-

Kahnawake Mohawks in 1869

398-7100), open Tuesday to Sunday just across Rue Sherbrooke from the McGill University campus. The heart of its collection is a glorious hodgepodge of artifacts collected by a lawyer named David Ross McCord (1844-1930). He was an inveterate pack rat with a passion for anything that had to do with life in Canada — books, photographs, jewellery, furniture, clothing, guns, old documents, paintings, toys, porcelain. And he gave all this to McGill University so it could open a museum of social history. Some of the best exhibits are the collections of Indian and Inuit artifacts. These aren't limited to the ubiquitous west coast and Arctic art, but include tools and weapons and intricately decorated clothing. The museum also has one of the best photographic archives in Canada, with more than 70,000 pictures. Some of the most interesting come from the studio of William Notman, a photographic pioneer who captured life in Victorian Montreal. Notman's work includes lots of exterior pictures, families tobogganing, soldiers marching and members (several hundred of them) of the posh Montreal Amateur Athletic Association posing in snowshoeing regalia on the slopes of Mount Royal. The remarkable thing about these pictures is that all the figures were photographed individually in a studio and then painstakingly assembled onto the exterior background.

Inset: Iroquois beadwork

Earliest Montreal

Musée d'Archéologie

Musée d'Archéologie Pointe-à-Callière, in the middle of Vieux-Montréal, at 350 Place Royale, (514-872-9150), probes a little deeper — literally — into the city's history. It's housed in a startlingly modern building on the waterfront that looks rather like a concrete ship. It's quite a tall building, but the guts of the museum are in the basement where archeologists have dug their way through several layers of settlement to the remnants of the city's earliest days. You can wend your way down to the banks of a long-filled-in river where early settlers used to trade with the local Indians, visit the oldest Catholic cemetery on the island and examine the foundations of an 18th-century waterfront tavern. A tunnel connects the museum to the Old Customs House in Place

Royale, a fine old building with a huge gift shop.

Château de Ramezay at 280 Rue Notre-Dame E. (514-861-3708) is one of the few reminders the city has of the French regime. This mansion was built in 1702 by Claude de Ramezay, Montreal's 11th governor, and its interior reflects the grace and tastes of the early-18th-century elite. The most magnificent room is the Nantes Salon, which is decorated with intricately carved panelling by the French architect Germain Boffrand. The uniforms, documents and furniture on the main floor reflect the life of New France's ruling classes, while several rooms in the cellars depict the more ordinary doings of humbler colonists. But the museum's collection is fairly eclectic. One of its most prized possessions, for example, is a bright-red automobile that was produced at the turn of the century by the De Dion-Bouton company.

SALLE DE NANTES AND BEDROOM, CHÂTEAU RAMEZAY

At first, the exhibits in the Centre d'Histoire de Montréal at 335 Place d'Youville, (514-872-3207) a 19th-century firehouse, seem to cover much the same ground as those at the Château de Ramezay and the Musée d'Archéologie Pointe-à-Callière. That's a misleading impression, however, as the focus here is fixed firmly on everyday life. One of the most effective parts of the museum are the exhibits on city life in the 1930s and 1940s. You can sit in a period living room and listen to a play-by-play of a Canadiens hockey game or step into a phone booth and eavesdrop while a young factory worker tries to make a date with the shop clerk he adores.

A Tale of Two Women

One of the unique things about Montreal history is the large and acclaimed part that women have played in it. Two women in particular were absolutely vital to the city's development — Jeanne Mance, who co-founded the original settlement of Ville-Marie with Paul de Chomedey, Sieur de Maisonneuve, and Marguerite Bourgeoys, the colony's first schoolteacher and now a canonized saint. Both women were feisty, devout and determined; they left behind concrete reminders of their presence: Jeanne Mance's Hôtel-Dieu hospital still serves

CENTRE D'HISTOIRE DE MONTRÉAL

the city's sick, and the religious order that Marguerite Bourgeoys founded still runs schools and colleges across Canada. Several museums offer insights into the lives of these remarkable and indomitable women.

Maison Saint-Gabriel, 2146 Place Dublin (514-935-8136), is an isolated little fragment of New France lost among the apartment buildings of working-class Pointe St-Charles. It was a farm when the formidable Marguerite Bourgeoys bought it in 1668 as a residence for the religious order she had founded in 1655. The house, rebuilt in 1698 after a fire, is a fine example of 17th-century architecture, with thick stone walls and a steeply pitched roof built on an intricate frame of heavy timbers. Marguerite Bourgeoys and her tireless sisters worked the farm and ran a school on the property for Indian and colonial children. They also housed and trained the filles du roy (the king's daughters), orphaned young women sent to New France by Louis XIV to be the wives and mothers of his new colony. The house's chapel, kitchen, dormitory and drawing rooms are full of artifacts from the 17th, 18th and 19th centuries including a writing desk the saint actually used. There's a smaller museum dedicated to Marguerite Bourgeoys and her mission in North America attached to the chapel of Notre-Dame-de-Bon-Secours in Vieux-Montréal. It too is worth a visit.

Musée des Hospitallières is located at 201 Ave. des Pines O./W., (514-849-1919). Jeanne Mance was as pious as her friend, Marguerite Bourgeoys, and even more important to the establishment of a colony on Montreal Island. But she never joined or founded a religious order, so she left behind no band of sisters to promulgate her memory. She did, however, bring the Religeuses Hospitallières de Saint Joseph to Montreal in the mid-1600s to run Hôtel-Dieu, the hospital she'd founded. And while the sisters no longer run the hospital, they still maintain this small but charming museum that reflects Jeanne Mance's zealous spirit. Books, documents and artifacts from the early days are on display and there is a sometimes chilling exhibit on the history of medicine and nursing.

Great Personalities

Montreal's history is filled with colourful characters — strongman Louis Cyr, hockey player Maurice (Rocket) Richard, artist Marc-Aurèle Fortin and Mayor Camilien Houde, who spent time in an internment camp for his opposition to conscription during the Second World War. Every one of them would be worthy of a museum, but only a few have permanent exhibitions in their honour.

The Sir George-Étienne Cartier historic site at 458 Rue Notre-Dame E. (514-233-2292 or 1-800-463-6769), is the most elaborate museum dedicated to a single individual. George-Étienne Cartier (1814-73) was largely responsible for persuading French Canada to join the new Canadian confederation in 1867, arguing that a federal system would give French Canadians the powers necessary to protect their language, religion and culture. The national historic site comprises two adjoining greystone houses the Cartier family owned on the eastern edge of Vieux-Montréal. One is dedicated to Cartier's career as a lawyer, politician and railway-builder. One of the exhibits gives visitors the opportunity to sit at a round table with plaster models of the Fathers of Confederation and listen in either French or English to a very good summary of the founding of Canada. The second house, on the other side of a covered carriageway, focuses on the Cartiers' domestic life and the functioning of an upper-middle-class family in the mid-19th century. Visitors wander through formal rooms full of fussy, overstuffed furniture, listening to snatches of taped conversation from "servants" gossiping about the lives of their master and mistress.

Musée du Bienheureux Frère André (Oratoire Saint-Joseph de Mont-Royal, 3800 Rue Queen Mary, 514-733-8211), tucked away in St. Joseph's Oratory, is a little museum dedicated to the diminutive man who started the whole project — Brother André Bessette. Models, photographs and documents chronicle his early life and a shrine containing his embalmed heart is testiment to the reverence in which he is still held. The office where Frère André worked, the room where he slept and the hospital room where he died have been reconstructed and preserved. Not a bad monument for a man who was born in abject poverty and never held a job more important than porter in a classical college.

LA COMPAGNIE FRANCHE DE LA MARINE

Le Monde de Maurice (Rocket) Richard (corner of Ave. Pierre-de-Coubertin and Rue Viau, 514-251-9930) isn't really a museum at all, just a room tucked way in the Maurice Richard arena. One of the most exciting hockey players who ever lived probably deserves much more, but the exhibits do reverently trace the great man's life and career.

FORT DE L'ÎLE-SAINTE-HELENE

Marc-Aurèle Fortin is the only Quebec artist with his own museum (Musée Marc-Aurèle Fortin at 118 Rue St-Pierre, 514-872-9150). And he deserves it. The man virtually invented Quebec landscape painting. He also pioneered the painting of images on a black background — a technique that has been abused by schlock merchants ever since. No one, however, has painted grander trees than Fortin.

MILITARY ADVENTURES

Old Fort and Stewart Museum (Île Ste-Hélène, 514-861-6701). The Fort de l'Île-Sainte-Hélène was built in 1825 to protect Montreal from an American attack that never came. Its red stone walls enclose a grassy parade square that is

At play in the Old Fort

used today by members of the Olde 78th Fraser Highlanders and the Compagnie Franche de la Marine, re-creations of two 18th-century military formations that fought each other over the future of New France. The fort also houses the Musée Stewart, a small but excellent historical museum with an interesting collection of 17th- and 18th-century maps, firearms and navigational instruments. Its costumed guides give an accurate, unsentimental and yet quite humorous account of the first encounters between Europeans and Native North Americans.

Trade and Commerce

Lachine Canal

A cyclist can coast comfortably into Montreal's industrial past by following the bike path along the Lachine Canal from the Vieux-Port to Lac St-Louis. The canal, built to

allow shipping to avoid the treacherous Lachine Rapids, was supplanted by the St. Lawrence Seaway in the 1950s and has become a kind of long, thin and very popular park. Near the end of the trail in the lakeside suburb of Lachine is the Lachine Canal Interpretation Centre (514-637-7433), which houses an interesting display on the building and operation of the canal. Further along the Lachine waterfront at 1255 Blvd. St-Joseph is an old stone warehouse with a cumbersome name — Fur Trade in Lachine National Historic Site. Constructed in 1802 as a trading depot, today the building offers displays on the trade that created Montreal's wealth. Because of its position west of the trade-blocking rapids, Lachine became a prosperous trading town. One of its oldest houses, built in 1670 by merchants Jacques Le Ber and Charles LeMoyne, is now the Musée de Lachine (110 Chemin LaSalle, 514-634-3471, extension 346) with historical exhibits and an art gallery.

Stones and Laughter

Not all city museums are dedicated to Montreal's history. There are art museums (see Galleries), museums that focus on nature (see Natural History) and some museums that are just difficult to categorize.

North Façade from Entrance Gate, Canadian Centre for Architecture

The Canadian Centre for Architecture at 1920 Rue Baille (514-939-7026) is a place for serious scholars. Its library has more than 165,000 volumes on various aspects of architecture and the Centre's collection of plans, drawings, models and photographs is the most important of its kind in the world. It also has six well-lit exhibition rooms for rotating exhibits that range from the academic to the whimsical. Recent shows have focussed on doll houses, miniature villages and American lawn culture. All this is housed in an austere, modern building that embraces a grand old mansion built in 1874 for the family of the president of the Canadian Pacific Railway, Sir Thomas Shaughnessy. The house is open to visitors and has a remarkable art nouveau conservatory with an intricately decorated ceiling. The CCA's most playful exhibit, however, is outside — the architecture designed by artist Melvin Charney. It's stuck in an unlikely spot, between two highway ramps across busy Blvd. René-Lévesque and separated from the museum itself, but its whimsical bits and pieces of architecture perched in unlikely places is a delight.

TOP: CANADIAN CENTRE FOR ARCHITECTURE MIDDLE: BOOKSTORE AT THE CCA

The International Museum of Humour at 2111 Blvd. St-Laurent (514-845-4000) opened in 1993 as an outgrowth of the city's Just For Laughs Comedy Festival, and it seems appropriate somehow that one of the world's few museums dedicated to laughter is housed in an old brewery. The museum uses film clips and old movie sets to explore the history of comedy.

SHAUGHNESSY HOUSE TEA ROOM AT THE CCA

GALLERIES

EILEEN TRAVERS

TOP: JEAN-NOËL DESMARAIS AND BENAIAH GIBB PAVILIONS

MIDDLE: JEAN-NOËL DESMARAIS PAVILION, EXTERIOR

BOTTOM: JEAN-NOËL DESMARAIS PAVILION, INTERIOR

Discovering art in the Paris of North America is as easy as grabbing a beret, a croissant and a subway map. Faced with more than 19 museums and dozens of galleries, choosing a starting point might prove to be your most difficult decision. But if pondering over a Mantega or perusing a roomful of Dali and Kandinsky prints is on your agenda, Montreal's Museum Mile on Rue Sherbrooke O./W. should be your first stop.

Before you go, you may want to purchase the Montreal museums pass (514-845-6873). It covers 19 art, science and historical museums and exhibitions throughout the city. Prices range from $15 to $60 for adults and families for one to three days of museum hopping.

The fine arts museum, Musée des Beaux-Arts de Montréal at 1379-80 Rue Sherbrooke O./W. (514-285-1600), the oldest art museum in Canada (1860) has accumulated more than 25,000 works in its permanent collection. In 1991 more than half of the museum's collection was moved to the Jean-Noël Desmarais pavilion across Rue Sherbrooke from the Benaiah Gibb pavilion. Designed by architect Moshe Safde, the Desmarais pavilion is a harmonious blend of old and new. The building integrates the façade of an apartment block dating to 1905 with a dozen different materials, from steel to glass, to create a balance between the surrounding Gothic churches and Victorian houses and the streamlined downtown office buildings.

Once inside the new pavilion, stop by a gift shop that rivals the Louvre's. The museum has commissioned Quebec artists to replicate selected items from its permanent

L'ETANG AUX ANTILLES BY JAMES WILSON MORRICE AT THE MUSÉE DES BEAUX-ARTS DE MONTRÉAL

collection in jewellery, sculpture and ceramics. This pavilion also houses a wing for special exhibitions. Shows have included 200 sculptures and paintings by Alberto Giacometti, masterpieces from the Guggenheim and exhibitions of works by Lichtenstein, Colville, Magritte and Modigliani. The museum also features the oldest art library in Canada, with a collection of 74,000 books and more than 54,000 auction catalogues. The library is open to the public on Wednesday afternoons; visitors should phone on Monday or Tuesday to make an appointment.

Visit the museum's Canadian section for a trip into history. Offerings in the collection's prints section range from the sketch books of James Wilson Morrice to the drawings of Paul-Èmile Borduas, the leader of the 1940s "Montreal movement." Inuit and Amerindian art forms a large part of the collection. Wind through the halls to view carvings of the Okvik, Thule and other prehistoric cultures. The work of Povungnituk artist Joe Talirunili includes his 1964 stone sculpture The Migration, depicting a group of families who, marooned on an ice floe, build a boat. Contemporary Canadian art is represented by the clean, geometric abstractions of Guido Molinari and the Plasticiens and the magical realism of Alex Colville. Several works by Montreal artist Betty Goodwin are alone worth the visit, especially to gaze at her haunting 1986 chef d'oeuvre Carbon, which features carbonized figures suspended in a heavenly space.

From the Middle Ages to 20th-century modernists, the museum's European collection includes such treasures such Bernat Martorell's 15th-century painting of the Annunciation, Tilman Reimenschneider's Renaissance lindenwood statue of

St. Sebastien, Rembrandt's Portrait of a Young Woman and the 19th-century Renoir portrait Head of a Neapolitan Girl. Sit and stare at the moody hues of Cézanne's Roadway in Provence or contemplate Tissot's October. Then visit the 20th-century collection, which includes works by Dali, Feininger, Matisse, Picasso and Rouault.

For decorative art, venture into the Asian section to see the world's largest collection of Japanese incense boxes. The Clemenceau collection sits among a wider range of Japanese tea and wine vessels and lacquer items. Nearby is a small but deliciously thorough collection of Korean art, from prehistoric pottery to a 17th-century Yi dynasty porcelain jar. The decorative-arts collection also includes 256 groups of Chelsea, Worcester, Derby and Wedgwood pieces as well as an extensive display of 18th- and 19th-century glassware from across Europe. Sections dedicated to ancient Greek and Roman works, 1,300 years of Islamic art and a small but representative selection of Coptic tiles should not be missed. More than 300 Chokwe and Umbundu artifacts make up part of the section's African display, along with masks, portraits and textiles from Nigeria and Zaïre.

Stand in front of the Musée d'Art Contemporain de Montréal, 185 Rue Ste-Catherine O./W. (514-847-6212) and look up to see a pair of lips perched atop the entrance. The lips belong in the

JEUNE FILLE AU CHAPEAU **BY PIERRE AUGUSTE RENOIR AT THE MUSÉE DES BEAUX-ARTS DE MONTRÉAL**

ANCIENT EGYPTIAN CAT

catalogue of Montreal artist Geneviève Cadieux's work and are just one of the features welcoming visitors into the museum's eclectic collection of contemporary art. Painter, teacher and art critic John Lyman founded the Contemporary Art Society of Montreal in 1939, initiating an entirely new approach to art in Canada which bucked the trend of "souvenir painting" being produced at the time by the Group of Seven.

MUSÉE D'ART CONTEMPORAIN DE MONTRÉAL, EXTERIOR (ABOVE) AND INTERIOR (BELOW)

From Lyman's society sprang a growing interest in contemporary art, which finally found a permanent home at the museum. The building shares a plaza and ground-floor entrance with Place des Arts, a complex that includes performance halls which the Montreal Symphony Orchestra and Les Grands Ballets Canadiens call home. Waltz through the museum's spacious lobby, which is decorated like a steel dream. Among the more than 5,000 works in the museum's permanent collection are classic examples of major art movements from the last 60 years, including the works of Picasso, Lichtenstein, Warhol and Mapplethorpe. The New York School of abstract expressionism, pop art, minimalism and post-painterly abstraction are represented in the works of Hans Hoffman's Classic Fragments, Jim Dine's Bolt Cutters, Carl André's Newbrugkwerk Dusseldorfgewidmet and Jules Olitski's Radical Love. More than 60 percent of the permanent collection is dedicated to Quebec artists. A special section contains 75 paintings by Montreal artist Paul-Emile Borduas.

Walk downstairs to the basement level of the museum where the multimedia room offers exhibitions, dance performances, theatre pieces and seminars led by artists. The museum's video art collection has been growing since 1979 and includes Robert Fillou's Teaching and Learning as Performing Arts, Part II, and Intercept the Rays by Nan Hoover. The museum also mounts exhibitions from the Guggenheim, New York's Museum of Modern Art and the Oxford Museum in England. Past shows have featured works by Paul Klee and Robert Doisneau.

Musée Marc-Aurèle Fortin can be found at 118 Rue St-Pierre (514-845-6108), just a block south of Place d'Youville in Vieux-Montréal, next door to the Grey Nuns' first hospital in Montreal, built in the 1700s. This is a two-storey gallery dedicated to the kaleidoscope country landscapes of Marc-Aurèle Fortin, where exposed brick walls are a suitably homey backdrop for more than 60 of the artist's paintings and engravings. This is the only museum in Quebec devoted exclusively to the work of one artist, and Fortin's masterpieces provide a glimpse of life in Quebec throughout the century. Fortin was a master of landscapes, the "black" technique and watercolours that capture the Laurentian landscape, village scenes and billowing elm trees. His work resembles stained-glass panels, with deep blues, greens and reds taking over the canvas.

Fortin's fascination with trees dominates many of his landscapes as he captures the Quebec countryside in both summer and winter. Crisp winter blues and greys decorate Montagne Blue and Messe de Minuit. Dozens of shades of green fill the the Ste-Rose and Île-des-Soeurs rooms. Walk downstairs to the Sainte-Rose room, named after the village where Fortin lived and painted. Here the museum mounts temporary exhibitions. Previous exhibits have included works by Claude Monet and landscape painter Mireille Tessier Bourbeau. Fortin created more than 2,000 paintings, engravings and sketches before his death in 1970. To get a sense of the artist's love for nature, stand before The Big Tree and take in the detailed foliage, billowing clouds and a magical path to an enchanted countryside.

Perusing art galleries sprinkled along Rue Sherbrooke O./W. and through the maze of lanes and alleys in Vieux-Montréal is a treasure hunt for both the beginner and the connoisseur. Browsers or buyers can select from traditional and contemporary galleries to find some of the best art Montreal has to offer. The Walter Klinkhoff gallery at 1200 Rue Sherbrooke O./W. displays a smattering of contemporary art, Post-impressionist Canadian paintings and works by the Group of Seven. Stop in also at the Waddington and Gorce Gallery at 1446 Sherbrooke. In Vieux-Montréal, Isart,

SCULPTURE INSTALLATIONS BY PIERRE GRANCHE, MUSÉE D'ART CONTEMPORAIN DE MONTRÉAL

MUSÉE MARC-AURÈLE FORTIN

a performance space at 263 Rue St-Antoine O./W., doubles as a gallery for new local artists. Venture into the heart of Vieux-Montréal to see an extensive collection of Inuit art and sculpture at the gallery Le Chariot at 446 Place Jacques-Cartier.

The Leonard and Bina Ellen Gallery is located at Concordia University, 1400 Blvd. de Maisonneuve O./W. Of the city's four university art galleries, this downtown treat ranks number one for its dedication to presenting the work of new artists. Located in Concordia's Webster Library, the gallery functions like a small museum. The permanent collection contains more than 2,000 works. Exhibits featuring the work of upcoming artists are mounted throughout the year.

Although from the exterior Èdifice Belago, 372 Rue Ste-Catherine O./W., appears to be a diamond in the rough, inside lies an gem for art enthusiasts. The third to fifth floors hold a virtual shopping mall of contemporary art galleries and exhibition spaces. If time is short, make sure you visit a few of the galleries. Most exhibits are shown from Tuesday to Saturday, but phone first to confirm opening hours. Start with the fifth floor and work downwards. In between, you'll find at least 10 exhibition spaces featuring solo or group shows alongside established galleries showcasing the work of more well-known artists.

Take the freight elevator to the fifth floor and turn left to reach Galerie René Blouin. Among Blouin's more renowned artists is Montreal great Betty Goodwin. Down the hall at Galerie Trois Pointes, painter Harlan Johnson is just one of the artists recently exhibited. Try the Optica Centre for Contemporary Art, also on the fifth floor. This government-funded gallery, which opened in 1972 and moved to its current address in 1997, is dedicated to promoting Canadian artists and features upcoming painters, sculptors and photographers in its spacious loft.

WALTER KLINKHOFF GALLERY

Also on the fifth floor are the offices of the Montreal Association of Contemporary Art Galleries, where visitors can find out about the latest openings around town. Suites located on the fifth through third floors offer a cornucopia of collections. Recent exhibits featured the photographs of Denis Lévesque-Huberdeau, the sculptures of Jean-Louis Èmond and installations by Magli Bouteloup.

Those less enamored of contemporary art can visit Dominion Gallery at 1438 Rue Sherbrooke O./W. for a selection of more traditional work. Situated in a Victorian mansion, the Dominion is a landmark among commercial galleries. Known in the 1950s and 1960s as the first stop in Montreal for art collectors, the Dominion Gallery is still a must-see for classical art collectors.

NATURE & NATURAL HISTORY

ANASTASIA MICHAILIDIS-RISACHER

There are the obvious ways to slip away from the bright lights and hard excitement of the big city. You can hike up Mount Royal, for example, or take the Métro to Île-Ste-Hélène for a picnic. But there are other, more exotic ways to get a taste of the wild in Montreal. One of the best is the Biodôme (4777 Ave. Pierre-de-Coubertin near the Olympic stadium tower, open daily, 514-868-3000). From the outside, Montreal's most popular natural-science museum

THE OLYMPIC STADIUM AND BIODÔME

is shaped a bit like a bicycle helmet. This isn't as odd as it sounds. It was originally built as a stadium for the Olympic bicycle races during the 1976 Games. Its transformation into an ecological museum that re-creates four different ecosystems found in the Americas is remarkable. The animals and most of the plants are real, but the landscape they live in — the cliffs, caves, rocks and even some of the enormous trees — are made of concrete. The rocks conceal most of the water and heating systems that keep the ecosystems functioning and the enormous concrete trees emit warm, moist air to maintain the proper humidity.

The Biodôme attracts a million visitors a year, a lot of

them winter-weary Montrealers who are drawn to the museum's Tropical Forest, where the temperature never dips below 25 degrees Celsius and the air is thick with the scent of vegetation. Dozens of animals creep, crawl and scurry amid all that vegetation, most of them quite freely, but the more ferocious — the anaconda, piranha and poison-arrow frogs — are safely behind glass. Many of the residents of the Tropical Forest belong to endangered species — the hyacinth macaw, for example, which is the world's largest species of parrot, as well as the golden lion tamarin, a cute little primate that has become scarce in its native Brazil. Through its involvement in the global Species Survival Plan, the Biodôme breeds endangered animals in captivity with the ultimate goal of reintroducing them into the wild.

TROPICAL FOREST AND LAURENTIAN BEAVER IN THE BIODÔME

Spring comes slightly earlier in the Biodôme's Laurentian Forest than it does in its natural counterpart north of Montreal. But, like the real thing, this exhibit changes with the seasons. Plants become dormant toward the end of the summer, the leaves on the live hardwood trees turn red and yellow and drop off in the fall, and leaves and blossoms reappear and the cycle begins anew in the spring. Among the inhabitants of this ecosystem are dozens of species of fish, along with reptiles, birds, and mammals such as beavers, porcupines and lynx.

The main feature of the St. Lawrence Marine Ecosystem is a glass-walled tank holding 2.5 million litres of sea water produced by the Biodôme itself. As you stroll by, you can spot 20 different species of fish including cod, halibut and salmon. Eventually, the pathway leads to a saltwater marsh and past a rocky shore bottom filled with starfish, sea anemones and crabs. The subpolar regions of

ST. LAWRENCE MARINE ECOSYSTEM IN THE BIODÔME

the Arctic and Antarctica are both represented at the Biodôme's Polar Ecosystem. You'll find puffins at the subarctic exhibit, while the subantarctic exhibit features those ever-lovable penguins. By the way, don't worry about getting cold. You can watch the antics of the birds from a glassed-in corridor that protects you from the rigours of these frosty climates.

POLAR WORLD PENGUINS AT THE BIODÔME

Another recommended stop is the Naturalia Discovery Room. Find it by walking in the green frog tracks. This is an exploration and discovery room where touching is encouraged. You can inspect a whale bone, stroke an otter pelt or examine a feather under a microscope. The nature guides on duty organize special games and demonstrations for children.

You can enjoy the Biodôme's ecosystems at your own pace. An easy-to-follow pathway leads you through the different environments. Information panels are posted along the way, and nature guides are on patrol to answer your questions. And if travelling from the humid heat of the tropical forest to the cool air of the Laurentian forest makes you hungry, there's a restaurant on site, as well as a souvenir shop where you'll find neat stuff like bat houses and bug-catching kits.

ST. LAWRENCE MARINE ECOSYSTEM

The Jardin Botanique de Montréal (4101 Rue Sherbrooke E. across the street from the Olympic stadium, open daily, 514-872-1400). If you visit during the summer, you're likely to come across at least one wedding party, posing for photographs in one of the 30 outdoor gardens. There are many stunning locations within the botanical

JARDIN BOTANIQUE: JAPANESE GARDEN (TOP), CHINESE GARDEN (MIDDLE), AND GREENHOUSE (BOTTOM)

garden's 185 acres. One of the most popular is the refined Japanese garden. Here, every plant and rock has been carefully placed to create a meditative atmosphere. An elegant pavilion at the entrance houses a library and a tearoom where the Japanese tea ritual is often enacted. This is also the site of the largest Chinese garden outside of Asia, as well as a garden featuring alpine plants and a superb rose garden filled with the perfume of 10,000 bushes.

If you want ideas for your own perennial garden, this is the place to come. And if you've wondered what cooking

herbs and medicinal plants look like before they're dried and stuffed into a jar, there's a collection of healthy, live specimens. There's also a garden of plants to avoid. No matter how good a diagram may be, it's much easier to identify poison ivy in the wild if you've already seen the live plant.

Since it opened in 1931, the Jardin Botanique has become one of the world's leading horticultural centres. There are 21,000 species on display. A miniature sightseeing train can help you cover the grounds quickly, or you can stroll at your own pace along one of the many nature trails.

When snow covers the outdoor gardens in the winter, the trails are taken over by cross-country skiers, but if you'd rather pretend you're in the desert or the tropics, you can amble through 10 connected greenhouses and admire the orchids, cacti and banana plants. The main greenhouse stages special annual events such as a pumpkin contest at Halloween and Christmas and Easter shows.

In the Chlorophyll Room children learn about plant life, and for adults there are horticultural clinics throughout the year. One of the most popular clinics is the mushroom-

identification session, which takes place in the fall.

Montreal's Insectarium, at 4581 Rue Sherbrooke E. on the grounds of the Jardin Botanique, open daily (514-872-1400), started with one man's personal fascination with bugs. For many years, Georges Brassard travelled the world collecting insects of every size, shape and colour. He identified and mounted thousands of specimens, but his spectacular collection was hidden like a buried treasure in his basement. Fortunately, he managed to persuade the city to build a museum to house it, and now anyone can see and learn about the creatures that some people have described as our rivals for control of the Earth.

INSECTARIUM INTERIOR AND EXTERIOR

Even if you've spent most of your life thinking that insects are repulsive, your loathing will turn to intrigue as you see their amazing variety. There are insects that look like green leaves, dry leaves, sticks or thorns and insects that reflect every colour of the rainbow. The colours and patterns of the butterflies and moths are stunningly beautiful. Many varieties of beetles have such brilliant metallic bodies that people make jewellery out of them, and you'll be astonished at how big some of them get.

Not all the insects are dead and mounted. The Insectarium has several live exhibits. Stroll through a room where butterflies fly freely from flower to flower, watch bees come and go through a glass-cased hive to the Jardin Botanique outside, or observe ants at work in a wall-length ant farm.

Every February the Insectarium becomes a restaurant of sorts, serving up delectable dishes such as biscuits made of ground-up beetles or chocolate-covered grasshoppers. Believe it or not, this event attracts 20,000 people every year. Yes, they do try the samples, and, although most prefer their insects in a disguised form, many happily crunch right into a cricket or gobble up some larvae. Tempted? Don't worry if you can't make it in February.

You can buy a cookbook specializing in insect cuisine at the Insectarium's boutique any time of the year.

Biosphère

Did you know that less than one percent of all the water on Earth is fresh and available for use by living organisms? And did you know that the water that was formed 3.8 billion years ago is the same water that exists today and will exist in the future? The water that made up a tear in Cleopatra's eye could be part of that apple you are about to bite into.

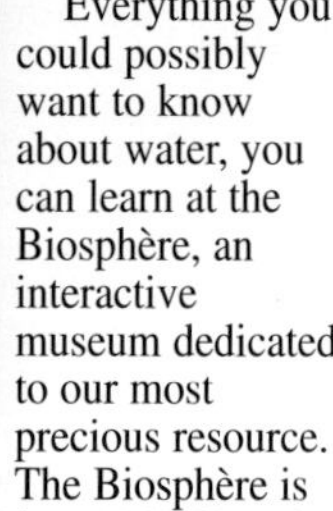

Biosphère

Everything you could possibly want to know about water, you can learn at the Biosphère, an interactive museum dedicated to our most precious resource. The Biosphère is on Île-Ste-Hélène, in the St. Lawrence River (160 Chemin de la Tour-de-l'Île, Île Ste-Hélène, open daily, 514-283-5000). The location is fitting because the St. Lawrence is one of the great rivers of the world, flowing out of the Great Lakes, which themselves make up one fifth of the world's supply of fresh water.

Interactive exhibits at the Biosphère

One of the drawbacks of this museum is that most of the fascinating facts about water are stored in computers. They are easy to operate, with touch-screen technology, but it's a slow process because you have to wait for the screens to refresh. A giant globe and large-scale models are more interesting for younger children. There are also guided tours and a multimedia show. One room features stacks of pastel towels for you to use after you've treated your tired feet to a refreshing dip in a pool of water.

FINDING OUT HOW WATER WORKS

As a member of the EcoWatch Network for conservation, the Biosphère has the lofty goal of encouraging environmental awareness through education. It shows us the cyclical nature of water: water evaporates into the sky, falls back to earth, penetrates plants and animals, flows through streams, is piped in and out of our homes, and returns to the water cycle. When it comes into contact with pollutants it picks them up and carries them along. Because we all share the water that is on this planet, the way each of us uses it affects the people who will come into contact with it down the line, and because that line draws a circle the people affected in the end could be ourselves.

The Biosphère is worth a visit for the simple admiration of the sphere itself. Buckminster Fuller's enormous geodesic dome was built for the United States Pavilion at Expo '67. A fire destroyed its acrylic skin in 1976, but left the impressive skeleton that surrounds the museum. The outdoor observation deck offers a great view of Montreal and the St. Lawrence River.

REDPATH MUSEUM

When you step through the heavy wood doors of the Redpath Museum of Natural History, you are transported to a time when museums were solemn warehouses of artifacts and knowledge. There are no interactive buttons to push, no multimedia screens or computers. Children and accompanying adults are expected to maintain a hushed tone and to refrain from touching the exhibits or leaning on the fragile glass cases. But despite all the rules, or perhaps even because of them, this little museum on the campus of McGill University is well worth a visit (859 Rue Sherbrooke O./W., open weekdays 9–5, Sundays 1–5, closed on public holidays and on Fridays during the summer months; 614-398-4086).

The Redpath Museum is one of the oldest in Canada. It opened in 1882, to preserve and display the collections of Sir William Dawson, a noted Canadian natural scientist and McGill's principal at the time. Then, as now, the museum existed primarily to serve the professors and students of McGill. It is a space for teaching, for laboratory research and for observation.

But the museum is also a public place and a visit here is interesting and enjoyable as well as educational. Children love it, and because it isn't too big it's the perfect place for that first museum visit. Watch their eyes light up in fascination as they climb the wide, wood-panelled staircase and find themselves standing next to a cross-section of the McGill University Founder's Elm. The tree was planted in 1790 and cut down 186 years later, in 1976. Its diameter is impressive but not nearly as grand as the cross-section on the next landing — a 533-year-old Douglas fir from British Columbia. It stands on its side, measuring about two metres in diameter.

On the second floor, there is a medium sized skeleton of a dinosaur and fossils with names like Ordovician invertebrates and Devonian vascular plants. There are also cases and cases of rocks and minerals, and who would have imagined that the shapes and colours of their crystals are as varied as flowers or butterflies? Don't be surprised if, soon after a visit here, you find yourself filling your living room with your own collection of rocks.

The animals in this museum are all dead and either mounted or in a jar. This gives them a rather spooky attraction, particularly if you stand and stare into their glassy eyes, as you can with an African mountain lion on the landing to the third floor. There are also many beautiful shells, a giant clam and a giant spider crab from Japan. In nature the crab lives in sand at a depth of 50 to 300 metres and its arm span is up to four metres.

My favourites are the ethnology exhibits on the third floor. There are mummies of people (two of them are females so it could be that once, long ago, they were also mommies) and mummies of animals: crocodiles, a falcon and a cat. One mummy is of a man in his early 30s. He probably never knew what was going to kill him 3,000 years ago, but a CT scan done at Montreal's Hôpital Saint-Luc in 1995 diagnosed a fatal infection from a dental abscess. There are also artifacts from more recent times. The Congo collection is from a turn-of-the-century medical expedition by a McGill professor of parasitology. It includes embroidered textiles, figurines, musical instruments and ornate tools and bowls.

REDPATH MUSEUM

The architecture of the Redpath Museum contributes to its overall appeal. It is an example of Greek Revival in North America and has the distinction of being one of the first Canadian buildings singled out for praise in the international architecture literature.

SHOPPING

MARK STACHIEW

If you were born to shop you should have been born in Montreal. The city has several distinct shopping districts that will satisfy any consuming desire. The biggest and best is Rue Ste-Catherine in the heart of downtown. It's where you'll find the flagship stores of the country's big department and chain stores as well as a galaxy of shops and boutiques. If the weather's bad, you can go below street level and get lost in a maze of malls that are part of Montreal's famous underground city.

Most visitors to the city eventually find themselves in Vieux-Montréal (Old Montreal), which has plenty of appealing shops. There are numerous art galleries and some antique shops as well as the ubiquitous souvenir shops that usually sell ersatz Canadiana consisting of T-shirts, mass-produced "Inuit" carvings and plastic totem poles made in Taiwan.

SHOPS ALONG RUE SHERBROOKE

Inspired by the elegant architecture of the old city, many tourists enjoy a visit to Antique Alley on Rue Notre-Dame O./W. Two long stretches between Ave. Atwater and Rue Guy boast a string of stores that stock antiques and collectibles that will fit all budgets and suitcases.

The Golden Square Mile in the downtown was so named because it was the favourite neighbourhood of the bankers and railway barons who built Montreal at the turn of the century. It's still a tony district and the shops along Rue Sherbrooke are among the city's finest. The same crowd that frequents these boutiques also patronize nearby Ave. Greene in Westmount, which features more exclusive ones.

If Sherbrooke and Greene haven't depleted your bank account, you should head uptown to Ave. Laurier. The stretch between Blvd. St-Laurent and Chemin de la Côte Ste-Catherine is home to many unique stores that will appeal to shoppers of all ages and budgets.

For the trendinistas, St-Laurent and Rue St-Denis are the streets to visit. Nestled among the ne-plus-ultra nightclubs and restos are a bevy of too-cool shops that always seem to be battling to be the first to spot the trends.

Hard-core bargain hunters should make an expedition to the Rue Chabanel area at the northern end of Blvd. St-Laurent. It's the home of the city's garment district and the showrooms in the factory buildings are filled with men's and women's fashions at wholesale prices.

EATON (TOP); THE BAY (MIDDLE); SIMONS (BOTTOM)

Before you lace up your most comfortable shopping shoes, remember these points. Most stores are open from 10 a.m. to 6 p.m. on weekdays, 10 a.m. to 5 p.m. on Saturday and noon to 5 p.m. on Sunday. If you're a foreign visitor, remember to save your receipts, because you can claim a refund on the 7 percent Goods and Services Tax when you leave the country. The GST is levied on just about all goods except certain groceries.

CLOTHING

If you're short on time you should start with the city's major department stores, which are all within a short walking distance of each other. Each has its own personality and people tend to be loyal to one, being tempted into another only when there is a sale.

The Bay is probably the most popular of the lot. It stocks clothing for the entire family, ranging from the most basic items to designer fashions. You can also find a wide variety of other items, as you would expect from a department store. This could be anything from perfume to housewares.

Eaton is The Bay's main rival, but it has recently changed its focus to slightly more upscale, with a greater emphasis on designer fashions, including local names such as Lino Catalano and Jean-Claude Poitras that appeal to young people. It is a great place to find interesting decorative items for the home. A special treat for Eaton shoppers is to have lunch in the 9th-floor restaurant, which is modelled after the art deco dining room of a great ocean liner.

Up the street is a department store that has been an institution in Quebec City for more than 125 years. Simons expanded into Montreal and moved into the old Simpsons building, which was left derelict for a decade — and they barely had to change the wording on the sign. Simons has clothing for everyone but its specialty is upscale women's fashions. Further along Ste-Catherine is Ogilvy. It's not really one store any more, but a collection of specialty boutiques that rent square footage on the floors of the venerable old department store. The emphasis is on women's fashion, but you'll find clothes for the entire family as well as other goods such as fine jewellery, perfume and even books.

The top of the market is Holt Renfrew. It sells top designer fashions from such names as Giorgio Armani and Chanel. It's near the Ritz-Carlton, one of Montreal's best hotels, so Holt's is where a lot of celebrities shop when they're in town shooting a movie. Bring your autograph book as well as your credit card.

Purse and pearls from Simons

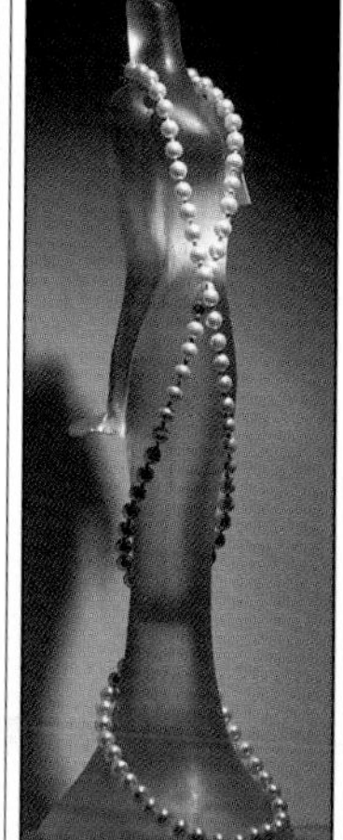

A quick glance at the glamorously dressed women walking down the city's streets as if they were runway models will convince you that the Montreal is serious about fashion. They don't call it the Paris of North America just because you can buy tasty baguettes.

If you're after the trendiest fashions, hit the friperies on Blvd. St-Laurent and Rue St-Denis. Scarlett O'Hara is a good place to start. It features its own funky and daring line of clothes as well as many used items. In a similar vein are Twist Encore and Friperie St-Laurent. Another shop on

Twist Encore

Friperie St-Laurent

Titanic

Mexx

Bluesonthegreen

top of the latest fashions is BCBG, which has boutiques on Ste-Catherine, Laurier and St-Denis. Slightly younger and cooler are Johnny Freddy, Rio, Titanic and Mode 2010. One World stocks plenty of the trendy stuff but also specializes in exotic fashions that can lead to ethnically confusing combinations — say, if you try to mix a pair of Guatemalan pants with a Tibetan sweater. Urban Outfitters is the safe and sanitized version of these trendy stores.

If you're less daring, stroll the many name-brand stores that line Ste-Catherine such as Gap, Jacob, Mexx, United Colours of Benneton and the Canadian chains Le Château and Tristan & America. Each offer, a range of styles for both women and men. Chances are, though, they stock pretty much the same stuff in their outlets all across North America and around the world. Still, there might be a price advantage. Less cool but still popular is Cache Cache. Think garden party. They have lots of casual long dresses with lots of flowers and frills. They also sell housewares and linens that evoke a simpler era. More grown up women's fashions can be found in two of Ave. Greene's nicest boutiques, Ingrid and Bluesonthegreen. They offer similar styles of clothing and the latter also has items for men and children.

A Canadian chain that has garnered world-wide attention for its elegantly casual clothing is Club Monaco. It also has a line of cosmetics. Another Canadian company, Roots, is known for its sporty clothing and fine leather goods. Among its most popular items are caps and jackets in the style of those that Roots supplied to Canada's Olympic athletes at the Nagano games. Both chains have multiple outlets in the city.

For denim, you could check out Parasuco, which has been making inroads with its fashionable jeans in the United States. They're worth visiting for their gorgeous store, which is housed in a beautiful old bank building. For denim bargains, visit Superior Pants. They specialize in Levis and will even hem your pants on the spot at no extra cost. For larger sizes, visit Addition-Elle. They cater to women who wear sizes 14+, or try Grand Mein, which is geared to women who are taller than 5'8".

ADDITION-ELLE

BRISSON & BRISSON

For a lark, visit Mode Derby. It sells young, casual fashions that are nothing special, but this hole in the wall is probably the city's smallest store. Most stores have changing rooms that are larger.

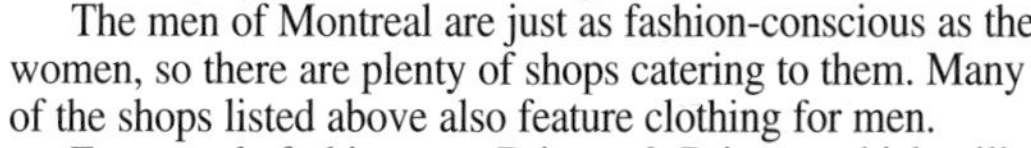

The men of Montreal are just as fashion-conscious as the women, so there are plenty of shops catering to them. Many of the shops listed above also feature clothing for men.

For upscale fashions, try Brisson & Brisson, which will outfit you in clothing from big-name designers. Speaking of designers, Polo Ralph Lauren has a shop on Rue Sherbrooke. Another alternative for high style is Pierre, Jean, Jacques on Ave. Laurier.

TIES AT A. GOLD & SONS

For something more mainstream, you can try any of the outlets of the large, national chains. For example, the large A. Gold & Sons outlet on Ste-Catherine stocks excellent quality suits and sweaters for men and women. Other choices include Bovet in the Eaton Centre and Old River.

Fashion sense starts at an early age in this city. There are many shops that sell miniature versions of the styles favoured by grown ups. You can buy fashionable togs for tykes at Jeunes d'ici or Oink Oink.

Cargo pants and paramilitary clothing are all the rage these days. There are numerous army surplus stores that can help you with the

OINK OINK

latest style. Try Surplus International, SOS Surplus or Soldats de la Mode (which is French for Soldiers of Fashion).

They may not be politically correct, but there's still a market for furs, especially in Montreal, a city that was built on the fur trade. There's a compact fur district downtown on rues St-Alexandre and Mayor. Any one of Diakomakis, Fourrures Nina Ricci or Maîtres Fourreurs de Montréal will outfit you with a fashionable fur coat. They have items for both men and women. Excelfur et Cuir deals in both furs and leather. Also for leather goods, Screaming Eagle, which has lots of tough biker gear, with more conservative clothing on the lower level.

LES SOLDATS DE LA MODE

SHOES

A few years ago Imelda Marcos was looking to buy a condo in Montreal. Could it have been because the footwear-collecting wife of the former Philippines dictator heard about the city's fabulous shoe stores? One of the city's most popular footwear shops, Tony Shoe Shop, stocks all the latest names such as Bally, Dr. Martens, and Bandolino. They are especially renowned for their inventory of hard-to-fit sizes, ranging all the way up to 13 G for women and 16 EEEE for men. They also have an annex filled with bargain shoes. Dozens of other outlets of the big-name shoe chains such as Browns, Aldo, Transit and Simard can be found in the city's main shopping districts and malls. If it's cowboy boots you're after, check out Marie Mode. They have a wide selection of footwear that will be perfect for your next visit to the rodeo. They also have other cowboy gear such as dusters, and even chaps.

JEWELLERY

The city's glittering array of jewellery stores is sure to tempt you. Start with Birks, a Montreal institution. Many an engagement ring and anniversary present has been bought here. Birks deals in fine-quality jewellery and also has a wonderful selection of silverware and china. On the same block is Hemsleys, a competitor worth visiting. They sell similar merchandise but offer less variety. A short walk away, Eliko specializes in watches. They've got them all: Rolex, Seiko, Swiss Army, Swatch, Tag Heuer, Fossil and more.

HEMSLEYS

A short distance east on Ste-Catherine, a number of small but excellent jewellers deal primarily in gold but sell various objects. Two of these are Bijouterie Élégant and Bijoux Marsan, but others in the area are also worth sampling. For something a little more specialized, visit AmberLux in Les Promenades de la Cathedrale. Their jewellery comes in

Bijoux Marsan

all shapes and sizes, but only one colour — amber. In a similar vein, Geomania, a boutique in the Eaton Centre, sells interesting jewellery made out of semi-precious stones and crystals. They also sell fossils.

If fine jewellery isn't your thing or if you're on a budget, take a walk through Phillips Square, which is in the shadow of the Birks building. When the weather is nice it's filled with artisans and entrepreneurs selling funky, one-of-a-kind pieces of costume jewellery.

Art

Art is a very subjective thing, so it's difficult to recommend any one gallery in Montreal, but it's a sure bet it won't take you very long to find one to suit your tastes. The two best areas for your quest are Rue St-Paul in Vieux-Montréal and Rue Sherbrooke O./W., downtown between rues de la Montagne and Guy. Both are lined with numerous galleries that are wonderful places to browse. Many galleries feature the canvasses and prints of established artists from Canada and abroad. Representative of the spectrum are Galerie Laroches and Galerie Parchemine in Vieux-Montréal and Galerie Walter Klinkhoff on Sherbrooke.

Galerie de Chariot bills itself as the largest gallery of Inuit art in Canada, with an exquisite collection of soapstone and whale-bone carvings from Canada's arctic communities. Take a look at what they have to offer before buying a cheap imitation in a souvenir shop. Artisinat Canadien and Artisinats Québécois feature crafts made by Canadian and Quebec artisans. They have a wide selection of beautiful objects such as sturdy wood carvings and fine pottery.

In the summer months Place Jacques-Cartier and parts of Rue St-Paul in Vieux-Montréal are filled with artists displaying their wares. You'll find reasonably priced watercolours and sketches of the city to take homes as souvenirs.

If your travels don't allow you the opportunity to shop in more exotic parts of the world, visit Born Neo Art Gallery or Artisans du Monde. The former stocks primarily African carvings and textiles, while the latter sells fascinating handicrafts hand-picked from bazaars and markets around the world.

For something a little out of the ordinary, head to Galerie Archeologica. Touring this store is like being in a great museum. Their specialty is bona fide ancient art works from places like Greece, Rome and Central America.

Middle: Galerie Laroche
Bottom: Galerie Parchemine

GIFT SHOP AT THE MUSÉE DES BEAUX-ARTS

For something a lot more affordable, the Musée des Beaux-Arts de Montréal has a fantastic gift shop. The selection is always changing, as it reflects the current exhibits on display at the museum of fine arts. They have posters, reproductions, art books and much more.

ANTIQUES

Antique Alley on Rue Notre-Dame is bliss for collectors of curios and artifacts from bygone days. Their inventories are always changing, so you never know what you'll find. "Antiquing" is a popular Sunday-afternoon pastime for Montrealers, so you may want to schedule your visit for the middle of the week to avoid the crowds. Typical of shops in the Alley are Antiques Hubert, C. Blain Antiquaire and Antiquités le Design. Le Village des Antiquaries concentrates several dealers under one roof. Some deal in old jewellery, others in furniture, still others in vintage clothing. There's something for everyone. Cascades Lounge specializes in antique toys such as Lionel train sets. Milord sells elegant European furniture, mirrors and the like. One person's castaway is another's antique. Located at the eastern end of Antique Alley, the Salvation Army's giant thrift store is like a year-round garage sale. Check out their "As Is" section for interesting finds.

There is a smattering of other antique stores around town, notably in Vieux-Montréal and on Ave. Greene in Westmount.

COLLECTIBLES

DOLL AT L'ARMOIRE AUX POUPÉES

If you're the sort of person who gets a thrill from buying a hockey stick autographed by Jean Béliveau or needs a certain 1941 issue of Life magazine to complete a collection, there are numerous shops to help feed your collecting obsession.

Sports collectors won't want to miss Lucie Favreau Sports Memorabilia. Even if you're not going to buy anything, it's worth taking a look at the amazing items she has in stock. It's like visiting a sports hall of fame.

A short walk down the street is Retro-ville, a paradise for people who collect the sort of items that are old but not old enough to be considered antique. They have old magazines, toys, neon signs, Coca-Cola collectibles and much, much more. Pause Retro is a similar sort of nostalgia store but with an emphasis on sports cards.

Doll collectors should take the time to visit L'armoire aux Poupées, a permanent display of antique dolls that also features a gift shop.

BOOKS

Montreal is a bibliophile's paradise. The western part of Rue Ste-Catherine has developed into a tidy little book district with a number of small, independent shops. They stock primarily used books of all genres, but each has its own specialty. Café Boooks (the three o's are designed to counteract the province's language laws which are not favourably disposed to English words) specializes in art books. (It is just off Ste-Catherine on Rue Stanley) Bibliomania is known for its books on antiques and collectibles. Vortex Books, nearby, is the spot for literary works. In the same neighbourhood are two specialty bookstores that deal in new titles. Nebula Books is the city's specialist for science fiction and fantasy, and also stocks a wide selection of mystery novels. Stage Theatre Book Shop sells plays and books about the theatre.

VORTEX BOOKS

There are two other unique bookstores worth mentioning. Double Hook on Ave. Greene in Westmount stocks exclusively books by Canadian authors, many of whom don't get wide distribution in the chain stores. Ulysses travel bookstore with outlets on Ave. du Président Kennedy and Rue St-Denis, stocks guidebooks and maps for just about every place on the planet.

The biggest bookstore in the city is Chapters' flagship store for Montreal on Rue Ste-Catherine. It has four floors of books and a comfortable, library-like atmosphere that encourages you to linger. The in-house Starbucks coffee shop makes it even more attractive. The store sells books on just about every topic imaginable. If they don't have it, they'll find out if it's in print and will order it for you. Chapters' competition includes the recently arrived Indigo Books in Place Montreal Trust, also on Ste-Catherine. They have a wide variety of books in stock and also sell fascinating objects for the home as well as cards, stationery and other paper items.

CHAPTERS

A pair of used-book stores worth mentioning are Cheap Thrills and S.W. Welch. If you're on the hunt for a hard-to-find tome, it's easy to while away many hours browsing in these stores.

HOUSEWARES

For one-of-a-kind items for your home, you'll want to visit Multi-Design International. MDI designs and manufactures funky household items ranging from the beautiful to the bizarre. You'll love their foot-high juicer, which looks like

NEBULA BOOKS

Indiport

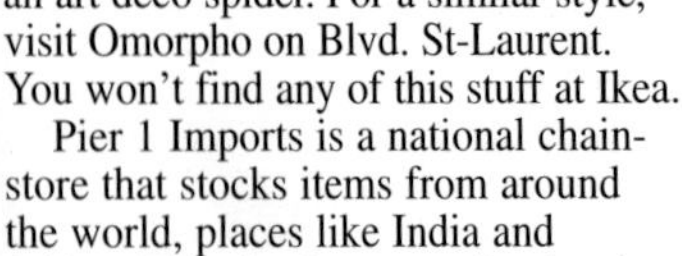

an art deco spider. For a similar style, visit Omorpho on Blvd. St-Laurent. You won't find any of this stuff at Ikea.

Pier 1 Imports is a national chain-store that stocks items from around the world, places like India and Africa. There's glassware, furniture and objets d'art.

For imported Persian carpets, check out Collage Tapis or Indiport. Kim Heng in Chinatown is where the city's Chinese restaurants do their shopping for tableware. They have everything from teapots to rice cookers and woks to chopsticks.

Electronics

Blvd. St-Laurent between Ave. du Président Kennedy and Rue Sherbrooke is home to numerous stores dealing in grey-market electronics such as TVs and DVD players. These are generally items that are semi-legally imported from the United States or other countries and sold at a discount. Great deals can be had if you know what you're buying, but ask about warranties. Often these goods are not meant to be sold in Canada. Some of the shops you can try are Alma Electronique, Distribution 2010 and Multi-Système Electronique. Many of these electronics shops are run by people who have a lot of experience bargaining in bazaars. Be prepared to haggle.

Omorpho

If you prefer reading prices on price tags, go to nearby Audiotronic or Dumoulin La Place. Both offer a similar range of consumer electronics at decent prices, and both also stock camera equipment. Audiotronic has another shop on Ste-Catherine near the behemoth Future Shop, part of a Canadian chain that sells low-priced computer equipment, home electronics and CDs.

Records

Music lovers can stock up on their favourite CDs in any of the many record stores in town. The biggest and loudest is HMV's main store on the corner of rues Peel and Ste-Catherine. There are three floors of selection and a bargain annex across the street. Sam the Record Man's main store, also on Ste-Catherine, is looking pretty shabby these days, but their prices are good and their selection is better. One of their closest competitors is Archambault much further east on Ste-Catherine. Besides CDs they have a large selection of sheet music and songbooks.

Dumoulin

Because Montreal is a mosaic of cultures, you can buy music from many different countries. A good spot for one-stop shopping is Rayon Laser on Blvd. St-Laurent. Specializing in worldbeat music, they've got something from everywhere, whether it be Afghanistan or Zambia.

Cameras

Camera buffs will want to visit Simon Cameras, It's an old-fashioned camera store that looks as if it hasn't changed since Kodak introduced its first Brownie. They have all the latest camera technology as well as an excellent selection of used equipment. Another good source of used equipment is York Bijouterie, a high-class pawn shop that also deals in musical instruments and jewellery. If you need something fixed, or have run out of film while visiting Vieux-Montréal, stop by Place Victoria Cameras. They'll have what you need and their service can't be beat.

Rayon Laser

Odds & Ends

Montreal boasts many odd but unique shops catering to diverse interests. For example, there are actually two boutiques that sell medieval fashions and accessories. Boutique Médiévale or Le Choppe du Dragone Rouge will outfit you in chain mail and size you for a broadsword, if that's what you're looking for. They also have interesting jewellery and household items.

Panel at Boutique Médiéval

Since Montreal is also home to the continent's only Formula One race, Le Grand Prix du Canada, and Quebec is the birthplace of a recent F1 champion, it's easy to see why there's a store dedicated to Formula One merchandise. It's called Boutique de la Formule 1. Car buffs can also have their appetites sated at Zone Automobile, which stocks magazines, books, posters, models and much more.

Everyone loves kites. Check out the ones on sale at Atelier-Boutique de cerfs-volants. They look more like works of art than something Charlie Brown would get stuck in a tree.

If you're flying in a more traditional manner, get yourself to Jet-Setter on Ave. Laurier, a store that caters to travellers. They have every sort of travel gadget imaginable, along with more traditional items such as suitcases, backpacks and outdoor wear. Another shop for travellers is Tilley Endurables, also on Laurier. They sell sensible travel clothing but are best known for their hats, which inspire cult-like devotion from their wearers.

What visit to Montreal would be complete without a visit to the home of its hockey heroes, the Canadiens? The Molson Centre souvenir shop should be on the itinerary of any sports fan. They have jerseys, books, photos and many items not found elsewhere.

Maybe it's the French influence, but Montreal has a shop that specializes in condoms. La Capoterie on Rue St-

Atelier-Boutique des cerfs-volants

Denis isn't a sex shop with gag gifts, but rather a place for playful couples to have fun shopping for contraceptives. Other odd shops include Mélange Magique, where witches and warlocks do their shopping. It has all manner of items for New Age spiritualists. And, as unlikely as it sounds, Sucré Bleue specializes in Pez dispensers and candies.

Festivals & Events

Bram Eisenthal

Montreal has its problems, economic and political, but no city in North America is better at throwing a party. It's a tradition that goes back at least as far as Expo '67, the world's fair that marked Canada's 100th birthday, and it continues to the present day. Every summer is filled with festivals that begin in late June and end about Labour Day.

The granddaddy of all these celebrations is the World Film Festival, founded by Serge Losique in 1977. This celluloid showcase presents a plethora of films from more than 60 countries. It's the only competitive festival in North America recognized by the International Federation of Film Producers Associations; winning films in competition receive the prestigious Grand Prix of the Americas and other prizes. Held the final week of August through Labour Day, the WFF screens some 400 films (250 features and 150 shorts) plus a dozen or so outdoor ones. Check the festival website at http://www.ffm-montreal-org or phone 514-848-3883 for more information. The city is rapidly becoming one of the main film-production locales in North America. In recent years stars like Marlon Brando, Richard Gere, Denzel Washington, Bette Midler, Ben Kingsley, Charlie Sheen, Mira Sorvino, Ewan McGregor, Aidan Quinn and Quebec's own Donald Sutherland have come to the city to work and play. During the film festival you can usually increase your odds of spotting a star by hanging around Blvd. St-Laurent after the show.

The first major event of the festival season is the Festival International de Jazz de Montréal, which fills the first two weeks of July with concerts and jam sessions. This is one of the premiere jazz fests around, attracting performers such as Manhattan Transfer, Chick Corea, Count Basie, Dave Van Ronk, France's Orchestre National De Barbes and Canada's hottest singer-pianist, Diana Kraoll. Virtually every big-name jazz entertainer or band

Festival International de Jazz

has appeared here since the festival's debut, and that includes many legends. In addition to ticketed events, there are more than 300 free outdoor concerts, some attracting as many as 100,000 people.

The Just For Laughs Comedy Festival hasn't been around as long as the other two. It began as a humble, two-night French-language show that attracted little attention, and it laboured for the first couple of years in the shadow of the jazz festival. But its two founders — Gilbert Rozon and Andy Nulman — have turned it into the most important festival of its kind in the world. Just For Laughs fills two weeks in July with more than 1,300 shows and performances, indoors and out. Many of the performers are household names — people like Jerry Seinfeld, Tim Allen, Roseanne Barr, Michael Richards, Drew Carey, John Candy, Rowan (Mr. Bean) Atkinson, Sandra Bernhard, Sinbad, Mary Tyler Moore, Marcel Marceau and the late George Burns — but this is also where many new comics get their first real recognition. Canadians like Mike McDonald and Bowser and Blue, for example, make a point of appearing as often as they can. Book early if you're thinking of attending, especially for the French and English Gala performances and the most popular events. The festival has a website at www.hahaha.com.

JUST FOR LAUGHS COMEDY FESTIVAL

While these three festivals attract most summer tourists to the city, there are a slew of smaller events year-round that add to the charm and excitement of this city that never sleeps, where joie de vivre brings people back year after year. The event that opens the summer season is arguably the most beautiful to gaze at — the Benson & Hedges Fireworks Competition. Incendiary masters from around the world light up the night skies over Montreal every weekend from early June to mid-July, with some mid-week displays thrown in. These have become so popular that the best viewpoint, the Jacques-Cartier bridge, is often clogged with spectators and closed to traffic from 10 p.m. to midnight. Prizes are awarded to the winning entries.

BENSON & HEDGES FIREWORKS COMPETITION

If hot-air ballooning is your passion, you mustn't miss the Festival des Mongolfières, held at nearby St-Jean-sur-Richelieu (half an hour south by car, over the Champlain bridge). Enthusiasts assemble from all over to share some hot air, fly their colourful contraptions and fill the skies with yet more beauty for all to behold. You can take a ride in one for a fee, weather permitting. This festival is held the middle of August.

For something a little more traditional, try the Festival de la Gibelotte in Sorel, a 90-minute drive downriver from Montreal. Gibelotte is a robust stew made with barbotte, a fatty, flaky species of catfish that lives in the waters around the Îles de Sorel. Every August, the cooks of the town make gallons of the stuff and serve it up with bread and locally brewed beer in one of the finest and most cheerful street festivals in the province.

Beer lovers can also attend Montreal's Mondial de la Bière festival (514-722-9640), a five-day outdoor extravaganza that attracts some 25,000 brew fans. It's held in mid-June at the Jacques-Cartier pier in the Vieux-Port, and provides you an opportunity to sample beer from breweries like McAuslan's (St. Ambroise) and Les Brasseurs du Nord (the Boréale line). The Ontario-based Sleeman Brewing and Malting Company has been making sudsy waves in the field and is well represented here. You'll also find many American and European brands.

Lovers of modern dance will certainly hip-hop over to the Festival International de la Nouvelle Danse, held for 10 days in early October — just when dancing is starting to seem a great way to beat the approaching winter chill. Some of the finest and most renowned performers and troupes, like the Quebec-founded La La La Human Steps, can be found here.

LES FRANCOFOLIES DE MONTRÉAL

Outdoor urban events proliferate during the summer. Two of the best are the Tour de l'Île de Montréal and Les Francofolies de Montréal. The first is the world's largest gathering of cyclists, attracting some 40,000 riders over a 66-kilometre route through the city in early June. The Tour generally marks the end of the Montreal Bike Fest, held the preceding week (514 521-8687). Les FrancoFolies are equally impressive, bringing some 1,000 musicians into the open at Place des Arts. Rock, pop, hip hop, jazz, funk, and latin music are just some of the rhythms you'll hear in late July and early August, en francais, of course (514 876-8989).

Finally, back to film festivals. You just can't escape them. Some of the others held throughout the year include the Montreal International Festival of Cinema and New

Media (www.fcmm.com), previously held during the summer but now moved to the fall to avoid scheduling clashes with the major competition. This festival features unusual films as well as interesting venues, virtually every place but movie theatres. A New York version of this event has been held as well.

Cinemania (514-288-4200) celebrates French films with English subtitles. Maidy Teitelbaum, the wife of an entrepreneur who owns a large chain of lingerie stores, loved French films and wanted to share that joy with other English-speaking movie fans, so she and a tiny staff cobbled this festival together on a shoestring budget. It has become quite respectable after several years and is worth a visit if you're in Montreal in November. Teitelbaum is showing more and more premiéres (11 in 1998), often with the stars and directors in attendance. The venue is the Musée des Beaux-Arts de Montréal.

The Jewish Film Festival is a small event that showcases the best of international filmmaking. Movies presented by creator/president Susan Alper feature viewpoints representative of Jewish culture, with topics such as the Holocaust, Israel and modern Jewish issues. The festival runs in March, coinciding with a similarly named but unrelated event in Toronto.

Finally, one of my personal favourites is Fant-Asia, the International Festival of Fantastic Cinema (www.fantasiafest.com). It started in 1996 primarily as a vehicle for Asian action and fantasy films and rapidly became a celebration of international horror, sci-fi and fantasy, a lot like France's defunct Avoriaz Festival used to be. Screenings, in the classic old Imperial Theatre, are generally sold out. Many premières feature the directors. This month-long festival begins the middle of July, which should add to your sweet dilemma: How many festivals can I possibly attend? Just ask yourself how much fun you want to have and act accordingly. In Montreal, fun is strictly de rigueur. Bonne chance, mes amis.

TOUR DE L'ÎLE DE MONTRÉAL

DINING

MONIQUE POLAK

GARDEN ROOM AT LES CAPRICES DE NICOLAS

Montreal is a great city for food. It could be the French influence or the long, cold winters — but Montrealers love to eat. Nothing stops us from indulging our gourmet tastes. Not ice storms, not even politics. You'll notice that life here revolves around eating. We spend an inordinate amount of time shopping for food — picking out just the right shallots, going from one specialty shop to the next in pursuit of cheese, baguettes, coffee and wine. We also talk endlessly about food, and of course we love to go out to eat. What distinguishes dining out in Montreal from dining out in other major cities is that there's so much good food. It's everywhere. And you don't have to pay a fortune to sample it. Though Montreal has its share of pricey restaurants, there are plenty of inexpensive alternatives.

Historically, Montreal has been known for its French cuisine. Today there are still plenty of French restaurants — though many of them have been influenced by the latest trends in Thai and California cuisine. The many immigrants to Montreal have also brought their own unique flavours to the city. Just follow your nose to find delicious Greek, Italian, Chinese, Indian, Vietnamese and Caribbean food.

Part of the joy of visiting Montreal is discovering some of these places. One thing is certain: you'll be back for more.

BREAKFAST AT BEAUTY'S

BRUNCH

Sunday brunch is a Montreal tradition. And in summer, when the weather's good, every day is a Sunday.

Expect a line that heads out the front door and onto nearby Rue St-Urbain if you turn up at

Beauty's later than 10 a.m. on a weekend. Located at the foot of Mount Royal on Ave. Mont-Royal O./W. Beauty's has been a hit with Montrealers since it opened in 1942. Owner Hymie Sckolnick — whose nickname, Beauty, explains the name of the restaurant — still turns up most days, though his son, also named Hymie, manages the place. Everything here is sold à la carte so expect to pay extra for your freshly squeezed orange juice. The most popular item on the menu is the Beauty's Special, a bagel sandwich filled with cream cheese, lox, tomato and onion. If you're too hungry to survive the line it'll take you less than five minutes to walk to Dusty's on Ave. du Park. The food is similar and just as good, but you won't be able to say you had breakfast at Beauty's.

Chez Cora Déjeuners

Though sophisticated Montrealer diners disapprove of food chains, a new breakfast chain has been drawing crowds. With more than a dozen locations on Montreal island, Chez Cora Déjeuners offers a variety of hearty breakfasts, most of them served with an artful — and abundant — arrangement of fresh fruit. Downtown, there's a Chez Cora on Rue Stanley. Everything sounds so good on the colourful menu that it'll be difficult to choose, but you might try the french toast made with zucchini bread.

Or you can go for something completely different: dim sum breakfast in Chinatown. "Dim sum means 'touch your heart,'" says Chuck Kwan, owner of La Maison Kam Fung, the most popular dim sum spot in town. "We Chinese eat dim sum for breakfast, lunch and as a snack," says Kwan. We consider it a good sign that most of the diners here are Chinese. Located upstairs in a mini-mall, the restaurant is huge and unpretentious. Dim sum is available here seven days a week from 7 a.m. until 3 p.m. Waitresses go by with stainless-steel carts carrying a variety of exotic delicacies. You wave them over to get what you want. Each item costs between $2 and $3.50, but beware — with so much temptation the bill climbs quickly. You mustn't miss the steamed shrimp dumplings, rice rolls or bean curd with vegetables. Go for the sesame seed balls for dessert.

If you prefer to sleep in, Café Santropol on Rue St-Urbain opens at noon. In summer, try to get a spot in the garden — an urban paradise complete with small pond, chimes and bird feeders. The specialty here is huge healthy sandwiches made with thick slabs of pumpernickel bread. The Midnight Express is filled with cream cheese and peanut butter, the Killer Tomato with cream cheese and sun-dried tomatoes. They sound odd, but they taste delicious.

QUICK EATS

SCHWARTZ'S

At some Montreal landmarks you can order take-out as well as eat on the premises. But though the service is fast, this ain't fast food.

Forget your diet and order your smoked meat medium when you go to Schwartz's delicatessen on Blvd. St-Laurent. Built in 1930, this old-fashioned deli has long, plain tables at which customers literally rub elbows. To pass for a local, order a cherry Coke and pickles on the side.

Arahova Souvlaki is probably Montreal's best-known souvlaki joint. The original Arahova, located on Rue St-Viateur O./W. in Montreal's Mile End district, has been around since 1972. Two others have opened recently, one in the heart of downtown on bustling Rue Crescent. A combo plate with souvlaki, salad and fries goes for $6.50. What makes Arahova souvlaki so good? "The secret is our tzatziki sauce. It's yogurt-based, with garlic, cucumber and salt," says Nick Koutroumanis, whose father began the business.

ARAHOVA SOUVLAKI

Drive slowly on Ave. Victoria in the Côte-des-Neiges district or you might just miss The Curry House. The decor is pretty humdrum, but the Caribbean food here is out of this world. Try the roti — curried meat and potatoes served in a chapati, or Indian flatbread. If you're feeling brave, go for the jerk chicken. You'll need a piña colada — or two — to wash it down. Luckily, a piña colada here costs only $2.95 — and it's the best-tasting one this side of Jamaica.

FAMILY FARE

For homestyle Italian cooking, try Trattoria La Rondine on Chemin de la Côte-des-Neiges at the corner of Chemin de la Côte Ste-Catherine. You'll feel right at home in this pretty restaurant where big green plants fill the many windows. All the recipes come from Maria Casullo, who owns the restaurant along with her husband, Paul. The menu features designer pizzas such as the Mona Lisa, which has artichokes, mushrooms, black olives, mozzarella cheese and Maria's tomato sauce. Cooked with a touch of wine, the spaghetti bolognese is another winner. Don't leave without trying Maria's desserts. Her chocolate mousse cake decorated with ribbons of semi-sweet chocolate is a delight, but leave a little room for her chocolate almond brittle — it's too good to share.

TRATTORIA LA RONDINE

It's a bit of a trek, but Restaurant Daou on Rue Faillon in Montreal's east end is worth it. This family-owned Lebanese restaurant has been around since 1975. The atmosphere is informal with long tables set close together. Begin with

…URANT DAOU

the fatouch salad — morsels of cucumber, parsley, tomato, onion and toasted pita in a dressing of olive oil and lemon. Proceed directly to the marinated breast of chicken. Shadia Daou, one of the four sisters who run the restaurant, won't divulge the secret spices used in the marinade. "But the chicken marinates for a couple of days," she says mysteriously.

If you have a craving for Indian food, try La Maison du Curry (not to be confused with the previously mentioned Curry House). Located downtown on Rue Bishop in what might be described as a hole in the wall, this restaurant serves food that is authentic and spicy. Try the onion bajis or samosas — phyllo triangles stuffed with vegetables and meat — as an appetizer. The butter shrimp and butter chicken are the most popular main dishes. Be sure to order them spicy. Served with aromatic basmati rice, the shrimp and chicken will transport you directly to India. The nan bread here is also first class. Wash the whole thing down with a British beer.

BYOB

BYOBs, or bring-your-own-bottle establishments, abound in Montreal. They help keep dinner prices down, making fine dining accessible to the budget conscious. And because Quebec liquor stores carry an excellent selection of French wines, some from lesser known regions like the Loire valley and Languedoc, you can treat yourself to a nice bottle of wine. Consider it a good investment.

One BYOB that everyone's raving about is Restaurant le P'tit Plateau. Located on Rue Marie-Anne E. near Rue St-Denis, this elegant yet cosy restaurant seats only 42 people. This explains why you need to reserve a week in advance — 10 days in advance for a weekend rendez-vous. The table d'hôte that includes soup or salad, main course and coffee, tea or tisane for $17.95 to $22. There are three items that the young Bordeaux-born chef and owner, Alain Loivel, has to keep constantly on the menu in order to meet customer demand: cassolette d'escargots, confit de canard and mille-feuilles aux deux saumons. Doesn't everything sound delicious en français? The snails are served in a creamy garlic sauce with fresh parsley, the duck is cooked in its own oil in the traditional style of southwestern France and the salmon dish features thin slices of potato, fresh salmon, spinach and smoked salmon layered together and encircled by French beans.

FOUR-STAR DINING

FOOD AT LES CAPRICES DE NICOLAS

If you have money to burn — or are in the mood to splurge — there are plenty of four-star restaurants in Montreal just waiting for you.

For a special occasion try Le Passe-Partout. Located west of downtown on Blvd. Décarie, this restaurant, attached to a fine French bakery, seats 32. The pastel-pink walls are decorated with Intaglio prints collected by Suzanne Baron-Lafrenière, whose husband, James McGuire, is chef. The restaurant is open only three evenings a week — Thursday through Saturday — but is also open for lunch Tuesday through Friday.

McGuire's menu changes with the season. "Just as a baker has flour to work with or a winemaker has grapes, the idea is to make the best of the best produce," says McGuire, whose face takes on a beatific look when he contemplates food. His salmon appetizer, lightly salted and smoked on the premises is irresistible. Main-course specialties include breast of Barbarie duck cooked with black cherries and red snapper served in a red wine sauce. For dessert, try the Tarte Tatin, an upside-down apple tart topped with caramelized sugar. A wide selection of wines are available. Every evening, McGuire selects two wines — he matches them with the menu — which he makes available by the glass. On your way out, don't be surprised if you're presented with a loaf from the couple's boulangerie. Expect dinner for two at Le Passe-Partout to cost between $80 and $90 before wine, tax or tip.

TOQUÉ!

Toqué! has been attracting a lot of attention since it first opened in the mid-90s. Located on Rue St-Denis, this striking restaurant — the walls are covered in red velvet and some of the furnishings are chrome — seats 65. Chef Normand Laprise is known for his market cuisine. Like McGuire's, his menu changes constantly and relies heavily on local produce. The word toqué is Québécois slang and means stubborn — but in a good way. According to

Laprise's business partner, Christine Lamarche, that's exactly how the couple feel about food. "The emphasis here is on food. Almost all of the vegetables we use are organic," says Lamarche. Delicacies include rare yellowfin tuna tempura — tuna served in a light batter with a vinaigrette of baby leeks, celery root and French beans with Chinese garlic, accompanied by roasted peppers and fresh raspberries. Another specialty is roasted leg of Quebec lamb. The lamb is carefully deboned with all traces of fat removed and served medium rare in its own juices garnished with sautéed yellow and white carrots, fava beans and two kinds of beet. For dessert Lamarche recommends the hazelnut biscuit and lemon cream. Dinner for two is \$100 to \$110 before wine, tax or tip.

Private room at Les Caprices de Nicolas

The most recent arrival on the four-star dining scene in Montreal is Les Caprices de Nicolas, located downtown on Rue Drummond. There are three dining rooms from which to choose — each decorated with paintings by well-known contemporary Quebec artists. The garden room, a covered atrium with a fountain, is particularly delightful. One room is a private salon. Here too the menu is constantly changing, but signature dishes include Le Caviar — a ravioli-like appetizer made with caviar, fresh salmon and lemon sauce. Another popular appetizer is the foie gras — pan-seared duck liver served with roasted fig and thinly sliced French fingerling potatoes marinated in a truffle vinaigrette, served with a currant coulis. For your main dish, consider the milk-fed veal loin, roasted and served with caramelized jus.

Food at Les Caprices de Nicolas

"Don't confuse jus with sauce. Jus is lighter than sauce," warns owner Dan Medalsy. A dessert that will make you think you've died and gone to heaven is the dish of seven scoops of homemade ice cream and sherbet. The sherbet flavours include basil and watermelon, and the vanilla ginger ice cream is divine. Dinner for two will set you back some $100 to $110 before wine, tax or tip.

DINING ROOM AT MILOS

Profusion has been causing quite a stir since opening in 1998. Located in the slick Bell amphitheatre building on Rue de la Gauchetière, this restaurant is reminiscent of a luxury liner. There's a wood and metal ramp and the floors are made of mahogany. As the name suggests, fusion cuisine is the specialty here. As an appetizer, try the spinach salad with mango; for the main course, the pheasant cooked in cassis is hard to resist. Rumour has it this place serves the best sushi in town. Dinner for two is about $90 before wine, taxes or tip.

On the more established side, Montrealers have been coming to Chez La Mère Michel at 1209 Rue Guy for over 30 years. Specialties of the house include Lobster soufflé nantua and barquette alsacienne, and the fish (try the Skate) is brought in fresh each day. Caribou and bison appear as seasonal dishes. The wine list is large and reasonably priced, before adding it to the $120 or so you will spend for two.

Where do Paul Newman and Bette Midler hang out when they visit Montreal? At Milos Restaurant, an upscale version of the traditional Greek psarotaverna, located just north of Mount Royal on Ave. du Parc. There's no better fish restaurant in town. Start with an appetizer of crab cakes — they're served with a light mustard sauce. Grilled octopus is another specialty, but most customers order fish by the pound. They choose it themselves from what looks like an open market at the back of the dining room. Imported from as far away as Tunisia and Greece, your fish is grilled whole, then deboned before being served up on a platter. Dinner for two starts at about $100 before wine, taxes or tip. Don't forget to check out the bathrooms downstairs — they're the swankiest in all of Montreal.

You may find yourself a little too close to your neighbours at Mediterraneo, on 3500 Boul. St-Laurent, but the service here is superb and the food worth the wait. Chef Claude Pelletier is at his best with fish — tuna, char, and snapper — but the lamb with rosemary and hazelnuts is every bit as scrumptious. The wine list is a good fit to the menu, which will set you back about $120 before you indulge in a Californian chardonnay.

The Mobil Travel Guide keeps awarding five stars to the Beaver Club, a Montreal dining institution. There's some squabbling about whether the food served here is really that good, or whether it's the elegant atmosphere and fine service that appeal. Located in the main lobby of the Queen Elizabeth Hotel, the Beaver Club first opened in 1958 but has its roots in the 18th-century fur trade. The walls are done in brick and oak panelling; there's an open rotisserie by the restaurant's back wall. Specialties include roast prime rib of beef and rack of lamb. Charles Ploem, the maître d'hôtel since 1962, recommends the filet of caribou served in the Grand Veneur style — in a sauce of cherries and red wine. Jacket and tie are required for men. Dinner for two runs about $100 before wine, taxes and tip.

THE BEAVER CLUB

Lastly, if you feel like a short excursion, Au Tournant de la Rivière is a just reward for those who can find it, at 5070 Rue Salaberry in Carignan. (Take Boul. Décarie south to Hwy. 10 east; turn west at Exit 22 and then immediately take the right turn for Sherbrooke; then make a left on Boul. Brunelle: the restaurant is at Brunelle and Salaberry in a converted barn behind a farmhouse.) The atmosphere is luxurious and the service first-rate. Chef Jacques Robert gives conventional dishes the kind of treatment that makes them exceptional, but much of which can be prohibitively priced. Still, don't miss the chocolate soufflé before you wend your way back to the city.

NIGHT LIFE

SEAN FARRELL

WINNIE'S AND THURSDAY'S ON RUE CRESCENT

Some winters ago a blizzard descended on both Montreal and Toronto with particular ferocity. It closed businesses, snarled traffic and crippled transit systems in both cities. Thousands of commuters were stranded in subway stations and bus terminals. Toronto responded by closing all the bars early. Montreal responded by allowing the bars to stay open all night long. Montreal's not just a city that never sleeps; it's a city that never hibernates. Wander down St-Denis or along Ste-Catherine late on a January night and the streets are nearly as crowded with celebrants as they are in July or August. In winter, of course, the bars and clubs themselves retreat behind their steamy front windows, but at the slightest hint of spring, all that life pours out onto the terraces where the view of life's passing parade is livelier and more varied. There are a number of distinct districts, all with their own feel and ambience.

A good place to start is the corner of rues Peel and Ste-Catherine. There's not much here in the way of watering holes except for the somewhat grungy Peel Pub. But if you walk west three blocks you come to Rue de la Montagne (often called Mountain St.) — the eastern edge of the downtown night scene and what could be called the Anglo playground of Montreal. There are bars and restaurants on Ste-Catherine, but the real action is on the cross streets that run north-south between Blvd. René-Lévesque and Rue Sherbrooke. Mountain, Crescent, Bishop and Mackay are lined with fine old greystone buildings that were once the town homes of the comfortably middle class and are now the stomping grounds of the footloose and fancy-free.

HURLEY'S

HARD ROCK CAFÉ

Winter or summer, these four streets are always bustling with pedestrians edging their way past lineups outside clubs. Cars cruise by slowly, not for safety but so their occupants can see and be seen. The trendiest of these streets is probably Crescent — although that could change at the drop of a hemline. It's the home of such well-established clubs as Thursday's, Winnie's and Sir Winston Churchill Pub. It also has a Hard Rock Café for those who like their fun American style. Those who like it with a Celtic flavour can try Hurley's just south of Ste-Catherine.

The clubs on Bishop are generally less formal than those on Crescent. Below Ste-Catherine is a good place to catch a live performance by a local rock band, at a club like Déjà-Vu, or to just kick back at Charlie's American Pub. Rue Bishop is also the home of the Comedyworks, one of two top places for nightly comedy performances. The other is the Comedy Nest just to the south in the Nouvel Hotel on Blvd. René-Lévesque.

The downtown scene is not strictly limited to the Rue Crescent area. Clubs sprout up in the most unlikely places. Planet Hollywood, for example, opened in 1998 in Place Montreal Trust, a glitzy shopping centre on Ste-Catherine east of Peel. And a few long-time favourites have survived far from the main stream. Biddle's on Rue Aylmer above

FIDDLERS AT McKIBBIN'S IRISH PUB

Le Swimming

Président-Kennedy is a grand place to go for an evening of jazz and a plate of ribs. And the unprepossessing Old Dublin on Rue University — it's painted an obscene shade of green and fronts a parking lot — rivals Hurley's for the Irish crowd.

The other great centre for nightlife is 14 blocks east of Peel. It follows the twin corridors of Blvd. St-Laurent and Rue St-Denis. This area is more franco than anglo, although once again it is best to avoid sweeping generalizations. It is also best to avoid the southern end of St-Laurent at night unless your taste runs to sleazy strip clubs and ladies of the evening in outrageous attire. But north of Rue Sherbrooke, the Main — as St-Laurent is often called — is lined with clubs and cafés. For a bit of people watching, try the Shed. College kids are particularly fond of a dance club called Angel's and the live bands at Café Campus a block east of St-Laurent on Rue Prince Arthur. Just north of Prince Arthur is the cleverly named Le Swimming. This is a pool hall for the young and beautiful, hence the punny name. If you're looking for a sports bar, go further up St-Laurent, above Ave. des Pins,, to Champs where you're sure to see whatever game it is that you want to catch. Club Balattou, on St-Laurent just south of Ave. Mont-Royal, will have you dancing all night to African rhythms.

Pool at Le Swimming

Rue St-Denis is seven blocks east of St-Laurent and many of the streets that link the two thoroughfares — Mont-Royal, Rachel and Prince Arthur, for example — are alive with restaurants and cafés. St-Denis itself throbs with a jazzy Latin beat. Bars like the enormously popular Grand Café and the more modest Le Central have live jazz bands, while Les Beaux Esprits includes blues in the mix.

Angel's

East of St-Denis, clustered along Ste-Catherine between Rue Amherst and Ave. Papineau, is le Village, the city's

Casino de Montréal

gay district. Sky features techno-pop music and L'Entre-Peau stages transvestite shows. The leather crowd tend to favour La Track, and the intellectual types — real and pseudo — congregate in Le California. Vieux-Montréal has never developed much of a nightlife but a couple of places are worth mentioning. Both are on Rue St-Paul O./W. L'Air du Temps is one of the city's finest jazz clubs, while the nationalist crowd likes to gather in Aux Deux Pierrots to sing along with some of Quebec's best performers.

If you fancy fighting crowds of hopeful local residents, a trip out to the phenomenally popular and très élégant Casino de Montréal on Île-Ste-Hélène is in order. It's open 24 hours a day and is always packed with people who take pleasure in throwing their money away. There's no accounting for taste.

Montreal can't match New York or Toronto for English-language theatre, but it does lead the continent in French-language productions. Théâtre du Nouveau Monde stages the classics, Théâtre de Quat'Sous experiments with cerebral plays and Théâtre du Rideau Vert offers modern French repertoire. The Centaur Theatre in Vieux-Montréal is the heart of what English-language theatre there is, although touring Broadway productions often make summer stops at Théâtre Saint-Denis and Place des Arts.

Centaur Theatre

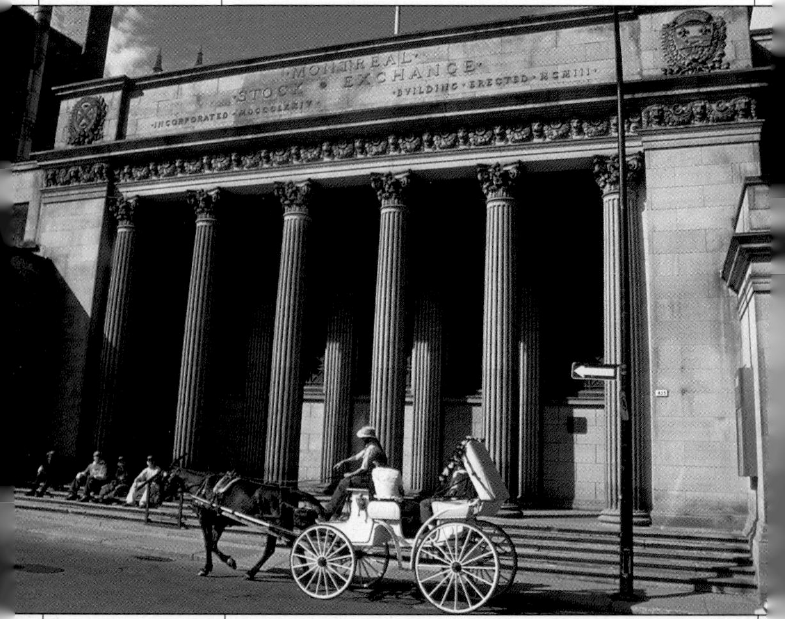

Montreal by Area

OLD MONTREAL

SEAN FARRELL

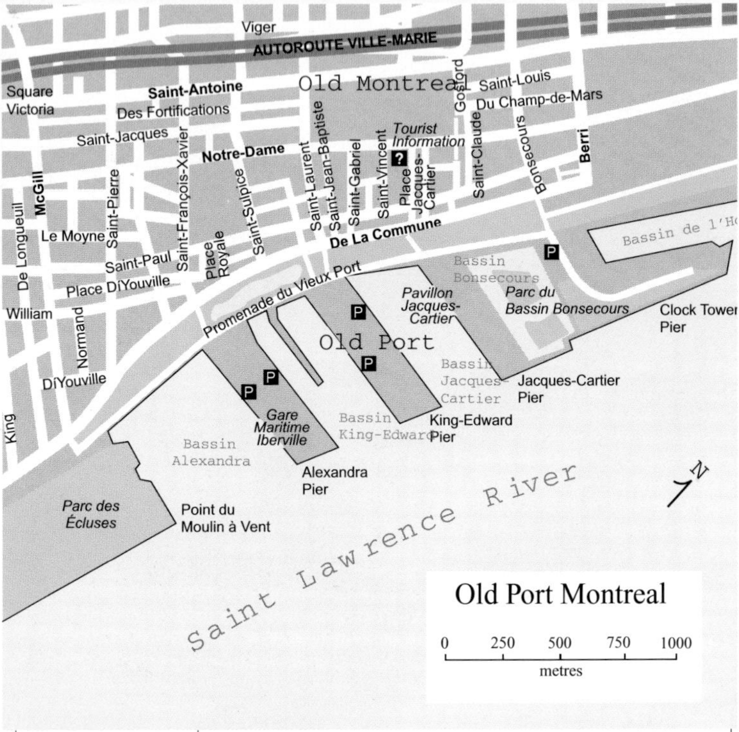

18TH CENTURY MARKET

Montreal's first pious settlers had dreams of establishing a new civilization founded on Christian principles when they straggled ashore in 1642. They christened their collection of rude dwellings Ville-Marie in honour of Christ's mother and set out to convert the Indians. There's nothing left of that old settlement but the name but there's still plenty of history in Vieux-Montréal (Old Montreal), the little chunk of land that stretches along the waterfront from Rue McGill in the west to Rue St-Denis in the east. This was the heart of the city's commercial and political life until the end of the 19th century. Today it thrives in its new role as the city's centre of tourism.

You can, if you wish, rattle along the cobbled streets in a horse-drawn carriage or rumble along them on a tour bus, but there's really no need. The district's easy to get to by Métro — get off at the Square-Victoria, Place d'Armes or Champ-de-Mars station —

Place Jacques-Cartier

and small enough to be explored on foot. So put on a good pair of walking shoes and step out. Most of the history you'll see is 19th century, but there's a generous scattering of 18th-century gems and many of the later buildings rest on 18th-century foundations.

Place Jacques-Cartier, near the Champ-de-Mars Métro station, is a good place to start, for two reasons: first, there's a tourist office on the northwest corner of the square where you can pick up a copy of a booklet that outlines a self-guided walking tour; and second, Place Jacques-Cartier is one of the prettiest and liveliest squares in the whole city. It stretches from Rue de la Commune on the riverfront north to Rue Notre-Dame, and its whole length is lined with restaurants and snack bars with terraces that open on to the square. In summer, jugglers, fire-eaters and musicians amuse the crowds and the whole area is bright with flowers. The column at the north end of the square bears a statue not of Jacques Cartier, as you might expect, but of Admiral Horatio Nelson. It was erected in 1809 to celebrate Nelson's victory over the French fleet at Trafalgar.

French seamanship does get its due in Place Vauquelin on the other side of Rue Notre-Dame. This little square and its fountain are named for the French admiral who defended Louisbourg. Just beyond Place Vauquelin is a flight of stone steps that leads down to Champ de Mars, a handsome green space that used to be a parking lot and

Hotel de Ville

before that a parade ground. It's now used occasionally for public gatherings. Archeologists have also excavated the foundations of the walls that used to surround the old city.

Captains of commerce fled Vieux-Montréal long ago, but the district is still the heart of civic and legal activity. The Second Empire wedding cake on the east side of Place Vauquelin, for example, is city hall, and the balcony above the main door is where Charles de Gaulle made his infamous "Vive le Québec libre!" speech in 1967. If you look west along Notre-Dame you will see three courthouses — two on the north side of the street and one on the south side. They are the old courthouse, the old new courthouse and the new new courthouse. Only the last is still active as the Palais de Justice and you should have no trouble picking it out. It's the big modern slab that doesn't belong.

Far handsomer is the Château de Ramezay, right across from city hall. It was built in 1705 as a residence for the city's governor and looks a little like a Norman castle. It houses a museum with an extensive collection of art, furniture and documents dating from the 18th and 19th centuries. A five-minute stroll east along Notre-Dame to Rue Berri brings you to two grand old buildings that used to be train stations. The Dalhousie station on the southeast corner of Berri and Notre-Dame linked Montreal to Vancouver, while the Viger station on St-Antoine at Berri served points to the east.

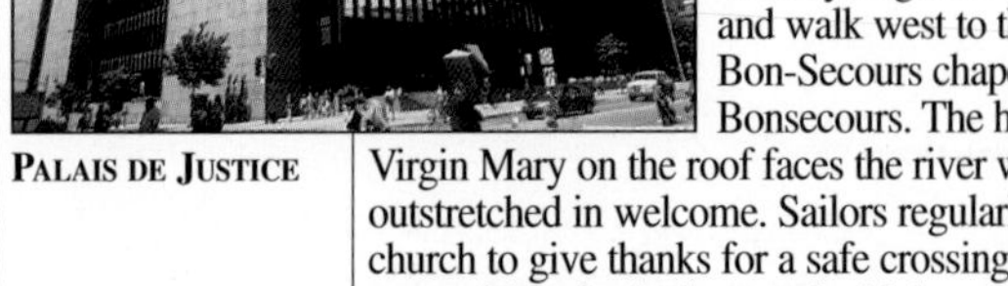

Palais de Justice

Walk south on Berri, stopping to visit the lovingly restored home of Sir George-Étienne Cartier, the man who led Quebec into Confederation in 1867. When you get to Rue St-Paul turn right and walk west to the Notre-Dame-de-Bon-Secours chapel at the foot of Rue Bonsecours. The huge statue of the Virgin Mary on the roof faces the river with its arms outstretched in welcome. Sailors regularly visited this little church to give thanks for a safe crossing. The beautifully restored interior is decorated with lamps in the form of model boats, left as gifts by grateful mariners.

Across St-Paul at the corner of Bonsecours is one of the finest samples of 18th-century architecture in Montreal, the greystone Maison du Calvet, built in 1725. Pierre du Calvet was a merchant and ardent admirer of the American Revolution, and Benjamin Franklin was a regular visitor. The long, low building with the tin-roofed dome next to the chapel is the Marché Bonsecours. The market has had a number of incarnations over the years, serving at various times as a concert hall and even as city hall, but it has returned to its original purpose as a marketplace, featuring a number of lovely boutiques and exhibitions.

A short stroll west and you're back at the southern end of Place Jacques-Cartier. Walk another 50 metres or so and turn left down Rue St-Vincent, a narrow lane jammed with artists and artisans peddling their wares. When you get back to Rue St-Paul, take a careful look at the buildings on the south side of the street. Merchants once coveted these places. They could take in their goods directly from the docks along Rue de la Commune behind their shops and sell them to the customers they received on the fashionable St-Paul side.

NOTRE-DAME-DE-BON-SECOURS CHAPEL

Waterfront Rue de la Commune, from Berri to the Lachine Canal, connects Vieux-Montréal with the Vieux-Port. Many of the buildings on de la Commune still display the names of the businesses once housed there with what is

left of old signs painted on the brick or stone walls. A few blocks to the west along de la Commune sits Pointe-à-Callière, the site where Paul de Chemodey, Sieur de Maisonneuve, and his brave followers landed in 1642. The

WATERFRONT RUE DE LA COMMUNE

triangular building with the lookout tower is an archeological museum built over an excavation of the site. Visitors can actually wander among the various layers of development, from the 17th century to the Victorian age. The museum is linked underground with the Old Customs House, which houses one of the finest museum gift shops in the city.

The Centre d'Histoire de Montréal, just a few blocks away in the heart of Place d'Youville, is housed in a beautifully restored fire station. It presents a folksier view of Montreal history, with exhibits that highlight day-to-day life. The museum houses a collection of objects and models that tell the story of Montreal from its foundation to the present day.

POINTE-À-CALLIÈRE

Walk north on Rue St-Pierre and you come to some imposing stone ruins. This is all that's left of one of Montreal's first hospitals, built by the Frères Charon. In 1747 it was taken over by one of the heroines of city history, Ste-Marguerite d'Youville, founder of the Grey Nuns. Three blocks further north is Rue St-Jacques — or St. James St., as it was known when it was the financial capital of Canada. The business barons who worked in the grand old buildings that line the street from Victoria Square to Place d'Armes controlled three quarters of the country's wealth. And if you think they were a stodgy lot, take a closer look at the buildings. They're decorated with a fanciful array of stone cherubs, naked goddesses and lots of granite grapes and vines. Some, of course, are simply grand; the Royal Bank monolith at the corner of St-Pierre, for example, was the tallest building in the British Empire when it was completed in 1928.

Just across the street from the Royal Bank is the World Trade Centre, one of the district's newest and most imaginative developments. It was created by glassing over Fortifications Lane, a fetid, narrow alley that traced the route of the old walls. This resulted in a thin, six-storey mall linking two rows of decaying buildings (which the developers sandblasted into respectability). Throw in a a luxury hotel, a link to the Métro and a magnificent black-marble fountain, and presto: a delightful interior space with a food court and a row of boutiques. The graffiti-covered slab of concrete at the east end of the centre is a section of the Berlin Wall, a gift from Berlin on the occasion of Montreal's 350th birthday in 1992.

A block east of the World Trade Centre is the old city centre, Place d'Armes. The heroic stone figure in the middle of the square is of Paul de Chomedey, Sieur de Maisonneuve, the leader of the first settlers. He's surrounded by a bewildering array of architecture. The domed Greek temple behind him is the Bank of Montreal's head office (the interior also resembles a Greek temple). The redstone building on his left is the city's first skyscraper and the soaring black tower on his right is the headquarters of the Banque Nationale. But it's the the magnificent Gothic façade he's looking at that gets all the attention from tourists. This is Basilique Notre-Dame-de-Montréal, possibly the most famous church in Canada. The interior is a vast blue cavern studded with 18-karat-gold stars and dimly lit by a row of stained-glass windows crafted in Limoges. The reredos with its life-sized tableaus from the Old Testament is a display of virtuoso wood carving. The Sacred Heart chapel behind the main altar is as large as some churches and more ornate than most. Thousands of Montrealers have been married in that chapel. Spend an hour at the basilica before going home. If you're lucky, the Montreal Symphony Orchestra will be practising in the sanctuary and you can watch and listen. Or there might be a string quartet playing on the plaza in front. Or you can just sit and meditate and let the colours soak in to your soul.

PLACE D'ARMES

Old Port

Sean Farrell

Promenade du Vieux-Port

Montreal is an island city in the middle of the St. Lawrence River and is still one of Canada's most important ports. Nowhere is the city's bond to the sea more apparent than at the lively Vieux-Port (Old Port) along the southern edge of the old city. This strip of docks is no longer the commercial heart of Montreal — the big container ships and bulk carriers of modern trade load and unload at more modern wharves further east — but it has become one of the most popular parks in Montreal. And it's popular all year round. In February it's the site of the annual Fête des Neiges and its huge skating rink is used all winter long.

But the place really blossoms in summer. On warm summer days and late into the evening, the Promenade du Vieux-Port that runs the length of the waterfront from the Lachine Canal in the west to the Clock Pier in the east is crowded with strollers, inline skaters and cyclists. Whole families glide by in pedal-driven vehicles that look like a cross between a

Old Port at night

HABITAT '67

horseless carriage and a surrey with a fringe on top. The less energetic rumble by in little motorized trains that run tours all along the waterfront. This is also where Montreal celebrates Canada Day with concerts and dances that last well into the night.

Sometimes a wedding cake of a cruise ship will be docked at the Iberville pier at the western end of the Vieux-Port just south of Pointe-a-Callière, the site of Montreal's founding in 1642. Cruise passengers are among the best accommodated of Montreal's visitors, living in floating luxury with a view of the river and Île Ste-Hélène. And all this is just an easy walk from the sights of Vieux-Montréal. Visiting warships also use the docks when they pay courtesy calls on the city, and so do the tall ships that some countries use as training vessels for their navy cadets. The latter add a real 19th-century flavour to the port.

The best way to get here is by Métro. Get off at Square-Victoria and walk south on Rue McGill to the waterfront. It's a bit of a hike, but it's better than trying to park a car on Rue de la Commune (impossible) or in one of the Vieux-Port's parking lots (costly). If you do come by Métro, a good place to start exploring the Vieux-Port is at its western end, at Parc des Ècluses (Locks) in the shadow of the great grain elevators. This marks the entrance to the Lachine Canal, a 19th-century engineering marvel that took ships past the Lachine Rapids. The St. Lawrence Seaway has rendered it obsolete but its grassy banks form a kind of long, thin park that ends on the shores of Lac St-Louis. The canal's bicycle path is also the source of many of the bikes coasting along the waterfront.

Look across the Alexandra basin and you'll see a building that looks a bit like a cliffside pueblo dwelling in the American Southwest. It's even the right colour to blend in with the Arizona desert. This is Habitat '67, built for the Expo '67 world's fair by architect Moshe Safdie as an experiment in modular, moderately priced housing. Its waterfront address makes it a little less modest than Mr. Safdie planned. It's the most impressive building on Côté-du-Havre, a long, thin park that leads to the Concorde bridge and Parc des Îles.

Walk west past the Iberville pier to the King Edward pier at the foot of Blvd. St-Laurent. This is home to a variety of activities. One of its busiest attractions is

IMAX MOVIE THEATRE

OLD PORT MARINA

something called the S.O.S. Labyrinthe, an ever-changing maze of mirrors that is popular with both young children and the young at heart. The mile of passageways is regularly changed in order to present a fresh challenge to frequent visitors. To add an even greater measure of difficulty, try it after sunset. As the operators like to point out, no flashlight provided. Good luck. The pier also has a pair of IMAX movie theatres. These special-format movies are shot with oversized film and shown on gigantic screens that often make you feel like you are part of the action. The theatre generally schedules a double-bill for its screenings and alternates between screenings in English and French. The films are guaranteed to assault your senses though you might want to think twice if you suffer from motion sickness — the illusion is that effective.

In May 2000, The IMAX theatres will be incorporated into the Centre iSci (sic), a complex that will fill the Quai King Edward. The centre will combine education (interactive science exhibits and space for exhibitions and displays on science and technology), food (bistros and family restaurants) and shopping (a gift shop and a craft market with 17 outdoor stalls).

The King Edward pier and its eastern neighbour, the Jacques-Cartier pier, frame a marina full of pleasure craft. It's a popular place to do some people watching or a bit of daydreaming, especially over some of the bigger yachts or sailboats berthed there. But if you want to do a bit of boating you don't have to own one of the luxury yachts. The western side of the Jacques-Cartier pier is lined with opportunities. You can chug along the river on an ersatz paddle-wheeler or do high-speed 360-degree turns on a speed boat. The glass-topped Bateau-Mouche — it looks a lot like those boats that cruise the Seine in Paris — offers dinner cruises on the river. The best deal, however, are probably the little ferries that take pedestrians and cyclists to Île Ste-Hélène and Longueuil on the south shore. One of the more unusual ways to tour the Vieux-Port and Vieux-Montréal is on the Amphi-Bus, which leaves from the Jacques-Cartier pier. As its name suggests, this odd machine is part boat and part bus. It has both wheels and propellers and offers visitors an amphibious view of the waterfront. The Jacques-Cartier pier also has a boutique, restaurant and washroom facilities, which makes it a good place for a pit stop.

BONSECOURS BASIN

On the east side of the Jacques-

CLOCK PIER

Cartier pier is the Bonsecours basin where you can pilot your own boat. OK, its only a pedal boat and you can't go beyond the boundaries of the basin, but it's a good place to laze away a summer afternoon. There's a lovely little park in the middle of the basin, a kind of grassy island linked to the mainland by narrow footbridges.

The last pier is the Clock Pier on the eastern edge of the Vieux-Port. It was once called the Victoria Pier, and it's shaped a little like a crooked thumb with the tip pointing east, down the river. If your trip so far has been uneventful and you're getting bored, this might be a good place to stop and check out the Saute-Moutons jet boats in the basin between the thumb and the mainland. Saute-Moutons — literally "jumping sheep" — is the French term for rapids, and these big, flat-bottomed boats will take you upriver for a wet and wild ride in the Lachine Rapids. There aren't many major cities where you can do this kind of thing without going beyond the city limits. Though not cheap, it'll satisfy your need for an adrenaline rush. But be warned — you will get wet. Walk along the pier — don't forget to wave to the people returning from their jet-boat ride with their hearts in their throats — to the clock tower that gives the pier its name. If you want to hear your own heart pound, climb its 192 steps for a fantastic view of the waterfront and its surroundings. You don't have to count your steps most of the way up because each stair is numbered, except for the top ones, which form a tight, spiralling staircase opening on to the top deck. There isn't room for more than a few people at a time to stand and enjoy the view, but it's worth the effort to climb all those stairs if you want to get a new and different perspective on Montreal. The tower was built in 1922 to honour the merchant mariners who kept the supply lines open to Europe during the First World War. The pier itself is the prettiest on the waterfront. The little park at its western end is set aside for kite-fliers, and the benches and rock gardens at the eastern end under the clock are popular with the crowds who come out on weekends to watch the fireworks competitions. It's a good place to finish up and try to remember where you left your car.

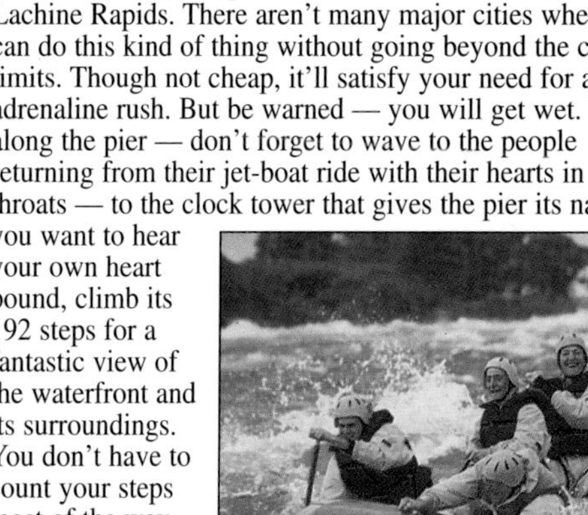

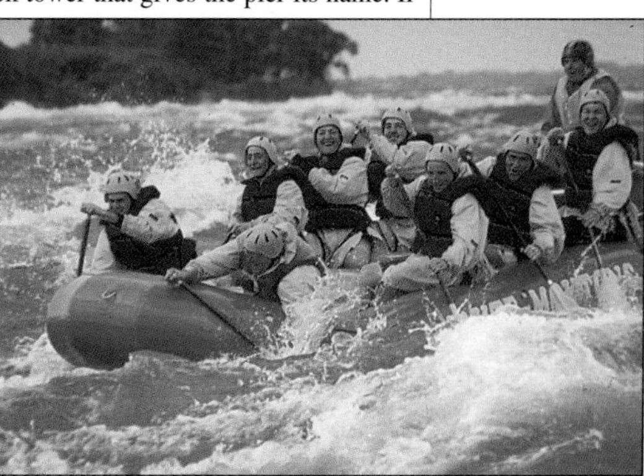

PADDLING THE LACHINE RAPIDS

Downtown & Ste-Catherine's

Pierre Home-Douglas

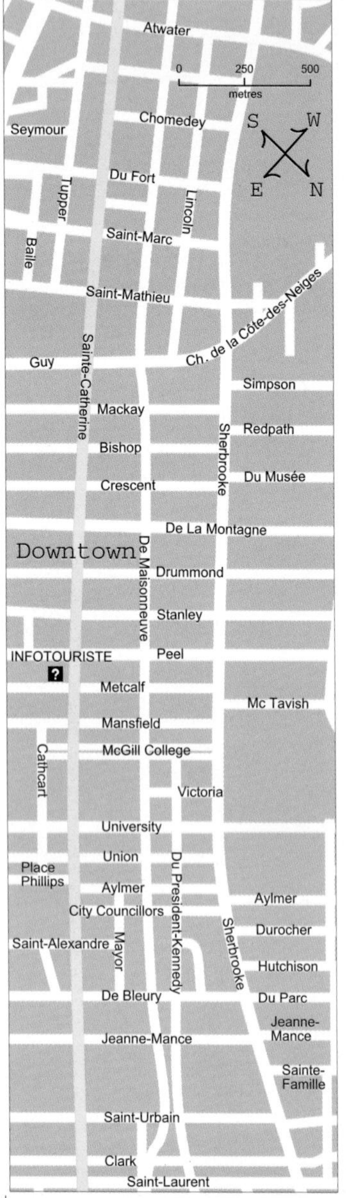

Every great city has its main shopping street where locals and visitors throng to shop, stroll, people watch and tap into the spirit of the town. London has its Oxford Street, New York its Fifth Avenue, Toronto its Yonge Street. In Montreal it's Ste-Catherine, a gritty, jaunty strip of flash and dash that cuts a 15-kilometre swath right through the metropolis, from the affluent enclave of Westmount in the west to the factories and row housing of the working-class east end. In between lies a world of upscale boutiques, grand old department stores, seedy striptease joints, quirky shops, restaurants of every ethnic type imaginable. And people. Plenty of them. At just about any hour of the day or night you'll find Montrealers milling about, heading off to a rendezvous at a nearby bar, stopping for a café au lait, checking out the latest fashion trends or just, well, living. Rue Sherbrooke, a couple of blocks to the north, may offer more refinement, more Old World gentility, but if you want to feel the real pulse of the town, head for Ste-Catherine and take a walk.

At its western end Ste-Catherine begins where it merges with Blvd. de Maisonneuve, a few yards from the

Le Mélange Magique

Vendôme Métro station. But for most Montrealers the route kicks into high gear at Atwater, a couple of kilometres east. The intersection was once hockey mecca in this hockey-mad town. Here stands the Montreal Forum (2313), home for more than 70 years to one of the most storied franchises in sports: the Montreal Canadiens. The fabled building closed in 1996 when the team shifted to new digs at the Centre Molson. Somehow it all seemed depressingly fitting. Once a thriving shopping and entertainment area, this stretch of Ste-Catherine seemed to suffer more than most parts of Montreal when the economy of the city turned sour during the 1980s and early '90s. Locals watched as store after store was either boarded up or torn down. Gone were the venerable Texan Steak House and Toe Blake's Tavern. To many observers, the Forum's closing seemed the final nail in the coffin.

But then, Lazarus-like, the street started to make a comeback. New shops emerged, like March Almizan (2167), which sells imported spices and such Middle Eastern specialties as fig marmalade and halvah and Lily's Garage Sale (1946), which offers a permanent fix for garage-sale devotees. Other stores, like Garnitures Dressmaker (2186), endured despite the economic roller-coaster ride. This shop has been at the same address since the late '50s, sewing up a storm and dispensing craft supplies ranging from wall stencils to a wide selection of feathers, beads and ribbons. And then word came that the Forum, after serving a brief stint as a key location for an $80-million feature film, Snake Eyes, was destined to become an entertainment centre with two dozen cinemas. There was life in the old town after all.

GARNITURES DRESSMAKER

If you happen to have missed breakfast, take a side trip one block north on Lambert-Closse to Casse-Croûte au Coin (2212 Lambert-Closse). Regulars still call it Moe's after its owner until the late '70s. When the Forum was in full swing across the street you would often see visiting

MOE'S

SEVILLE THEATRE

hockey players eating huge breakfasts on game day. Regular patrons included Wayne Gretzky and Mario Lemieux — plus roadies, circus workers, even a rock star or two. Today it's still a good bet for a cheap breakfast. And it's open 24 hours a day.

Another landmark just to the east of the Forum on Ste-Catherine is the Seville Theatre. Back in the '40s and '50s, some of the top entertainers in the world belted out tunes from the stage here, megastars like Frank Sinatra and Sarah Vaughan. Later it was turned into a much-loved repertory cinema. Then the boards went up on the doors and windows and the building lay dormant for more than a decade as preservationists fought to keep the wrecking ball at bay. Finally word came that it too will be saved — converted into boutiques and offices.

STE-CATHERINE WEST OF GUY

Over the years, the strip from Ave. Atwater to Rue Guy has evolved into a magnet for Montreal book lovers. Some call it Bookstore Row. Here you'll find everything from Westcott Books (2065), its shelves piled high with quality used books for every taste, to Le Mélange Magique (1928), Quebec's largest English-language occult and metaphysical bookstore. Two tiny and very selective book shops are worth a visit. Argo, which deals in new books, is a Montreal institution, while the more recently established Vortex offers a range of hand-picked literary titles. And don't forget Librairie Nebula (1832), with the best sci-fi selection in town. There are also a couple of magazine shops that can satisfy just about any taste. Mediaphile (1901), for example, offers hundreds of mags to hungry readers and will allow you to order from a list of 10,000 titles. The owners also indulge in a little side business, selling top-notch cigars from Cuba, Jamaica and several other countries at reasonable prices.

MEDIAPHILE

Probably the most successful part of the recent regeneration of this stretch of Ste-Catherine is the Faubourg (1616), a food bazaar with a difference. Opened in the late '80s, the Faubourg features a ground floor that is a funky mix of food shops and boutiques. The top floor offers a raft of ethnic take-out foods from more than 20 nations, running the gamut from Szechuan to sushi. Locals stop by on Sunday morning for their paper and a cup of cappuccino and to sit by the windows that face out onto Ste-Catherine. Light streams in from the skylights in the festive atrium, where 20-foot kites dangle from the ceiling. On

THE BAGEL PLACE

the way out you can watch bagels being baked or pick up some tasty cheeses at La Fine Gueule.

A couple of blocks east of Guy, Ste-Catherine intersects two streets filled with some of Montreal's best-known watering holes. Rues Bishop and Crescent rank as one of the hippest areas in Montreal for trendy young Anglos to sit and chat and drink away the evening. A constantly replenishing young crowd keeps things hopping here, particularly on Friday and Saturday nights. Among the best-known spots are Sir Winston Churchill Pub (1455 Crescent), reputedly David Letterman's favourite place to meet people in Montreal; Hurley's Irish Pub, which sells more draft Guinness than any other bar in North America; Grumpy's (1242 Bishop), where you might find novelist and essayist Mordecai Richler holding court with media luminaries; and Brutopia (1219 Crescent), which offers live music and some of the best home-brewed beer in town.

LA FINE GUEULE

The block between rues Crescent and de la Montagne is dominated by Ogilvy (1307), one of the grand dames of Montreal's department stores. Founded in 1866 by James Angus Ogilvy, the store received a much-needed facelift in the 1980s, when the five-floor edifice was converted into a series of upscale boutiques. Old-timers still bemoan the loss of the basement cafeteria, where you used to see old ladies hunched over their cup of tea, as they wiled away the hours. But there have been welcome additions, including the Nicholas Hoare bookstore, which draws two thumbs up from book lovers all over town. And some traditions still endure: every day at noon a kilted bagpiper marches through the main floor playing his pipes; and in December locals line the snowbound sidewalk in front of the store with their children to view the elaborate Christmas scene on display in the Ogilvy windows.

SIR WINSTON CHURCHILL PUB

NICHOLAS HOARE BOOKSTORE

There's more history in this area than even most Montrealers realize. Half a block south on de la Montagne stands a row of mid-19th-century townhouses. Next door to number 1181 is where Confederate President Jefferson Davis lived after the American Civil War. Davis's house was ripped down in the 1950s to make way for an alley (this was at a time when preserving the past carried little weight in Montreal), but the limestone buildings on the right that once adjoined it are identical to the ones in which Davis spent two years before leaving to live out his final years in Mississippi.

STE-CATHERINE AND PEEL

Ahead lies one of the busiest stretches of Ste-Catherine. Montrealers have long considered the intersection with Peel as the absolute dead centre of town. The stores along this stretch are decidedly more upscale than those to the west. Names like Benetton, Gap and Mexx display the latest fashions to the crowd strolling by. Or pop across the street and head upstairs to Basha (930), a Lebanese restaurant that offers tasty, filling meals like plates of shish taouk chicken and shawarma beef for around $6.

GAP

One block further east, take a look up Ave. McGill College, the closest thing Montreal has to a Champs-Elysées. This is one of the best views in the city, with the copper-roofed buildings of McGill University at the top of the street, behind the curved entrance of the Roddick Gates, with Mount Royal in the background. At Christmas time, Ave. McGill College is lit up with innumerable small white lights. When the snow falls softly in the evening the street looks like a fairyland.

Next is Montreal's largest department store, Eaton (677). The venerable institution boasts the usual array of merchandise, from electronics to high fashion, but it's real attraction lies on the ninth floor in a restaurant called Le 9e. This isn't your typical department store eatery. Le 9e is an art deco masterpiece designed by Jacques Carlu, who styled it after the dining room on the passenger ship Île de France, Lady Eaton's favourite ocean liner. The room features marble columns, two large murals and space for 600 diners, and it makes an ideal spot to take a break from sightseeing and revive yourself with afternoon tea.

Still, it's not all chic restaurants and upscale stores in this part of the town. The stretch from Guy to University has its share of Danseuses Nues/Nude Dancers signs. And right across the street from Eaton is probably the best-known strip joint in town, Super Sexe (696), which features in at least one piece by Hunter S. Thompson. The famed gonzo journalist didn't mention it, but it's hard to imagine he wasn't impressed by the fact that someone standing in front of the Super Sexe can divert their glance from the large red letters boldly proclaiming its attractions and catch a glimpse of one of Montreal's best-loved churches, Christ Church Cathedral, less than half a block away.

Christ Church Cathedral at 1440 Ave. Union, fronting on Ste-Catherine, is a neo-Gothic masterpiece. It was designed in the 1850s by Frank Wills, a native of a town that has an impressive cathedral of its own — Salisbury, England. Christ Church is topped by a graceful spire made of aluminum, which replaced the original stone one after it was discovered that its weight threatened the structure. In 1986 the church leaders leased the rights to their lot to developers, who then propped up the entire cathedral on huge steel posts and dug out enough space underneath to squeeze in a 100-store mall, Les Promenades de la Cathédrale. Some may have decried the move as selling out, but parishioners in the late 21st century may have the last laugh. That's when the lease expires and the

CHRIST CHURCH CATHEDRAL

Promenade and the soaring glass tower called La Maison des Coopérants directly behind the Cathedral become church property.

Christ Church faces Phillips Square or Carré Phillips, a small patch of green on Ste-Catherine. Also facing the square are Birks (1240 Carré Phillips), one of Canada's oldest jewellers and a favourite for bridal registries in the city, and the Bay department store (585), a red sandstone beauty dating back to 1886 with a regrettably ugly steel-covered walkway that encircles the building. Beyond Phillips Square, Ste-Catherine dips down slightly to Rue Jeanne-Mance, where Place des Arts, home to the Montreal Symphony Orchestra, and Complexe Desjardins gaze down from opposite sides of the street. During the Montreal

BIRKS

international jazz festival every July this is ground zero for a couple of weeks of some of the best music on the planet. The surrounding streets are wall-to-wall people as far as the eye can see, everyone swaying to the beat of an astonishing array of free outdoor concerts.

There are still more than five kilometres to go until Ste-Catherine runs into Rue Notre-Dame at the eastern end of Montreal's docks and calls it quits. But, quite frankly, it's not really worth the walk — with one exception: Henri-Henri, 189 Ste-Catherine E. at the corner of Ave. Hôtel-de-Ville, is a hat store that has been in business since 1932 and is still one of the best places in town — if not in all of Canada — to pick up a $400 borsalino or a beret straight from France. Just ask patrons like Donald Sutherland and Charlie Sheen, who drop in here when they're filming in Montreal. Henri-Henri is exceptional — and yet it's also typical in a way: another little jewel that pops out on Rue Ste-Catherine when you least expect it.

PLACE DES ARTS

SHERBROOKE ST.

DONNA MACHUTCHIN

Montrealers are fervent about their city and its history, as developers have discovered to their peril. Rue Sherbrooke, downtown Montreal's most elegant thoroughfare, is testament to that: A few high-rises loom along the street in the area between rues Guy and University, but their blandness serves to emphasize the charm of the old houses that have survived. Zoning laws have kept many of these from being demolished and they provide a measure of European elegance and keep the scale human.

Sherbrooke runs through the centre of the Square Mile, where shipping, sugar, fur-trade, railway and brewery magnates built their mansions in the 19th and early 20th centuries when Montreal was the premier city in Canada. In 1840 the street (formerly called Rue Ste-Marie) was extended east and west from the city core and re-named after Sir John Coape Sherbrooke, who was Governor-in-Chief of British North America in 1816–1818. Now it extends 22 miles through the city. It's a street with panache and style. Each season offers a fresh view of its compelling reaches and a walk along it is the perfect way to get to know Montreal and its moods. There are explantory bronze placques at some sites.

Start your walk at Ave. Atwater. On the northeast corner of Sherbrooke and Atwater is a prime example of how

MANOIR DE BELMONT

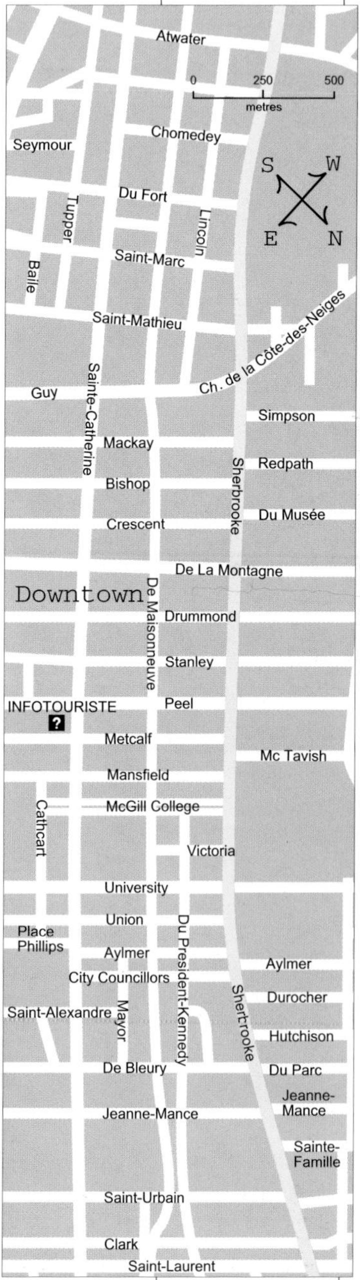

LE GRAND SÉMINAIRE

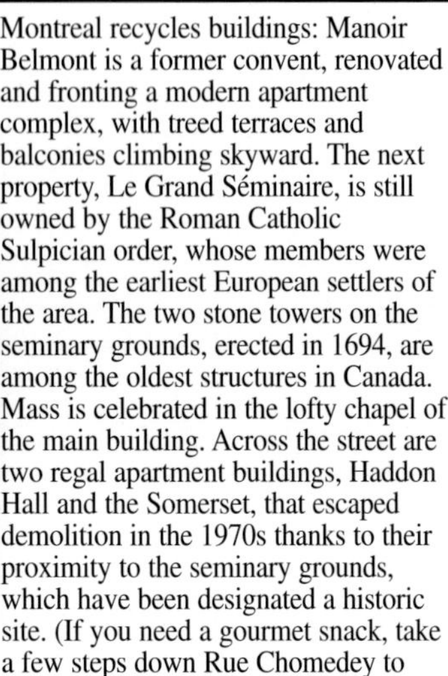

Montreal recycles buildings: Manoir Belmont is a former convent, renovated and fronting a modern apartment complex, with treed terraces and balconies climbing skyward. The next property, Le Grand Séminaire, is still owned by the Roman Catholic Sulpician order, whose members were among the earliest European settlers of the area. The two stone towers on the seminary grounds, erected in 1694, are among the oldest structures in Canada. Mass is celebrated in the lofty chapel of the main building. Across the street are two regal apartment buildings, Haddon Hall and the Somerset, that escaped demolition in the 1970s thanks to their proximity to the seminary grounds, which have been designated a historic site. (If you need a gourmet snack, take a few steps down Rue Chomedey to Charcuterie L'En Cas, tucked into the side of Haddon Hall, and pick up a little something. Specialties include fresh croissants, prepared salads, an excellent choice of cheeses and even take-out crème caramel.) The Haddon apartments and others farther east attest to the livability of downtown Montreal.

In the next block is the Masonic Temple, built in 1930, with its impressive neo-Grecian façade. At Rue St-Mathieu the Hôtel Château Versailles stands on both sides of Sherbrooke — the older, Edwardian building on the north side offers rooms with high ceilings and lots of architectural detailing, while the 1960s annex across the street houses a very good restaurant, the Champs Elysée. Past the hotel is a block of tidied up greystone houses with high stoops. They are home to Ex Libris, a good second-hand bookstore; the cosy Bistro Europa, which offers inexpensive pasta and pizza; and Galerie Tansu, which sells lovely Japanese antiques and furniture. Oh, and Kayakqua, where you can buy a kayak if you're so inclined. Diagonally across the corner of Sherbrooke and Rue Guy (which is called Ave. de la Côte-des-Neiges above Sherbrooke), stands the Linton Apartments, built in 1912, another fine example of residences for the carriage trade.

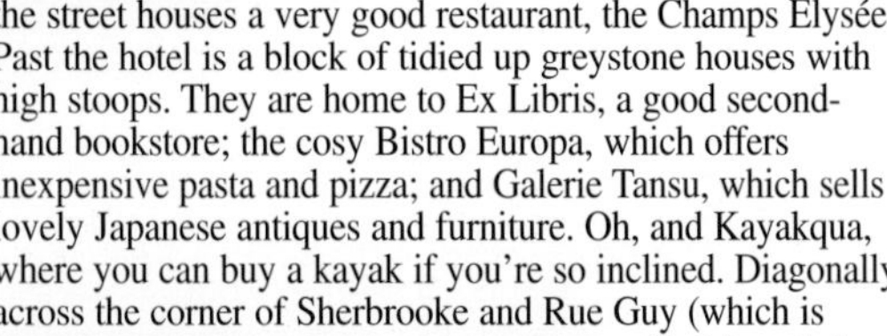

HADDON HALL

GALLERIE TANSU

The streets past Guy that run north from Sherbrooke provide access to the flank of Mount Royal, and some streets end in flights of stairs leading into the treed side of that lofty, benign presence that is Montreal's best-known landmark.

LINTON APARTMENTS

The section of Sherbrooke from Guy to Peel is rife with art galleries and delightful shops, and if you go even just half a block south on any side street you'll come to more boutiques and some very good restaurants. Be sure to be on the lookout for restaurants too, that are tucked into buildings such as Maison Alcan further along.

MAISON ALCAN

On Sherbrooke near Rue Simpson, Bice is a pricey place for Italian food, Première Moisan nearby offers special breads, pastries and gourmet snacks, and Il Cortile, hidden in the Passage du Musée near Rue Mackay, provides good food and atmosphere in a pretty courtyard café. On the north side of Sherbrooke at Redpath is the magnificant Church of St. Andrew and St. Paul — nicknamed the A & P. It is the regimental church of the Black Watch of Canada. On the first Sunday of May the regiment attends the morning service and then marches along Sherbrooke, pipes skirling, to the armoury on Rue Bleury.

The Musée des Beaux-Arts comprises two buildings, one on either side of Sherbrooke. The building on the north side, which houses the museum's permanent collection, opened in 1912; the other, designed by Moshe Safdie and opened in 1991, has garnered mixed reviews but houses excellent exhibitions as well as a boutique full of treasures and books devoted to fine art. Just past the museum is the Romanesque Erskine and American Church. The building dates from 1894 and has 18 Louis Comfort Tiffany stained-glass windows, transferred from the original Erskine Church and installed in the 1930s.

ERSKINE AND AMERICAN CHURCH

On the south side of the street along to Rue de la Montagne are haute-couture boutiques such as Chanel and the posh confines of Holt Renfrew, for expensive, chic clothes and accessories. Holt Mens offers deluxe shopping too. Across the street, the Château Apartments provide shelter for the well to do. The Ritz-Carlton Hotel stands proudly in the next block, with its garden restaurant open in summer. Nearby, the august bulk of the Mount Royal Club provides a less public

refuge for members of the establishment. Maison Alcan was once a hotel and now houses boutiques, offices and a restaurant, Brûlerie St-Denis, which serves bistro-style fare and a vast assortment of coffees in an inner courtyard graced with colourful wall hangings. On the north side, near Rue Stanley, Chez Georges serves French cuisine, steaks and fish; in summer its pretty terrace provides green niches and an elevated view of the passers-by.

Ritz Carleton Hotel

Further along, past the corner of Rue Peel, the campus of McGill University begins, with a sweep of lawn above the Roddick Gates. The university was founded in 1821 through a bequest of funds and 46 acres from wealthy landowner James McGill. The university is internationally renowned, especially in life sciences, architecture, music and law. The quadrangle, a welcoming space at any time, borders on Sherbrooke and is surrounded by buildings of various styles. In summer huge old trees shelter the grass, provinding a lounging spot for students and anyone else who wants to enjoy tranquillity amid the bustle of the city. Beyond the buildings of the university to the north are the Victorian Gothic towers of the Royal Victoria Hospital and the castle-evoking turrets of the city reservoir. The campus is a grand place to stroll, especially in autumn when the leaves are turning or on a snowy winter evening at dusk. There are often concerts during the school year in Redpath Hall on the west side of the grounds.

Statue of James McGill

Look south of the university's Roddick Gates and you'll see wide Ave. McGill College leading to busy Rue Ste-Catherine. In summer the mall is blossom bright, and in winter the trees are festooned with tiny lights and a huge Christmas tree graces the plaza of Place Ville-Marie.

Paragraph Bookstore, at the corner of Sherbrooke and McGill College, contains a good selection of reading material and a café. It's popular with downtowners and both local and visiting literati. Look carefully at the houses east of Ave. McGill College and you will see that they provide the façade of a tall office building. Their formal ornamentation is a sharp contrast to the latter's strong angular modern lines — the old and deservedly treasured fronting the new. Further east on the south side of Sherbrooke is the McCord Museum, housing many artifacts pertaining to Montreal's history and a small boutique where you can pick up something reminiscent of the city. Exhibitions here focus on Montreal's social history and are worth a visit.

Just past the corner of University and near the end of this little tour is Royal Victoria College, home to McGill University's faculty of music. Check the daily newspaper for concerts here (presented in Pollock Hall) — from chamber music to jazz. That quirky juxtaposition reflects Sherbrooke blue-blood past and stylish present, its delights and diversions.

St-Laurent & St-Denis

Catherine Boucek

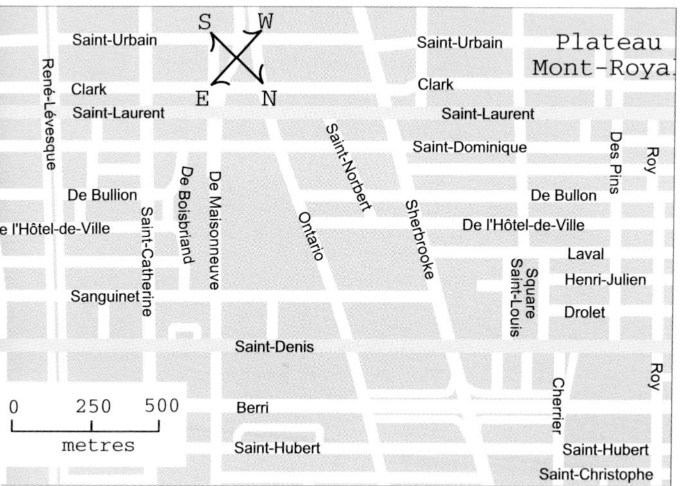

Blvd. St-Laurent is the traditional dividing line between Montreal's two solitudes — the French community to the east and the English community to the west. At least that's the way it's usually described. But of course no city divides quite as neatly as that, and St-Laurent itself is a multicoloured strip that has been home to just about every ethnic wave that has swept over Montreal since the immigration boom of the 1800s. Its denizens speak Cantonese, Yiddish, Portuguese, Greek, Spanish, Italian and Thai. Polish sausage shops and Latin salsa bars share street space with noodle restaurants and posh French restaurants.

St-Laurent begins where Montreal began, at the Vieux-Port, but its first few blocks pass through one of the duller parts of the old city, and the street doesn't really get interesting until it cuts its way along the eastern edge of Montreal's small but vibrant Chinatown.

Start your trek at Rue Viger, and try to time your walk to coincide with lunch, when the bustle is at its peak and you can stop to sample some Chinese delicacies. Restaurants, grocery stores and shops line Rue de la Gauchetière — a pedestrian mall just off St-Laurent. A good place to stop and people-watch is

Chinatown

LATIN QUARTER, ST-DENIS

the zen-like Dr. Sun Yat Sen Park at the corner of de la Gauchetière and Clark. One of Montreal's most famous restaurants is just north of Chinatown, in the seamy strip of stores, strip clubs, peep shows and nightclubs that line St-Laurent between Blvd. Réné-Lévesque and Rue Sherbrooke. Although "restaurant" is perhaps too grand a word for the Montreal Pool Room, a small, badly lit hole in the wall that doesn't even have pool tables any more. Its fame and fortune rest on its "stimés," a soggy delicacy created by stuffing a steamed weiner in a steamed bun and covering it with onions, mustard and coleslaw. Served with "frites" (french fries) and a Coke, this meal is the stuff of legend.

North of Blvd. de Maisonneuve at 2111 St-Laurent is the International Museum of Humour, which grew out of Montreal's Just For Laughs comedy festival — the largest comedy festival in the world. The museum focuses on the history of humour and it might be well worth checking out whatever exhibit might be on or catching a comedy act in the museum's 250-seat cabaret theatre.

Further north, in the stretch between Rue Sherbrooke and Ave. des Pins, are some of the trendiest boutiques, restaurants and bars in Montreal. The languorous and the beautiful haunt this area, showing off the latest fashions. But so do a more humbly attired mix of students, business people and artists, who all congregate in the outdoor cafés and bars. During the day shoppers fill the grocery stores and swish boutiques, and at night the party crowd lines up outside the hot nightclubs, hoping for a nod of approval from the bouncers who guard the doors against the uncool. Just as hot as some of the clubs are the sausage sandwiches at Slovenia, an ideal stop for a snack. If you'd prefer a cool juice, try Granos, a cute little restaurant just north of Rue Prince Arthur.

S.W. WELCH BOOKSELLER

Before you venture any further north, stop to enjoy the ambience of Prince Arthur. Nothing compares to strolling east along this pedestrian thoroughfare on a warm summer evening and stopping at any one of the several Greek restaurants for dinner on the terrace. Most of these restaurants have a bring-your-own-wine policy — meaning they don't have a liquor licence so you have to bring some with you. There's a dépanneur (convenience store) on the strip that sells wine until 11 o'clock at night. Prince Arthur ends at Carré St-Louis a beautiful square surrounded by the comfortable Second Empire homes built in the 19th century to house Montreal's bourgeoisie. The park is a great place to escape the bustle of St-Laurent for a minute or two, sit on a bench and watch the world go by.

In the Main's Portuguese district

Back on St-Laurent, continue north. As you approach Ave. des Pins, swish shops begin to make room for stores whose window displays haven't changed since the 50s. This stretch was once the centre of Jewish life in Montreal. Thousands of immigrants from Romania, Poland and other Eastern European countries moved into the area late in the 19th century, establishing shops, schools and synagogues. This area inspired the book *The Apprenticeship of Duddy Kravitz* by Montreal writer Mordecai Richler. Montreal poets Leonard Cohen and Irving Layton were also inspired by the colourful character of St-Laurent. Much of the Jewish community has dispersed to more affluent neighbourhoods, but the legacy of that era lives on. La Vieille Europe just up from Ave. des Pins, for example, is an authentic Central European grocery store rich with the smell of cheese, salami, loose tea and sweets. Next door, at Warsaw, a grocery-cum-housewares store, visitors can wander through aisles displaying canned goods, wicker furniture and knick knacks. Don't let the messiness dissuade you; bargains can be found here — it's a treasure hunt. Across the street, St. Lawrence Bakery sells crusty European sourdough breads, pastries and sweet rolls. Try the sticky cinnamon rolls. Perhaps the most famous eatery on the block is Schwartz Hebrew Delicatessen. If it's too crowded, you can always head across the street to the Main Restaurant for equally good — some say better — smoked meat. Moishe's, perhaps Montreal's most famous steak house, is next door to Schwartz's.

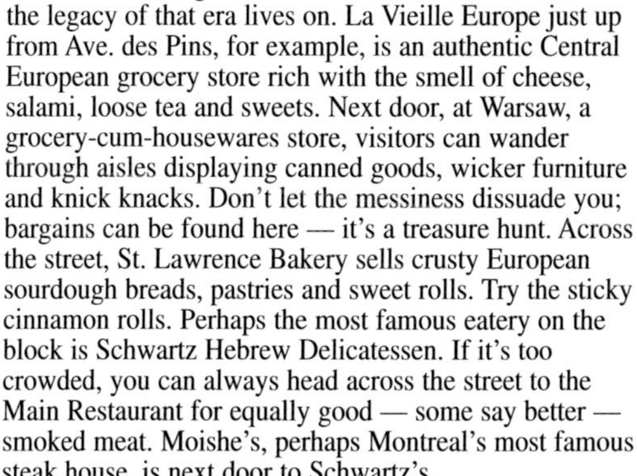

S.W. Welch Bookseller is a cosy place to flip through rare and second-hand titles.

At the corner of Marie-Anne and St-Laurent is a beautiful little blue-tiled park where old men gather to talk and children come with their mothers to play. This is the heart of the Main's Portuguese district. But like most other parts of St-Laurent this isn't the exclusive jurisdiction of any one ethnic group. Portuguese tapas restaurants and grocery stores rub shoulders with places like Bagel Etc., a trendy bagel eatery and favourite of night owls.

Several blocks north of Ave. Mont-Royal you'll find a handful of reasonably priced Indian restaurants between Laurier and St-Viateur, as well as an assortment of Italian, Thai and other choices. Puca-Puca, just south of St-Viateur, is a large, lively and inexpensive Peruvian restaurant popular among area residents.

Much further north, if your feet aren't too sore (or if you'd rather take the No. 55 bus), is Little Italy and more consolation for your stomach. Stop off at Fruiterie Milano and browse the selections of pasta, cheese, antipasto and sweets that make this the best Italian grocery in town.

This is where the locals go to shop. If the weather's nice don't miss Marché Jean-Talon, Montreal's largest outdoor produce market. Growers set up their kiosks in the square, while bakeries, butcher shops and restaurants line the streets around.

Now you could take the Métro back downtown, but why not get off at the Laurier station, walk west a block or two and explore Rue St-Denis? Whereas St-Laurent still shows its working-class roots, St-Denis is all European elegance. Stop off for a bite at the Galaxie Diner at the corner of Rue Gilford. This shiny retro diner was trucked in from Boston and restored. It serves the usual burgers, fries and deli fare. Or stay on the Métro until you come to Mont-Royal Station. From Ave. Mont-Royal south to Rue Sherbrook, St-Denis is a mix of high-priced boutiques, gourmet restaurants and trendy shops. If browsing and shopping are your pleasure, there's no place like this.

Latin Quarter, St-Denis

Don't miss Essence du Papier between rues Rachel and Duluth for beautiful stationery, journals, fancy pens and other writing implements. Zone is a whimsical two-storey housewares boutique. You can find everything from chandeliers to shower curtains. It's all cutting-edge stylish and often affordable.

Below Rue Sherbrook the street takes on another look. This is where students from the nearby Université du Québec à Montreal hang out. The result is predictable — lots of bars and coffee shops.

Just below Blvd. de Maisonneuve at the National Film Board of Canada, seeing the move of your choice is a piece of cake. A robot selects the video disc and puts it in the player. All you have to do is relax in your comfortable viewing chair. Movies are also shown in the 140-seat theatre.

Student life along St-Denis

Excursions

Sarah Waters

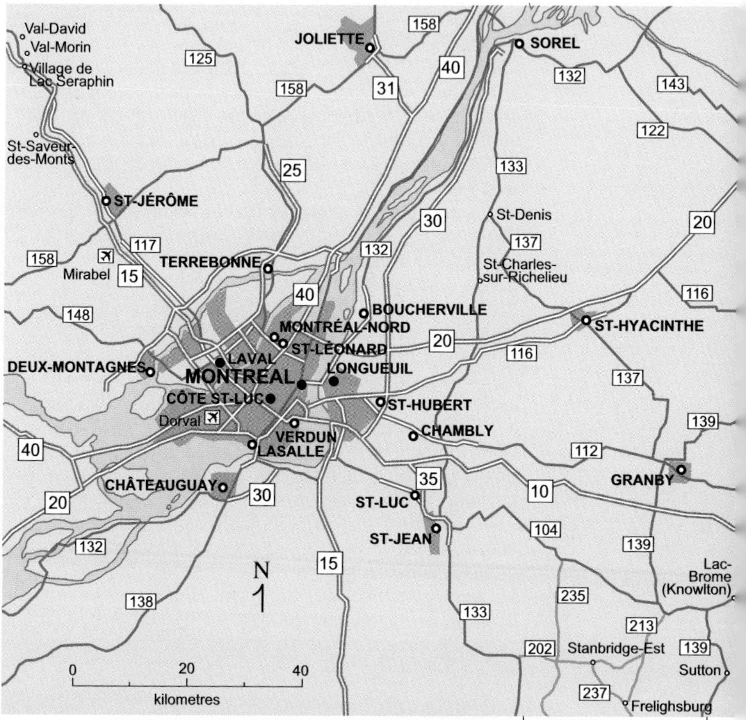

One of the surprising things about Montreal is just how easy it is to get out of it. You can drive for days in places like Toronto and still be surrounded by suburban sprawl. Drive for just 20 minutes and you're out of Montreal and in rolling countryside, two hours and you're in the wilderness of the northern Laurentians — if the traffic's flowing on the bridges, that is. The choice of day trips is pretty extensive.

Forts and Patriots

One of the simplest and best excursions is to drive downriver to Sorel and then follow the Richelieu river south through some of the province's richest farmlands and orchards to the American border at Lacolle. The valley is not only rich agriculturally. The Richelieu was one of the most important waterways of New France. It led to the rich trading areas around Lake Champlain and the Hudson River and was much coveted by the European powers vying for hegemony in the region — France, Britain and Holland. As a result, the valley is also rich in history.

Entrance to Fort Lennox

You could start your journey with a cruise of the Sorel islands, an enchanting little archipelago in the St. Lawrence that's alive with waterfowl and fish. But that would take at least a couple of hours and if time is limited it might be best to start south through the valley. Follow Highway 133 toward Chambly. This route is sometimes called the Chemin des Patriotes (Patriots' Road) in honour of the men and women who joined Louis-Joseph Papineau in the 1837 rebellion against imperial rule. The rebels fought two important battles in the valley — they faced down the British at St-Denis-sur-Richelieu and were driven off in a skirmish at St-Charles-sur-Richelieu.

There are many reminders of the revolt along the road. The route is marked with signs bearing the image of an armed rebel in tuque and a ceinture fléchée (a colourful woven sash), and just outside St-Denis-sur-Richelieu at 610 Chemin des Patriotes, (450-787-3623) is an early-19th-century home that is now Maison Nationale des Patriotes. Exhibits and audio visual shows — in French only — recount the rebellion and the battles. In St-Denis itself the insurgents' green, white and red tricolour flies over a monument erected in their honour in 1987. The nearby church has twin towers, one of which houses the liberty bell that called the rebels to battle. The next landmark is a natural one — Mont St-Hilaire, a steep, 1,300-foot peak that soars abruptly out of the rolling countryside. Its lower slopes are covered with apple orchards and its upper reaches are heavily forested. Most of the mountain belongs to McGill University but an area of about six square kilometres is open to the public. You

FORT CHAMBLY

can park your car halfway up the mountain and follow a series of paths to the summit for sweeping views of the valley and Montreal. The mountain was once the estate of Andrew Hamilton Gault (1882–1958), who founded Princess Patricia's Canadian Light Infantry.

Further upriver lies Chambly, an important trading and defence centre during the French regime. Captain Jacques de Chambly built the first French fort here in 1665 to defend Montreal against Indian and later British attack. The stone successor of that humble wooden stockade still guards the Chambly rapids, the northernmost of a series of military strongholds along the river. Fort Chambly (450-658-1585) has been restored to its 18th-century appearance and stands in a pleasant park by the river. It serves as an interpretation centre with displays and programs illustrating military and farming life in the 18th and 19th centuries.

Chambly is also the northern end of the Chambly canal (450-658-6525), a 19-kilometre waterway that skirts a series of rapids and leads to the industrial city of St-Jean-sur-Richelieu. Today it's used only by pleasure craft and the towpath has been converted into a pleasant bicycle path. From Chambly the road heads south through St-Jean-sur-Richelieu to the next fort on the route — Fort Lennox (450-291-5700), which was built by the British in 1802. It sits on an island — Île-aux-Noix — in the middle of the river, and as if that weren't enough water protection, a wide moat surrounds its star-shaped fortifications. Displays and costumed actors capture the tough life of a 19th-century British regular on colonial duty. The last fort on the river is the two-storey blockhouse at Lacolle, which is still pocked with bullet holes from the War of 1812.

BARRACKS INTERIOR AT FORT LENNOX

Not all the valley's attractions are military. The surrounding countryside is full of orchards and many growers make their own ciders, which you can stop and sample. Many of the village churches are quite beautiful, and are decorated by some of Quebec's leading artists. The ones in St-Hilaire and St-Matthias are especially worth visiting.

NORTHERN PLAYGROUND

The Laurentian Mountains have been Montreal's backyard for decades. Attempts in the late 19th and early 20th centuries to settle these low-lying rocky hills didn't work out very well — the soil was often too thin for farming — but the region found its real wealth in recreation.

The hills, lakes and rivers of the region attract hikers, hunters, fishermen, canoeists, kayakers, cross-country skiers and mountain-bikers, not to mention artists and photographers. Downhill skiing in Canada can trace its roots to the Laurentians, which

LAURENTIAN COLOUR

had the country's first mechanical lifts. And just in case all these natural pastimes aren't enough, entrepreneurs have filled the valleys with golf courses, go-cart tracks, bungee towers and a dizzying array of bars, boutiques and fine restaurants.

MONT-ROLLAND ON THE P'TIT TRAIN DU NORD

One of the best ways to explore the region is on two wheels. Parc du P'tit Train du Nord — Quebec's longest bicycle trail — follows an abandoned railway line from St-Jérôme 200 kilometres north to Mont Laurier. Its gentle

SAINT-SAUVEUR-DES-MONTS

grade takes cyclists through some of the region's prettiest countryside and most charming villages. The 20-kilometre stretch between St-Sauveur and Ste-Agathe is thick with restaurants, cafés and bed & breakfasts as well as Laurentian scenery. Further north, the landscape gets wilder and the bicycle traffic thinner. North of Labelle, you

EN ROUTE ALONG THE P'TIT TRAIN DU NORD

can cycle for miles with just the birds for company.

But the car-bound can explore the Laurentians as well. A good place to start is St-Sauveur-des-Monts, which was once a simple ski village with a single hotel, a couple of watering holes and a few restaurants. It has developed into a major resort choked with condos and trendy bars that throb with life all year round. Traffic on the main street in July, when the sidewalks are full of stylish diners and shoppers, can be as thick as it is on Rue Ste-Catherine in Montreal. This might not sound like much of a wilderness escape, but it is an exciting place to be. The frenetic pace eases considerably as you drive north on Highway 117.

From Ste-Agathe the road snakes through Val Morin and Val David, villages every bit as attractive as St Sauveur, surrounded as they are by hills and lakes. They too have their pleasant little restaurants and bars, plus a couple of first-class inns, Val Morin and Val David have somehow escaped the feverish development that has marked the recent history of their more southerly neighbour.

MONT-TREMBLANT RESORT

Follow Highway 117 to St-Jovite and then take Highway 327 to the Mont Tremblant ski resort. Mont Tremblant, with a vertical drop of 2,131 feet, is the highest mountain in the Laurentians, and it was legendary travel writer and ski buff Lowell Thomas who first suggested turning it into a ski hill. It has had its struggles since then, but in September 1991 it was bought by Intrawest, the company that developed Blackcomb on the west coast. Intrawest has since spent billions of dollars turning the mountain into a year-round resort. It has opened new ski trails and added a gondola and several high-speed chairlifts. It has also built a spectacular golf course, opened

a couple of resort hotels and re-created a miniature version of Quebec City at the base of the mountain. Mountain bikers use the lifts and ski trails in summer, and thousands of leaf-peepers ride the chairs to the top every fall for endless vistas of gold and crimson hills. The resort is also the setting of a summer blues festival and classical music concerts (1-800-461-8711).

MONT-TREMBLANT PROVINCIAL PARK

Beyond the resort, the road turns into Mont Tremblant provincial park (819-688-2281), a 1,500-square-kilometre wilderness of rivers, lakes and mountains. The road, which is closed in winter, follows the Rivière Diable (Devil's River), a well-named waterway punctuated with falls and rapids. The scenery here is some of the most wildly beautiful in Quebec. Well worth a stop are Chute du Diable (Devil's Falls) and Chute aux Rats (Muskrat Falls) and there's a beautiful beach on Lac Monroe. The park has hiking trails and facilities for canoeists and campers.

From St-Donat-de-Montcalm, take Highway 329 south to Ste-Agathe and from there follow Highway 117 or Highway 15 (the Laurentian Autoroute) back to Montreal.

LOYALIST COUNTRY

After the American Revolution, colonists who wished to remain loyal to the British Crown fled north to Canada and settled in parts of Quebec, New Brunswick and Ontario. They brought with them their language, their Protestant faith and their culture. In Quebec they were allowed to establish townships in the great chunk of land along the American border between the Richelieu and Chaudière rivers. This was unsettled land beyond the reach of the French parishes. Its gently rolling countryside punctuated by the northern reaches of the Appalachian Mountains made it ideal for farming and the new settlers prospered.

CANTONS DE L'EST

The area is now known as the Eastern Townships (Cantons del'Est, or Estrie) and its towns and villages look more like New England than New France. They're full of fine brick and clapboard homes built on the British model with central hallways and formal front rooms. But that look is deceiving. The Loyalist pioneers and the British and American settlers who followed them into this rich and fertile land are now outnumbered by their French neighbours. The blend, however, is harmonious. Townshippers of both cultures can usually switch from one language to the other with ease and agility.

One way to get a taste of this varied and beautiful region is to drive east on Highway 10 (the Eastern Townships Autoroute) to Exit 90 and then follow Highway 243 south along the shores of Lac Brome to Knowlton, a pleasant 19th-century town full of fine brick buildings. The streets are lined with boutiques and restaurants, and there is a summer theatre that specializes in English-language comedies and mysteries. The lakeshore is lined with mansions that are the summer homes of Montreal's elite.

HIKING IN THE CANTONS DE L'EST

From Knowlton follow Highways 104 and 215 to Sutton, another pretty little Loyalist town, but the homes here are mostly white clapboard with wrap-around verandhas and fanciful towers and gables. Its main street, too, has an assortment of restaurants and boutiques. Just outside town is Mont Sutton, a major ski resort whose lifts offer fall and summer visitors a great way to view the surrounding countryside.

From Sutton drive west on Highway 237 through Frelighsburg, a beautiful village of brick homes cupped in the Pike River valley, to Stanbridge East, a good place to stop for a picnic. The village doesn't offer much in the way of restaurants, but it does have a delightful little Anglican church and an old grist mill, general store and barn that are now a museum of pioneer life (450-248-3153). The land across the river from the mill has been turned into a wonderful little park.

From Stanbridge turn east again on Highway 202 and drive through Quebec's wine country to Dunham.

ANTIQUES IN KNOWLTON

Mountains protect this gentle piece of land from the northern winds and capture the southern sun, creating a microclimate warm enough to make the growing of grapes just possible. Most of the vineyards along the road sell their produce in on-site boutiques and some have little wine bars and even restaurants.

From Dunham you can follow Highways 202 and 139 north back to the Autoroute and home to Montreal.

OTHER SUGGESTED DAY TRIPS

Terrebonne, a pretty little town on the Mille-Îles river north of Montreal, is in the heart of a fertile farming area. Its wealth, however, comes from the river, which 19th-century merchants harnessed to power grist and flour mills to process grain and sawmills to cut lumber. Much of this heritage is preserved on Île des Moulins, a kind of industrial theme park — carefully preserved flour mills and sawmills as well as Canada's first industrial bakery, built in 1802 to supply hard biscuit for voyageurs and trappers. The old seigneurial office serves as an interpretation centre and the "new mill," built in 1850, houses a theatre, a cultural centre and an art gallery. This is all open from mid-May to Labour Day. (450-471-0619).

The industrial town of Trois-Rivières sits at the confluence of the St. Lawrence and Mauricie rivers. (The Mauricie splits into three channels just before it empties into the St. Lawrence, hence the town's misleading name.) Its chief industry is pulp and paper and the odour of sulphur often hangs heavy in the air, but the visitor who overcomes that will find much to charm. Trois-Rivières is older than Montreal and its historic section is full of 18th- and 19th-century treasures.

MISSISQUOI MUSEUM IN STANBRIDGE EAST

QUEBEC CITY'S BEST

QUEBEC CITY'S TOP ATTRACTIONS

SARAH WATERS

THE TERRASSE DUFFERIN

"I would rather be a poor priest in Quebec [City] than a rich hog merchant in Chicago"

— English poet Matthew Arnold (1822–88)

There are many who might challenge Matthew Arnold's implied criticism of Chicago, but few would disagree with his praise for Quebec City. It is truly one of the most dramatic and most beautiful of North American cities. It's also one of the oldest, and beauty and history are a potent mix when it comes to entrancing visitors.

Most people arrive in Quebec City by car, usually from the west, driving through a dreary wasteland of suburbs, industrial buildings and snarling freeways. Not the most promising approach, but probably the most efficient. If you can manage it, though, arrive by train. That way you alight in Quebec City's magnificent old château-like station, which is within strolling distance of the old city and the waterfront. Check your bags, then head for the docks and take the ferry to Lévis. It costs $3 return for a foot passenger and the trip is worth every nickel. Try not to look behind you on the way out. That way you can pretend on the way back that you're arriving in Quebec City for the first time by boat — the absolute-best way to approach it.

LÉVIS FERRY

A couple of things make this a dramatic experience. First, the river narrows sharply at Quebec, from a broad expanse of more than a kilometre of brown and slightly brackish water to a stream just a few hundred metres wide — small enough to be covered by cannon fire. In fact, the city's name comes from a Huron word meaning "where the river narrows." And then there's the 100-metre sheer cliff of Cap Diamant that splits the city horizontally into two.

If you have time and money, you don't have to fake this marine approach. A few cruise ships make regular stops in Quebec City, especially in the fall when they bring passengers up the St. Lawrence River to oohh and ahhh at the fall colours, but that's a limited option.

THE FUNICULAR

One thing you get from the river is a kind of two-level history lesson. On top of Cap Diamant are the walls and turrets of Haute-Ville or Upper Town. At the foot along the river's edge are the narrow streets and tall stone houses of Basse-Ville or Lower Town. Just before the Conquest, the governors, priests and army commanders lived in Haute-Ville. The merchants, tradesmen and labourers (as well as the thieves and hookers) scrabbled for a living with varying degrees of success down on the riverfront in Basse-Ville. After the Conquest, nothing changed much, except that Haute-Ville aged gracefully and Basse-Ville degenerated into an industrial slum, a state from which it was rescued only a couple of decades ago.

Today the two areas are connected by several streets (avoid them), 28 stone staircases (use them for going down) and the funicular, a kind of outdoor elevator that delivers an easy ride up and great views of the river for just $1.

Haute-Ville is of course the more famous of the two towns. It's the one with the walls and the cannons and most of the restaurants and sidewalk cafés. It's full of nooks and crannies and tiny laneways that shoot off at unexpected angles. It's like something Walt Disney might have designed, except that when Disney designed something he generally took the reality out. Quebec doesn't. Those quaint cobbled streets are jammed every day with cars, pedestrians and horse-drawn calèches. Dépanneurs (convenience stores) still sell beer and tinned beans from cramped quarters in centuries-old buildings. (No, they haven't all been taken over by trendy restaurants, arty boutiques and souvenir shops

THE CHÂTEAU FRONTENAC

THE GRAND SÉMINAIRE

selling rude T-shirts and cutesy mugs.) And the Château Frontenac, the huge, copper-roofed castle sitting in the middle of all this, belongs not to Cinderella but to Canadian Pacific and is arguably Canada's best-known hotel.

Haute-Ville was the centre of intellectual and religious life during New France's salad days in the 18th century. The Grand Séminaire — Canada's first institution of higher learning, which evolved into Université Laval in the 1850s — was founded in 1663 by Bishop François de Laval. The glittering cathedral once ruled a diocese that stretched as far south as New Orleans.

Quebec City's story, however, really began in Basse-Ville in 1608. The gentry and the clergy moved up the hill later only because they feared English aggression. Cap Diamant was safe, they thought — easier to defend and well out of the range of the Royal Navy's guns. But Samuel de Champlain built New France's first permanent settlement on the flats between the cliffs and the river. Under the French regime the area became the centre of commercial life in the colony. Later, in 1686, the colonists erected a bust of Louis XIV, the Sun King, in the great cobbled square and Place du Marché became Place Royale. This was the first area in Basse-Ville to be rescued from centuries of squalour. The 17th- and 18th-century homes have been restored, the altar in the church of Notre-Dame-des-Victoires once again glitters with gilt and fresh paint, and in the summertime musicians and dancers perform near the Sun King's bust.

PLACE ROYALE

Just to the west, on the thin strip of land between Cap Diamant and the ferry docks, is the Quartier Petit-Champlain. It too was once a slum, its narrow streets lined with decaying buildings that dated back to the 17th and 18th centuries. But it too has been rescued. The cobblestones have been cleaned up, the old homes sand-blasted back to respectability, and it looks much as it did in the 18th century, except that the lighting's better and so are the drains. In one of those beautifully

CANNON ON TERRASSE DUFFERIN

restored homes you can get on the funicular at the end of a long day and ride slowly back to the lordly heights of Terrasse Dufferin.

CALÈCHE

Several bus companies offer tours of Basse-Ville and Haute-Ville, but as long as you're healthy you're much better off exploring the old city on foot. The buses — even the mini-buses — have trouble navigating the narrow streets, especially in summer when the streets are crowded. Frankly they're also a bit of an eyesore. The horse-drawn carriages that line up outside the Château Frontenac and just inside the Porte St-Louis fit in better with their surroundings and, to those with a sense of romance are worth their rather steep price. Incidentally, everyone — tourists and local residents alike — call these vehicles calèches, although most of them are in fact victorias. A true calèche has only two wheels. But the only transportation aids you'll need as long as you're reasonably fit are a pair of sturdy shoes and a good map. Stop in the tourist-information centre on Place d'Armes across from the Château Frontenac to pick up a guide and check out the schedules for things like the son-et-lumière shows at Cathédrale Notre-Dame and in Basse-Ville. Then take the Casse-Cou (Breakneck) stairs down to Basse-Ville.

ESCALIER CASSE-COU

If you're a determined walker, you can probably cover Basse-Ville in a day, even with a ferry ride and a leisurely browse through the antique shops along rues St-Paul and St-Pierre and a visit to the church of Notre-Dame-des-Victoires, Place Royale and the farmer's market on the waterfront. But it would be more practical to set aside a day and a half if you plan even a modestly long stop at the Musée de la Civilisation.

A thorough exploration of Haute-Ville could take considerably longer. Visitors should tour the cathedral, the Château Frontenac, the walls and the Citadelle. Throw in an absolutely mandatory stroll along Terrasse Dufferin and you've still barely scratched the surface. There's still the Anglican Trinity Cathedral, the Grand Séminaire du Québec and the Monastère des Ursulines with its chapel and museum. And no exploration of the city should stop at the walls. Stroll west on Grande-Allée beyond the Porte St-Louis and you can get a feel for Canada's precarious future. On your left is the magnificent expanse of the Plains of Abraham where Canada's ethnic conundrum began, and on your right is the Second Empire grandeur of the Hôtel du Parlement, where Quebec's Assemblée Nationale might very well end it.

MONASTÈRE DES URSULINES

Heritage & Architecture

Sovita Chander

The Walls of Quebec

You can't turn around in Quebec City without bumping into a story about the past. After all, this is where French colonists staked their first permanent settlement in the New World. Consequently the city possesses a unique architectural heritage dating from its founding in the early 17th century. Most remarkably, much of this heritage is intact. For instance, it is the only city north of Mexico to have preserved its military fortifications, which comprises a wall surrounding Vieux-Québec (the old city). Practically all 11 square kilometres of the old city and beyond has a monument, building, park or residence with something to say. Some shout their visual wares, beckoning travellers with grandiose façades and far-flung reputations. Others sit squarely, solidly, stating their place in the history of everyday life. The rest whisper, yielding their rewards only through patient inquiry and observation.

Notre-Dame-des-Victoires

Quebec City's history, and even prehistory, begins in what is now known as Basse-Ville, or Lower Town, along the banks of the St. Lawrence. And the heart of Basse-Ville, historically speaking, is Place Royale, which has been an important commercial site for at least 2,000 years. Indians used it first, as a trading post, part of a vast network that covered all North America. When Jacques Cartier sailed up the St. Lawrence River in 1534 he landed near the site and found the Iroquois village of Stadacona, a thriving settlement of 500 souls. The Iroquois were gone when Samuel de Champlain arrived in 1608 to establish the first French settlement and open trade with the Indians. Europeans were eager to establish a fur trade for a simple yet lucrative reason: fashion. Beaver fur made a luxuriously fine felt for the men's hats that were de rigueur for much of the period.

There's nothing left of Champlain's original settlement. Fire destroyed much of it in 1682 and colonial and religious officials built a church dedicated to the Virgin Mary — now called Notre-Dame-des-Victoires — on the ruins. The parishioners of the settlement had long petitioned the Church for a place of worship in Basse-Ville, for the trip to the cathedral in Haute-Ville was arduous in wintertime.

NOTRE-DAME-DES-VICTOIRES, INTERIOR

Looking beyond Notre-Dame-des-Victoires, we find the rest of Place Royale, which became the trading hub of New France and was where merchants lived and worked. During the British regime (from the Conquest in 1759 until Canadian Confederation in 1867) Place Royale continued to function as a commercial centre, particularly during the Napoleonic Wars. With Baltic supplies of timber cut off by Napoleon, the British navy turned to their North American colonies for shipbuilding materials. After the wars Quebec City merchants and shipbuilders continued to play a key role in the domestic economy, and in time Quebec City came to have the largest port in British North America. Until the 1860s, when shipbuilders began turning from wood to steel, Place Royale was at the heart of the economy of the city and the colony. From the 1860s on, the square served local needs, remaining a marketplace. Over the course of the 20th century the area declined and Place Royale faded away into a mere shadow of its former self. In 1950 the Quebec government began work on rediscovering and re-establishing this heritage site. Over the next 15 years extensive work by archeologists, historians and museum professionals returned Place Royale to its former place as a vibrant public space.

The information centre for Place Royale, Maison Thibaudeau at 215 Rue March-Finlay (418-643-6631) is also an annex of the Musée de la Civilisation. This is a relative latecomer to the Place Royale.

MAISON THIBAUDEAU

The prominent Quebec City architect Joseph Ferdinand Peachy constructed what was originally known as the Thibaudeau Building in 1880, when it was one of the largest warehouses in the district. Guided tours are available year-round (reservations are required out of season), as is detailed information about the surrounding buildings and displays. Interesting sites include Maison Chevalier, featuring a display of 17th- and 18th-century domestic life; Maison Paradis, featuring artisans displaying work and demonstrating techniques; and Parc de l'UNESCO, a small playground built when UNESCO declared the old city a world heritage site, featuring structures based on a maritime theme.

TOP: MAISON CHEVALIER
MIDDLE: MAISON CHEVALIER, INTERIOR

From Place Royale you can easily walk to Rue du Petit-Champlain, the first street in Quebec City. In the 17th and 18th centuries this narrow lane was the main street of the town, with businesses and residences lining each side. Nowadays, after the 1977 revival of the street and surrounding neighbourhood by artisans and business people, you can find high-quality crafts made in Québécois, Native and Inuit traditions. From Petit-Champlain, you can cut across to Rue Dalhousie where the Lévis-Québec ferry docks. The ferry itself may not be of historic interest, but it does offer a spectacular view of old Quebec. In winter, the ride turns into suitable entertainment for children (and some adults), as they watch the boat glide through the ice floes. Although the chunks of ice are blasted down to a safe, navigable size, they are still large enough to awe.

RUE PETIT-CHAMPLAIN

Further along at 85 Dalhousie is the Musée de la Civilisation, the province's main ethnographic museum. It was designed by architect Moshe Safdie to echo the heritage of Quebec City. Three historic buildings were integrated into the museum: Maison Estèbe, Maison Pagé-Quercy and the site of the First Bank of Quebec. Maison Estèbe and Maison Pagé-Quercy were both built after 1750 by local merchants for use as their residences; at the time, merchants would have stored their goods at home. The

ESCALIER CASSE-COU

Bank of Quebec was founded in 1818, but the original building, not to mention the bank itself, had long since disappeared by the time the museum was built. The terraced waterfall at the main entrance makes reference to the city's natural landmarks — the river and the cliff. Lastly, the bell tower, or campanile, evokes the church steeples scattered throughout the old city.

From Basse-Ville, there are two picturesque ways to reach Haute-Ville, or Upper Town. The first is to walk up the Escalier Casse-Cou (Breakneck Stairs), one of the more than 20 staircases that link Haute-Ville and Basse-Ville. The stairs, which are as steep as their name suggests, ascend from Rue du Petit-Champlain. The ironwork was constructed in 1893, designed by the architect Charles Baillairgé (who was descended from a prominent Quebec City family of master builders and architects going back to the previous century), but the staircase has been in use since the 17th century. From these stairs, you have to walk another couple of hundred metres uphill along the Côte de la Montagne. If this sounds intimidating, you have a second option: the funicular, or cable car, which was renovated in the late 1990s. The lower station is at 16 Petit-Champlain and is known as Maison Louis-Jolliet. The house was built in 1683 by Louis Jolliet, the first European to reach the Mississippi River. The upper station opens onto Terrasse Dufferin, built in 1878 and named for the governor-general of Canada in 1872–78. Lord Dufferin persuaded city officials to launch the beautification project that ended up preserving the fortified walls surrounding the city.

JARDIN DES GOUVERNEURS

The multilayered, copper-roofed structure adjacent to Terrasse Dufferin is the Château Frontenac. This landmark was built in 1893 as a luxury hotel by the Canadian Pacific Railway. The site had previously housed several generations of governors under both French and British regimes. Up the hill from Terrasse Dufferin is the Jardin des Gouverneurs, flanked by the Château Frontenac and two residential streets. Originally enclosed and part of the governor's residence during the 18th century, it is now a

Séminaire du Quebec

public park. The Wolfe-Montcalm monument at the entrance to the park commemorates the generals of both sides in the 1759 Conquest, when the colony passed from French to British hands. From this location you can head in a number of different directions to see several key religious structures.

When religion played a greater role in public life, these buildings were important symbols of status, power and prestige. The cathedral of the Roman Catholic archbishop of Quebec is the Basilique Notre-Dame-de-Québec at 16 Rue de Buade. The original church was built in 1647, but one look will tell you that this is not a 17th-century structure. The church has been rebuilt several times, most recently in 1922 after a fire. The Ursuline convent at 12 Rue Donnacona houses the Ursuline nuns, a teaching order. They run the oldest private girls' school in North America, founded in 1639. Much of the grounds are off-limits to visitors, but you can visit the chapel and the museum. Holy Trinity Anglican Cathedral at 31 Rue des Jardins was built in 1804 to serve the spiritual needs of the English elite. Captain William Hall and Major William Robe, both of the Royal Artillery, designed the cathedral in the classical tradition embodied by two London churches, St. Martin-in-the-Fields and Marylebone Chapel, both by architect James Gibbs. (Many colonial builders were inspired by Gibbs's 1728 Book of Architecture, in which he published his technical drawings.)

The Séminaire du Québec at 2 Côte de la Fabrique is a vast assembly of buildings that used to house Université Laval before it moved to the suburb of Ste-Foy. The seminary was founded in 1663 by Quebec's first bishop, François de Laval, to train priests locally; it is oldest post-secondary teaching institution in North America. At least two portions of the complex are of interest to visitors. The first, the Vieux-Séminaire, is made up three wings — the Aile de la Procure, the Aile de la Congrégation and the Aile des Parloirs — that date from the late 17th century with some portions rebuilt over the course of the 19th century. The other site worth a visit is the Musée de l'Amérique Française, which comprises four seminary buildings; the entrance is located at 9 Rue de l'Université. The museum, which is now affiliated with the Musée de la Civilisation, is home to a collection of religious artifacts, including rare 18th- and 19th-century silver objects from England, France and Quebec. Also part of the museum is the seminary's Chapelle Extérieure, which was deconsecrated in 1992. Many

Musée de l'Amérique Française

original features of the late-19th-century reconstruction of the chapel, including the spectacular trompe-l'oeil ceiling and stained-glass windows, remain in excellent condition.

Moving west through the old city, we find the Literary and Historical Society of Quebec, founded by Lord Dalhousie in 1824. The society was one of a few institutions to attract both English and French elites to its meetings and lectures. The library of the society also had a surprising number of women among its members. In Victorian times it was rare for proper women of the middle and upper classes to venture beyond the domestic sphere, but lending libraries like this one provided some intellectual stimulation. The society is housed in a former prison completed in 1814. The architect François Baillairgé, an ancestor of the Charles Baillairgé who designed the Breakneck Stairs, constructed the prison in accordance with the enlightened principles of the day, following the ideas of British prison reformer John Howard.

CHAPELLE EXTÉRIEURE AT THE MUSÉE DE L'AMÉRIQUE FRANÇAISE

At the western edge of Haute-Ville, down the hill from the Literary and Historical Society, you will find Parc de l'Artillerie, which provides an ideal introduction to the military history of the city, including detailed information about the fortifications and walls. The fortifications form a 4.6-kilometre wall around Haute-Ville, extending from the Citadelle on the Plains of Abraham to the Prescott gate in the east to the St-Jean, Kent and St-Louis gates to the west.

PORTE ST-LOUIS

The Quebec Arsenal at the main entrance to the park houses a scale model of Quebec City dating from 1808. From the old city, exit at the St-Louis gate and follow the Grande Allée, and you'll find yourself at the parliament buildings. Several buildings and monuments make up this historic site. The imposing main parliament building was completed in 1886, designed by the architect Eugene-Étienne Taché in the French Empire style. The statues surrounding the quadrangle's outer walls are a veritable who's who of Quebec history, ranging from Comte de Frontenac, one of the first governors of New France, to Robert Baldwin, co-premier of the United Canadas in the mid-19th century. The interior is open to the public through guided tours.

PARLIAMENT BUILDING STATUE

Beyond the old city and its impressive adjuncts such as the parliament buildings, there are subtle rewards for

ST. MATTHEW'S CHURCH

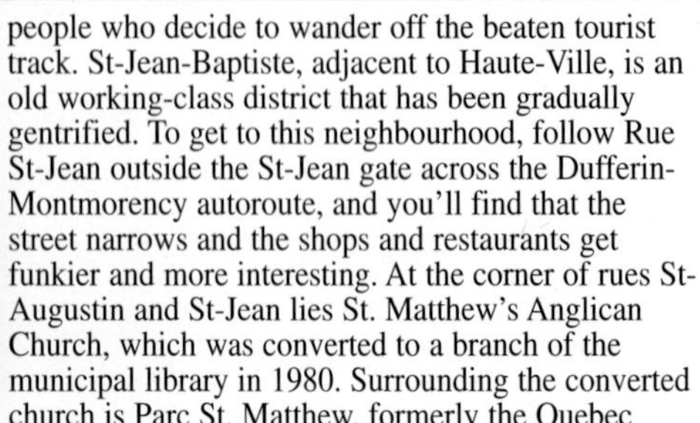

people who decide to wander off the beaten tourist track. St-Jean-Baptiste, adjacent to Haute-Ville, is an old working-class district that has been gradually gentrified. To get to this neighbourhood, follow Rue St-Jean outside the St-Jean gate across the Dufferin-Montmorency autoroute, and you'll find that the street narrows and the shops and restaurants get funkier and more interesting. At the corner of rues St-Augustin and St-Jean lies St. Matthew's Anglican Church, which was converted to a branch of the municipal library in 1980. Surrounding the converted church is Parc St. Matthew, formerly the Quebec Protestant Burying Ground, which was in use from 1771 to 1860. Captain Thomas Scott, the younger brother of Sir Walter Scott, is buried just inside the main entrance. The park is open from May to November.

ÉGLISE ST-JEAN-BAPTISTE

Further along Rue St-Jean, the local Catholic parish church, Église St-Jean-Baptiste, occupies the block between rues Ste-Claire and Deligny. The current building was completed in 1884, designed by Joseph Ferdinand Peachy, after a fire destroyed its predecessor. The ornate exterior, designed in the French Second Empire style, echoes aspects of Parisian churches from the same period. It can accommodate up to 3,000 worshippers. If you wander through the residential part of the neighbourhood, be sure to head down the hill to the martello tower on Rue Lavigeur just to the west of Rue Racine. It is one of the least known, least publicized parts of the fortifications; the interior is not open to the public, but there is a lookout.

A guidebook can get you oriented in Quebec City, but you're sure to discover even more by exploring yourself. You could spend months here and still find surprises at the end of your stay.

MARTELLO TOWER ON RUE LAVIGEUR

Festivals & Events

Sarah Waters

Dogsled races at the Quebec Winter Carnival

Many people in traditionally Catholic countries or regions tend to enter the penitential season of Lent with a hangover and something worth repenting. That's because they've partaken of that grand tradition — the pre-Lenten carnival, or Mardi Gras. This one last, glorious blowout, often lasting a couple of weeks, once prepared the devout to endure the 40 days of fasting and mortification that led up to the glory of Easter.

Lent is less rigorous than it used to be, and not as widely observed even in devout countries, but the Carnival tradition persists. There are street parties, fireworks and parades — often featuring thousands of nubile young women dressed in little more than glitter and spangles — and people eat too much, drink too much, sing too much and pursue romance with commendable vigour. All this is very well in places like New Orleans, Rio de Janeiro and Nice. But Quebec City has managed to create a similar bacchanalia, complete with street parties and parades, in one of the harshest climates in the world.

Dozens of imitators have sprung up across Canada —

Montreal's Fête des Neiges and Ottawa's Winterlude, for example. But Quebec City's is the granddaddy of them all. The first winter carnival was held in 1894. It was a fairly modest event with some religious overtones. But it had a parade, as well as a ball for the elite and street parties for humbler folk. The round of parties and suppers with the occasional sporting event made for a pleasant and heart-warming break in the middle of a brutal winter, and the city continued the tradition sporadically for several decades. But it wasn't until 1955 that the carnival became an annual event, thanks to the members of the city's chamber of commerce who were looking for a way to perk up the anemic midwinter economy and attract some visitors. The chamber beefed up the parade and the balls and came up with the idea of breaking the city into regions represented by duchesses from whose ranks the carnival queen would be selected. The chamber also introduced Bonhomme Carnaval, the event's enduring mascot. He's supposed to be a snowman and his tuque and ceinture fléchée (a colourful woven sash) add a dash of Quebec patriotism.

BONHOMME CARNAVAL

Both Bonhomme and the carnival are enduring symbols of Quebec's hardy resolve to enjoy life, and they continue to brighten the dead of winter with two weeks of parties and sporting events that attract more than 100,000 fun-seekers. That's not to say the carnival hasn't had its problems, but since 1996 the organizers have been making serious efforts to revitalize their big party and clean up its sometimes riotous image. One of the oddest changes has been to the name. The organizers managed to entice one of the world's biggest food companies to climb aboard as a sponsor, so now the party is officially known as the Carnaval de Québec Kellogg's. Is nothing sacred? That means a definite emphasis on good, clean family fun, so, along with the traditional balls and street parties, there are more kid-friendly activities: an ice park on the Plains of Abraham with slides and rides, for example, and junior lessons in ice sculpting. Kellogg's involvement also means that Bonhomme Carnaval, the traditional pudgy snowman with the big smile, has to share the spotlight with characters like Snap, Crackle and Pop. The cereal trio pop up all over the place, and they march in the big parade along with Bonhomme, the carnival queen and brass bands. But most of the traditional events — dogsled races, ice-sculpture contests, boat races across the half-frozen St. Lawrence, ski and snowmobile races, street parties — are still going strong (418-626-3716).

The two other most venerable events on Quebec City's social calendar are the Concours Hippique de Québec (the

Carnival spectacle

Quebec Horse Show) in late June or early July and Expo-Québec, the province's biggest agricultural fair, in August. The horse show is the first event in the equestrian World Cup, and it attracts some of the best horsemen and horsewomen in the country and indeed the world. They gather on the Plains of Abraham behind the armoury for five days of exquisite dressage. This is pretty serious, classical stuff, and a lot of the finer points might well be lost on all but the cognoscenti. But the setting and the steeds are magnificent and the jumping competitions are spectacular.

Expo-Québec (418-691-7110) has been held for more than 50 years and fills the grounds near the Colisée de Québec with prime livestock, especially beef cattle, and agricultural exhibits. It comes with all the usual bells and whistles of a major country fair — a midway, shows and horse-pulling contests. Expo runs in conjunction with the Carrefour Agro-Alimentaire (418-522-8811), a kind of food fair that showcases all the culinary specialties of the region. It includes competitions, demonstrations by some of the province's best chefs and of course tastings.

Middle and bottom: Expo-Québec

A newer event that has grown into the city's biggest party is the summer festival, Festival d'Été de Québec, (888-992-5200) which is held in early July. This is the largest festival of French-language performing arts and street theatre in North America. There are hundreds of acts — singers, dancers, jugglers, clowns, acrobats, magicians — and most of the shows are free of charge and in the open air. The narrow streets and cobbled squares of the old city as well as the open parkland of the Plains of Abraham, provide some of the finest stages in North America for this sort of event.

Other summer events are the Fêtes de la Nouvelle France (418-694-3311) in early August, which recall the era of the French regime with military displays, parades and re-enactments, and Plein Art, a 10-day crafts exhibition held in a tent on the esplanade near the parliament buildings.

A couple of events held just outside the city are also worth considering. The Grands-Feux Loto-Québec (1-800-923-3389 or 418-523-3389) take place at the end of July and the beginning of August. These fireworks displays are staged in a spectacular setting, on parkland at the foot of Montmorency Falls. One of the best observation points is the St. Lawrence River, so the area around the falls fills with boats whose lights twinkle and flash in the darkness, adding to the show.

Just a few miles further downstream lies the shrine of Ste-Anne-de-Beaupré (418-827-3781), built in honour of the mother of the Virgin Mary. St. Anne's feast day is celebrated on July 26 with due religious ceremony — solemn Masses and rosary recitations — but it is also something of a festival. Gypsies and some Native tribes hold St. Anne in particular esteem, and they flock to the site in late July. Many of the Indians celebrate in traditional costumes and the Gypsies often arrive in caravans of mobile homes.

The last major event of the summer is the Festival International du Film de Québec (514-843-3883), a week-long celebration of some of the best Canadian and foreign films. It starts in late August and ends around Labour Day.

Fall comes relatively early to the Quebec City region and the leaves start to turn as early as mid-September. The city celebrates this with a Festival des Couleurs (418-827-4561) on nearby Mont Ste-Anne, a 2,000-foot ski hill that affords a dramatic view of the surrounding countryside. Another fall event that has been turned into a festival is the return of the snow geese. Great clouds of these magnificent white birds, which spend their summers at the northern tip of Baffin Island, descend on the marshes and farmlands near the city to stock up on carbohydrates before continuing their flight to their winter nesting grounds on the Atlantic shores of the Carolinas. One of their favourite stopovers is Cap Tormentine and the local residents celebrate their visit with the Festival de l'Oie des Neiges de Saint-Joachim (418-827-4808). Every morning the birds fly off in their thousands to forage for food and every evening they return to spend the night in huge colonies. Sandwiched between those two natural events are shows, craft displays and guided walking tours of the birds' favourite haunts.

FESTIVAL D'ÉTÉ DE QUÉBEC

Shopping

Lorraine O'Donnell

Charlevoix socks at Lambert & Co.

Do you wonder what really makes this city tick? It's money, of course. Don't be fooled by the grand edifices dedicated to religion and learning and governance. Quebec also thrives on commerce, and it is full of stores. To really know the place, then, you have to go shopping. In so doing, you will discover hidden treasures. Quebec has wonderful things to buy, especially local products that you might fancy for mementoes. There are antique and newly handcrafted household goods brimming with local character. There is clothing made and worn by Quebecers because it suits their boiling summers and freezing winters. And there are the products of many artists and artisans: paintings, sculpture, jewellery.

But shopping in a foreign place is about more than buying goods. It also allows you to encounter local people going about their business, and to see what they eat, wear and use to work and play. It even takes you off the beaten track, into interesting neighbourhoods. There are boutiques and malls, discount stores and department stores, ranging from humble to upscale, dusty to dazzling.

The brief guide that follows introduces you to some of the worthwhile places to shop in Quebec. It is organized by district, starting with the old city centre, where you will most likely be spending a lot of time, and moving outward to some of the other areas that also merit a look.

Rue St-Louis

Old City Centre

In Vieux-Québec (the upper part of the old city centre) you can find all kinds of souvenirs. For kitschy knick knacks and T-shirts, look into the shops on Rue St-Louis. Nearby Rue du Trésor is an open-air market of locally produced visual art including images of the city. If you cross onto Ste-Anne at No. 34,

you'll find fun 3-D puzzles of the Château Frontenac at Au Grand Carrousel. The parallel street, de Buade, has a store featuring children's clothing by local designers, Chez Marie-Alexandre, (No. 43, second floor), and a tobacconist, J.E. Giguère (No. 61), selling reasonably priced Quebec-made pipes (as well as Cuban cigars). Over on Côte de la Fabrique is a small branch of the Simons department store (No. 20), known for its house

SWEATER AND MOCCASINS AT LA CORRIVEAU

brands of women's and men's clothing, especially sweaters and hats. Down the street, you can buy fine handmade sweaters and moccasins at La Corriveau (No. 24) and jewellery at Zimmermann (No. 46). Around the corner on Garneau you can obtain colourful striped wool socks in the old Charlevoix style at Lambert & Co. (No. 42), and a selection of hats from Quebec at Bibi & Co. (No. 40). Turn onto the main shopping street of the area, St-Jean, and there's everything from candy to more clothes. Librairie Pantoute (No. 1100) sells English-language guidebooks for the region.

LAMBERT & CO.

Shopping in the lower section of the old city (Quartier du Petit-Champlain, Vieux-Port) is more varied. Although the Quartier du Petit-Champlain may look discouragingly touristy, in fact many locals come here to buy high-quality goods, such as Quebec designer clothes at Oclan (No. 52 Blvd. Champlain). All kinds of handicrafts, ranging from lace to glassware, and art, including sculpture and paintings, are featured. Sculpteur Flamand at 49 du Petit-Champlain features wood carvings in the traditional Québécois style, while down the street La Soierie Huo at No. 91 sells graceful, modern hand-painted silk scarves.

In the Vieux-Port area is Rue St-Paul, famous for good-quality antique and used furniture stores. Everything from rustic pine to groovy plastic is available. Gerard Bourguet Antiquaire at No. 97 sells 18th- and 19th-century pine furniture, while Décenie at No. 117 features re-upholstered vinyl pieces from the 1960s. Nearby is the Marché du Vieux Port at 160 Quai

DRESS AT OCLAN

St-André, open from March through November. Although this might feel a bit modern and stuck in the middle of nowhere, the farmers' produce is fresh and some nice handicrafts such as handwoven table linens are available.

Antiques on Rue St-Paul

Suit at Oclan

Basse-Ville (Lower Town)

The differences between the old city centre and Lower Town are many, and nowhere does this become this more apparent than in the stores. If you consider the old centre dishearteningly bourgeois, then Basse-Ville, being gritty, not pretty, is the place for you. It's an old working-class district, now also populated by artists, youths and recent immigrants, and its stores are unpretentious and eclectic.

Southwest of the train station at 915 Rue St-Vallier E. is the wonderful thrift shop Comptoir Emmaus, four giant floors of inexpensive used clothing, books, furniture and housewares. Here you can find that pineapple-shaped ashtray you always wanted. The 2nd-floor pneumatic-tube system for making change is fun.

On Rue St-Joseph is the Mail Centre-Ville. Billed as the longest covered street in the world, this mall has little else to boast about. With the tony exception of Laliberté at No. 595, whose fur coats are famous (you can even visit its fur workshop), most of the mall's department stores have closed. Left is a miscellany of fairly downscale restaurants and shops, and dollar stores selling cheap housewares, novelties and toys. Still it's a good place for finding bargains on bad-weather days.

Leaving the mall, go west on St-Joseph to find stores selling used furniture, clothes and books. X20 at No. 200 sells its own line of funky streetwear. Turn onto St-Vallier O./W. to visit a number of East Asian and Latin American import stores and restaurants (around Nos. 100-500). There's also Magasin Latulippe at No. 637, with its enormous selection of workwear and outdoor wear, including great warm hats. A worthwhile detour: see and sample the bright rows of cupcakes and other baked goods at Royaume de la Tarte (402 des Oblats at Durocher).

Haute-Ville (Upper Town)

Right outside the old city walls is the shopping centre Place Québec at 880 Dufferin-Montmorency. It houses 40

Handmade paper at Copiste du Faubourg

stores and restaurants and useful services like a post office, but its dreariness might put you off.

Much more engaging is Rue St-Jean west of Côte d'Abraham, the commercial heart of the friendly St-Jean-Baptiste neighbourhood. On this colourful street, cafés peacefully co-exist with upscale sex shops (gay and straight) and stores selling cool clothing, local and imported furniture and decorative items, and fine food, including the oldest grocery store in North America, J.A. Moisan at No. 699. Of special note are the astonishing arrays of rubber stamps at Paradis des Ètampes (No. 603) and of handmade paper at Copiste du Faubourg (No. 545).

Continuing west down St-Jean/Ste-Foy, you come to Cartier, which serves the somewhat richer, older, more orderly clientele of the Montcalm neighbourhood. As well as many restaurants, cafés and specialty food shops, Cartier has a number of fine women's fashion boutiques. One with consistently attractive collections is Boutique Paris Cartier at No. 1180. The mini-mall Halles le Petit Cartier at No. 1191 will interest gourmets. On René-Lévesque just west of Cartier are some exclusive Quebec designer boutiques. Pop into Autrefois Saïgon at No. 55 to see an intriguing line of women's clothing made here but with an East Asian flavour.

Suburbs

To really cover the Quebec shopping scene, do as the residents do: go to the suburban malls. These are omnipresent, enormous and convenient. They sell all kinds of clothing, household items and food, and they have good parking facilities as well as services like stroller rental. Plus, they offer shelter and entertainment of sorts when it's too cold to be outside, a feature appreciated by the elderly and parents of young children. What they lack is local flavour and charm. Probably the most interesting is Galeries de la Capitale (5401 des Galeries), because of its enormous indoor playground featuring a roller-coaster. For sheer size, visit Place Laurier in the suburb of Ste-Foy (2700 Laurier). Weighing in at 350 stores, it's the largest shopping centre in eastern Canada. Close by, Place Sainte-Foy, at 2452 Laurier has big department stores including another Simons, while the huge Ailes de la Mode at 2450 Laurier offers a shuttle service to downtown hotels.

But all is not hopelessly suburban in Ste-Foy. Witness the lively outdoor food and flea market on Roland-Beaudin, open every Sunday from May to early October. You can browse and haggle your way through reams of the lovely stuff cast off by people anxious to mine new quarry at — where else? — the nearby malls.

DINING

SARAH MORGAN

RESTAURANTS ON GRANDE-ALLÉE

Dining in Quebec City is not quite the varied adventure it is in Montreal. The ethnic mix of the Vieille-Capitale is not as exotic as that of its upriver rival. And Quebec City has a problem — it attracts far more tourists in the summer than it really has room for, so that at the height of the season quality can suffer a little. The same can be said of the bacchanalian fortnight in February known as the winter carnival.

But the city does have more than its share of fine chefs, and they ply their ancient trade in some pretty sumptuous locales. It's hard to beat the stone-walled mansions of Haute-Ville and Basse-Ville for atmosphere. And if you're willing to take a short drive into the country, you can dine in a manor house on Île d'Orléans or in a mansion that served as a love nest for Queen Victoria's father and his mistress.

The best place to start is right in the city. And as long as you're in Quebec City, you might as well start with a view. There is, of course, the Astral, the rotating restaurant on top of Loew's Le Concorde Hotel at 1225 Place Montcalm (418-647-2222). It's just another slick hotel restaurant, but the food is good and the view is magnificent. The hotel is just west of the city walls so diners can take in the old city, the waterfront, the river (atwinkle with ships and boats), and the towers and turrets of the Château Frontenac.

For something more traditional but still with a view, you could try the Café de la Terrasse at the base of those towers and turrets (1 Rue des Carrières, 418-692-3861). Its big bay windows give diners a wonderful view of lovers and families strolling by on terrasse Dufferin with the river and the city of Lévis in the background. The food is standard continental and the location makes it very popular in

CAFÉ DE LA TERRASSE

LE PARLEMENTAIRE

summer. You can drop in for afternoon tea between 2:30 and 5. Of course, view isn't everything, even in Quebec City where it's hard to find a bad one. Politics, for example, can make for interesting table chatter, especially if you choose to stop for lunch in the Le Parlementaire (418-643-6640), the dining room of the Assemblée Nationale. It's open to the public and is reasonably priced. The decor is grandiose and you never know who might be at the next table.

LA BASTILLE CHEZ BAHÜAUD

GRANDE TABLE SERGE BRUYÈRE

If your objective is as much to people-watch as it is to satisfy your hunger, there are dozens of terrace restaurants from which to choose. There's a whole row of them on Grande-Allée just west of the Assemblée Nationale, housed in fine old stone houses with large front yards transformed into giant terraces ideal for people-watching. Even Burger King has a spot here, in case you want to combine fast food with a little quality café life. None of these places are renowned for their food, however. It's competent at best. What you pay for on Grande-Allée is location. If you really like to dine al fresco, you can get better food in a sylvan setting at the la Bastille Chez Bahüaud located ar 47 Ave. Ste-Geneviève (418-692-2544). Tables are set amid tall trees in a pleasant garden setting.

And then there's haute-cuisine for those for whom food really is the thing. Quebec City's reputation for fine dining rests on the efforts of a handful of very good restaurants. The best-known of these is Grande Table Serge Bruyère located in a 150-year-old building at 1200 Rue St-Jean (418-694-0618). It serves specialties like scallop stew with watercress and duckling with blueberry sauce. The prices at the Grande Table are as rich

INSIDE LAURIE RAPHAËL

as the sauces. If you want to sample simpler fare of the same quality, try the dishes at the Petite Table in the same building. The complex also includes a café, a food store and a catering service.

There are other restaurants in the same class. Laurie Raphaël at 117 Rue Dalhousie (418-692-4555) boasts one of the best chefs in the province, Daniel Vèzina, who adds his own distinctive touch to an international menu and delights in experimenting with both traditional dishes like scallops or ris de veau and the latest delicacies such as ostrich. Le Champlain in the Château Frontenac hotel (418-692-3861) serves classic French dishes in one of the city's most lavishly decorated rooms, and La Closerie at 996 Blvd. René-Lévesque O./W. (418-687-9975) hides a first-class kitchen and an intimate dining room behind a rather bland exterior.

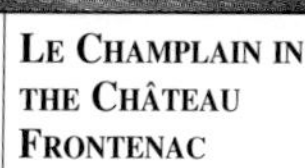

LE CHAMPLAIN IN THE CHÂTEAU FRONTENAC

LE SAINT AMOUR

The Saint Amour at 48 Rue Ste-Ursule is in a class with the Grande Table and is also one of the most romantic restaurants in the city. It has its own chocolaterie on the premises (and everyone knows what an effect chocolate can have on the romantic heart) as well as a glassed-in terrace decorated with plants and flowers that's open year-round.

The restaurant with the most romantic history, however, is probably the dining room in the Manoir Montmorency (418-663-3330) overlooking the falls of the same name. The manoir itself is a rambling wooden building with verandhas and cupolas that the Duke of Kent and his mistress used as a summer hideaway when he commanded the Quebec garrison. The Duke later returned to England and fathered Queen Victoria.

Quebec City does beat Montreal roundly in one category — traditional Québécois cuisine. Finding a good tourtière or salmon pie in Montreal is difficult enough; anything more elaborate is virtually impossible. But the Quebec City region has three good restaurants with menus that any 18th-century habitant would find familiar. Two of them are out of town, but the grandest is in the heart of Haute-Ville at 34 Rue St-Louis. This is Aux Anciens Canadiens (418-692-1627), housed in a fine 17th-century building. The chefs here simmer ham in maple syrup and bake beans with chunks of salt pork and molasses. For dessert, try the blueberry pie. The two other traditional restaurants are Auberge Baker in the Château-Richer at 8790 Ave. Royale (418-824-4852), which serves game dishes in a stone-walled room with a fireplace; and L'Âtre on Île d'Orléans, at 4403 Chemin Royale in Ste-Famille (418-829-3474), which is located in an ancient stone house and features staff dressed in traditional costume.

Two reasonably priced restaurants with good food and atmosphere can be found in Basse-Ville. Le Cochon Dingue at Blvd. 46 Champlain (418-692-2013) is a lot of fun. The name means "crazy pig," and the restaurant is housed in an 18th-century stone building with flagged floors and period decor. The menu focuses on well-prepared bistro food (mussels and fries, steak and fries, creative burgers, homemade quiche) served with speed and panache, and the desserts could turn anyone into a pig. (This outfit has two other outlets in Quebec City of the same quality and eccentric style, but this one is the best.) Bistro Sous le Fort (48 Rue Sous-le-Fort, 418-694-0852) is a bit more austere in its decor but the food is both good and plentiful.

So while Quebec City may lack the dazzling array of cultures of the metropolis, its chefs have carved out a place for themselves on the province's culinary map. For the most part they concentrate on the basics — good local produce skilfully prepared — but they bring to the craft a particularly Quebec City flavour, emulating, perhaps, the great regional chefs of Provence or Normandy rather than the masters of Paris.

AUX ANCIENS CANADIENS

Quebec City by Area

LOWER TOWN

LOUISA BLAIR

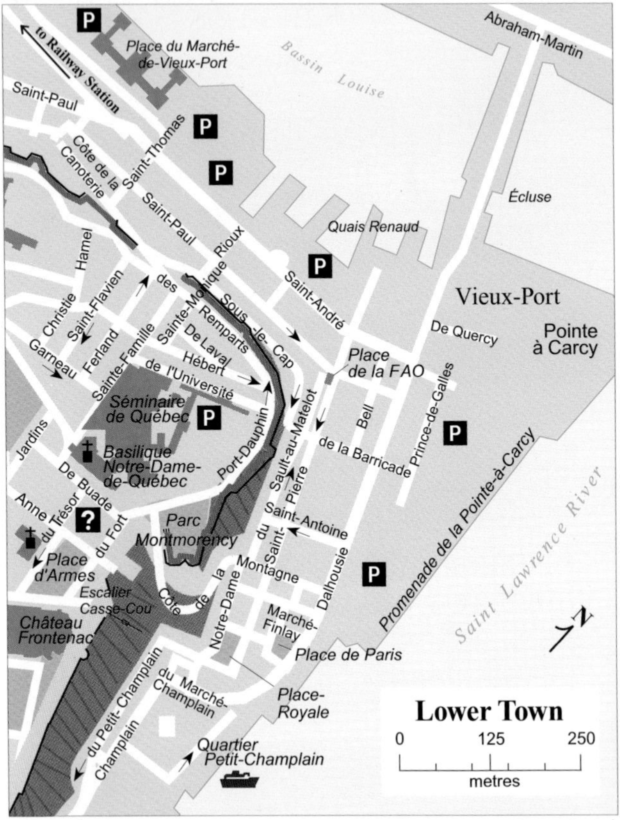

To many people the name Vieux-Québec means the walled city on the hill — with its warren of narrow, twisted streets spreading out from the castle-like bulk of the Château Frontenac. But in fact Haute-Ville is the newer part of the old city. To introduce yourself to Quebec's real birthplace, stand on Terrasse Dufferin at the edge of Haute-Ville and look over the wrought-iron guardrail. The steep roofs below cover some of the oldest buildings in North America. In 1608 Samuel de Champlain landed down there on the narrow strip of land between the St. Lawrence River and the cliff, cut down some trees and built himself a trading post. That first rude settlement comprised a moated manor house and some storehouses and outbuildings. Fire and war have destroyed any trace of Champlain's post, but many of the walls and foundations of the current buildings date to the prosperous days of the early 1700s.

PLACE DE PARIS

As recently as the 1970s, Basse-Ville (Lower Town) was a rundown slum. Then Quebec developed a fervour for its architectural heritage and set about restoring the district. The work began in Place Royale, a cobbled open square presided over by a bust of Louis XIV, the Sun King. Place Royale was a marketplace long before the French arrived. Various Indian tribes began meeting there as early as 2,000 years ago. The new settlers began to use it as a marketplace in 1673. The restorers certainly succeeded in recapturing the look of the French regime, but unfortunately they also managed to suck much of the life out of the place. It now looks rather like a film set, and on most summer days it's difficult to find anyone in the vicinity who isn't carrying a camera.

Notre-Dame-des-Victoires

Still, the church on the square, Notre-Dame-des-Victoires, is worth battling the crowds for. It was built in 1687 and was a favourite of New France's first bishop, François de Laval. Hanging from the ceiling is a replica of the boat Brézé, one of the few examples left of the ex voto offerings that were the fashion among the devout Breton sailors who arrived in Quebec. When caught in one of the frequent storms in the Gulf of the St. Lawrence, they would promise the saint that if she delivered them safely they would build an exact replica of their boat in her honour. This church also has an unusual altar; it is shaped

Batterie Royale

NEW CUSTOMS HOUSE

RUE ST-ANTOINE

like a fortress.

Just down the hill from Place Royale is Place du Paris, a once bustling colonial market now dominated by a chunk of modern sculpture that, according to rumour, has been repeatedly mistaken for a public washroom. It was a gift from the city of Paris and provides a little comic relief for tourists before they solemnly turn their attention to the nearby Batterie Royale, a fortified promontory dating from 1691, topped with 10 French cannons. The river used to lap at the foot of this promontory at high tide, a reminder that Quebec's grandeur was built on the maritime trade.

Between 1797 and 1897 Quebec's 40 shipyards turned out 2,500 ships. The Quartier du Petit-Champlain, hugging the cliff to the west, was where the shipsmiths, spar- and block-makers, riggers, chandlers and tow-boat owners lived. Restored by a citizens co-operative, this area still has life in it and is worth a wander for the craft shops, cafés and atmosphere.

MUSÉE DE LA CIVILISATION

On the other side of Basse-Ville, the restored Vieux-Port offers something of a relief from the tourist throngs in Place Royale. Sit down on one of the benches facing the water and watch the yachts, freighters and cruise boats dodge each other in the busy harbour. Stubby blue and white ferries plough back and forth between the port and Lévis on the south shore. For just a few dollars the ferry ride gives you an unparalleled view back at the city, the great offices of Quebec's first industrialists along Rue Dalhousie and above them the green turretted roofs of the Château Frontenac and the silver spires of the

Séminaire du Québec. If you walk east along the shore, you can rent a bicycle near the Agora (an outdoor amphitheatre) and ride the extensive bike paths all around the port and, if you like, right out to Beauport.

DRESS AND HEARSE, MUSÉE DE LA CIVILISATION

The magnificent "New" Customs House (built in 1856) at 2 Quai St-André is still what it claims to be, and glares across at the equally magnificent Société des Ports Nationaux (1914) at 10 Rue de Quercy. Between them is a restful little park with fountains and rows of mountain ash trees. Behind you, the imposing buildings of the old financial district tower over the narrow streets of Sault-au-Matelot, St-Antoine and St- Pierre. Until the 60s, this was the Wall Street of Quebec; it even had its own stock exchange for a few years. Now there's not a bank to be seen — just restaurants, hotels, art galleries and one of the most interesting museums in Canada, the Musée de la Civilisation at 85 Rue Dalhousie.

MARCHÉ DU VIEUX-PORT

The museum, built in 1988, was designed by Moshe Safdie to blend in with the old buildings that surround it. With a special mission to explore Québécois culture and its relationship to the world, the museum consists of 11 exhibition spaces arranged around a vast bright entrance hall, which in turn is dominated by a cement sculpture in pools of water representing the spring breakup on the St. Lawrence River. There's too much concrete here, but lots of light and life. Aside from permanent, temporary and travelling exhibitions, there are concerts, film screenings, poetry readings and political debates: a museum that has managed to turn itself into a truly vibrant cultural centre. Don't miss the fabulous dressing-up room in the basement, with extraordinarily creative costumes for adults and children alike. Across the street, Robert Lepage, Quebec's internationally renowned playwright, was inspired to add some blocks of black granite to the back of the old fire station at 103 Dalhousie, and has made it the home of his production company, Ex Machina. All his shows are created, rehearsed and produced here, but this is not a performance space.

Vieux-Port

After visiting the museum, take a walk along Sous-le-Cap, a dark, narrow street hugging the cliff, criss-crossed with picturesque stairways and galleries. When the river was higher this was the only route around the shore and in the early 19th century it was a fashionable address. The Marché du Vieux-Port is the next stop. Here you can buy a snack from the farmers of Île d'Orléans, whose descendants sold their wares in Place Royale during the French regime. As you munch your apple take a look at the station, built to resemble a château. Step inside and look up at the magnificent skylight with its stained-glass map of North America. The Centre d'Interprétation du Vieux-Port at 100 Rue St-André, an eyesore run by Parks Canada, reflects the importance of Quebec's maritime history as both a port and a shipbuilding centre. In the 19th century it was one of the five most important ports in the world, and in 1833 the Royal William, built here, was the first ship to cross the Atlantic powered solely by steam.

Cartier St-Roch

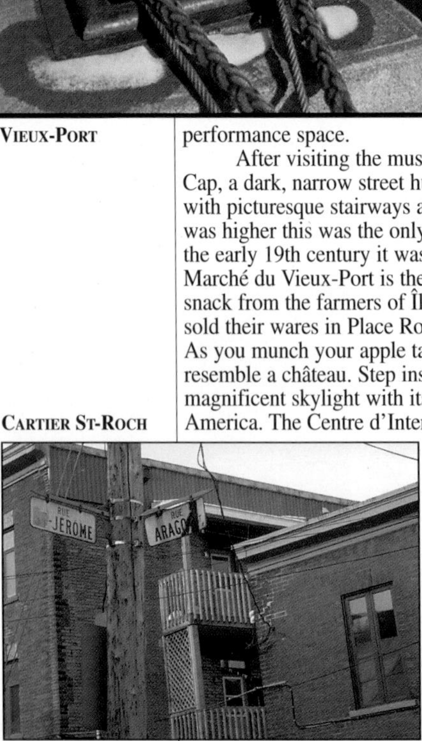

Beyond the Dufferin-

HÔPITAL GÉNÉRALE

Montmorency viaduct is another Basse-Ville, vibrant with life, struggling with poverty and devoid of tourists. This is the Quartier St-Roch, a working-class district whose gritty charm has had a little recent buffing. There's the very modern Bibliothèque Gabrielle-Roy, for example, built in 1988, and the beautifully restored Édifice de la Fabrique at 255 Blvd. Charest E., which houses Université Laval's school of fine art. A lot of people still call the latter gem Dominion Corset. Don't laugh: in its heyday this factory employed over a thousand single women, who produced as many as 21,000 corsets and brassières per day.

The smaller back streets of St-Roch and the neighbouring St-Sauveur district are worth exploring. The tightly packed housing on streets like Jérôme, Arago and du Roi in St-Roch and Aquéduc, des Oblats and Victoria in St-Sauveur are a jumble of styles. Tiny old houses with mansard roofs are jammed in among those from every successive era. The winding Rue St-Vallier leads to one of the outstanding legacies of the French regime, the Hôpital Générale at 260 Blvd. Langelier. It was founded in 1692 by Quebec's second bishop, Jean-Baptiste de la Croix de Chevrières de Saint-Vallier, and still looks after the poor and dying. With a little advance notice (418-529-0931), sisters from the Augustinian order, which has been running the place for 300 years, will give you a guided tour of the fascinating museum and the beautiful Notre-Dame-des-Anges chapel, Quebec's best-kept secret.

Just remember: the old walled city has 4,000 residents and four million tourists per year. It's gorgeous, but save some time for the Lower Town, and don't stop at the viaduct if you want to get a sense of what Quebec is really all about.

NOTRE-DAME-DES-ANGES

PPER TOWN

MARY ANN SIMPKINS

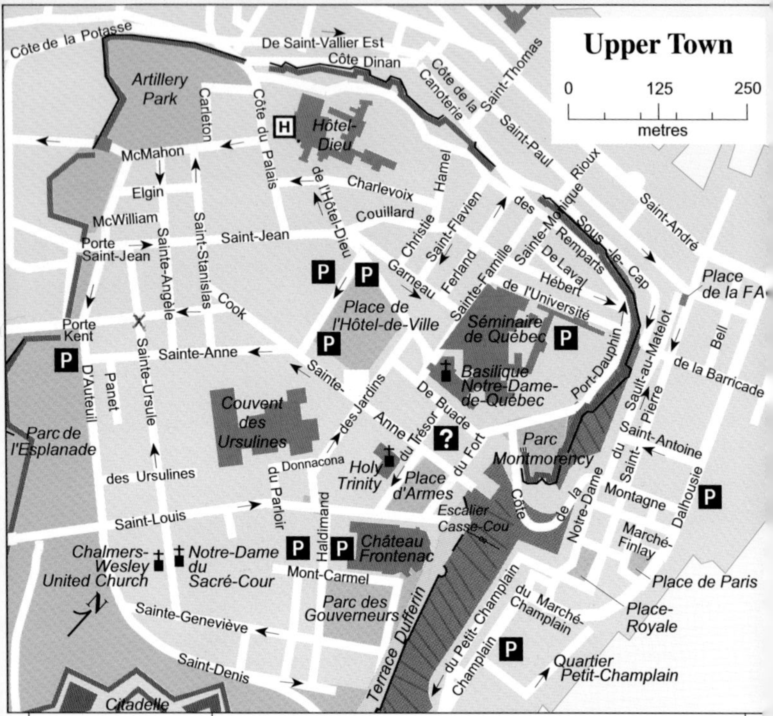

The doughty French settlers who founded Quebec City in the 17th century built their homes and warehouses with convenience in mind, not security. Theirs was a trading venture, after all, and what better place to build it than on the banks of the St. Lawrence River where boats and canoes could easily land? A few skirmishes with English fleets, however, revealed their vulnerability, and soon the colonists hacked a trail up the sheer rock face of the heights and founded Haute-Ville, or Upper Town, in 1620.

PLACE D'ARMES BEFORE THE CHÂTEAU FRONTENAC

At the top, Samuel de Champlain built a small fortress where his statue now stands, between the Château Frontenac hotel and a wildly modernistic globe that commemorates UNESCO's decision to designate the entire old city a World Heritage Site. Champlain's statue faces Place d'Armes, the military parade ground during both the French and British regimes. The park is a good starting point for touring Haute-Ville. And there's really only one way to accomplish this: on foot. Most tour buses are too big to navigate the more interesting streets and the horse-drawn calèches cover only part of the route.

So lace up your most comfortable shoes, pick up a free city map at the tourist bureau facing the square, and set out. You can easily walk the route in an hour, but that includes no stops along the way. Better to set aside most of a day and do the place thoroughly. Start at the turretted Musée du Fort on the corner of the square, where taped commentary and lights flashing on a panoramic model of the city chronicle the military skirmishes for Quebec. Much livelier is Québec Expérience at 8 Rue du Trésor. Blazing guns, gushing water, 3-D figures and other special effects give you dramatic snapshots of the city, from the first explorers to the present day.

The English-speaking population of Quebec City has dwindled considerably since the mid-1800s, dropping from half the population to less than two percent today, yet three of the churches in Upper Town are anglophone. The one you see backing onto the northeast corner of Place d'Armes is Holy Trinity Cathedral, the mother church of the Anglican diocese of Quebec and the first Anglican cathedral built outside the British Isles. King George III, no doubt unclear on Canada's timber resources, shipped over oak from Windsor Castle's royal forest for construction of the pews. A balcony pew has been reserved since 1810 for royalty or royalty's representative. Guided tours of the cathedral, offered daily from May to Thanksgiving, in October, recount the fascinating history behind some of the memorial plaques and the burial of the Duke of Richmond under the main altar. Craftsmen set up shop in the church grounds in the summertime, but artists hang their paintings and engravings of Quebec City year-round on the walls lining Rue du Trésor, which leads eastward from Place d'Armes and was where the early colonists came to pay their taxes to the governor of New France.

At the end of this short street, turn left on de Buade to reach the entrance to the Basilique Notre-Dame-de-Québec, the cathedral of the Roman Catholic archdiocese. The glorious

HOLY TRINITY CATHEDRAL

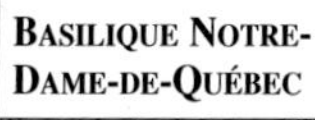

BASILIQUE NOTRE-DAME-DE-QUÉBEC

BASILIQUE NOTRE-DAME-DE-QUÉBEC, INTERIOR

interior is lavishly decorated with statues, stained glass and a sumptuous gilded canopy over the main altar. The church's side chapel holds a resting bronze figure representing Quebec's first bishop, François de Laval, who is entombed, with more than 900 other souls, in the church's crypt. In summer the church stages Feux Sacrés, an impressive sound-and-light show that focuses on the building's architectural and religious history. (Keep an eye on the weekly Chronicle-Telegraph, which is the city's only English-language paper, distributed free in tourist bureaus in summer. It often offers two-for-one coupons for Feux Sacrés.)

The ornate iron gate next to the cathedral guards the Séminaire du Québec, founded by Bishop Laval in 1663 to train priests for the parishes of New France. The first institution of post-secondary education in North America, it eventually evolved into Université Laval. In 1954, the university moved to modern quarters in suburban Ste-Foy but the old Séminaire still houses the architecture school. It also houses the Musée de l'Amérique Française, which traces more than three centuries of French history and culture in North America through temporary and permanent exhibitions that include ornate silver chalices, carved wood religious sculptures, and Canadian and European paintings. Don't miss the seminary's stunning external chapel with its Second Empire trompe-l'oeil interior and Canada's largest collection of relics.

MUSÉE DE L'AMÉRIQUE FRANÇAISE

Opposite the basilica, Quebec's city hall once again flies the Canadian flag. After the failure of the Meech Lake constitutional amendments, Mayor Jean-Paul L'Allier ordered the flag removed. Angered by this action, three French Canadian veterans rose early

HÔTEL DE VILLE (CITY HALL)

Convent of the Bon-Pasteur

each morning for a brief flag-raising ceremony. A new council voted in 1998 to reinstate Canada's national emblem.

Follow the seminary's high stone wall down Rue Ste-Famille to the end. At this point, if you turn right on Ave. des Remparts you'll come to Montmorency park, which has been lined with a row of British cannons since 1832. The guns had enough force to shoot cannonballs across the St. Lawrence into Lévis, from which the British bombarded the city in 1759, destroying many houses. Those facing the river were mainly rebuilt in the same architectural style, using the original foundations and walls.

If you turn left at the end of Ste-Famille, you'll reach one house that survived the British bombardment, the home of the Marquis de Montcalm, the general in charge of the French forces. A plaque identifies the burgundy-painted house. The wood facing was installed over the stone around 1850 as protection against the fierce northeasterly winds. Go back up Rue St-Ferland and just before turning the corner onto Rue Couillard you'll see a small doorway on your right. It leads into the convent of the Bon-Pasteur and was used by unwed mothers-to-be who needed the nuns' help but wanted to avoid the prying eyes on the more public Rue Couillard. The 19th-century convent is now a museum and you can enter through the front door, no matter what your condition. Rotating and permanent exhibits fill three floors and friendly nuns will play an English video about their order for you and answer questions about the displays ranging from the cloth-enclosed nuns' rooms to religious art.

It's hard to avoid the influence of nuns in Quebec City. After the church established a presence in the colony, dozens of religious orders poured into the city. One of the first to arrive was a group of Augustinian nuns who opened a hospital in 1644, the first in North America north of Mexico. Hôtel-Dieu still operates, as does the adjoining convent with its free museum. Ring the bell at 32 Rue Charlevoix, next to the small church

Hôtel-Dieu hospital

beside the massive greystone hospital, for entry to the small Musée des Augustines. The treasures include 17th-century Louis XIII furniture donated by the French governor's wife and medical equipment spanning the centuries — a lovely example of the earthenware fountains and basins that were to be found in each hospital room, a late-17th-century syringe made of bone and wooden shoes worn by surgeons in the operating rooms.

Rue St-Jean was the city's fashionable shopping street from the late 1800s to the 1950s, but now it's a mishmash of souvenir shops, clothing stores and restaurants. Walking past these toward the St-Jean gate, you'll reach Parc de l'Artillerie on the right. This national historic site run by Parks Canada transports you back into Quebec's military history, a passage reinforced by guides acting as characters in the different periods. The reception centre for the complex is the Federal Arsenal, a turn-of-the-century munitions factory that closed in 1964. A short walk away looms the imposing Dauphine redoubt. The French began building the whitewashed fort in 1712, later turning it into barracks. Inside you'll find French soldiers but also a cook from the Royal Artillery Regiment. After the Conquest the redoubt housed British troops. Be sure to visit all four floors: each represents a separate era. A British military captain of the 1830s lives amidst elegant furnishings in the cottage on another side of the parade grounds.

Rue St-Jean

Convent of the Bon-Pasteur

On the other side of Rue St-Jean, Rue d'Auteuil runs parallel to the city's walls. Haute-Ville was the preserve of religious organizations, the city's administration and the wealthy, as you can see at No. 69 d'Auteuil, considered Haute-Ville's most beautiful house. Any similarity between it and Ottawa's parliament buildings is understandable: this was the residence of their builder, Thomas McGreevy. In contrast to the flamboyance of McGreevy's home, Chief Justice Sewell chose the stolid English Palladian style for his residence, erected in 1803 at the corner of d'Auteuil and St-Louis.

The St-Louis gate on Rue St-Louis is the principal entrance to Vieux-Québec. When the British garrison departed, the city tore down many gates. Some people clamoured for the walls to be demolished as well, but the governor-general at the time, Lord Dufferin, persuaded them to save the

NO. 69 RUE D'AUTEUIL

walls and had this gate and others rebuilt. The road left of the gate leads to the Citadelle. On the right, dug into the wall, is the magazine the British used to store gunpowder. It serves as an interpretation centre with a scale model of the city depicting the evolution of the walls, from those constructed by the French in 1690 to those put up by the British in 1790.

Back on Rue St-Louis, head for the city centre. At Rue Ste-Ursule make a short detour to your right and take a peek into the church of Notre-Dame du Sacré-Coeur. Its richly coloured stained-glass windows diffuse a gentle light onto walls crammed with marble plaques giving thanks for favours granted. Across the street, Chalmers-Wesley United Church offers free Sunday-night concerts in summer on their century-old organ.

NOTRE-DAME DU SACRÉ-COEUR

Returning to St-Louis, keep your eyes peeled for a souvenir of the British bombardment: a cannonball lodged in the base of a tree. Turn left on Rue Donnacona and you come to the great sprawl that is the Monastère des Ursulines, home to an order of nuns who arrived in Quebec City in 1639 led by the indomitable Marie de l'Incarnation. Its stone walls still house the oldest continuously operating girls' school in North America, a beautiful chapel and a delightfully eclectic museum. The four rooms of the Musée des Ursulines display the parchment signed by Louis XIII approving the opening of a monastery and school in New France, altar cloths finely embroidered with silk and gold thread, and porcupine-needle baskets. Further down Rue St-Louis are some of Haute-Ville's oldest houses. The white house with the steep red roof at No. 34, for example, was constructed in 1677. It's now the restaurant Aux Anciens Canadiens. The stately white building with blue trim at No. 25 was built about 1650 and is where the French formally surrendered the city to the British in 1759. Oddly enough it now houses the French consulate.

The Château Frontenac only emerged as the city's most recognizable symbol in 1893. William Van Horne and other businessmen had the turretted, copper-roofed hotel constructed on the site of the demolished governor's palace. Actually there were two palaces here. French governors had greatly expanded Champlain's small fort and enforced it with stone. The English governor, however, refused to live in the Château and had another built. The wooden boardwalk in front of the Château is called Terrasse Dufferin, fitting recognition for Lord Dufferin's foresight in saving the only fortified city remaining in North America.

The Walls and Beyond

Sarah Waters

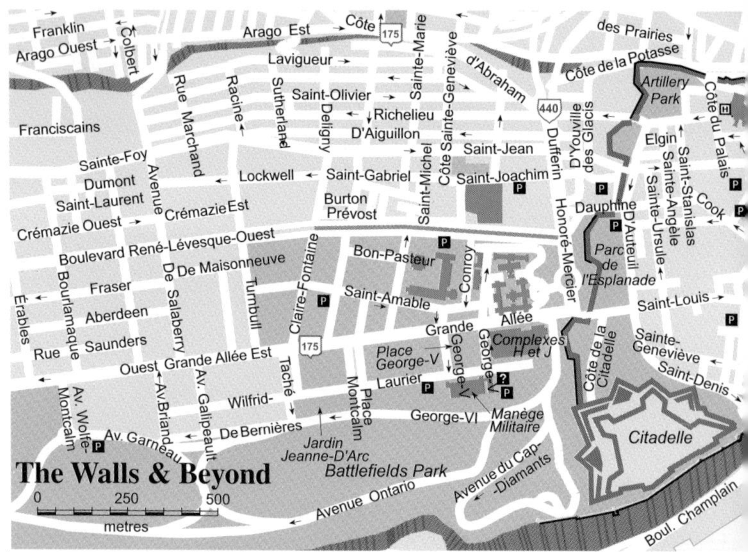

There's something very seductive about the walls of Vieux-Québec. Tourists have been known to disappear behind the Porte St-Louis never to re-emerge until it's time to go home. And they no doubt have a wonderful time exploring the cobbled streets and 18th-century buildings of the old city.

But their view of Quebec will be somewhat skewed and one-dimensional. Staying behind the walls is a delightful but limiting experience. To get the whole picture, you have to abandon the security of the walled city and explore the city's other facets.

A good way to start is to explore the fortifications themselves, to skirt the edges of the historic city, as it were, before venturing out onto unprotected turf. There are two parts to this exploration: the walls and the citadel. Let's start with the walls. The city has always been fortified — it would have been madness not to have some

Cannon along the walls of Quebec

kind of protection — but the French authorities didn't begin the present walls in earnest until after British troops took Louisbourg on Cape Breton Island in 1745. It turned out to be a bit late. The walls were still unfinished when General James Wolfe conquered the city in 1759, and it was left to the British to complete them. By the late 19th century, North America was a fairly peaceful place and the walls didn't really have much military purpose any more. But Lord Dufferin, Canada's governor-general from 1872 to 1878, thought they added a certain romance to the old city and insisted they be preserved. In fact he ordered that they be refurbished and that all the advance defences be torn down to expose the splendour of the walls. So Quebec owes much of its French-regime charm to the whimsical tastes of an English aristocrat.

An interpretation centre run by Parks Canada at 100 Rue St-Louis gives an excellent overview of the history of the fortifications and their construction. From there it's a short stroll to the Porte St-Louis for a tour of the ramparts. This is the most impressive section of the fortifications. It faces west over what was once open ground and the most vulnerable to attack. The wall here is 1.5 metres thick and close to five metres high. Two ornate main gates — the St-Louis and the St-Jean — puncture its stone solidity. At the northern end of the section is Parc de l'Artillerie, a pleasant green space that holds relics of some of the oldest parts of the fortifications. The park's old foundry has a beautiful scale model of what Quebec City looked like at the beginning of the 19th century. Nearby is the Redoute Dauphine, parts of which date to 1713. Beyond the park the fortifications swing east along the clifftops overlooking Basse-Ville. The cliffs provided a natural defence, so the walls here are not much more than chest high, but they're studded with cannons and mortars. Follow the walls along Ave. des Remparts, and you'll eventually come to the

FORTIFICATIONS OF QUEBEC

REDOUTE DAUPHINE

INSIDE THE CITADELLE

Château Frontenac. Just in front of the château is Terrasse Dufferin, a wide boardwalk along the cliffs that leads to the narrower and more precipitous Governor's Walk, which in turn leads you to the next stop on the tour: the Citadelle de Québec.

This star-shaped fortress is kind of a middle ground between the old city and the wider metropolis beyond. It is still part of Vieux-Québec but is linked to the rest of the city by being a part of the fortifications that extend beyond the walls: it's a post-Conquest addition. The British built the citadel between 1820 and 1831 to defend the city against an American attack that never came. It represents the apogee of 19th-century fortifications, with low-lying walls half-hidden behind gentle grassy slopes designed to absorb cannon shot and force attackers to expose themselves to withering fire from the fort. It is still an active military post, home to the Royal 22e Régiment — the "Van Doos" — who keep a battalion on station year-round. Two unflinching infantrymen in red tunics and tall bearskin hats guard the handsome main gate — the Porte Dalhousie — and visitors must join a guided group to tour the interior. You'll be

BAND OF THE VAN DOOS ON PARADE

FORMER GOVERNOR-GENERAL'S RESIDENCE

somewhat limited in what you can see. The chapel — once a powder magazine — and the governor-general's residence are off-limits, as are the barracks. However, visitors do tour an old military prison that now houses part of the Van Doos' museum — arms, uniforms, medals, etc. — and get a magnificent view of the old city from the King's Bastion and a sweeping one of the river from the Prince of Wales's Bastion.

MONUMENT ON THE PLAINS OF ABRAHAM

The western walls of the fort overlook the Plains of Abraham, now National Battlefields Park, which should be your next stop. This is the biggest urban park in Canada, with 107 hectares of gently rolling greenery laid out on the clifftops overlooking the St. Lawrence. If it's a fine day, plan to spend a couple of hours exploring its nooks and crannies as you wander westward. It could be said that Canada's fate was sealed on this pleasant tract of land on September 13, 1759, when General James Wolfe and his battle-hardened Scots and English soldiers defeated a French garrison force commanded by the Marquis de Montcalm. The battle claimed the lives of both commanders and essentially ended French dreams of a North American empire. Reminders of the park's martial past litter the landscape in the form of old cannons, plaques and monuments to both leaders and several panels describing the battle. Two later military relics are the martello towers, which now house exhibits on military engineering and (of all things) meteorology. These round stone towers, named for the man who designed them, were cutting-edge military technology when they were built in the early 1800s as outer defences for the citadel. The walls that face away from the citadel are solid and thick to fend off attack. The walls facing the citadel, however, are much thinner and could be easily destroyed by the citadel's cannon so that attackers could never use them for defence. For something a little less militaristic, pause at the Jardin Sainte-Jeanne-d'Arc. This flower-filled oasis with its statue of the Maid of Orleans is located at the entrance to the park between Ave. Taché and Place Montcalm. It certainly looks peaceful, but it was planted in honour of the soldiers of Nouvelle France who died fighting General Wolfe. The saint it's named for led an army and is entrusted with guarding the valour of French arms.

MARTELLO TOWER ON THE PLAINS OF ABRAHAM

One way to find out more about the park and its history is to visit the Musée du Québec on Ave. Wolfe-Montcalm right in the middle of the park. The Centre d'Interprétation du Parc des Champs-des-Batailles, on the ground floor of the museum's handsome Édifice Baillairgé, features a mockup

JARDIN SAINTE-JEANNE-D'ARC

of the battle and exhibits on the evolution of the site. It also offers guided tours of the park (418-648-4071).

Don't leave without visiting the museum itself. It has one of the finest art collections in Canada — more than 22,000 pieces that illustrate the development of painting, sculpture and decoration in Quebec from the 18th century to the present. One of its most notable treasures is Charles Alexander Smith's Assemblée des Six Comtés. It's an important portrayal of Canadian history that shows rebel-leader Louis-Joseph Papineau addressing a crowd during the 1837–38 insurrections against British colonial rule. The museum's collection includes landscapes, portraits, documents and a fascinating exhibit of religious art and artifacts drawn from churches all over the province. But the Musée du Québec is not all art. One of its two buildings — the Édifice Baillairgé, a beautiful Renaissance-Revival structure — was designed in 1871 by renowned architect Charles Baillairgé to serve as a prison. The museum has preserved a whole cell block and uses it to portray prison life in the 19th century.

When you emerge from the museum — and to do the place justice, this should be several hours after you enter — walk down Ave. Wolfe-Montcalm and turn right on to Grande-Allée to head back toward the old city. This stretch of Grande-Allée is about as stately and elegant a street as any in North America. It's lined with some fine old homes, churches and public buildings in styles that range from neo-Gothic to Beaux-Arts with a heavy dose of Second Empire, which was very popular with the 19th-century bourgeoisie who made their homes here. Recent commercial and government efforts to participate in this architectural display have marred the grace of the street somewhat, with contributions from the glitter-and-glass school of architecture (commercial) and the bunker style of construction (government). But try to ignore them and keep your eyes on the gems.

CAFÉ ON GRANDE-ALLÉE

At No. 115, for example, is something that looks like a country cottage with its steep roof and dormer windows but which is, in fact, a city house built in 1850. It's named Maison Krieghoff for its most famous resident, the painter Cornelius Krieghoff, who lived in it off and on in 1859 and 1860. Next door, at

No. 111, is the graciously proportioned Ladies' Protestant Home with its massive cornice and lantern. No. 82 is a piece of pure Regency, the Maison Henry-Stuart, with its row of french windows and massive overhanging roof. Maison Henry-Stuart with its pretty gardens is open to the public, and they even serve afternoon tea here (418-647-4347).

MAISON KRIEGHOFF

The fanciful jumble of towers and battlements at 530 Grande-Allée that looks a little like a fortress is, in fact, the church of Saint-Coeur-de-Marie built by Eudist priests in 1919. Further west and just two blocks north of Grande-Allée at 1080 Rue de la Chevrotière is a far more significant religious building. It's the motherhouse of the Soeurs du Bon-Pasteur (Sisters of the Good Shepherd), a religious order dedicated to the education of abandoned and delinquent girls. Its austere walls hide one of the most exuberantly beautiful places of worship in the city, a neo-Baroque chapel designed by Charles Baillairgé. Its narrow nave soars several storeys and a beautifully gilded 18th-century retable rests on the main altar.

MUSÉE DU QUÉBEC

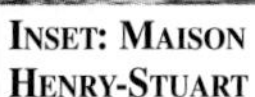

INSET: MAISON HENRY-STUART

Just across the street from the nuns' residence is one of those ugly government buildings — Édifice Marie-Guyart. This one, however, has a saving grace. Its top floor, the 31st, is an observatory with a magnificent, 360-degree view of the city and the surrounding countryside. There's a fee to get in, but it's worth it (418-644-9841).

SOEURS DU BON-PASTEUR CHAPEL

Back to Grande-Allée and continue the trek east and you come to the very heart of the Quebec government — the Hôtel du Parlement where the province's legislature, the Assemblée Nationale, meets in Second Empire splendour. The building faces the walls so to get to the main entrance you have to skirt its southern side. The grim bronze personage standing in the garden is one of Quebec's most notorious premiers, Maurice (Le Chef) Duplessis, who governed the province for much of the 1930s, '40s and '50s.

To appreciate the beauty of the

Hôtel du Parlement walk all the way down to Ave. Dufferin. Turn left and walk to the front gates and take a look. What you see is a history lesson. Eugène-Étienne Taché, the architect who designed the building in 1875, went out of his way to showcase the men and women who built the province. Bronze statues of people like Samuel de Champlain, Paul de Chomedey, Sieur de Maisonneuve, Marguerite Bourgeoys and Jeanne Mance fill 22 niches along the façade and up the sides of the central tower. An Indian family in bronze poses at the main door and just below them an Indian fisherman stands at the edge of a fountain with his spear poised to catch a fish. In less politically correct times — say, in the late '70s — this door was called the Porte des Sauvages, or Door of the Savages. You don't hear that term much any more.

HÔTEL DU PARLEMENT

There are frequent tours of the building and it's worth going inside even if it's just to see the two parliamentary chambers. The ornate Red Room on the left of the main door used to be the meeting place of the appointed Legislative Council. When that was disbanded, the room became the main meeting room of parliamentary commissions and committees. Laws are actually hammered out in the Blue Room on the right of the main door. This isn't quite as ornate as the Red Room and the colour scheme is a little less florid, but it's pretty fancy. The painting above the speaker's chair depicts the Debate on Languages in 1793 that resulted in French gaining official status in what was a British territory. Between the two chambers is the Beaux-Arts parliamentary dining room, which is open to the public (418-643-7239).

When you exit the Hôtel du Parlement you'll almost be back at the Porte St-Louis, but before you return to the charms of the old city, take a look across Grande-Allée at the Manège Militaire, or Armoury. It, too, was designed by Eugène-Étienne Taché. The pleasant green space in front of it is Place George V and the monument in the middle was erected in memory of two British soldiers who died fighting a fire in Faubourg St-Sauveur in 1889.

MANÈGE MILITAIRE

Excursions

Mary Ann Simpkins

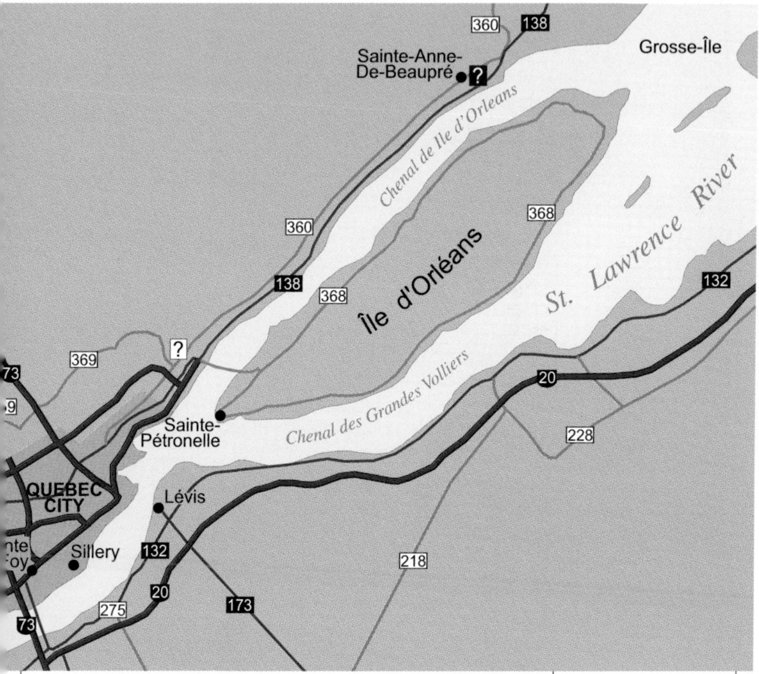

The area around Quebec City, beyond the old walls and Grand-Allée, is rich in history and natural beauty. Within a short distance of the citadel are marvellous gardens, a waterfall higher than Niagara Falls, a shrine that attracts pilgrims from all over the world and a traditional Indian village.

Take Sillery, for example, just west of the Plains of Abraham, where the governor-general of the United Province of Canada had his home in the 1800s. In those days nearly half the city's population was English-speaking and the wealthy ones lived in grand homes near the vice-regal residence. Fire destroyed the residence in 1966 and the grounds became a public park — the Bois-de-Coulonge (1215 Chemin St-Louis), which is filled with flower gardens and walkways to some great viewing spots over the St. Lawrence.

Fire also wrecked a smaller home on the estate. A replica was erected in 1929. Villa Bagatelle (1563 Chemin St-Louis) is a rare example of rural Quebec Gothic architecture. The barren, modernized interior that features rotating exhibits on aspects of Quebec society is overshadowed by the English-style garden, which demonstrates the diversity possible in a

Villa Bagatelle

small space. The wooded oasis is crammed with more than 350 varieties of exotic and indigenous plants, from apple trees to forsythia, along with two rock gardens, a stream and a pond.

The governor-general's summer residence was a few kilometres away, in the centre of Sillery. Additions over the years have turned Domaine Cataraqui (2141 Chemin St-Louis) into an elegant neo-classical villa. Purchased by the provincial government after the death of the last owner, Catherine Rhodes, the house was restored to the style of the 1930s when she lived here with her husband, the artist Henry Percyval Tudor-Hart. Some furnishings, photographs and paintings belonging to the couple remain in the house, which also serves as the provincial government's official reception centre and as an art gallery, hosting three major exhibitions a year.

DOMAINE CATARAQUI

Just as elegant are other buildings on the estate such as the stable and Tudor-Hart's studio. The artist treated the front lawn as a canvas, using dynamite to duplicate the contours of waves rippling through the St. Lawrence, visible at the end of the property. You can easily spend an hour wandering among the flower beds and along trails through a forest of catalpa, Japanese ginkgo and other species. This is an idyllic setting for the various musical groups that perform Wednesday evenings and Sunday mornings in summer.

Nearly directly below, at the base of the cliff, at 2320 Chemin du Foulon, is the Maison des Jésuites. The Jesuits set up their first permanent mission in North America beside the St. Lawrence where Native people fished for eel. Fire demolished the original home. The present stone house was built around 1730, with the second floor being added about 100 years later. Inside are photographs, amulets and other artifacts unearthed on digs here and a copy of a 1769 romance novel written by a resident, Frances Brooke — this was the first English-language book published in Canada. The Jesuits tried to persuade the Montagnais, Algonquin and Attikamek nations to settle among them, but only a few stayed here permanently. The Amerindian camp in the back yard is a reminder of their presence, as are the wooden crosses across the street in the Indian cemetery.

Back up the cliff, nearly adjacent to the bridges connecting the north and south shores, is the Aquarium du Québec. The collection of more than 3,500 specimens ranges from pythons to piranhas. Small outdoor pools are the year-round home of the seals that perform in two shows a day. Rivalling the exhibits is the aquarium's location on the edge of a forested cliff. There's an excellent view of the river and Quebec Bridge (the world's longest cantilevered

bridge). A stroll through the woods brings you to a picnic area, a hatchery for rainbow trout, a skeleton of a whale at the exhibit on the St. Lawrence and the old toll station for crossing the river.

LAVAL UNIVERSITY

A few blocks north, opposite three large shopping centres, is Université Laval's Roger Van Den Hende garden at 2480 Blvd. Hochelaga, named for its founder, a professor of ornamental horticulture. The garden ranks as one of eastern Canada's most beautiful. From May to September the public can tour the six hectares, filled with more than 2,000 plant species from Europe, Asia and North America, an arboretum, and a water garden. The highlight for many visitors is the extensive rose garden. The more than 200 different types, from shrub to hybrid teas, have unusually vibrant colours, a result of the area's cold nights.

JARDIN VAN DEN HENDE

In Charlesbourg, the Jardin Zoologique du Québec at 9300 Rue de la Faune is popular not just with children but also with photographers looking for a place to shoot wedding pictures. That's because the zoo is also a horticultural park with flower beds, a lake inhabited by flamingoes, a river with ducks and swans, and two waterfalls. Trolleys (rides begin at the entrance) circle the park without stopping. Walk instead, following moose tracks and bear paws painted on the paths. The six-kilometre route goes by most of the 600 animals. Besides moose, polar bears and pythons, there are farm animals and a petting zoo. A guide inside one old stone house — from the days when a mink farm was located here — might also offer you a chance to caress an African cockroach. Falcons and vultures soar overhead in the summer birds-of-prey show.

TRADITIONAL HURON VILLAGE

On leaving the zoo, drive east to reach Wendake reserve, the only Huron reserve in Canada. Converted by the Jesuits and allied with the French, the Huron left what is now Ontario more than 300 years ago to settle here. A wooden palisade circles the re-created traditional Huron village, which offers a glimpse into the lives of the ancestors of the present residents. Inside the longhouse a full-sized doe

hangs from the rafters and someone might be tanning a beaver skin by the smokehouse. In one building costumes help explain the differences between the various nations. The village restaurant serves typical aboriginal food and its row of tiny shops sell everything from herbal remedies to recordings of Huron music. The Traditional Huron-Wendake Village is open year-round, with dance and song performances from May to September.

Montmorency Falls

Île d'Orléans, a small island a 15-minute drive east of Quebec City, remains rooted in the past. The entire island was named an historic district by the Quebec government in 1970. The first settlers arrived in 1649 and most buildings date from the 18th and 19th centuries. Driving the 67-kilometre road around the island reveals a bucolic landscape, a vista of farms, stone manors and churches interspersed with a few artisans practising time-honoured crafts.

When he set out to conquer Quebec in 1759, General James Wolfe set up his headquarters at the western tip of Île d'Orléans, in Ste-Pétronille, the smallest of the island's six parishes. His takeover of the island wasn't always peaceable. The Manoir Mauvide-Genest in St-Jean, for example, rated the finest example of rural architecture under the French regime, still bears the pockmarks of British cannon fire in its stone walls. The Norman-style manor is today a museum and restaurant.

Elsewhere on the island, the Parc Maritime de Saint-Laurent celebrates the shipbuilding heritage of St-Laurent parish with exhibits and on-site demonstrations of wooden boat-building, a blacksmith demonstrates traditional techniques at the Forge à Pique-Assaut and weavers spin rugs at the Economusée du Tapis in St-Pierre. To see other works by local craftsmen, visit the parish church, Canada's oldest village church.

On the mainland, just east of the Île d'Orléans bridge, Montmorency Falls plunges 83 metres, a drop nearly one and a half times greater than that of Niagara Falls. For a superb view, cross the pedestrian bridge suspended over the falls. The cable car offers another panorama, as well as an alternative to climbing the 400 stairs connecting the upper and lower boardwalks. Perched on top of the cliff close to the falls is a Palladian-style villa, a replica of the original constructed around 1783 for the governor of Quebec, later rented by the Duke of Kent. A small museum tells the history of the graceful white wooden building, which also houses an art gallery, bar and restaurant. Sunday buffet is popular with local residents.

SAINTE-ANNE-DE-BEAUPRÉ BASILICA

Further east, along Highway 138, sits Sainte-Anne-de-Beaupré basilica. Pilgrims have been coming to this site since 1658; it is considered the oldest Christian shrine in North America. And they're still coming, more than a million of them a year, to pray inside the most recent church on this site: a concrete edifice warmed by glimmering mosaics, carved stones and 200 stained-glass windows. In summer, evening candlelight processions sometimes wind over the nearby hillside, where life-sized bronze figures line the Way of the Cross. On the opposite side of the basilica, the round Cyclorama features a museum and a panoramic painting of Jerusalem. One floor covers the history of the pilgrimages, displaying photographs along with earrings, necklaces and other offerings to St. Anne. The second floor displays the church's treasures, from silver chalices to an 18th-century gilded altar.

WINTER FUN AT MONT SAINTE-ANNE

The shrine and its little town sit at the foot of Mont Ste-Anne, an 800-metre-high mountain that offers some of the best alpine and cross-country skiing east of the Rockies. The resort has 56 downhill trails totalling 84 kilometres. Thirteen percent of them are classified as extremely difficult. The cross-country network, the largest in Canada, has 223 kilometres of trails, while a large funpark and two halfpipes lure snowboarders. At the base of the mountain are a skating rink and ski museum. In summer, mountain-bikers and hikers take over the trails, sightseers ride the lifts and golfers play on the two courses gracing the foot of the mountain.

SKIING AT MONT SAINTE-ANNE

Cycling Mont Sainte-Anne

In summer, take the ferry across from Quebec City to Lévis and catch a shuttle bus that meanders around the city. Among the stops is Fort No. 1, built early in the 19th century to fend off an American attack that never came. The guides who lead tours wear costumes modelled on the uniforms of the Royal Engineers, but the fort is no longer a military installation. It was used as a storage depot for ammunition through two world wars and was finally decomissioned in 1948.

East of Lévis, close to the town of Montmagny, sits Grosse Île. For more than 150 years the small island was the main gateway to Canada for thousands of immigrants and the quarantine station for those afflicted with cholera, typhoid and black plague. A sense of sadness pervades this final destination for so many. The largest graveyard is known as the Irish Cemetery. Most of the more than 5,000 men, women and children buried here were fleeing the Irish potato famine. The sightseeing trolley also visits the Celtic Cross, the Catholic church, the hospital, and the Disinfection Building where pipes over narrow shower stalls sprayed each ship passenger with mercury chloride. The only way to reach this island operated by Parks Canada is on licensed boats. Tour operators offer packages from Montmagny, nearby Berthier-sur-Mer and Quebec City. The tours last around three hours. There are picnic tables and the hotel has a cafeteria.

East of Ste-Anne-de-Beaupré, villages cling to cliffs overlooking the St. Lawrence. This area has long been a magnet for artists — even the smallest village boasts a gallery. The scenic landscape leads to Pointe-au-Pic, where a turretted stone castle, Manoir Richelieu, was recently renovated to celebrate its 100th anniversary. Opposite the hotel, try your luck at the casino. Or hop aboard a boat for a whale-watching tour or a ride down the majestic Saguenay fjord.

Golf at Mont Sainte-Anne

Listings: Contents

GETTING THERE

MONTREAL

Located along the shores of the St. Lawrence River, Montreal is easy to get to by air, highway, rail and water.

BY AIR

- Dorval International Airport: Located 18 kilometres west of downtown Montreal, the airport is accessible from highway 20 and by commuter train or shuttle bus. Since 1997, the airport handles regular scheduled flights from local to international destinations. Some thirty-four major airlines offer regularly scheduled flights. For information call 514 633-3105.
- Mirabel Airport: Located 58 kilometres north of downtown Montreal, this airport serves charter air traffic and cargo flights. Taxis and shuttles to downtown hotels and Central Station are available. The airport serves Air Transat, Canada 3000, Cubana Airlines, Royal and Sky Service. For information call 450 476-3010.

BY ROAD

By car or by bus, travellers can reach Montreal by several major routes. Highways 20 and 40 enter Montreal from the west. Hwy. 20 also enters Montreal from the northeast, hugging the shores of the St. Lawrence River. Hwy. 10 enters Montreal from the east over the Champlain Bridge. Hwy. 15 runs towards Montreal from Quebec's southern border shared with New York State and from the north. Out-of-town buses arrive and depart from the Montreal Bus Terminal at 505 Boul. de Maisonneuve E. Adirondack Trailways offers rides to New York City and Orléans Express Coach Lines covers Quebec City and other destinations. From May to October, the Rout-Pass entitles holders to unlimited bus travel for 15 consecutive days in Quebec and Ontario. Call the station at 514 281-2281 for bus company fares and schedules.

BY RAIL

Train travellers arrive at Central Station, 895 Rue de la Gauchetière O./W. Montreal is served by the VIA Rail Canada System, the network that provides all rail service throughout Canada. Amtrak provides daily service to New York and Washington. VIA Rail offers a Canrailpass, valid for one month, which allows the holder to 12 days of train travel across Canada. Central Station is located across from the Hilton Montréal Bonaventure. The station also serves commuter rail lines and is connected by indoor tunnels to Montreal's subway system and several underground shopping centres. Call 514 989-2626 for train schedules and fares.

QUEBEC CITY

Located 253 kilometres northeast of Montreal along the St. Lawrence River, Quebec City is easily accessible by air, road and rail.

BY AIR

Jean-Lesage International Airport: The airport is located 16 kilometres from downtown Quebec City along route 138 Boul. Wilfrid-Hamel and autoroute 540. The airport offers scheduled flights with Air Alliance, Air Canada, Air Nova, Canadian International, Canadian Air, Air Atlantic, Northwest Airlink and charter flights with Aeropro, Aviation Portneuf and Aviation Roger Forgues. For information on flights, call Transports Canada 418 640-2600. A taxi costs about $25 from the airport to downtown. The Maple Leaf Sightseeing Tours and Dupont provide shuttle services for $8.50 one way or $16 round trip. Call 418 649-9226 for shuttle schedules.

BY ROAD

Quebec City is served by highway 20 by the south shore of the St. Lawrence River and hwy. 40 from the north. Buses arrive at the Bus Terminal at 320, Rue Abraham-Martin.

Intercar Côte-Nord links Quebec City with several northern towns and Orléans Express Coach Lines link the city with the rest of Quebec. From May to October, the Rout-Pass entitles holders to unlimited bus travel for 15 consecutive days in Quebec and Ontario. Call 418 525-3000 for information.

BY RAIL

Via Rail Canada offers daily service between Quebec City and Montreal with regular and first class cars. Call 418 692-3940 for information and reservations. Trains arrive and depart from Gare du Palais at 450 Rue de la Gare-du-Palais in downtown Quebec City. Call 418 524-4161 for information.

TRAVEL ESSENTIALS

MONEY

Currency can be exchanged at any bank at the prevailing rate. If you use a small local branch, it's best to call ahead to confirm their capacity to exchange, on the spot, any currency other than American funds. There are currency exchange booths at the airport. Banks are generally open from 10 a.m. to 4 p.m. Units of currency are similar to those of the United States, excepting the Canadian one-dollar (loonie) and two-dollar (twoonie) coins.

Most major North American credit cards, including American Express, Carte Blanche, Diners Club, EnRoute, MasterCard and Visa, are accepted almost everywhere. Traveller's cheques can be cashed in major hotels, some restaurants and large stores. Many stores and services will accept U.S. currency, but the exchange rate they offer may vary greatly. Since there are no laws enforcing foreign currency rates of exchange, we strongly recommend that you convert to Canadian funds before you make your purchases.

American visitors may also use bank or credit cards to make cash withdrawals from automated teller machines that are tied into international networks such as Cirrus and Plus. Before you leave home, check with your bank to find out what range of banking services its cards will allow you to use.

PASSPORTS

American citizens need only a proof of citizenship, such as a birth certificate or a voter's registration card. Naturalized U.S. citizens should carry a naturalization certificate. Permanent U.S. residents who are not citizens are advised to bring their Alien Registration Receipt Card. Citizens of all other countries, except Greenland and residents of St. Pierre et Miquelon, must bring a valid passport. Some may be required to obtain a visitor's visa. For details, please consult the Canadian embassy or consulate serving your home country.

CUSTOMS

Arriving

As a nonresident of Canada, you may bring in any reasonable amount of personal effects and food, and a full tank of gas. Special restrictions or quotas apply to certain specialty goods, and especially to plant-, agricultural - and animal-related materials. All items must be declared to Customs upon arrival and may include up to 200 cigarettes, 50 cigars, 400 grams of manufactured tobacco, and 400 tobacco sticks. Visitors are also permitted 1.14 litres (40 oz.) of liquor or wine, or 8.5 litres (24 x 12-oz cans or bottles) of beer.

You may bring in gifts for Canadian residents duty-free, up to a value of $60.00 (Canadian) each, provided they do not consist of alcohol, tobacco, or advertising material.

For more detailed information, please see the federal Customs (Revenue Canada) website (www.rc.gc.ca), the Customs information booklet "I DECLARE", or contact Revenue Canada, Communications Branch, Ottawa, Ontario K1A 0L5, by phone at 613 957-0275, or by fax at 613 957-9039.

Departing

For detailed customs rules for entering or re-entering the United States, please contact a U.S. Customs office before you visit the province of Quebec. Copies of the U.S. customs information brochure "Know Before You Go" are available from U.S. customs offices or by mail.

Travellers from other countries should also check on customs regulations before leaving home.

TAXES

Most goods and services are subject to a federal tax (GST) and a provincial tax (PST) in Quebec. Foreign residents may be entitled to certain tax rebates on tourism-related goods and services. For more information, ask for the Tax Refund for Visitors booklet, or contact Revenue Canada, Visitor Rebate Program, Ottawa ON K1A 1J5, by phone at 613 991-3346 or 1-800-668-4748 in Canada.

Goods and Services Tax (GST)

The federal Goods and Services Tax is 7%. This is a value-added consumption tax that applies to most goods, purchased gifts, food/beverages, and services, including most hotel and motel accommodation.

Provincial Sales Tax (PST)

The Quebec provincial sales tax is 7.5%. A PST refund form can also be obtained by contacting Revenue Quebec at 514 873-4692 or ask a retailer for a form.

GETTING ACQUAINTED

TIME ZONE

Montreal and Quebec City fall within the Eastern Standard Time Zone.

CLIMATE

Here are average Montreal temperatures, highs and lows; fluctuations from the norm are common:

January	21°F to 5°F -6°C to -15°C
February	25°F to 7°F -4 °C to -14°C
March	28°F to 19°F -2 °C to -7°C
April	52°F to 34°F 11°C to 1°C
May	66°F to 45°F 19 °C to 7°C
June	73°F to 55°F 23 °C to 13°C
July	79°F to 59°F 26°C to 15°C
August	77°F to 57°F 25 °C to 14°C
September	68°F to 48°F 20°C to 9°C
October	55°F to 39°F 13°C to 4°C
November	41°F to 28°F 5°C to -2°C
December	27°F to 12°F -3°C to -11°C

Average annual rainfall: 28.98"/73.63 cm.

Average annual snowfall: 84.33"/214.2 cm.

Average temperatures are +5.4C (41F) in spring, +19.4C (66.2F) in summer, +11.4C (51.8F) in autumn, and -6.1C (21.2F) in winter.

The average temperatures, highs and lows, in Quebec City are:

January	18°F to 1°F -8°C to -17°C
February	21°F to 3°F -6°C to -16°C
March	32°F to 16°F 0°C to -9°C
April	46°F to 28°F 8°C to -2°C
May	63°F to 41°F 17°C to 5°C
June	72°F to 50°F 22°C to 10°C
July	77°F to 55°F 25°C to 13°C
August	73°F to 54°F 23°C to 12°C
September	64°F to 45°F 18°C to 7°C
October	52°F to 36°F 11°C to 2°C
November	37°F to 25°F 3°C to -4°C
December	23°F to 9°F -5°C to -13°C

Average annual rainfall: 34.69"/88.13 cm.

Average annual snowfall: 132.67"/337 cm.

Average temperatures are +3.2C (37.4F) in spring, +17.7C (64.4F) in summer, +9.5C (50F) in autumn, and -8.3C (17.6F) in winter.

GUIDES AND INFORMATION SERVICES

Tourisme Québec operates more than 200 tourist information offices provincewide to provide regional information and seven Maison du tourisme, which offer more extensive services for visitors. For information call 1-800-363-7777 (Canada and the United States) or write to info@tourisme.gouv.qc.ca or Tourisme Québec: at P.O. Box 979, Montreal QC H3C 2W3, Fax: 514 864-3838. Also, visit on the web at www.tourisme.gouv.qc.ca for comprehensive information about accommodations, camping and attractions throughout the province of Quebec, including Montreal.

MONTREAL

- Greater Montreal Convention and Tourism Bureau: 1555 Rue Peel, Suite 600, Montreal QC H3A 1X6; 514 844-5400; 1-800-363-7777 (North America) Fax: 514 844-5757, www.tourisme-montreal.org. For regional information.

- Maison du tourisme: 1001 Square Dorchester, Montreal QC H3B 1G2; 514 873-2015; 1-800- 363-7777 (North America). The Infotouriste Centre handles travel planning, hotel reservations, car rentals, attractions and guided bus tours.
- Tourist Information Centre of Old Montreal: 174 Rue Notre-Dame E. Near Métro Champs-de- Mars. Drop in at the centre for bus maps, road maps, telephone cards, Museums Passes and bicycle path passes as well as brochures about attractions. Or visit its Website at www.montrealcam.com to see Montreal in real time by the Greater Montreal LiveCam Network.
- Ville de Montréal: Montreal City Hall, 275 Rue Notre Dame E., Montreal QC H2Y 1C6, 514 872-3355.

QUEBEC CITY

- Office du tourisme et des congrès de la Communauté urbaine de Québec: 899 Rue St-Joseph E., Second Floor, Quebec City QC G1K 8E2; 418 522-3511; Fax 418 529-3121
- Maison du Tourisme: 12 Rue Ste-Anne. Located across from the Château Frontenac, the Infotouriste Centre provides extensive local information plus hotel and car rental reservations. Mailing address: Tourisme Quebec, C.P. 979, Montreal QC H3C 2W3, or www.tourisme.qc.ca.
- Transport Canada Airport Information: Information available on the airport, flights and tourist attractions. Call 418 640-2600.
- Ville de Québec: Quebec City Hall, 43, Côte de la Fabrique, Quebec City QC G1R 5M1. Urban Life Interpretation Centre of the Ville de Québec, 418 691-7630.

LANGUAGE

Most Montrealers speak English, but when travelling through some areas of the province, you might as well be in France. But unlike speaking French in Paris, using a phrase or two en français will most likely get a cheer of praise by most French-speaking Quebecers.

GETTING AROUND

TRAVELLING IN MONTREAL AND QUEBEC CITY

Montreal is an island connected to the mainland by bridges to the north and south of the city. The city is served by the Ville Marie Expressway which leads to highways 10, 15 and 20 to travel west and east. The Decarie Expressway leads to hwy. 40 going north and west.

If you're a member of any recognized auto club affiliates (AAA, CAA, etc.), the CAA-Quebec will provide all club services. In Montreal, call 514 861-9663 or 1-877-832-6744. In Quebec City, call member services at 418 624-0708 or emergency services at 418 624-4000.

PUBLIC TRANSPORTATION

MONTREAL

The Société de Transport de la Communauté urbaine de Montréal (STCUM) operates from 5:30 a.m. to 12:30 a.m. Some bus lines run all night. The subway system consists of four Métro lines and covers 65 kilometres across 65 stations, with free transfers to 140 bus lines. Exact fare is required. Free maps, discount tickets and day passes are available at all Métro stations and in many convenience shops. At the time of publication, one adult ticket is $1.90 or $8.25 for six tickets. The Tourist Card is available at the Infotouriste Centre at 1001 Square Dorchester, the Tourist Information Centre at 174 Rue Notre-Dame E., or at Metro Berri-UQAM for unlimited travel for one day for $5 or for three days for $12. Call A-U-T-O-B-U-S (514-288-6287) for bus lines, schedules and information.

Commuter Buses and Trains

Regular train service to Montreal's suburbs operates from Central Station and from Windsor Station. Call 514 288-6287 for train schedules for both stations. Regular bus service on the South Shore run from Metro Longueuil (450 463-0131) and in Laval from Metro Henri Bourassa (514 688-6520).

A ferry service offers rides to pedestrians and cyclists from the Old Port to the Parc des Îles, Longueuil, Promenade Bellerive in East Montreal, and Île Charron from mid-May to mid-October. Call 514 281-8000 for information.

QUEBEC CITY

The Société de transport de la Communauté urbaine de Québec operates bus lines throughout Quebec City. Fares at the time of publication are $1.85 for adults and $1.25 for children. Day passes are available. Call 418 627-2511 for information.

A Winter Shuttle, the HiverExpress, operates daily from downtown Quebec City to Ste-Foy hotels and to a number of outdoor activity sites. Call for reservations at 418 525-5191.

The Société des traversiers du Québec operates year-round daily ferry services from Quebec City to Levis, across the St. Lawrence River. For information call 418 644-3704 or 418 837-2408.

CARS AND RENTALS

Most foreign driver's licenses are valid in Quebec. Non-resident drivers and passengers of automobiles licensed in Quebec are entitled to the same compensation from the Société de l'assurance automobile du Québec as Quebec residents if they are injured in an accident in the province. Other non-resident accident victims, including pedestrians, cyclists and drivers of cars not licensed in Quebec can be compensated in inverse proportion to their responsibility for any accidents. Owners of vehicles driven in Quebec must have at least $50,000 in liability coverage. For additional information, contact the Societé de l'assurance automobile du Québec at 418-528-3100.

Distances are indicated in kilometres and speed limits in kilometres per hour. One kilometre equals about 5/8 of a mile. To convert from kilometres to miles, multiply kilometres by 0.6. To convert from miles to kilometres, multiply miles by 1.6. Metric measurements are used for motor fuel. One litre equals about one-quarter of an American gallon, or about one-fifth of an Imperial gallon.

Speed limits on highways and main roads are 100 km/h maximum and 60 km/h minimum. The provincial police prohibit possession of a radar detector, whether connected or not, and fines range from $500 to $1,000. Turning right on a red light is strictly prohibited everywhere in Quebec except when allowed by an additional green arrow at a stoplight.

Seatbelt use by passengers and drivers is mandatory.

MONTREAL

- Alamo Rent-a-Car, Dorval Airport, 514 633-1222, www.goalamo.com
- Avis Rent-a-Car, 1225 Rue Metcalfe: 514 866-7906, www.avis.com.
- Hertz Canada Ltee., 1073 Rue Drummond: 514 938-1717, Website: www.hertz.com.
- Pelletier Car and Minibus Rental, 3585 Rue Berri: 514 281-5000, Website: www.nacra.net.
- Sako Location d'Autos Inc., 2350 Rue Manella, Town of Mont-Royal: 514 735-3500, Website: www.sako.com.

Consult the Yellow Pages for more agencies.

QUEBEC CITY

- Discount Location, 1-800-263-2355.
- Hertz Canada, 1-800-263-0678; Tilden, 1-800-387-4747.
- Via Route, 418 692-2660.

Consult the Yellow Pages for more agencies.

TOURS

MONTREAL

- Autocar Connaisseur Grayline. Sightseeing tours on board a replica of Montreal's street cars of the past. Infotouriste Centre, 1001 Square Dorchester; 514 934-1222.
- Autocar Royal Tour de Ville. Bilingual city tours with ten stop-off points. Infotouriste Centre, 1001 Square Dorchester; 514 871-4733.
- Aventure Boréale Inc. Day-trips to countryside. Downtown departures for canoeing, fishing, hiking in the

summer and dogsledding, ice fishing, snowmobiling, and snowshoeing in the winter. Transportation and meals included. 514 271-1230.

- La Balade du Vieux-Port. A bilingual guided tour of the Old Port's past. 514 496-7678.
- Bateau-mouche au Vieux-Port de Montréal. Tour the city in a glass-roofed boat for spectacular views. Jacques-Cartier Pier at the Old Port. 514 849-9952, www.bateau-mouche.com.
- Delco Aviation Lteé. See Montreal from a seaplane in the summer or try hydraskis in the winter. 450 663-4311.
- Flowers Aviation Inc. Cessna 206 seaplanes tour regions throughout the province. 514 727- 6486.
- Following the Footsteps of La Bolduc. A walking tour traces the stomping grounds of the famous Quebec singer Mary Travers, nicknamed la Bolduc, in the Hochelaga-Maisonneuve district. Leaving from Maisonneuve Market Place. 514 256-4636.
- Guido Nuncheri, the Stained Glass Alchemist. Peruse Nuncheri's stained glass masterpieces in Montreal churches in four neighbourhoods. Leaving from Maisonneuve Market Place. 514 256-4636.
- Guidatour. Daily walking tours of Old Montreal from June through October. Tickets on sale at Notre Dame Basilica. Private guided tours of Montreal and environs available in several languages. 514 844-4021 or 1-800-363-4021.
- Interactive Tour of the Old Port. From May to September, pick up a phone from the Cellcom booth and dial #PORT to experience an interactive tour of the harborside. Next to the La Balade platform at the Old Port. For more information, call 514 496-7678.
- Montreal AML Cruises. Sail on the St. Lawrence River on guided tour boats or dinner cruises. Bilingual guides. 514 842-3871, 1-800-667-3131, www.croisieresaml.com.
- Montreal Guide Service. Multilingual guided tours tailored for individuals or groups. 514 342-8994, www.total.net/~montreal.
- Old Montreal Ghost Trail. Meet some of the city's most famous ghosts on an evening walking tour. 514 868-0303.
- Les Services de Calèches et traîneaux Lucky Luc. Tour Montreal in your own horse-drawn carriage, sleigh or long coach. Door-to-door. 514 934-6105.
- Vélo Aventure Montréal Inc. Rental and sales of bicycles and in-line skates plus bicycle tours. Located at the Convoyeurs Pier at the Old Port. 514 847-0666.
- Vélo-Tour Montréal. Bicycle rentals and tours in English, French and Spanish. 99 Rue de la Commune O./W.; 514 236-8356.

QUEBEC CITY

- Aéro Québec Inc. See the city by seaplane. 418 872-0206.
- Belle Epoque calèches et Tramway royal. Horse-drawn buggies offer tours for small groups. 418 687-9797.
- Calèches du Vieux-Québec. Horse-drawn carriages of the Old Town. 418 683-9222.
- Corporation du tourisme religieux de Québec. Walking tours of religious sites. 418 694-0665.
- Héli-Express. See Quebec City from above on a helicopter tour. 418 877-5890.
- Maple Leaf Sightseeing Tours and Dupont offer a variety of bus tours. 418 649-9226.
- Old Quebec Tours. Bus tours for small groups of the city and environs. Whale watching tour available. 418 664-0460
- Québec Historical Society. Walking tours to discover the city's past. 418 692-0556.
- Visite historique de Québec. Bus tours cover historical landmarks. 418 656-4245.

ACCOMMODATION

What follows is a good cross-section of the accommodation options Montreal and Quebec City offers.

Montreal has more than 23,000 rooms to suit every taste and every budget. The Greater Montreal area offers comfortable and convenient accommodations for groups of any size in hotels, motels, apartment hotels, bed and breakfast homes, college dormitories, campgrounds and resorts. The major hotel chains are represented in the city, as well as a range of lesser-known but equally comfortable establishments.

The majority of these establishments are located in the downtown core, near the subway system. Many are within walking distance of the major convention sites and shopping areas.

The Quebec government is responsible for regulating and supervising hotel establishments and campgrounds, as well as issuing permits. Non-Canadian residents can receive a cash rebate of the federal goods and services tax (GST) and the provincial sales tax (PST) on short-term accommodations and on some purchases.

Infotouriste offers a hotel reservation service for Montreal and Quebec City. Contact them at 1001 Square Dorchester, Montreal QC H3B 1G2; 514 873-2015; 1-800-363-7777 (North America).

Approximate prices are indicated, based on the average cost, at time of publishing, for two persons staying in a double room (excluding taxes): $ = $50-$90; $$ = $90-$180; $$$ = above $180.

If you're travelling at the last minute or looking for hotel savings during the off-season, try using the services of the Diner's Club Hotel Savings Hotline at 1-800-567-8850. The service does not require that you be a Diner's Club user. It offers a range of hotel options at good rates for same-day accommodation. However, during busy periods you can't rely on this service to have any inventory of rooms. The service does not help if you're booking in advance, though it can give you an idea of how low a specific hotel will go when it is not too busy.

For the locations of downtown hotels in Montreal, see the map on page 10.

MONTREAL

Hotels: Dorval Airport

- Day's Inn Montreal Aéroport, 4545 Chemin Côte-Vertu O./W., St-Laurent QC H4S 1C8; 514 332-2720, 1-800-325-2525, Fax: 514 332-4512. Conference rooms, public transportation nearby. $$
- Econo Lodge Aéroport, 6755 Chemin Côte-de-Liesse, St-Laurent QC H4T 1E5; 514 735- 5702, 1-800-553-2666, Fax: 514 340-9278. Airport shuttle, conference room, outdoor swimming pool, nearby golf course. $$
- Four Points Hotel Dorval, 6600 Chemin Côte-de-Liesse, St-Laurent QC H4T 1E3; 514 735- 7788, 1-800-325-3535, Fax: 514 735-8515. Five minutes from airport. Family and corporate rooms. Indoor pool and water slide. $$
- Holiday Inn Aéroport-Montreal, 6500 Chemin Côte-de-Liesse, St-Laurent QC H4T 1E3; 514 739-3391, 1-800-361-5430, Fax: 514 739-6591, E-mail: hiairport@interfusion.net. Eight minutes from airport. Fifteen minutes from downtown. Free airport shuttle. Tropical garden, indoor and outdoor poor, sauna, whirlpool. $$
- Hotel Ramada Aéroport Montreal, 7300 Chemin Côte-de-Liesse, St-Laurent QC H4T1E7; 514 733-8818, 1-800-318-8818, Fax: 514 733-9889. Airport shuttle, conference rooms, outdoor pool, near golf course. $$
- Montreal Aéroport Hilton, 12505 Chemin Côte-de-Liesse, Dorval QC H9P 1B7; 514 631- 2411, 1-800-445-8667, Fax: 514 631-0192. Free airport shuttle. $$$
- Quality Hotel Aéroport Montreal, 7700 Chemin Côte-de-Liesse, St-Laurent QC H4T 1E7; 514 731-7821, 1-800-553-2666, Fax: 514 731-1538. Airport shuttle, babysitting, conference rooms, near golf course, spa/fitness center, outdoor pool. $$

Hotels: Mirabel Airport

- Le Château de l'Aéroport-Mirabel, 12555 Rue Commerce A-4, Mirabel Airport, Mirabel QC J7N 1E3; 450 476-1611, 1-800-361-0924, Fax: 514 476-0873. Airport shuttle, indoor pool, conference rooms, babysitting, non-smoking rooms, spa. $$
- Motel au P'tit Sapin, 16033 Boul. Curé-Labelle (route 117), Mirabel QC J7Z 5T4; 450 432- 0606, Fax: 450 432-4691. Airport shuttle, near gold course. $
- Motel Moulin Rouge 1993, 13219 Boul. Curé-Labelle (route 117), Mirabel QC J7J 1H1; 450 430-2062, Fax: 450 435-8415. Airport shuttle, non-smoking rooms, snowmobiling services, nearby cross-country skiing and golf course, outdoor pool. $$

Hotels: Downtown Montreal

- Appartement-Hôtel Le Riche Bourg, 2170 Ave. Lincoln, Montreal QC H3H 2N5; 514 935-9224, 1-800-678-6323, Fax: 514 935-5049. Indoor pool, gym. $$$, **Map 1**
- Appartements Touristiques du Centre-Ville, 3463 Rue Ste-Famille, Suite 008, Montreal QC H2X 2K7; 514 845-0431, Fax: 514 845-0262. Fitness centre, indoor pool, some rooms with cooking facilities. $
- Auberge de la Fontaine, 1301 Rue Rachel E., Montreal QC H2J 2K1; 514 597-0166, 1-800-597-0597, Fax: 514 597-0496. Conference rooms, bicycle rentals. $$
- Auberge du Parc, 5500 Rue Sherbrooke E., Montreal QC H1N 1A1; 514 256-5500, 1-800-470-5500. Airport shuttle, indoor pool, fitness center, conference rooms. $$
- Auberge le Jardin d'Antoine, 2024, rue St-Denis, Montreal QC H2X 3K7; 514 843-4506, 1-800-361-4506, Fax: 514 281-1491. Airport shuttle. $$
- Best Western Europa Centre-Ville, 1240 Rue Drummond, Montreal QC H3G 1V7; 514 866-6492, 1-800-361-3000, Fax: 514 861-4089. Airport shuttle, babysitting, spa/fitness centre, conference rooms, some rooms with cooking facilities. $$, **Map 2**
- Best Western Ville-Marie Hôtel et Suites, 3407 Rue Peel, Montreal QC H3A 1W7; 514 288-4141, 1-800-361-7791, Fax: 514 288-3021. Conference rooms, some rooms with cooking facilities, fitness centre. $$$, **Map 3**
- Le Centre Sheraton, 1201 Boul. René-Lévesque O./W., Montreal QC H3B 2L7; 514 878- 2000, 1-800-325-3535, Fax: 514 878-2305. Corporate rooms, business center, computer hook-ups, spa/fitness centre and lounge. $$$, **Map 4**
- Château Royal Hotel Suites, 1420 Rue Crescent, Montreal QC H3G 2B7; 514 848-0999, 1- 800-363-0335, Fax: 514 848-9403. Cooking facilities in all rooms, babysitting. $$$, **Map 5**
- Day's Inn Montréal Centre-Ville, 215 Boul. René-Lévesque E., Montreal QC H2X 1N7; 514 393-3388, 1-800-668-3872, Fax: 514 395-9999. Conference rooms. $$, **Map 6**
- Hilton Montréal Bonaventure, 1 Place Bonaventure, Montreal QC H5A 1E4; 514 878-2332, 1-800-267-2575, Fax: 514 878-3881. Airport shuttle, conference rooms, rooftop garden with indoor and outdoor pools. $$$, **Map 7**
- Holiday Inn Montréal-Midtown, 420 Rue Sherbrooke O./W., Montreal QC H3A 1B4; 514 842-6111, Fax: 514 842-9381. Airport shuttle, indoor pool, conference rooms, fitness centre. $$$, **Map 8**
- Hôtel Château Versailles, 1659 Rue Sherbrooke O./W., Montreal QC H3H 1E3; 514 933-3611, 1-800-361-7199, Fax: 514 933-6867. European charm, airport shuttle, near museums. $$, **Map 9**
- Hôtel Courtyard Marriott Montréal, 410 Rue Sherbrooke O./W., Montreal QC H3A 1B3; 514 844-8855, 1-800-449-6654, Fax: 514 844-0912. Airport shuttle, indoor pool, spa/fitness centre. $$$, **Map 10**
- Hôtel de la Couronne, 1029 Rue St-Denis, Montreal QC H2X 3H9; 514 845-0901. Airport shuttle, some rooms with shared bathrooms. $
- Hôtel Delta Montréal, 475 Ave. Président-Kennedy, Montreal QC

H3A 1J7; 514 286-1986, 1- 800-268-1133, Fax: 514 284-4342. Conference rooms, babysitting, indoor and outdoor pools, spa/fitness centre. $$$, **Map 11**

- Hôtel de Paris, 901 Rue Sherbrooke E., Montreal QC H2L 1L3; 514 522-6861, 1-800-567- 7217, Fax: 514 522-1387. Airport shuttle, bicycle rentals. $$
- Hôtel du Fort, 1390 Rue du Fort, Montreal QC H3H 2R7; 514 938-8333, 1-800-565-6333, Fax: 514 938-2078. Conference rooms, babysitting, fitness centre. $$$, **Map 12**
- Hôtel du Manoir Saint-Denis, 2006 Rue St-Denis, Montreal QC H2X 3K7; 514 843-3670, 1-888-567-7654, Fax: 514 844-2188. Restaurant on premises. $
- Hôtel du Parc, 3625 Ave. du Parc, Montreal QC H2X 3P8; 514 288-6666, 1-800-363-0735, Fax: 514 288-2469. Airport shuttle, babysitting, conference rooms, spa/fitness centre, cooking facilities in some rooms. $$$, **Map 13**
- Hôtel Dynastie, 1553 Rue St-Hubert, Montreal QC H2L 3Z1; 514 529-5210, Fax; 514 695- 1167. Near amenities. $
- Hôtel Gouverneur Place Dupuis, 1415 Rue St-Hubert, Montreal QC H2L 3Y9; 514 842-4881, 1-888-910-1111, Fax: 514 842-1584. Airport shuttle, babysitting, conference rooms, indoor pool. $$$, **Map 14**
- Hôtel Inter-Continental Montréal, 360 Rue St-Antoine O./W., Montreal QC H2Y 3X4. 514 987-9900, 1-800-361-3600, Fax: 514 847-8730. Conference rooms, babysitting, indoor pool, fitness centre. $$$, **Map 15**
- Hôtel Lord Berri, 1199 Rue Berri, Montreal QC H2L 4C6; 514 845-9236, 1-888-363-0363, Fax: 514 849-9855. Airport shuttle, conference rooms, near bus terminal, fitness centre. $$, **Map 16**
- Hôtel Maritime Plaza, 1155 Rue Guy, Montreal QC H3H 2K5; 514 932-1411, 1-800-363- 6255, Fax: 514 932-0446. Airport shuttle, conference rooms, indoor pool, near golf course. $$$, **Map 17**
- Hôtel de la Montagne, 1430 Rue de la Montagne, Montreal QC H3G 1Z5; 514 288-5656, 1- 800-361-6262, Fax: 288-9658. Classic rooms, airport shuttle, conference rooms, babysitting, outdoor pool, swanky lobby bar. $$$, **Map 18**
- Hôtel Montréal Crescent, 1366 Boul. René-Lévesque O./W., Montreal QC H3G 1T4. Conference room, near amenities. $$, **Map 19**
- Hôtel Wyndham Montréal, 1255 Rue Jeanne-Mance, P.O. Box 130, Montreal QC H5B 1E5; 514 285-1450, 1-800-361-8234, Email: info@wyndham-mtl.com. Business centre. Coffeemaker, voice mail, dataport, iron and ironing board in every room. $$, **Map 20**
- Loews Hôtel Vogue, 1425 Rue de la Montagne, Montreal QC H3G 1Z3; 514 285-5555, 1-800-465-6654, Fax: 514 849-8903. Conference rooms, babysitting, bicycle rentals, fitness centre. $$$, **Map 21**
- Marriott Château Champlain, 1 Place du Canada, Montreal QC H3B 4C9; 514 878-9000, 1-800-228-9290, Fax: 514 878-6777. Airport shuttle, massage, hairdresser, sauna and fitness centre indoor pool and babysitting. $$$, **Map 22**
- Novotel Montréal Centre, 1180 Rue de la Montagne, Montreal QC H3G 1Z1; 514 861-6000, 1-800-221-4542, Fax: 514 861-0992. Airport shuttle, conference rooms, babysitting, fitness centre. $$$, **Map 23**
- Quality Hotel (Journey's End), 3440 Ave. du Parc, Montreal QC H2X 2H5; 514 849-143, 1-800-465-6116, Fax: 514 849-6564. Babysitting, restaurant on premises. $$, **Map 24**
- The Queen Elizabeth Hotel, 900 Boul. René-Lévesque O./W., Montreal QC H3B 4A5; 514 861-3511, 1-800-441-1414, Fax: 514 954-2258. Conference rooms, airport shuttle, fitness centre, express check in/out, indoor pool. The Beaver Club dining room. $$, **Map 25**

- Radisson Hôtel des Gouverneurs, 777 Rue University, Montreal QC H3C 3Z7, 514 879-1370, 1-800-333-3333, Fax: 514 879-1761, E-mail: ventes@radissonmontreal.com. Near Old Montreal, convention centre, World Trade Centre and the Stock Exchange Tower. Offers the city's only revolving rooftop restaurant. Two telephones, voice mail, computer data ports in each room. $$$, **Map 26**
- Ritz-Carlton Kempinksi, 1228 Rue Sherbrooke O./W., Montreal QC H3G 1H6; 514-842- 4212, 1-800-363-0366. Old world elegance, with shops and restaurant serving breakfast, lunch, dinner and afternoon tea. $$$. **Map 27**

Bed & Breakfasts

Montreal has hundreds of bed and breakfast rooms available in many locations. There are also several services that cater to finding visitors accommodations that suit their needs. Stay in a loft in Old Montreal or a Victorian mansion in Westmount as an alternative to hotels.

- Angelica Blue Bed & Breakfast, 1215 Rue Ste-Élisabeth, Montreal QC H2X 3C3; 514 844- 5048, Fax: 514 844-2114. Non-smoking rooms, pets allowed, meals served. $
- Au Chat qui Rêve, 23 Ave. Laurier E., Montreal QC H2T 1E4; 514 276-8755. Meals served, non-smoking rooms. $
- Le Beau Soleil, 355, Rue St-Paul E., Montreal QC H2Y 1H3; 514 871-0299. Meals, no credit cards, non-smoking rooms. $
- Bed & Breakfast de Chez-Nous, 3717 Rue Ste-Famille, Montreal QC H2X 2L7; 514 845- 8008. Near Prince Arthur area. Studios and fully furnished apartments can accommodate as many as six people. 3 rooms. 10 suites. $
- Bed & Breakfast City-wide Network, C.P. 575, Snowdon Station, Montreal QC H3X 3T8; 514 738-9410, 1-800-738-4338, Fax: 514 735-7493, Email: info@bbmontreal.com. Downtown condominiums to Victorian mansions in tony Outremont and Westmount. 30 rooms. 5 suites. $-$$
- A Bed & Breakfast - A Downtown Network, 3458 Ave. Laval, Montreal QC H2X 3C8; 514 289-9749, 1-800-267-5180, Fax: 514 287-7386, Email: mariko@bbmontreal.qc.ca. Downtown, Old Montreal, Latin Quarter locations. Non-smoking rooms and handicapped facilities available. 50 rooms. 6 suites. $
- Bonheur d'Occasion, 846 Rue Agnés, Montreal QC H4C 2P8; 514 935-5998. Meals, no credit cards. $
- Carole's Purrfect B & B, 3428 Rue Addington, Montreal QC H4A 3G6; 514 486-3995. Meals, pets allowed, no credit cards, non-smoking rooms. $
- Chambre avec Vue/Bed and Banana, 1225 Rue de Bullion, Montreal QC H2X 2Z3; 514 878- 9843, Fax: 514 878-9843. Meals, no credit cards, non-smoking rooms. $
- Couette et Café Cherrier, 522 Rue Cherrier, Montreal QC H2L 1H3; 514 598-5075, Fax: 514 982-3313. Meals and bistro on premises. $
- Daisy's Suites, 1599 Rue Panet, Montreal QC H2L 2Z4; 514 521-5846. Meals, no credit cards, non-smoking rooms. Open seasonally. $
- Gîte Montreal Centre-Ville, 3462 Ave. Laval, Montreal QC H2X 3C8; 514 289-9749, 1-800- 267-5180, Fax: 514 287-7386. Meals, non-smoking rooms. $
- Gîte Toujours Dimanche, 1131 Rue Rachel E., Montreal QC H2J 2J6; 514 527-2394, Fax: 514 527-6129. Meals, no credit cards, non-smoking rooms. $
- La Maison du Jardin, 3744 Rue St-André, Montreal QC H2L 3V7; 514 598-8862, Fax: 514 598-8862. Meals, no credit cards. $
- A Montreal Oasis, 3000 Chemin de Breslay, Montreal QC H2X 2G7; 514 935-2312, Fax: 514 935-3154, E-mail: bb@aei.ca. Rooms in downtown, Old Montreal and Latin Quarter with or without private bath. Open fireplace, terrace and gourmet breakfast. 20 rooms. $
- Relais Montréal Hospitalité, 3977 Ave. Laval, Montreal QC H2W 2H9; 514 287-9635, 1-800- 363-9635, Fax: 514 287-1007. Rooms

near Old Montreal for smokers and non-smokers in furnished apartments rented on short- and long-term basis. $

- Welcome Bed & Breakfast, 3950 Ave. Laval, Montreal QC H2W 2J2; 514 844-5897, 1- 800227-5897, Fax: 514 844-5894, E-mail:bbvenue@mlink.net. Country inn ambience located downtown. $

Hostels & College Residences
Almost all of the residences listed below are available in summer only, but they provide a safe, economical alternative to hotels. Make sure you book in advance.

- Auberge Alternative du Vieux-Montréal, 358 Rue Saint-Pierre, Montreal QC H2Y 2M1; 514 282-8069. Open year-round. $
- Auberge de Jeunesse de l'Hotel de Paris, 901 Rue Sherbrooke E., Montreal QC H2L 1L3; 514 522-6861, 1-800-567-7217, Fax: 514 522-1387. Open year-round, no credit cards, three meals served daily, pets allowed. $
- Auberge de Jeunesse de Montreal/Hostelling International, 1030 Rue Mackay, Montreal H3G 2H1; 514 843-3317, 1-800-663-3317, Fax: 514 934-3251. Breakfast and dinner served daily. $
- Auberge Montpetit, 3431 Rue Aylmer, Montreal QC H2X 2B4; 514 845-3984. No credit cards, open year-round. $
- Chez Jean, 4136 Rue Henri-Julien, Montreal QC H2W 2K3; 514 843-8279. Meals, no credit cards, pets allowed. $
- Collège Français, 5155 Rue de Gaspé, Montreal QC H2T 2A1; 514 495-2581, Fax: 514 271-2823. Summer only, dormitory. $
- Concordia University, 7141 Rue Sherbrooke O./W., Montreal QC H4B 1R6; 514 848-4757, Fax: 514 848-4780. Summer only, dormitory, meals served daily, no credit cards. $
- Le Gîte de Parc Lafontaine, 1250 Rue Sherbrooke E., Montreal QC H2L 1M1; 514 522-3910. Open year-round, meals, no credit cards. $
- McGill University Residences, 3425 Rue University, Montreal QC H3A 2A8; 514 398-6367, Fax: 514 398-6770. Summer only, dormitory. $
- Résidence Lallemand - Collège Brébeuf, 5625 Ave. Decelles, Montreal QC H3T 1W4; 514 342-1320, Fax: 514 342-6607. Summer only, dormitory. $
- Université de Montréal, Services des Résidences, 2350 Boul. Édouard-Montpetit, Montreal QC H3C 3J7; 514 343-6531, Fax: 514 343-2353. Summer only, breakfast and lunch served daily. $
- Université du Québec à Montréal, 303 Boul. René-Lévesque O./W., Montreal QC H2X 3Y3; 514 987-6669, 1-888-987-6669, Fax: 514 987-0344. Summer only, cooking facilities, indoor pool, three meals served daily. $
- Y.M.C.A. de Montréal (Succursale Centre-Ville) 1450 Rue Stanley, Montreal QC H3A 2W6; 514 849-8393, Fax: 514 849-8017. Residences for men and women, three meals served daily. $
- Y.W.C.A., 1355 Boul. René-Lévesque O./W., Montreal QC H3G 1T3; 514 866-9941, Fax: 514 866-4866. Women's residence, three meals served daily, pets allowed. $

QUEBEC CITY

Hotels: Downtown

- Château Frontenac, Rue des Carrières, Quebec QC, G1R 4P5; 418 692-3861, 1-800-441-1414, Fax: 418 692-1751. The crème de la crème of old world style. Airport shuttle, babysitting, conference rooms, non-smoking rooms, indoor pool, fitness centre. $$$
- Days Inn Québec Le Voyageur, 2250, Boul Ste-Anne, Quebec QC, G1R 1Y2; 418 661-7701, 1-800-463-5568, Fax: 418 661-5221. Conference rooms, non-smoking rooms, indoor/outdoor pool, near golf course. $$
- Hôtel Château Bellevue, 16, Rue de la Porte, Quebec QC, G1R 4M9; 418 692-2573, 1-800-463-2617, Fax: 418 692-4876. Mid-sized hotel, babysitting and near transportation. $$

- Hôtel Château Laurier, 695 Grand Allée E., Quebec QC G1R 2K4; 418 522-8108, 1-800-463-4453, Fax: 418 524-8768. Mid-sized hotel, babysitting, non-smoking rooms. $$
- Hôtel Clarendon, 57 Rue Ste-Anne, Quebec QC, G1R 3X4; 418 692-2480, 1-800-463-5250, Fax: 418 692-4652. Airport shuttle, conference rooms, babysitting and near transportation. $$- $$$
- Hôtel du Capitole, 972 Rue St-Jean, Quebec QC, G1R 1R5; 418 694-4040, 1-800-363-4040, Fax: 418 694-1916. Mid-sized hotel, babysitting, conference rooms, non-smoking rooms. $$$
- Hôtel Dominion 1912, 126 Rue St-Pierre, Quebec QC, G1R 4A8; 418 692-2224, 1-888-833-5253, Fax: 418 692-4403. Mid-sized hotel, conference rooms, non-smoking rooms. $$$
- Hôtel Loews Le Concorde, 1225 Place Montcalm, Quebec QC, G1R 4W6; 418 647-2222, 1-800-463-5256, Fax: 418 647-4710. Airport shuttle, babysitting, conference rooms, non-smoking rooms, outdoor pool, fitness centre. $$-$$$
- Hôtel Manoir Victoria, 44 Côte du Palais, Quebec QC, G1R 4H8, 418 692-1030, 1-800-463-6283, Fax: 418 692-3822. Airport shuttle, babysitting, conference rooms, non-smoking rooms, indoor pool, fitness centre. $-$$$
- Hôtel-Motel Le Gîte, 5160 Boul. Wilfrid-Hamel, Quebec QC, G2E 2G9; 418 871-8899, 1-800-363-4906, Fax: 418 872-8533. Mid-sized hotel, babysitting, conference rooms, non-smoking rooms, outdoor pool, cooking facilities in some rooms. $-$$$
- Hôtel Normandin, 4700 Boul. Pierre-Bertrand, Quebec QC, G2J 1A4; 418 622-1611, 1-800-463-6721, Fax: 418 622-9277. Mid-sized hotel, conference rooms, non-smoking rooms, snowmobile rentals. $$
- Hôtel Quality Suites, 1600 Rue Bouvier, Quebec QC, G2K 1N8; 418 622-4244, 1-800-267-3837, Fax: 418 623-8857. Babysitting, conference rooms, non-smoking rooms. $$
- Hôtel Ramada Québec Centre-Ville, 395 Rue de la Couronne, Quebec QC, G1K 7X4; 418 647-2611, 1-800-267-2002, Fax: 418 647-4317. Airport shuttle, babysitting, conference rooms, non-smoking rooms, indoor pool, fitness centre. $$
- Québec Hilton, 1100, Boul. René-Lévesque E., Quebec QC, G1R 4X3; 418 647-2411, 1-800-447-2411, Fax: 418 647-2986. Babysitting, conference rooms, non-smoking rooms, outdoor pool, spa/fitness centre. $$-$$$
- Radisson Gouverneur Québec, 690 Boul. René-Lévesque E., Quebec QC, G1R 5A8; 418 647-1717, 1-800-910-1111, Fax: 418 647-2146. Airport shuttle, conference rooms, non-smoking rooms, outdoor pool, spa/fitness centre. $$-$$$

Bed & Breakfasts

- Acceuil B & B Bourgault Centre-Ville, 650 Rue de la Reine, Quebec QC G1K 2S1; 418 525-7832. Meals, pets allowed, no credit cards, cooking facilities in some rooms. $
- À la Maison Tudor, 1037 Rue Moncton, Quebec QC G1S 2Y9; 418 686-1033, Fax: 418 686-6066. Meals, non-smoking rooms. $
- Chez Monsieur Gilles, 1720 Chemin de la Canardière, Quebec QC G1J 2E3; 418 821-8778, Fax: 418 821-8776. Meals, non-smoking rooms, near skiiing and golf course. $
- Hayden's Wexford House B & B, 450 Rue Champlain, Quebec QC G1R 2E3; 418 524-0524, Fax: 418 648-8995. Meals, non-smoking rooms, near skiiing. $
- Le Krieghoff Bed & Breakfast, 1091 Ave. Cartier, Quebec QC G1R 2S6; 418 522-3711, Fax: 418 522-3711. Meals. $
- La Maison d'Élizabeth et Emma, 10 Rue Grande-Allée O./W., Quebec QC G1R 2G6; 418 647-0880. Meals, no credit cards, non-smoking rooms. $
- La Maison Historique James Thompson, 47 Rue Sainte-Ursule, Quebec QC G1R 4E4; 418 694-9042. Meals, no credit cards. $

- La Trappe Touriste, 555 4ieme Ave., Quebec QC G1J 3A1; 418 648-9876. Meals, no credit cards, non-smoking rooms. $

Hostels & College Residences

- Association Y.W.C.A. de Québec, 855 Ave. Holland, Quebec QC G1S 3S5; 418 683-2155, Fax: 418 683-5526. Near transportation. $
- Auberge de la Paix, 31 Rue Couillard, Quebec QC G1R 3T4; 418 694-0735. No credit cards. $
- Centre International de Séjour de Québec, 19 Rue Sainte-Ursule, Quebec QC G1R 4E1; 418 694-0755, Fax: 418 694-2278. Meals served. $
- Hôtellerie pour Hommes, 14 Côte du Palais, Quebec QC G1R 4H8; 418 692-3956, Fax: 48 694-1452. Residence for men, meals, no credit cards. $
- Résidence du Collège Mérici, 757, 759, 761 Chemin Saint-Louis, Quebec QC G1S 1C1; 418 683-1591, Fax: 418 682-8938. Open seasonally. Cooking facilities in all rooms. $

DINING

MONTREAL

Montreal boasts some of the finest restaurants in North America. With a huge cultural diversity, there is something for everyone. The following is a select list of the restaurants available. The restaurants are listed by ethnicity (eg. French) and by general type (eg. Brunch) and then alphabetically.

Approximate prices are indicated, based on the average cost, at time of publication, of dinner for two including wine (where available), taxes and gratuity: $ = under $45; $$ = $45-$80; $$$ = $80-$120; $$$$ = $120-$180; $$$$$ = over $180. Meals served are indicated as: B = breakfast; L = lunch; D = dinner; S = snacks; Late = open past midnight. Credit cards accepted are also indicated: AX = American Express; V = Visa; MC = MasterCard.

AMERICAN

- Biddle's Jazz & Ribs, 2060 Rue Aylmer; 514 842-8656. Best live jazz in Montreal featuring Charlie Biddle.
  L/D, Late, $, AX/MC/V.
- Hard Rock Café, 1458 Rue Crescent; 514 987-1420. Rock and Roll theme restaurant featuring classic American cuisine, memorabilia and music, and really cool merchandise.
  L/D, Late, $, AX/MC/V.
- Nickels, 1384 Rue Ste-Catherine O./W. 514 392-7771. Burgers and smoked meat extraordinaire.
  L/D, Late, $, AX/MC/V.

CHINESE

- Aux Délices de Szechuan, 1735 Rue St-Denis; 514 844-5542. Sumptuous décor, culinary artwork, efficient service.
  D, $, AX/MC/V.
- Chez Chine (Holiday Inn Select Montréal Centre-Ville), 99 Ave. Viger O./W.; 514 878-9888. Montréal's finest authentic Chinese restaurant.
  B/L/D, $-$$, AX/MC/V.

FRENCH

- Restaurant le P'tit Plateau, 330 Rue Marie-Anne E.; 514 282-6342. Open Tues. to Sat. Elegant but cosy spot where French dishes are served. Bring your own wine.
  D, $, V.
- Restaurant Champs Elysées (Château Versailles Hôtel & Tour), 1800 Rue Sherbrooke O./W.; 514 939-1212, 1-800-361-7199, Email: versaill@montreal.net.ca. Excellent French wine selection. Jazz on Sat.
  B/L/D, $$, AX/MC/V.
- Alexandre, 1454 Rue Peel; 514 288-5105. 12 tap imported beers. Regional cuisine. Typical Parisian brasserie.
  L/D, L, $, AX/MC/V.
- Café de Paris / Le Jardin du Ritz (Ritz-Carlton Montréal Hotel), 1228 Rue Sherbrooke O./W.; 514 842-4212. Email: Ritz@citenet.net. Welcoming atmosphere and impeccable service, afternoon tea.
  B/L/D, $$, AX/MC/V.
- Claude Postel Restaurant, 443 Rue St.Vincent; 514 875-5067. Exquisite French cuisine and excellent crème brulée.
  L/D, $$, AX/MC/V

GREEK

- La Cabane Grecque, 102 Rue Prince-Arthur E.; 514 849-0122 Fax: (514) 849-3879. A family restaurant with steak and seafood specialities. BYOB
  L/D, Late, $, AX/MC/V.
- Restaurant Minerva, 17 Rue Prince-Arthur E.; 514 842-5451. Steak, seafood, Italian and Greek cuisine.
  L/D, Late, $, AX/MC/V..

INDIAN

- Hello India, 1422 Rue Stanley; 514 288-7878. Variety of mild and spicy dishes.
  L/D, $, AX/MC/V.
- Raga Buffet Indien, 3533 Chemin Queen-Mary; 514 344-2217. Vegetarian and tandoori cuisine. Worth the hike for the buffet.
  L/D, $, AX/MC/V.
- Restaurant Le Taj, 2077 Rue Stanley; 514 845-9015. Tandoori and vegetarian cuisine. Grilled specialities, plus a shop selling Indian artifacts.
  L/D, $, AX/MC/V.

ITALIAN

- Bocca d'Oro, 1448 Rue St-Mathieu; 514 933-8414. Exotic menu, romantic atmosphere, great food.
  L/D, L, $, AX/MC/V.
- Hostaria Romana, 2044 Rue Metcalfe; 514 849-1389. Continental cuisine, fish and seafood, and music nightly.
  L/D, $, AX/MC/V.
- Il Cavaliere (Hôtel Lord Berri), 1199 Rue Berri; 514 845-9236. Cosy atmosphere, exceptional Italian cuisine.
  B/L/D/, $, AX/MC/V.

JAPANESE

- Katsura, 2170 Rue de la Montagne; 514 849-1172. Traditional cuisine, private tatami rooms, sushi bar.
  L/D, $$, AX/MC/V.
- Koji's Kaizen - Treehouse Sushi Bar and Restaurant, 4120 Rue Ste-Catherine O./W., Westmount; 514 932-5654. Email: kaizen@total.net. Sushi and sashami. Live jazz from Sun. to Tues.
  L/D, $$, AX/MC/V.

RUSSIAN

- La Métropole, 1409 Rue St-Marc; 514 932-3403. Great food, excellent Russian tea and pastries, weekend music shows.
  L/D, $$, AX / V.
- Troïka, 2171 Rue Crescent; 514 849-9333. Flavoured vodkas. Russian musicians.
  D, $$, AX/MC/V.

SPANISH

- Casa Galicia, 2087 Rue St-Denis; 514 843-6698. Lively weekend flamenco shows and tasty appetizers and main dishes.
  Sun. Dinner only, L/D, $$, AX/MC/V.

VIETNAMESE

- La Merveille du Vietnam, 4526 Rue St-Denis; 514 844-9884. Steak, seafood and Chinese cuisine.
  L/D, $, AX/MC/V.

BRUNCH

- Beauty's, 93 Ave. Mont-Royal; 514 849-8883. This hip hangout serves up tasty diner fare.
  B/L, $, AX/MC/V.
- Café Santropol, 3990 Rue Saint-Urbain; 514 842-3110. Massive portions served in this urban oasis that opens a garden terrace in summer months.
  L/D, $.
- Chez Cora Dejeuners, 1425 Rue Stanley; 514 286-6171. Hearty breakfasts served with plenty of fresh fruit.
  B/L, $, AX/MC/V.
- Dusty's, 4520-B Ave. du Parc, 514 276-8525. Diner specials.
  B/L/D, $.
- La Maison Kam Fung, 1008 Rue Clark; 514 878-2888. Dim sum delights.
  B/L/D, $, AX/MC/V.

CAFÉS

- Art Folie (Notre-Dame-de-Grâce), 5511 Ave. Monkland; 514 487-6066, Fax: (514) 487-4226. Closed Mon. Paint-your-own-ceramics café.
  S, $, V.
- Café Cherrier, 3635 Rue St-Denis; 514 843-4308, Fax: 514 844-3273. European-style brasserie serving Italian and Californian cuisine.
  B/L/D, Late, $, AX/MC/V.
- Le Jardin Nelson, 407 Place Jacques-Cartier; 514 861-5731, E-mail: jardin.nelson@videotron.ca. Summer outdoor courtyard. Musicians serenade at this pancake house.
  L/D, Late, $, AX/MC/V.

FAMILY FARE

- Maison du Curry, 1433 Rue Bishop; 514 845-0326. This hole in the wall serves up authentic, spicy Indian fare and cool British beers.
  L/D, $, AX/MC/V.
- Marché Mövenpick Restaurant, 1 Place Ville-Marie, 514 861-8181. A new dining experience: a dozen stands offer everything fresh, from sushi and pasta to ice cream sundaes and fresh juices is available on one bill.
  B/L/D, Late, AX/MC/V.
- Restaurant Daou, 519 Rue Faillon E.; 514 276-8310. Lebanese dishes made from family recipes are served in an informal dining room.
  L/D, $, AX/MC/V.
- Trattoria La Rondine, 5697 Chemin de la Côtes-des-Neiges; 514 731-7833. Family recipes for pasta, pizza and pastries.
  L/D, $, AX/MC/V.
- La Capannina, 2022 Rue Stanley; 514 845-1852. Friendly family restaurant. Specialities: fresh pastas and seafood.
  L/D, $, AX/MC/V.

FONDUES

- Fonduementale, 4325 Rue St-Denis; 514 499-1446. Ideal for group dining in a relaxed atmosphere.
  D, $, AX/MC/V.
- La Fonderie, 964 Rue Rachel E.; 514 524-2100. Chinese and swiss fondues.
  D, $, AX/MC/V.

QUICK EATS

- Arahova Souvlaki, 480 Boul. St-Laurent; 514 282-9717. Serving up its succulent souvlaki with secret tzatziki sauce recipe since 1972.
- Le Commensal McGill, 1204 Ave. McGill College; 514 871-1480. Excellent view of the avenue. Ongoing hot, cold and dessert buffet. Pay by the weight concept. Other locations at 1720, 5043 Rue St-Denis, 3715 Chemin Queen-Mary.
  L/D, $, AX/MC/V.
- The Caribbean Curry House, 6892 Ave. Victoria; 514 733-0828. Caribbean-style jerk chicken, curried meat and potatoes and pina coladas.
- The Montréal Beer Museum, 2063 Rue Stanley; 514 840-2020. Beer collection in showcases, important beer selections, monthly theme, beer and food menu change to adapt to the theme.
  L/D, Late, $, AX/MC/V.
- Schwartz's Montreal Hebrew Delicatessen, 3895 Boul. St-Laurent; 514 842-4813. Quintessential smoked meat sandwich joint.
  L/D, $.

FOUR-STAR DINING

- Au Tournant de la Rivière, 5070 Rue Salaberry, Carignan; 514 658-7372. Call for directions (or check the dining chapter in this guide) to find this superb restaurant located in converted barn.
  D, $$$$, AX/MC/V.
- The Beaver Club, The Queen Elizabeth Hotel, 900 Boul. René-Lévesque O./W.; 514 861-3511. Closed Sun., Mon. p.m. and holidays. Elegant atmosphere with open rotisserie and specialities including prime rib of beef and rack of lamb.
  L/D, $$$, AX/MC/V.
- Chez La Mère Michel, 1209 Rue Guy; 514 934-0473. A fine restaurant of longstanding reputation; the food is expensive but reliable; seasonal dishes include bison and caribou.
  L/D, $$$, AX/MC/V.
- The Globe, 3455 Boul. St-Laurent; 514 284-3823. Snazzy bistro with designer customers and Chef David McMillan's serious, modern cooking, which makes the best of local produce.
  D, $$$, AX/MC/V.
- Le Mitoyen, 652 Place Publique, Ste-Dorothée; 514 689-2977. A short drive north out of Montreal brings you to this charming restaurant; try the rack of québécois lamb. Hot bread and sweet butter accompany each meal.
  D, $$$, AX/MC/V.
- Le Muscadin, 100 Rue St-Paul O./W.; 514 842-0588. Old elegance in Old Montreal; you can't go wrong here: veal, lamb, beef and sole are all exceptional, and wine list is arguably the best in the city.
  L/D, $$$, AX/MC/V.
- Les Caprices de Nicolas, 2072 Rue Drummond; 514 282-9790. Garden room with atrium, private salon. Signature dishes include caviar appetizers, foie gras, milk-fed veal loin and homemade ice cream and sherbet in basil and watermelon and vanilla ginger.
  L/D, $$$, AX/MC/V.
- Les Halles, 1450 Rue Crescent; 514 844-2328. A great start for those who are new to Montreal with a trustworthy (if pricey) à la carte; the menu douceur at lunchtime is a bargain.
  L/D, $$$$, AX/MC/V.
- Mediterraneo, 3500 Boul. St-Laurent; 514 844-0027. You'll be jammed next to your neighbour but eating well and served with panache; try the seared tuna or the Arctic char. The wine list suits the fare perfectly.
  D, $$$, AX/MC/V.
- Milos Restaurant, 5357 Ave. du Parc; 514 272-3522. Upscale traditional Greek food and fish by the pound.
  L weekdays/D, $$$, AX/MC/V.
- Le Passe-Partout, 3857 Boul. Decarie; 514 487-7750.This tiny 32-seat restaurant attached to a French bakery is open Thursday through Saturday for dinner, Tuesday through Friday for lunch. Menu changes with the season, a selection of two wines match the menu nightly.
  L/D, $$$, AX/MC/V.
- Profusion, 1000 Rue de la Gauchetière; 514 399-1122. Luxury liner style dining with fusion cuisine specialities such as spinach salad with mangoes, pheasant cooked in cassis and sushi.
  L weekdays/D, $$$, AX/MC/V.
- Restaurant Toqué!, 3842 Rue St-Denis; 514 499-2084. Sultry decor, market cuisine, organic vegetables. Specialties include roasted leg of Quebec lamb, rare yellowfin tuna tempura, and for dessert, hazelnut biscuit with lemon cream.
  D, $$$, AX/MC/V.

QUEBEC CITY

- L'Astral (Hôtel Loews Le Concorde), 1225 Place Montcalm; 418 647-2222. Great view in this rotating restaurant. International cuisine and Saturday night buffets.
  Brunch/L/D, $, AX/MC/V.
- La Bastille Chez Bahüaud, 47 Ave. Ste-Geneviève; 418 692-2544. Great food at tables set in tree-filled garden.
  L/D, $$, AX/MC/V.
- Manoir Montmorency, 2490 Ave. Royale, Beauport; 418 663-3330. Most romantic restaurant in town. Overlooks falls from a rambling wooden building.
  Brunch/L/D, $$, AX/MC/V.

- Le Parlementaire, Hôtel du Parlement; 418 643-6640. Open Tues. to Fri. 8-2:30. The dining room of the Quebec government is decorated in Beaux-Arts splendor. Regional cuisine.
  B/L, $, AX/MC/V.

CAFÉS AND BISTROS

- Bistro Sous le Fort, 48 Rue Sous-le-Fort; 418 694-0852. Good and plentiful dishes, but austere decor.
  L/D, $
- Café de la Terrasse, 1 Rue des Carrières; 418 692-3861. Standard continental fare and afternoon tea.
  L/D, $.
- Le Cochon Dingue, 46 Boul. Champlain; 418 692-2013. The name means "crazy pig" and the bistro fare includes steak and fries, burgers and mussels.
  Brunch/L/D, $, AX/MC/V.

REGIONAL FLAVOUR

- L'Âtre, 4403 Chemin Royale, Île d'Orléans, 418 829-3474. Traditional cuisine served by costumed staff.
  L/D, $$, AX/MC/V.
- Auberge Baker, 8790 Ave. Royale, Château-Richer; 418 824-4852. Serves game dishes in stone-walled room with a fireplace.
  Brunch/L/D, $$, AX/MC/V.
- Aux Anciens Canadiens, 34 Rue St-Louis; 418 692-1627. A menu including ham simmered in maple syrup, baked beans and blueberry pie is served in this 17th-century restaurant with five theme dining rooms.
  L/D, $$, AX/MC/V.

FOUR-STAR DINING

- Aspara, 71 Rue d'Auteuil; 418 694-0232. First-prize winner at the Gala de la Restauration de Quebec for exotic cuisine. Chef Beng an Khuong offers the best of Vietnamese, Thai, and Cambodian cooking.
  L/D, $$$-$$$$, AX/MC/V.
- Grande Table Serge Bruyère, 1200 Rue St-Jean; 418 694-0618. Specialties include scallop stew and duckling with blueberry sauce.
  L/D, $$$, AX/MC/V.
- Le Champlain (Château Frontenac), 1 Rue des Carrières; 418 692-3861. Serves classic French cuisine in lavish dining room.
  B/L/D, $$$, AX/MC/V.
- La Closerie, 996 Boul. René-Lévesque O./W.; 418 687-9975. Bland exterior, first-rate cuisine and intimate dining room.
  L/D, $$$, AX/MC/V.
- La Taniere, 2115 Rang Ste-Ange, Ste-Foy; 418 872-4386. A game restaurant with eight-course menu progressif; caribou, ostrich, venison, and rabbit are all at home here.
  D, $$$$, AX/MC/V.
- Laurie Raphaël, 117 Rue Dalhousie; 418 692-4555. Delicacies from scallops to ostrich. Sunday brunch.
  L/D, $$$, AX/MC/V.
- Le Continental, 26 Rue St-Louis; 418 694-9995. Classic menu, service and setting make this longstanding restaurant one of the best in the city. Try the rack of lamb, steak tartar, or Dover sole; superb wine list.
  L/D, $$$, AX/MC/V.
- Michelangelo, 3111 Chemin St-Louis, Ste-Foy; 418 651-6262. Salmon tartar or carpaccio with basil are hits at this new, expansive restaurant with a fabulous wine list.
  L/D, $$$, AX/MC/V.
- Saint Amour, 48 Rue Ste-Ursule; 418 694-0667. Excellent food and romantic surroundings with glassed-in terrace.
  L/D, $$$, AX/MC/V.

TOP ATTRACTIONS

MONTREAL

- Basilique Notre-Dame-de-Montréal. Most celebrated church in Canada. 110 Rue Notre-Dame O./W., Montreal QC H2Y 1T2; 514 842-2925 or 514 849-1070.
- Biodôme. Once the site of the 1976 Olympic bicycle races, it has been transformed into a recreation of four natural habitats, including a rain forest, a polar landscape and the St. Lawrence marine ecosystem. 4777 Ave. Pierre-de-Courbertin; 514 868-3000.
- Biosphère. An eco-museum. 160 Chemin Tour-de-l'Île, Parc des Îles; 514 283-5000.
- Casino Montréal. Open 24 hours. Île Notre-Dame; 514 932-2746.
- Jardin Botanique de Montréal. Gardens, greenhouses and an insectarium. 4101 Rue Sherbrooke E.; 514 872-1400.
- La Ronde amusement park. Rides and live entertainment all summer. Parc des Îles; 514 872-4537, 1-800-797-4537.
- Oratoire Saint-Joseph de Mont-Royale. Thousands make pilgrimages each year. 3800 Chemin Queen Mary; 514 733-8211.
- Stade Olympique, 4141 Ave. Pierre-de-Coubertin; 514 252-8687.

QUEBEC CITY

- Anglican Cathedral of the Holy Trinity. Modelled after London's Saint-Martin-in-the-Fields, the cathedral contains precious objects donated by King George III. 31, Rue des Jardins; 418 692-2193.
- Église Notre-Dame-des-Victoires. Oldest church in North America. Place Royale; 418 692-1650.
- Château Frontenac. Historic hotel built in 1893. 1, Rue des Carrières; 418 691-2166.
- The Citadel. Star-shaped fortification built by the British and still used by the military. Côte de la Citadelle; 418 694-2815.
- Hotel du Parlement. Built between 1877 and 1886, the parliament is used today by the provinical government. Grande Allée E.; 418 643-7239.
- Monastere des Ursulines. Oldest North American teaching institution for girls with adjacent museum. 12 Rue Donnacona; 418 692-4741.
- Notre-Dame-de-Québec Basilica. Richly decorated with gifts from Louis XIV. Oldest parish north of Mexico. 20 Rue de Buaude; 418 694-0665.
- Place Royale. Among North America's oldest districts with 400 years of Quebec history. Information Centre, 215 Rue du Marché-Finlay; 418 643-6631.

FESTIVALS & EVENTS

MONTREAL

January-February

- Harbin Ice and Lights Festival. Month-long event of ice sculpture exhibits. Botantical Gardens. 514 872-1400.
- Fête des Neiges. Month-long festival of outdoor activities, skating, slides, snow sculpture and more. Parc des Îles. 514 872-4537.

February

- Montreal Winter Festival. Activities held citywide. 514 872-1881

March

- Jewish Film Festival. For information, check listings in local newspapers.

April-May

- Vues d'Afriques. A multidisciplinary festival to showcase African and Caribbean cultural activities. Held at various locations. 514 284-3322

June

- Carifiesta. Annual Caribbean parade with costumes, food, music and dance held June 26. Downtown. 514 735-2232.
- Grand Prix Air Canada. Only Formula 1 race in North America. Gilles Villeneuve Circuit, Parc des Îles. 514 350-0000.
- Mondial de la Bière. Montreal's annual five-day outdoor beer festival. Jacques Cartier Pier. 514 722-9640.
- Montreal Chamber Music Festival. Ten days of outdoor concerts on Mount Royal by international musicians. Chalet de la Montagne. 514 489-7710.
- Le Tour de l'Île de Montréal. Annual 66-kilometre urban route; the world's largest. 514 521-8687.

June-July

- Benson & Hedges Fireworks Competition. Shows start Tuesdays and Saturdays. The Jacques Cartier Bridge is closed to cars during shows and offers excellent views. Île-Ste-Hélène. 514 872-4537.

July

- Fant-Asia International Festival of Fantasy and Action Cinema. The best Asian horror, sci-fi and fantasy films. Imperial Cinema, 1430 Rue Bleury. Website: www.fantasiafest.com. Call cinema for show times.
- Festival International de Jazz de Montréal. Ten days of concerts at outdoor and indoor venues. Many free events. 514 871-1881.
- Les FrancoFolies de Montréal. A week of music in the Place des Arts involving 1,000 performers from the entire contemporary musical spectrum. 514 876-8989.
- Just For Laughs Comedy Festival. Two weeks of more than 1,300 shows indoors and out. Website: www.hahaha.com. 514 790-HAHA.

August

- du Maurier Open. Canada's International Men's Tennis Championships. 514 790-1245.
- Festival de la Gibelotte. Participating venues serve up a robust stew made of catfish with locally-brewed beer at a giant street festival. Downtown Sorel (90 minutes downriver of Montreal).
- Festival des Montgolfières. About 150 hot-air balloons participate in the event. St-Jean-du-Richelieu (30 minutes south of Montreal). 450 347-9555.

August-September

- World Film Festival. Various theatres. Website: www.ffm-montreal.org. 514 848-3883. Autumn
- Montreal International Festival of Cinema and New Media. Unusual films at interesting venues. Website: www.fcmm.com. 514 843-4725.

October

- Black & Blue Festival. Among the world's most popular gay weekend-long parties to benefit AIDS research. 514 875-7026.
- Festival International de la Nouvelle Danse. Ten days of performances at various venues. 514 287-1423.

November

- Cinemania. A festival of French films with English sub-titles, which was founded by an English-speaking fan of French cinema. Musée des Beaux-Arts de Montréal. 514 288-4200.

QUEBEC CITY

January-February

- Carnaval de Québec Kellogg's. Mardi Gras blow-out for two weeks before Lent. The century-old annual carnival is known as the Mardi Gras of the north. Indoor and outdoor activities. 418 626-3716.

June-July

- Carrefour Agro-Alimentaire. A festival showcasing culinary specialties of the region. 418 522-8811.
- Expo-Québec. The province's biggest agricultural fair. Near Colisée de Québec. 418 691-7110.

July

- Concours Hippique de Québec. World Cup preliminary competition. Battlefield Park. 418 647-2727.
- Festival d'Été de Québec. Largest North American French-language festival of performing arts and street theatre. Various venues. 1-888-992-5200.
- Ste-Anne's Feast Day. On July 26, an annual pilgrimage attracts Native peoples, Gypsies and many others to the shrine of Ste-Anne-de-Beaupré for a religious ceremony and festival. 418 827-3781.

July-August

- Grands-Feux Loto-Québec. Fireworks displays. Montmorency Falls. 418 523-3389, 1-800-923-3389.

August

- Fêtes de la Nouvelle France. Military displays, parades and historical re-enactments plus a ten-day crafts exhibition. Near the Parliament Building. 418 694-3311.

August-September

- Festival International du Film de Québec. A week-long event with screenings of Canadian and foreign films. 418 848-3883.

September

- Festival des Couleurs. Outdoor activities and cultural events mark the beginning of fall and winter seasons. Mont Ste-Anne. 418 827-4561.

October

- Festival de l'Oie des Neiges de Saint-Joachim. This snow geese festival consists of watching thousands of birds fly off each morning and return each night, with activities and craft displays in between. Côte-de-Beaupré area. 418 827-4808, 418 827-3402.

MUSEUMS & GALLERIES

MONTREAL

MUSEUMS:

- Canadian Centre for Architecture, 1920 Rue Baille; Wed. to Fri. 11-6, Thurs. 11-8, Sat.-Sun. 11-5; 514 939-7000.
- Centre d'Histoire de Montréal, 335 Place d'Youville; Open daily 10-5 May to Sept. Off-season Tues. to Sun. 10-5; 514 872-3207.
- Château de Ramezay, 280 Rue Notre-Dame E.; June 1-Sept. 30, Tues. to Sun. 10-6, Off-season 10-4:30; 514 861-3708.
- Musée d'Art Contemporain de Montréal, 185 Rue Ste-Catherine O./W.; Tues. to Sun. 11-6. Wed. 11-9; 514 847-6212.
- Musée des Beaux-Arts de Montréal, 1379-80 Rue Sherbrooke O./W.; Tues. to Sun. 11-6. Wed. 11-9; 514 285-1600.
- Musée Juste Pour Rire - Just for Laughs Museum, 2111 Boul. St-Laurent; July to Sept. Tues. to Sun. 10-5. 514 845-4000, Website: www.hahaha.com.
- Le Monde de Maurice (Rocket) Richard, 2800 Rue Viau; Tues. to Sun. 12-6; 514 251-9930
- Maison Sir George-Étienne Cartier, 458 Rue Notre Dame E.; Seasonal, 10-12 and 1-5; 514 283-2282.
- McCord Museum of Canadian History, 690 Rue Sherbrooke O./W.; Tues. to Fri. 10-6, Sat.-Sun. 10-5; 514 398-7100.
- Musée d'Archéologie Pointe-à-Callière, 350 Place Royale; Tues. to Fri. 10-5, Sat.-Sun, 11-5; 514 872-9150.
- Musée du Bienheureux Frère André, Oratoire Saint-Joseph, 3800 Chemin Queen Mary; Open daily. May to Sept. 7-9; Off-season 7-5:30; 514 733-8211.
- Musée des Hospitallières, 201 Ave. Des Pins O./W.; Mon. to Fri 9-5; 514 849-1919.
- Musée Marc-Aurèle Fortin, 118 Rue St-Pierre; Tues. to Sun. 11-5; 514 845-9150.
- Stewart Museum, Île-Sainte-Hélène; May to Oct. daily 10-6, Thurs. 10-9, Off-season Wed. to Mon. 10-5; 514 861-6701.

GALLERIES:

- Dominion Gallery, 1438 Rue Sherbrooke O./W.; June-Sept. Mon. to Fri. 10-5, off-season Tues. to Sat. 10-5; 514 845-7471.
- Galerie Le Chariot, 446 Place Jacques-Cartier; Closed Jan. Year-round Mon. to Sat. 10-6, Sun. 10-3; 514 875-4994.
- Edifice Belgo, 372 Rue Ste-Catherine O./W.; call for opening hours at the following galleries. Most are open Tues. to Sat.; Galerie René Blouin, Suite 501, 514 393-9969; Galerie Trois Pointes, Suite 520, 514 866-8008; Optica, Suite 508, 514 874-1666.
- Isart, 263 St-Antoine O./W.; Gallery and performance art space. Call for shows. 514 878-1024.
- Leonard and Bina Gallery, 1400 Boul. de Maisonneuve O./W.; June-Aug. Mon. 11-3, Tues. to Thurs. 11-7, Sat. 1-5, closed Fri. and Sun., off-season Mon. to Fri. 11-7, Sat. 1-5, closed Sun.; 514 848-4750.
- Waddington and Gorce Gallery, 1446 Rue Sherbrooke O./W.; Wed. to Sat. 10-5, Tues. by appointment; 514 847-1112.
- Walter Klinkhoff Gallery, 1200 Rue Sherbrooke O./W.; June-Aug. Mon. to Fri. 9-5, off-season Mon. to Fri. 9:30-5:30, Sat. 9:30 -5; 514 288-7306.

QUEBEC CITY

MUSEUMS:

- Centre d'Interpretation du Vieux-Port. 100 Rue St-Andre. Quebec's maritime history. For schedule and rates call 418 648-3000.
- The Citadel. Côte de la Citadelle. Fortress built by the English and still an active military post. Guided tours of interior. Open daily. April to mid-May: 10-4. Mid-May to mid-June: 9-5. Mid-June to Sept.: 9-6. Oct.: 10-3. Nov. to April: Group reservations only. 418 694-2815.

- Hôpital Générale. 260 Boul. Langelier. With advance notice, sisters from the Augustine order which has run the hospital for 300 years, give guided tours of the grounds and the chapel. 418 529-0931.
- Maison Thibaudeau, 215 Rue March-Finlay. Annex of the Musée de la Civilisation built by architect Joseph Ferdinand. Guided tours of the Place Royale district available. Open daily May 5 to Sept. 27, 10-6. 418 643-6631.
- Musée de l'Amerique Française, 9 Rue de l'Université. Four seminary buildings contain religious artifacts, trompe l'oeil ceilings and 18th- and 19th-century objects from England, France and Quebec. Open daily June-Sept. 10-5:30, Off-season Tues. to Sun. 10-5. 418 692-2843.
- Musée des Augustines, 32 Rue Charlevoix. Located inside the Hôtel Dieu hospital, this tiny museum contains 17th-century Louis XIII furniture and medical equipment spanning centuries. Tues. to Sat. 9:30-12, 1:30-5, Sun. 1:30-5. 418 692-2492.
- Musée Bon-Pasteur, 14 Rue Couillard. Once a home for unwed mothers, now nuns run a guided tour of the grounds. Groups must reserve. For schedule, call 418 694-0243.
- Musée de la Civilisation, 85 Rue Dalhousie. Designed by Moshe Safdie, the museum contains three historic buildings and offers ten theme-oriented exhibitions. Open daily June 24-Sept. 7, 10-7, Sept.-June Tues. to Sun. 10-5. 418 643-2158..
- Musée du Fort, 10 Rue Ste-Anne. Chronicles Quebec's military battles. Open daily April-June 10-5, July-Sept. 10-8, Sept.-Oct. 10-5, Dec. 26-Jan 4 12-4, Feb.-Mar. Thurs. to Sun. 12-4. Rest of the year, by reservation only. 418 692-1759.
- Musée des Ursulines, 12 Rue Donnacona. Treasures include a parchment signed by Louis XIII, altar cloths and porcupine-needle baskets. May to Aug. Tues. to Sat. 10-12, 1-5. Off-season Tues. to Sat. 1-4:30, Sun. 12:30-5. 418 694-0694.
- Naval Museum of Quebec, 170 Rue Dalhousie. Open daily June-Sept. 10-5:30. Oct. to May. Mon. to Fri. 10-4:30. 418 648-4370.
- Québec Expérience, 8 Rue du Tresor. Special effects exhibition details life in Quebec from the first explorers onward. Daily May 15 to Oct. 15 10-10. Off-season Sun. to Thurs. 10-5, Fri. and Sat. 10-10. 418 694-4000.

GALLERIES:

- Galerie d'art du Petit-Champlain, 88 Rue du Petit-Champlain. Inuit art, lithographs and a vast selection of ducks. Daily (summer) 9-10, Off-season 10-5:30. 418 692-5647.
- L'Héritage contemporain, 634 Grande Allée E. Works of great Canadian painters. Daily June - Sept. 11:30-10, Oct.-May Mon. to Fri. 11:30-5:30, Sat.-Sun. 12-5. 418 523-7337.
- Galerie d'art Le Portal - Artour, 53 Rue du Petit-Champlain. Artists from Quebec and abroad. May 15-Oct. 15 daily 9-9, Off-season Sat. to Wed. 9-6, Thurs.-Fri 11:30-5:30. 418 692-0354
- Studio d'art Georgette Pihay, 53 Rue du Petit-Champlain. Painter/sculpture's workshop with permanent exhibitions. June 24-Sept. 30 daily 10-9. Off-season 9-5. 418 692-0297
- Galerie Linda Verge, 1049 Ave. des Érables. Contemporary art. Wed. to Fri. 11:30-5:30, Sat.-Sun. 1-5. 418 525-8393
- Galerie Madeleine Lacerte, 1 Côte Dinan. Contemporary art. Mon. to Fri. 9-5, Sat.-Sun. 1-5. 418 692-1566

NATURE & NATURAL HISTORY

- Biodôme. A recreation of a tropical rain forest, a glass-walled tank holding 2.5 million litres of sea water and wild life are some attractions. Open daily 9-5, summer hours 9-7. 4777 Ave. Pierre-de-Coubertin; 514 868-3000, Website: www.ville.montreal.qc.ca/biodome.
- Biosphère. An eco-museum with inter-active exhibits and multi-media presentations. June-Sept. Daily 10-5. Off season Tues. to Sun. 10-5. 160 Chemin Tour-de-l'Île; 514 283-5000.
- Jardin Botanique de Montréal. Stroll or take a site-seeing train through the garden's 185 acres. Open year-round 9-5, summer hours 9-7. 4101 Rue Sherbrooke E.; 514 872-4917, Website: www.ville.montreal.qc.ca/jardin.
- Montreal Insectarium. Butterfly house and other exhibits. Annual bug-eating festival. Open year-round daily 10-5, summer hours 9-7. Located on Jardin Botanique grounds, 4581 Rue Sherbrooke E.; 514 872-1400, Website: www.ville.montreal.qc.ca/insectarium.
- Redpath Museum of Natural History. Free admission to one of Canada's oldest museums. Open year-round. Mon. to Fri. 9-5, Sun. 1-5. Closed Fri. during summer months. 859 Rue Sherbrooke O./W.; 514 398-4086.

MONTREAL NIGHT LIFE

This list will help guide you through Montreal after dark. Refer to the Night Life section for more details and the map at the beginning of the book. Be sure to check local newspapers; there is something for everyone, from bazouki concerts to outdoor movies. For up-to-date listings, try the most recent edition of The Mirror or Hour weekly newspapers. Or try the French weekly Voir. All are available free of charge at many bars, shops and restaurants throughout Montreal.

DOWNTOWN

- Biddle's, 2060 Rue Aylmer; 514 842-8656. This Montreal jazz institution is home to bassist Charlie Biddle and his trio. Biddle's serves a mean plate of ribs to match the nightly shows.
- Charlie's American Pub, 1204 Rue Bishop; 514 871-1709. Kick back and listen to some American Pie tunes.
- Deja-Vu Bar, 1224 Rue Bishop; 514 866-0512. Catch a live rock band at this casual neighbourhood bar.
- Hard Rock Cafe, 1458 Rue Crescent; 514 987-1420. Rub elbows with the regulars and some surprise superstars, while enjoying drinks, food and rock n' roll.
- Hurley's Irish Pub, 1225 Rue Crescent; 514 861-4111. Celtic ambience with rowdy bar upstairs and mellow sitting room downstairs. Live music is almost always Irish.
- Peel Pub, 1107 Rue Ste-Catherine; 514 844-6769. A landmark drinking and eating hang out for regulars and college crowds with cheap beer and food. Open until midnight.
- Planet Hollywood, Place Montreal Trust, 1500 Ave. McGill College; 514397-9069. The glittered crowd hold private parties here but the public can always catch a glimpse of movie stars and their entourages.
- Sir Winston Churchill Pub, 1459 Rue Crescent; 514 288-3814. Be seen on the terrace of this raucous dance hall.

- Winnie's, 1455 Rue Crescent; 514 288-0623. Intense dancing to Top 40 tunes.

QUEBEC CITY

For concerts, movies, theatre and nightlife, check local newspapers, especially the weekly *Chronicle-Telegraph*, the city's only English-language paper. The *Chronicle-Telegraph* is distributed free in tourist bureaus.

SHOPPING

MONTREAL:

Antiques

- Antiques Hubert, 3680 Boul. St-Laurent, 514 288-3804. Vintage variety.
- Antiquites Le Design, 1604 Rue Notre-Dame O./W., 514 939-1594. Assortment of collectibles.
- C. Blain Antiquaire, 1904 Rue Notre-Dame O./W., 514 938-9221. Variety of items.
- Cascades Lounge, 2485 Rue Notre-Dame O./W. Specializes in toys.
- Galerie Tansu, 1622-A Rue Sherbrooke O./W., 514 846-1039. This museum-like shop sells Japanese antiques and furniture.
- Milord, 1870 Rue Notre-Dame O./W., 514 933-2433. Elegant European furniture and mirrors.
- Salvation Army, 1620 Rue Notre-Dame O./W., 514 935-7425. Check out "As Is" section in thrift shop.
- Le Village des Antiquaries, 1708 Rue Notre-Dame O./W. Several dealers under one roof.

Art

- Artisans du Monde, 123 Rue Laurier O./W., 514 272-7132. Crafts hand-picked from markets worldwide.
- Artisanat Canadien, Rue St-Paul E. Canadian crafts shop.
- Artisanat Quebecois, 2119 Rue St-Denis. Wood carvings and pottery by Quebec artists.
- Born Neo Art Gallery, 404 Rue St-Sulpice, 514 840-1135. African carvings and textiles.
- Boutique du Musée des Beaux-Arts, 1390 Rue Sherbrooke O./W., 514 285-1611. Shop reflects current exhibitions and offers posters, art books and more.
- Galerie Archeologica, Rue Sherbrooke O./W. Ancient Greek, Roman and Central American art works.
- Galerie Claude Lafitte, 1270 Rue Sherbrooke O./W., 514 842-1270.
- Galerie de Chariot, 446 Place Jacques Cartier, 514 875-4994. Gift shop sells Inuit art pieces.
- Galerie Elena Lee Verre, 1428 Rue Sherbrooke O./W., 514 844-6009.

- Galerie Laroches, 4 Rue St-Paul E. Canvasses and prints of established artists.
- Galerie Parchemine, 40 Rue St-Paul O./W., 514 845-3368. Canvasses and prints for sale.
- Galerie Walter Klinkhoff, 1200 Rue Sherbrooke O./W., 514 288-7306. Sells work by established artists.

Books
- Argo Book Shop, 1915 Rue Ste-Catherine O./W., 514 931-3442. A Montreal institution, deals in new books.
- Bibliomania, 1841 Rue Ste-Catherine O./W., 514 933-8156. Known for books an antiques and collectibles.
- Café Boooks, 140 Rue Stanley, 514 287-0029. Specializes in art books and used books.
- Chapters, 1171 Rue Ste-Catherine O./W., 514 849-8825. Four floors, discount section and a Starbucks coffee counter.
- Cheap Thrills, 1433 Rue Bishop, 514 844-7604. Good selection of used books.
- Double Hook, 1235-A Ave. Greene, 514 932-5093. Stocks books by Canadian authors.
- Ex Libris, Rue Sherbrooke O./W., 514 932-1689. Good selection of second-hand books.
- Indigo Books, Place Montreal Trust, 514 281-5549. Variety of books, cards, paper items and stationary.
- Nebula Books, 1832 Rue Ste-Catherine O./W., 514 932-3930. Science fiction and fantasy.
- Nicholas Hoare, 1366 Ave. Greene, 514 934-6046. Extensive selection. Daily tradition: kilted bagpipe player marches through main floor at noon.
- Paragraphe Books, 2220 Ave. McGill College, 514 845-5811. Near the university, the shop contains a wide selection of titles, plus a cosy coffee shop.
- Russell Books, 275 Rue St-Antoine O./W., 514 866-0564. Great for browsing through new and used selection.
- Stage Theatre Book Shop, 2123 Rue Ste-Catherine O./W., 514 931-7466. Plays and books about performing arts.
- Ulysses Bookstore, 560 Rue Président-Kennedy, 4176 Rue St-Denis, 514 843-9447. Travel, guide books and maps.
- Vortex Books, 1855 Rue Ste-Catherine O./W., 514 935-7869. Specializes in literary works.
- S.W. Welch, 3878 Boul. St-Laurent, 514 848-9358. Excellent selection of used books.
- Westcott Books, 2065 Rue Ste-Catherine O./W., 514 846-4037. Shelves filled with second-hand books.

Cameras
- Place Victoria Cameras, 495 Rue McGill, 514 842-4818. Equipment, film supplies and repairs.
- Simon Cameras, 11 Rue St-Antoine O./W., 514 861-5401. New and used equipment and film supplies.
- York Bijouterie, 1344 Rue Ste-Catherine O./W., 514 874-0824 . High-class pawn shop deals with cameras, musical instruments and jewellery.

Cigars
- La Casa del Habano, 1434 Rue Sherbrooke O./W., 514 849-0037. Handles importation of Cuban cigars.
- Cigar Emporium, 3525 Boul. St-Laurent, 514 281-6658. From inexpensive to top of the line smokeables.
- Cigars Vasco, 1327 Rue Ste-Catherine O./ W., 514 284-0475. Vast array of cigars.

Clothing
- A. Gold & Sons, 960 Rue Ste-Catherine O./W., 514 866-7711. Large outlet store has excellent quality suits and sweaters for men and women.
- Addition-Elle, 724 Rue Ste-Catherine O./W., 514 954-0087. Fashions for women wearing size 14 plus.
- BCBG, 1300 Rue Ste-Catherine O./W., 514 398-9130 . On top of the latest fashions.
- Bluesonthegreen, 1216 Ave. Greene, 514 938-9798. Fashions for women, men and children.

- Bovet, Eaton Centre, 514 849-9281. Men's suits and sweaters.
- Brisson & Brisson, 1472 Rue Sherbrooke O./W., 514 937-7456. Big name designers with matching price-tags.
- Cache Cache, 1051 Rue Laurier O./W., 514 273-9700. Long casual dresses, linens and housewares.
- Club Monaco, Rue 1455 Rue Peel, 514 499-0959. Canadian-owned company, trendy professional and casual clothing for men and women.
- Diakoumakos, 415 Mayor, 514 842-4846. Stylish fur coats.
- Excelfur et Cuir, 425 Rue Mayor, 514 849-1004. Fur and leather coats.
- Friperie St-Laurent, 3976 Boul. St-Laurent, 514 842-3893. Cool clothes, new and used.
- Gap, 1255 Rue Ste-Catherine O./W., 514 985-5311. Staples for a preppy wardrobe.
- Grand Mein, 4131 St-Denis. For women above 5'8".
- Guess, 1227 Rue Ste-Catherine O./W., 514 499-9464. Chain store sells jeans, casual wear and professional styles.
- Henri-Henri, 189 Rue Ste-Catherine E., 514 288-0109. One of the best hat shops in town, from Borsalino to berets, attract stars like Donald Sutherland and Charlie Sheen.
- Ingrid, 1225 Ave. Greene, 514 939-8888. Classy fashions for women.
- Jacob, 1220 Rue Ste-Catherine O./W., 514 861-9346. Reasonably-priced casual and professional fashions.
- Johnny Freddy, 3800 Boul. St-Laurent. Hip fashions for young people.
- Le Château, 1188 Rue Ste-Catherine O./W., 1310 Rue Ste-Catherine O./W., 514 866-2481. Reasonably priced stylish clothes for young women.
- Maîtres Fourreurs de Montréal, 1449 Rue St-Alexandre. Fur fashions.
- Mexx, 1125 Rue Ste-Catherine O./W., 514 288-6399. Chain store, casual wear and professional styles.
- Mode 2010, 2010 Rue St-Denis, 514 847-0006. Young, hip styles.
- Mode Derby, 1195 Rue Ste-Catherine O./W. Tiny shop chock full of casual clothes for young people.
- Oink Oink, 1234 Greene Ave., 514 939-2634. Cool newborn and children's clothes and some pricey designer wear plus piles of toys and gadgets in this kid-friendly shop.
- Old River, 1115 Rue Ste-Catherine O./W., 514 843-7828. Men's casual and formal wear.
- One World, 3982 Boul. St-Laurent, 514 287-1862. Exotic fashions and trendy clothes.
- Parasuco, 1414 Rue Crescent, 514 284-2288. Centre for jeans.
- Pierre, Jean, Jacques, 150 Rue Laurier O./W., 514 270-8392. Men's fashions.
- Polo Ralph Lauren, 1298 Rue Sherbrooke O./W., 514 288-3988. Classic and casual men's fashions.
- Rio, 3459 Rue St-Denis; 514 842-1692. Hip clothes for youths.
- Roots, 1223 Rue Ste-Catherine O./W., 514 845-7559, 716 Rue Ste-Catherine O./W., 514 875-4374, 4202 Rue St-Denis, 514 282-3331. Sporty clothes, caps and jackets.
- Scarlett O'Hara, 254 Ave. Mont Royal E., 514 844-9435. Features daring line of clothes as well as used items.
- Screaming Eagle, 1424 Boul. St-Laurent, 514 849-2843. Leather world.
- Titanic, 3794 Boul. St-Laurent. Trendy clothes for young crowd.
- Tristan & Iseut, 1101 Rue Ste-Catherine O./W., 514 289-9609. Chain store with casual and formal clothes for men and women.
- Twist Encore, 3974 Boul. St-Laurent, 514 842-1308. Funky new and vintage clothes.
- United Colours of Benneton, 1259 Rue Ste-Catherine O./W., 514 845-0178. European style casual clothes.
- Urban Outfitters, 1250 Rue Ste-Catherine O./W., 514 874-0063. Trendy urban wear.

Surplus Stores

- Les Soldats de la Mode, 3887 Boul. St-Laurent. Army surplus gear.
- Surplus International, 1431 Boul. St-Laurent, 514 499-9920. Cargo pants emporium.

- Surplus SOS, 1411 Boul. St-Laurent, 514 845-2405. Stylish surplus clothes.

Collectibles
- L'armoire aux poupees, 105 Rue St-Paul E. Permanent display of antique dolls and adjacent gift shop.
- Lucie Favreau Sports Memorabilia, 1904 Rue Notre Dame O./W., 514 989-5117. Like a visit to a sports hall of fame.
- Pause Retro, 2054-1 Rue St-Denis, 514 848-0333. Old toys, memorabilia and sports cards specialty.
- Retro-ville, 2652 Notre Dame O./W., 514 939-2007. Coca-Cola items, old magazines, toys and neon signs.

Department Stores
- The Bay, 585 Rue Ste-Catherine O./W., 514 281-4422. Fashions and more for the whole family.
- Eaton, 677 Rue Ste-Catherine O./W., 514 284-8484. More focus on upscale designer fashions and home items.
- Holt Renfrew, 1300 Rue Sherbrooke O./W., 514 842-5111. Top of the line fashions for men and women.
- Ogilvy, 1307 Rue Ste-Catherine O./W., 514 842-7711. Upscale women's fashions, fine jewellery, perfume, books.
- Marks & Spencer, 1500 Ave. McGill College, 514 499-8558. British chain store stocks Cheshire cheese, Shetland sweaters and more for reasonable prices.
- Simons, 977 Rue Ste-Catherine O./W., 514 282-1840. Upscale women's fashions and clothing for the whole family.

Electronics
- Alma Electronique, 1595 Boul. St-Laurent, 514 847-0366. Be prepared to haggle.
- Audiotronic, 368 Rue Ste-Catherine O./W., 1622 Boul. St-Laurent, 514 861-5451. Decent prices on home items and camera equipment.
- Distribution 2010, 2010 Boul. St-Laurent. Discount items.
- Dumoulin La Place, 2050 St-Laurent. Reasonable prices.
- Future Shop, 460 Rue Ste-Catherine O./W., 514 393-2600. Low-priced computer equipment, home electronics and CDS.
- Multi-Systeme Electronique, 1610 Boul. St-Laurent, 514 845-0059. Reasonable prices, open to haggling.

Housewares
- Collage Tapis, 1480 Rue Sherbrooke O./W., 514 933-3400. Imported Persian carpets.
- Indiport, 100 Rue St-Paul E., 514 871-1664. Persian carpets.
- Kim Heng, 1055 Boul. St-Laurent. Woks, chop sticks, tea pots, rice cookers and tableware supplier for local Chinatown restaurants.
- Multi-Design International, 273 Rue Laurier O./W. Funky household items.
- Omorpho, 3670 Boul. St-Laurent, 514 284-6110. Bizarre items for the home.
- Pier 1 Imports, 1321 Rue Ste-Catherine O./W., 514 985-2401. Chain store with wide selection of bohemian housewares.
- Zone, 4246 Rue St-Denis, 514 845-3530. Stylish and affordable wares, from chandeliers to shower curtains.

Jewellery
- AmberLux, Promenades de la Cathedrale, 635 Rue Ste-Catherine O./W.; 514 844 1357. Amber set in pieces of all shapes and sizes.
- Bijouterie Elegant, 377 Rue Ste-Catherine O./W., 514 844-2770. Gold objects and jewellery.
- Bijoux Marsan, 462 Rue Ste-Catherine O./W., 514 395-6007. Primarily gold.
- Birks, 1240 Phillips Square, 514 397-2511. Wide variety of fine-quality jewellery, silverware and china.
- Cartier, 1498 Rue Sherbrooke O./W., 514 939-0000. Fine jewellery.
- Eliko Les Montres, 680 Rue Ste-Catherine O./W., 514 875-6047. Specializes in watches: Rolex, Swiss Army, Swatch, Tag Heuer and more.
- Hemsley's, 660 Ste-Catherine O./W., 514 866-3706. Fine-quality jewellery, silverware and china.

- Geomania, Eaton Centre, 705 Rue Ste-Catherine O./W., 514 842-0446. Jewellery made of semi-precious stones, crystals and fossils.

Music
- Archambault, 175 Rue Ste-Catherine E., 514 281-0367. Large selection of CDs, sheet music and songbooks.
- HMV, 1010 Rue Ste-Catherine O./W., 514 875-0765. Three floors and a bargain annex across the street at 1035 Rue Ste-Catherine O./W., 514 844-0269.
- Rayon Laser, 3656 Boul. St-Laurent, 514 848-6300. Worldbeat music from Afghanistan to Zambia.
- Sam the Record Man, 399 Rue Ste-Catherine O./W., 514 366-8825. Good prices and excellent selection.

Shoes
- Browns, 1193 Rue Ste-Catherine O./W., 514 334-5000. Brand-name footwear for all occasions.
- Marie Mode, 469 Rue Ste-Catherine O./W., 514 845-0497. Cowboy boot specialists.
- Tony Shoes, 1346 Ave. Greene, 514 935-2993. Stocks latest styles plus hard-to-find sizes and bargain annex.

Odds & Ends
- Atelier-Boutique de cerfs-volants, 224 Rue St-Paul O./W., 514 845-7613. A must-see for kite lovers.
- Boutique de la Formule 1, 1182 Rue Ste-Catherine O./W., 514 861-9846. Grand Prix du Canada items.
- Boutique Médiévale, 122 Rue St-Paul E. Chain mail, broadswords and medieval regalia.
- La Capoterie, 2061 Rue St-Denis, 514 845-0027. Condoms in 21 flavours and other gag gifts.
- Le Choppe du Dragone Rouge 3804 St-Denis. Medieval outfits, jewellery and household items.
- Essence du Papier, Rue St-Denis, 514 288-9691. Stationery, journals and writing implements.
- Garnitures Dressmaker, 2186 Rue Ste-Catherine O./W., 514 935-7421. Open since the 1950s, this shop has an endless array of beads, feathers and ribbons.
- Jet-Setter, 66 Rue Laurier O./W., 514 271-5058. Luggage plus loads of travel gadgets.
- Kayakqua, Rue Sherbrooke O./W., 514 931-2082. A dazzling display of kayaks.
- Lily's Garage, 1946 Rue Ste-Catherine O./W. Cornucopia of second-hand treasures.
- Mediaphile, 1901 Ste-Catherine O./W., 514 939-3676. Hundreds of magazines on display, with order forms for 10,000 more, plus top-notch inexpensive cigars from Cuba and Jamaica.
- Mélange Magique, 1928 Rue Ste-Catherine O./W., 514 938-1458. New Age spiritualist items.
- Molson Centre Canadiens Boutique, Molson Centre, 514 989-2836. Jerseys, books, photos sold exclusively for the Habs.
- Pointe-à-Callière Museum, 150 Rue St-Paul O./W., 514 872-9149. Stocks unique reproductions, jewellery, pottery and toys.
- Sucré Bleue, 1701 Rue St-Denis. Specializes in Pez dispensers and candies.
- Tilly Endurables, 1050 Rue Laurier O./W., 514 272-7791.Travelwear, well-known for hats.
- Zone Automobile, 97 Rue Laurier O./W., 514 274-0404. Car buffs can find magazines, posters, models and more.

QUEBEC CITY:

OLD CITY CENTRE

Antiques
- Décenie, 117 Rue St-Paul; 418 694-0403. Re-upholstered vinyl furniture from the 1960s.
- Gerard Bourguet Antiquaire, 97 Rue St-Paul; 418 694-0896. 18th- and 19th-century pine furniture.

Art
- Sculpteur Flamand, 49 Rue du Petit-Champlain; 418 692-2813. Wood carvings.

Books
- Librairie Pantoute, 1100 Rue St-Paul; 418 694-9748. Selection of English-language guidebooks for the region.

Clothes
- Bibi & Co., 40 Rue Garneau; 418 694-0045. Hats galore.
- Chez Marie-Alexandre, 43 Rue de Buade; 418 694-9892. Children's clothes by local designers.
- La Corriveau, 24 Côte de la Fabrique; 418 694-0062. Handmade sweaters and moccasins.
- Lambert & Co., 42 Rue Garneau; 418 694-2151. Colourful wool socks.
- Oclan, 52 Boul. Champlain; 418 692-4690. Quebec designer clothes.
- Simons, 20 Côte de la Fabrique; 418 692-3630. Small branch of department store known for its own brand of men's and women's clothing, especially sweaters and hats.
- La Soierie Huo, 91 Rue du Petit-Champlain; 418 692-5920. Hand-painted silk scarves.

Jewellery
- Zimmermann, 46 Côte de la Fabrique; 418 692-2672.

Odds & Ends
- J.E. Giguère, 61 Rue de Buade;418 692-2296. Quebec-made pipes, Cuban Cigars and other tobacco products.

Toys
- Au Grand Carousel, 34 Rue Ste-Anne; 418 694-0539. 3-D puzzles.

LOWER TOWN

Clothing
- Cuirs Diva, 1100 Rue Bouvier; 418 626-3482. Leather fashions.
- Laliberté, 595 Rue St-Joseph; 418 525-4841. Workshop and store selling famous furs.
- Magasin Latulippe, 637 Rue St-Vallier; 418 529-0024. Large selection of workwear and outdoor wear, including great warm hats.
- X20, 200 Rue St-Joseph; 418 529-0174. Funky line of streetwear.

Odds & Ends
- Comptoir Emmaus, 915 Rue St-Vallier. E. Thrift shop heaven! Four floors of second hand clothes, books, furniture and housewares.
- Mail Centre-Ville, Rue St-Joseph; 418 648-9823. Billed as the world's longest covered street, with dollar stores, bargain shops and restaurants.
- Royaume de la Tarte, 402 Ave. des Oblats; 418 522-7605. Baked goods and decorated cupcakes.

UPPER TOWN

Antiques
- Antiquaire des héritiers, 5 Rue du Sault-au-Matelot; 418 694-2222.

Art
- Canadeau, 1124 Rue St-Jean; 418 692-4850. Amerindian art and Inuit sculptures.

Books
- Globe-Trotter 2000 - Librairie Ulysse, 4 Boul. René-Lévesque E.; 418 529-5349
- Librairie du Nouveau Monde, 103 Rue St- Pierre; 418 694-9475

Clothes
- Autrefois Saïgon, 55 Boul. René-Lévesque. Quebec-made women's clothing with an eastern touch.
- Boutique Paris Cartier, 1180 Ave. Cartier, 418 529-6083. Fine women's fashions.
- Logo Sport, 1121 Rue Saint-Jean; 418 694-9940
- Peau sur Peau, 70 Boul. Champlain; 418 692-5132.

Jewellery
- Pierres Vives Joaillerie, 231/2 Rue du Petit-Champlain; 418 692-5566.

Odds & Ends
- Boutique Médiévale Excalibor, 1055 Rue St-Jean; 418 692-5959. Medieval madness.
- Copiste du Faubourg, 545 Rue St-Jean; 418 525-5377. Handmade paper specialists.
- J. A. Moisan, 699 Rue St-Jean; 418 522-8268. Oldest grocery store in North America stocks large selection of fine foods.
- Paradis des Étampes, 603 Rue St-Jean; 418 523-6922. Huge choice of rubber stamps.

Shopping Centres
- Place Québec, 880 Ave. Dufferin-Montmorency; 418 529-0551. Rather dreary, but useful, with post office, 40 stores and restaurants.

SUBURBS

- Ailes de la Mode, 2450 Laurier, Ste-Foy; 418 652-4537. This fashion plaza offers shuttle service to downtown hotels.
- Galeries de la Capitale, 5401 des Galeries; 418 627-5800. Enormous roller coaster in indoor playground amidst dozens of shops.
- Place Laurier, 2700 Laurier, Ste-Foy; 418 651-5000. More than 350 stores under one roof is worth the trip.
- Place Ste-Foy, 2452 Laurier, Ste-Foy; 418 653-4026. Features department stores such as Simons.

INDEX

PHOTO CREDITS

T = top; C = centre; B = bottom.

Montreal

Photographs by Phil Carpenter, except for those listed below.

Anton's Photo Express: 95B; Association Touristique des Laurentides: 113B, 114T, C&B; Le Bateau-Mouche au Vieux-Port de Montréal: Yves Binette: 24B; Beaver Club: 80; Biodôme de Montréal: Julie D'Amour Léger: 49B, Sean O'Neill: 49T, 50T, C&B, 51T&B; Biosphère: 54C&B, 55T; Canadian Centre for Architecture: Michel Boulet: 42, Richard Bryant: 41, Robert Burley: 42B, Alain LaForest: 42C; Canadian Tourism Commission: Pierre St-Jacques: 16B, 17B, 20T, 22B, 40B, 95T; Les Caprices de Nicholas: 73T, 77T, 78T&B; Centre d'histoire de Montréal: 24C, 37B; Château Ramezay Museum: 28T, 37T&C; McCord Museum: 35T, C&B, 36T; Festival International de Jazz de Montréal: Jean-François Leblanc: 69T, Caroline Hayeur: 69B; Fort Chambly National Historic Site: 112; Les Francofolies de Montréal: 71; Just for Laughs Festival: Martin Savard: 70T; Milos Restaurant: 79; Missisquoi Museum: 118B; Mont-Tremblant Resort: 115T, C&B, 116B; Montréal Botanical Garden: 23T, 52T&B, 53T&B, Michel Tremblay: 52C; Montréal Museum of Fine Arts: 44, 45T&B, Timothy Hursley: 43T, Brian Merrett: 43C&B; Musée d'art contemporain de Montréal: Cöpilia: 46B, Caroline Hayeur: 47T, Richard-Max Tremblay: 46T, 47C; Notre-Dame Basilica: 29T; Old Port of Montréal Corp./A.P.E.S.: 23B, 93B, 94B, Anton Fercher: 95T, Denis Farley: 92; Parc des Îles de Montréal/Bernard Brault: 22C; Parc du Mont-Tremblant: Yves Boisvert: 116C; Pierre Pouliot: 116T; Parcs Canada: 111, 113T; Pointe-à-Callière Museum of Archaeology: 36T; Redpath Museum: 56B; Rivest, Giles: 39B; Simon, Paul 19; Société des casinos du Québec inc.: 22T; Stewart Museum at the Fort: 25C, 25B, 39T, 40T; Le Tour de l'Île de Montréal: Robert Laberge: 72; Tourisme Cantons-de-l'Est: 117T&B, Peter Quine: 118T; Tourisme Montréal: 11T, 20B, 70B, 91, Stéphane Poulin: 10, 27, 32T&B, 33B, 34, 36C, 54T, 85, 86, 87T&C, 89B, 107, 108T, Yano Philiptenenko: 18T; Ville de Montréal: Denis Labine: 25T; Johanne Palasse: 14T

Quebec City

Photographs by Théodore Lagloire, except those listed below.

Carnaval de Québec Kellogg's: 119, 131, 132, 133; ExpoCité: 133C&B; Festival d'été de Québec: 134; Fondation Bagatelle: 163, 164; Laurie Raphäel: 141T; Mont Sainte-Anne: Jean Sylvain: 12T, 13T, 167C&B, 168T&B; Musée de la Civilisation: 129T, 147T, 152C; Musée des Ursulines de Québec: 128T; Office du tourisme et des congrès de la Communauté urbaine de Québec: 165C&B

drew Cameron and Peggy McCalla